# The Cave of Heaven

Patrick Grainville

# THE CAVE OF HEAVEN

Translated by Dominic Di Bernardi

Dalkey Archive Press

Originally published by Éditions du Seuil


Library of Congress Cataloging in Publication Data
Grainville, Patrick, 1947-
[Caverne céleste. English]
The cave of heaven / by Patrick Grainville; translated by Dominic Di Bernardi.
Translation of: La caverne céleste.
I. Title.
PQ2667.R297A24 1990
843'.914—dc20 90-2762
ISBN: 0-916583-56-2 (cloth)
ISBN: 0-916583-68-6 (paper)

First paperback edition, 1991

Partially funded by grants from The National Endowment for the Arts and The Illinois Arts Council.

Dalkey Archive Press
1817 North 79th Avenue
Elmwood Park, IL 60635 USA

*Printed on permanent/durable acid-free paper and bound in the United States of America.*

# The Cave of Heaven

The voluptuousness of charging along the void of the gigantic highway. An asphalt desert drawn out like a boundless back. He felt as though he were inventing the landscape, creating his route solely by pressing the accelerator. Traffic was sparse. He'd chosen an uncrowded weekday and was sliding down this flawless toboggan course, a solid river quivering under the wheels. Now and then, defying the speed limits, he hit 110 MPH. The tensed, crackling vehicle emitted a curious moan, a death chirr. A paradoxical sensation of standing still seized the driver. Space and time contracted in a straight, vibrating line. The glass and metal capsule sustained this climactic velocity. It could all come undone, fly apart at any second. But the machine held up. Simon was thrust back against a sort of compact thrumming wall. He soon thought of nothing. His past evaporated and the panorama escaped his senses. His brain and body, lodged in the metallic pod, quit the realm of existence, entering a hard, atemporal zone. A cannonball purified to an absolute smoothness, shorn of regrets, desires, biographical anecdotes, the continuing saga of duration. Simon was clutched to this eternity. Suddenly, a song sprang from his throat, a cry as if his memory had been slain, crushed under his wheels. A gentleness invaded him. Without slowing down, he relaxed, lightened. And the stripped, ascetic condition of the automobile extended a promise of glory and aridity. He thirsted for a universe without compromise, a bone-dry cosmos in the guise of an enormous solar stone. And he knew, as the light sharpened into a brighter blue, that he was leaving the north behind him, the fleshy fields of grass, the babbling vegetation, that thick compost where he had been born: dense sudden showers of clay, a feast of dirt clods. Already outcrops of violet-tinged stone broke into view, and sterile horizons were unfurling. Simon's heart swelled. Rock orgies came to him in premonition. He was going to live in a large, bright expanse of gravel.

He arrived in Aguilar after dark. Consequently he saw nothing of the spaces where he was to conduct his investigation. This latter word stamped his assignment with a very solemn character. His newspaper had granted him a vacation that would keep him somewhat more on his toes than ordinary. During the course of these long weeks, he had to arrange for a few hours of work in view of producing a feature on the Aguilar cave and a five hundred thousand-year-old pithecanthropus whose skeleton had been discovered . . . *Cave, pithecanthropus, Aguilar, five hundred thousand years old* . . . These words immediately seduced him. In them he recognized the glamour of sunlight and dryness. He pictured some sort of archaic ossuary that would be perfect for taking him out of his element. It was night in Aguilar. And cave, mountains, the ruins of Cathar castles which, as he'd been told, adorned the jutting rock in the distance—these were all still invisible, steeped in the warm balmy darkness. He set down his bags at the only hotel in the village. The owner had gone to bed a while ago and was asleep. Simon had to call out several times. The man woke up and came down. He showed the traveler to a rather spacious but shabby room. The faded, tattered wallpaper pleased Simon. An odor of scorched dust hung in the air. The window was open on the deserted village, the streets blanched by moonlight. Simon, wired from his travel fatigue, no longer felt like sleeping. After the hotelier handed over a bunch of keys, Simon stepped softly down the stairs, opened the door and went out.

The uneven, patchily tarred street wound between the housefronts and farm porches. Simon liked the coarse crust of this roadway hammered by winegrowers' footsteps, stripping it smooth in places, or rubbing down the sidewalk curbs. A narrow passageway sculpted by life, molding itself to the least routine and passion. More a gallery than a street, a pebbly gully. Soon he was out in the country. The crickets riddled the shadows with their songs. A stubborn serenade transforming each molecule of darkness into a plangent needle. This proliferating hysteria was a new experience for Simon. The mute, damp northern nights had no inkling of this persistent din. Up there the sludge bogs you down. But here the night was studded with cries; a frenzied energy expended upon this great web of insomnia. Each lot of land possessed its frantic cricket. Simon walked amid drunken trumpeters and sentries. Then the echoes dulled, his hearing grew accustomed. The howling mosaic smoothed into a more serene, droning chant. This concealed landscape lay all about him. He would have liked to glimpse it through some miraculous fissure in the shadows. To be in league with the gods through some sacred cunning that allowed him a glimpse of this light-drenched land for one minute as if the sun were at zenith. He believed in the possibility of these sovereign triggers able to open mountains, revealing to a few celestial voyeurs their ruby-flowered bowels. For himself alone to transform moon into sun. He desired to be caught red-handed in a cosmic breaking and entering.

Short of pulling off such grandiose embezzlements, he left the road, followed a path among the vines, knelt on the ground and touched this unknown, invisible earth whose dry hot grain gave him chills. Somewhere, the cave gaped open. But nothing could indicate this fracture in the darkness. Slowly he gazed about, tried to discern this cavity in the rock. His rattled nerves peopled his mind with superstitions, innocent lusts. He breathed in the scent of this region for want of perceiving its lines, rifts and colors. The lizards slept under the stones, and beautiful snakes in sheaths of soil. An entire bestiary, with coppery scales, currency of asps, solar venom. For him night was always linked to some secret brilliance. Almost red stars: Altair, Antares in Scorpio echoed with their myriads the constellations of the crickets. Simon listened to the millions of stars singing and saw shimmering the beetles' golden pods under the vine stocks. The obscurity made strangely present the shadow of the first men. Espied from far back in the cave, what meaning did the circle of starry night possess? Shining points in a stone jaw . . . Canines of a thousand suns and molars of the sky. With what wild imaginings, what primitive anxieties, did they people this cavern opening through which the night flooded in, along with its noises, its thunders, its winged flights, its creeping breezes and astral bodies twinkling like animals' eyes? Stars identical to those brief bolts brought into being by banging quartz stones against each other, transforming them into weapons and tools. These primordial words moved Simon. By scratching the glebe he would have liked to bare the moonlit cavity preserving the first weapon and the first tool. Long before metal, long before fire. Still unformed objects in which only a trained glance could recognize the barest promise of human benefit. Stones where thought roams, rocks where the mind awakens. Ghosts in the cradle of the soil. Simon gladly would have slept the sleep of his ancestors in this mountain cave, halfway between the heavens and the earth, at the threshold of the visible, at the beginning of the world. Night was far advanced. The peasants were dreaming in the village of Aguilar. An empty room awaited Simon. But he remained stretched out under the soft leaves of the vineyard, amid the gnarled stocks and the Dionysian cymbals of the crickets. This is where daylight surprised him. He opened his eyes upon the amphitheater of the hills, the perpendicular rocks. The valley fashioned its hollow in this hard, bright casket. His heart beat before this bone-whiteness, these limestone skulls, these trunnions, these cliff roads, these scoured belemnite guards, these stone breasts crazed over with cracks and tortured with bumps and tendons. His gaze traveled along the vertical walls and gentle slopes. He spotted the cave hole, a dark patch in the pale greyness of a steep one hundred-yard rise. It was a suspended theater, a stage with a sunlit rim; then the cavity sank inward, forming a black niche. The night seemed to have taken refuge in this well up there in the sky. The mountain had swallowed the mass of shadows as if their immense opaque veils were needed to protect the dubious ancestral skeleton.

When Simon got back to the village, his trousers dusty, his hair studded with twigs, Alphonse the hotelier met him with an expression of surprise. But the man soon proved to have a cheerful nature. Simon benefited from a special goodwill extended by this obliging septuagenarian who was no longer made indignant by strange behavior. Very tall, dry, gnarled, with short close-cropped white hair, Alphonse's presence was imposing, a tireless cowboy. His red, fleshy lips added the touch of a bacchic grin to the physique of a Lyautey in retirement. His wife was a small, plump, white-haired woman. Alphonse warned Simon not to put any stock in this promising chubbiness. For Paula was fragile. Afflicted by a heart defect, she fainted for no reason and was required, every afternoon, to rest for three hours in her room. This necessity served Alphonse's interests. As soon as Paula had gone to bed, he left Lynne, a young waitress, to keep an eye on the hotel, and slipped away on a big black bicycle for the neighboring village. Simon soon learned that he met his mistress there, a woman thirty years younger. Simon took a shower, shaved, and went for a walk in the village. Life seemed peaceful here. Two or three teenage guys pulled up on their mopeds were trading wisecracks to fend off their boredom. A girl in skimpy yellow shorts walked up the street much to the boys' stupefaction. A few darkly garbed women, seated on chairs in front of their doors, watched the passersby while peeling vegetables or doing a little sewing. The row of old men on a bench were smoking. Their eyeballs darted in unison when an automobile halting at a red light allowed a peek at its cargo of half-dressed tourists, women in bright, very low-cut dresses or diaphanous bathing suits. At times, the door would open and a half-naked Parisian woman dashed toward the fountain right next to the beach. She filled a bottle with ice-cold water while the spray splashed her legs, riddling her flimsy attire with wet spots, tightening patches of fabric against her skin. The skewer of sages reached a peak of happiness. Simon was seduced by this small, vegetating, discreetly lecherous village. The desire to settle down on a bench took hold of him. He'd loiter there the whole afternoon long, in the shade of the plane tree, tossing out stray remarks, remembered bits and pieces, tranquilly rambling on until a stopped car made everybody hold their breath. Heaven-sent red light and fountain, traps fallen into by the shameless prey from northern cities. Blond damsels, caught in the snare. The desire to be old often took hold of Simon. A dream of calm immobility. He envied routine existences spent in contemplation. With pleasure he would have repeated the chain of identical gestures, engrossed by delicious redundancies, nestling down into a stretch of time free from any plans. To grow old all at once, through some magical metamorphosis, to go grey, wither, enlist a scrawny and passive torso in the row of half-doddering old men. To watch the others pass by, people in a hurry, unruly, harried, merchants madly scattering, barracks' rabble, flashy oddballs, space satellite guys, young executives with Kodaks and bosses with firm handshakes, little teenyboppers gaga about getting tans and driving fast, the curious, those who travel, who believe, who slam on their brakes at lights or shoot through them, those who run risks and accost . . . To squeeze onto a bench, turn to stone, a mummy of wrinkles . . . The burden of seeking, of time itself at last cast off. And then, perhaps, the unsurpassable voluptuousness of posing for a snapshot in front of a beautiful woman tourist who would take you for a local product, a picturesque inhabitant of this cracked, torrid land . . . A smile for the lady . . . And that bliss when she passes the camera to her husband and sits on the bench next to the old, very old Simon who'd seen wars, plagues, bad weather, floods, famines and phylloxera. The husband aims carefully at the couple, the woman wriggles at the side of this typical old man and Simon takes a tiny gander at her breasts. Her rebukes are a way of flattering him . . . oh the sly devil . . . And suddenly he gets a hard-on like the young man he really is. She sees the joyous spear sticking up under the large breeches. The lady's disconcerted, moved, perhaps indignant . . .

The village recedes, but already he knows its hues, its smells, its conserve of sounds. He touched the grain of its sun-heated walls. He crossed its large dresses of shadow under the trees. He divined its hidden inhabitants, its minuscule dramas, he distinguished voices behind the doors, he surprised faces at the windows. He'll go to the church soon, then to the bistro. He listens to the hum of this island, brown tile roofs, grey stones among which the living slowly move about. He climbs along an incline crowned with a boulder. He sits at the summit. The village huddles in the valley, interlocking its ossicles of houses. The colors belong to the surrounding scenery, interspersed with a rare, brighter stroke. Seedbed of tumbledown, heat-smitten houses, shriveled beneath the flames of the sky. And, all around, the gigantic enclosure of the slopes, limestone caryatids, this savagery of rock punctuated with stunted copses, bone-dry keeps, goiters full of cracks . . . and the cave of the first men.

On foot, Simon heads for the mountain. The vines decorate the slopes like paragraphs of writing. Simon likes their meticulous typography, their grim determination to stretch out, to conquer the inhospitable spaces, the peaks, the steep terraces. The bushes halt at thorny scrubland, chaoses of stone, crevassed plateaus, torpedoed with lines. Simon promises himself to wander about for hours on end, up there, where the winegrowing mania ceases, to lose himself in the kingdom of snakes and birds of prey. He would set out one morning and walk until nightfall without meeting another human being. And his chest would be transformed into arid burning rock. Finally, Simon saw himself going back down into the village, bearing this white-hot mineral torso. The superstitious villagers, reviving the glories of myth, would come up to touch his granite lungs, and lovers would carve the initials of their desire in his incorruptible flesh . . . He advances along the path. He took off his shirt. The sunlight clutches him. The ground is scorched. His heart beats very quickly. He adores this country, which purifies him. He is going to keep walking for a while. Sweat dampens his back, his stomach, and his skin darkens. Simon is happy. His roots are cut, his nostalgias have died. His life is beginning here in the furnace of the boulders. He lies down abruptly, rests a large stone on his chest, stretches out his arms and legs. He feels his bones under the weight of rock. He breathes almost normally. The sky spreads its wings, a gigantic blue buzzard. An emerald beetle pops up, scales his side. The shell shimmers like a jewel. Simon slowly lifts off the stone. He'll undergo the exercise again, longer next time. The task is to learn the secret of minerals, to earn their love. Simon reaches the foot of the rockface where the cave opens. He shuns an immediate climb. He procrastinates, plays with his desire. A small lake bathes the mountain base. The deep water is as black as the mouth of the cave. A large constriction blocks the far end of the basin, beyond which can be made out a narrow fault between two steep rises, probably the point where gorges begin. A lake, gorges, a cave . . . For Simon, it's a fantastic menu. Each of these elements is associated with a specific delight. He is going to savor this dry and tumultuous country where water gushes up, winds out in mineral trickles and fills hard hollow cisterns. A water that never slakes thirst, nor moistens soil, nor fosters any plant life but pours its cold current between quartz and limestone formations. This ground prohibits confusion, the murky northern matrimony between mist and alluvium. It organizes confrontations and contrasts: shadow-sunlight, water-rock, round cavities and aggressive reliefs. Simon takes off his trousers and dives into the stretch of water. His sunburnt body is gripped by the lake's metal. After the shell of sunbeams follows an armor of frost and shade. He's in pain, a power binds him, a large icy python. He struggles and gradually grows accustomed to this fatal sheath. Only his head sticks out, his eye peeled for the cave. A contorted path charges in fits and starts, zigzagging up the steep rise, exerting its muscles, hoisting itself step by step, spiraling in the air. It is near noon and no one would dare tackle the blazing wall. Simon enjoys being poised between cold and fire. He moves along the lake edges, his flesh glides through the black velvet of the waters. He belongs to the race of eels and congers. Up above, the opening captivates him. An overhanging rock, a celestial balcony where they once appeared, over five hundred thousand years ago, their simian silhouettes leaning toward the valley populated by moving herds of elephants and horses. He'd give his life to witness that, just for ten minutes, tumbling through time, a gliding vertiginous flight down a column of thousands of years. In passing, the stratum of the centuries, as when going down by elevator into a mine shaft, at top speed catching sight of the different levels, the superimposed gallery entrances and the swarms of active workers on every landing. At the bottom is the beginning. The lake of pure dark waters. Then the primeval mountain. The cave was less eroded then, its terrace was established ten or so yards in front of the present-day site. Five hundred centuries for wind and running water to devour ten yards . . . and for the ape to disappear from man's physiognomy. The ancestors approach the edge, and their gaze sinks into these anguishing waters where future divinities are slowly being forged. The gloomy eye of the lake fosters the birth of beliefs. The eye reflecting the cave, which rounds its unseeing orb in its stone skull. They . . . ephemeral hunters, links in a chain, moments, but with absolutely no knowledge of this, living the present perception, preparing their rudimentary weapons. No other world but their own. Past, distant future have no sense. They inhabit the house of the immediate, the very near future. They watch these waters where murky meanings stir, embryonic notions, conceptual macerations or phosphenes of logic . . . transparence and depth, mirror, opacity, magic of this substance that leaks, trickles out, slakes, invigorates, and where children die if they fall in. Liquid maw and womb of horror. They exist, they sense it, they shiver, they're hungry, they like to hunt down and slaughter animals. They glean pleasure from dominating the weak. They have no inklings of their own deaths. Grunting. Trading signs. Brains smaller than ours, diffusing a widespread impression of mystery. Their instinct gradually moves off center. Their desires are less rigorously bound to things. Thought slips between their sensations and the world. Thought, that lucid viper. They are nature's most intelligent creatures yet unaware of this fact. Cunning animals fear these splendid resourceful rivals. They are beautiful . . . They think at the water's edge. For the first time . . . The abstract already gnaws at them. Rather than in tooth or nail, their power resides in this capacity to cast off their own personalities and to create within this void, within this game, this impalpable zone germinating with all possibilities. The lake mirrors their gestures, their grotesque silhouettes, the waves sketch their thick, chinless, underhung pates, with that orbital ridge at the forehead base that makes them so obtuse, so haughtily browed . . . Do they have smooth or hairy faces? . . . Feelings haven't yet weakened their desires. But a tenderness at times lurks in their glances . . . At the edge of the abyss of love and death, they hesitate.

Simon emerges from the lake. He stretches out on a blue limestone slab, veined with white, almost no angles, like hardened mud preserving the gentleness of the hands that kneaded it. Simon gives up the idea of visiting the cave. He'll wait until tomorrow. He prefers examining it from a distance, inspecting the mountain surroundings, gathering red marble pebbles from the dried streambeds, and collecting bouquets of absinthe from their shores.

In the early afternoon he went back to the village. It's the moment Alphonse, forsaking his bedridden wife, takes his bicycle and rejoins his mistress. The tar oozes in the winding road baked by the tenacious sunlight. Wearing his cap Alphonse pedals along slowly. He never breaks a sweat. He's lived through much higher temperatures in Morocco long ago. Alphonse likes riding around while others are napping, when people as old as himself are vegetating in the shade of the plane tree. He passed in front of them just as he left the village. The fountain spluttering away, a chaos of bubbles and hushed babbling. They were asleep. Only the water was alive, musical, euphoric. Coming down from the mountain, it pierced the walls, singing inside the village, cradling the old men in their snooze.

As soon as he arrived, Yvette would close the grocery. She'd wrap him in her arms. He'd see her sweet, sensual shepherdess's face against his mouth. They'd move into the garden behind the house, under the almond tree. There they'd kiss. His old, lascivious caiman's torso pinned against Yvette's throat. She'd roll her hips and the black fur of her belly toward Alphonse's thighs, braids of flesh-stripped muscles, long pincers of love flanking his sex.

Simon is not alone in the room on the ground floor. There's a baby stroller in a cool corner. An infant is asleep . . . At eighteen the waitress Lynne got herself stuck with a kid by some guy passing through. She sees to the bar when Alphonse is away. A boy is listening to a record while playing pinball. The walls echo with a clangor of springs and brutal shocks, sporadically drowned out by a rock singer's high notes. The racket doesn't seem to bother the baby in the cradle. Lynne's a little shy. She's got big blue eyes, a mane of blond curls. On the small side, slim, with delicate skin. Simon feels like talking to her. She's a little bored in the village, but her melancholy is not excessive. In a few years, when the kid's gotten bigger, she hopes to go up to Paris, live at a girlfriend's place. Lynne still has dreams. The theater, beautiful shops, movies suddenly titillate her. She blushes slightly. From time to time desires pierce her. She'll forget everything. Prospects of a brighter future vanish in these irresistible cravings. That's how she got saddled with a kid. Simon picks up on this blend of chaste diffidence and passionate impulse. A book is left lying on the bar, some romance. Simon leafs through it, snatches two or three sentences which celebrate extraordinary lives, love at first sight, successful exploits foiling traps and tricks, the miracles of a charmed destiny. She serves the boy a Coke, then walks over to the cradle, takes out the kid, frizzy hair, pale complexion, who starts bawling. The youngster pinballs, the singer squeals, the child cries . . . But the clamor doesn't faze Simon. It's a quite harmless, limited ruckus. A fleeting hysteria, a trivial flood of sound. The village experiences a momentary pandemonium. Lynne undoes her vest. She's not wearing a bra, she holds out a slender breast, very downy, velvety, with a fat, pink, greedy tip which she pushes into the little one's mouth. The child falls mute. The teenager steals a glance. This crafty nipple is more enticing than the chicks in panties, fluorescent lights, leatherette shorts between the blinkers and electric circuits of the pinball machine. The baby's gluttonous cheeks pump the trickle of milk. The other breast can be made out in empty profile. Idle udder, outcast snout . . . And Lynne, like all women from the beginning, bends a tender gaze downward, with ecstatic expressions for this piglet born of her flesh, this leech sucking at her. Did the females of the caves love their brood? Little monkey-men, whimpering pithecanthropi pampered by thinking she-beasts. Up there the kids doze at their mothers' sides while the males attack bear and lynx. Now Lynne's subtle features. Wincing sensually when the child bites her breast. The process completed, she forces back her nipple. Buttons closed. Very sensible pullover, soft beige. Simon feels sorry. He'd like to pay her a compliment, tell her they're awfully pretty, so softly colored . . . Will I see them again soon, tell me when . . . He keeps quiet. He watches her intensely. She catches on, blushes. She has a weakness for strangers. The glamour of drifters. Simon's sort of good-looking. A touch of craziness in his face. His features slightly deranged. The orchestra conductors she sees on TV sometimes have these expressions, unbalanced sparrow hawks. Romantic. Chopin-Musset. Maybe Simon's sick. Come down to die here like the hero in *The Wild Ass's Skin.* She loved the movie, the sad young man, the pallid orgies . . . And then very beautiful, stark white death who kisses the angelic man's lips as a sign the end has come . . . She wondered what Simon was doing here. And despite her shyness, she felt such a sharp flash of curiosity that she asked him. He answered that he was doing a story on the Aguilar cave for a weekly Parisian magazine. "A story" lashed her with a gust of adventure. He was a reporter on the go, between two trains, two planes, in places where wars break out, catastrophes overwhelm people, like in Africa, Beirut, Iran, scarred populations, women veiled in black, long processions of fanatics . . . Lynne loved the news, the great ayatollah fascinated her, especially those implacable eyebrows . . .

A whimper for mercy was the only recourse after the verdict fell from that turban of death.

She confessed that she'd never gone up to the cave. He told her that in Paris he'd never set foot in the Sainte-Chapelle or the Moulin Rouge. She thought it wasn't the same thing. The cave was more scientific. But she'd visited the prehistoric museum located just outside the village. That had interested her a lot. The skull gave her a scare. She didn't like death's-heads. Simon announced that he'd be going to the museum very shortly, but that he preferred to see the cave first.

Simon still hesitated. He spent the late afternoon and evening reading Lynne's novel in his room. Failing to foster any daydreams, the story gave him two or three out-and-out hard-ons. Yet the tale was devoid of erotic descriptions. Stereotypes, artifices often had the power to arouse him. Duplicity made him erect, dishonest drag disguises, layered surprises as in a striptease show. Was he going to reveal the book's effect to Lynne? That would be a rather blunt way of broaching the subject. Lynne, your book gave me a hard-on because you read it in your own bed at midnight.

He still lingered the whole morning, whiling away the hours by chatting with Alphonse. He had picked the worst possible time. The sun directly overhead. He'd be alone. Maybe along the way he'd burn up, be transformed into a charred vine shoot. Who'd see him? Alphonse and Lynne would forget about this fleeting visitor. At first, he had to walk between the vines, follow long footpaths amid small glistening leaves. Simon was happy. Crickets everywhere, and their trilling, a magnificent obsession. Pointy sparrow hawks up in the blue. Trembling wings, beaks riveted groundward. Scrutinizing eyes. The ground granular, dried up. The yoke of the hills. Simon advances into the valley. After a little over a mile, the steep wall rises, Simon starts to climb. He's taken off his shirt, tied it around his waist. He presents a zinc torso to the motionless rocks and blazing rays. The narrow, intermittent path rears up step by step amid the fennel bushes, the arbutus, the thorny plants. Vegetation with very green ligula is interspersed with the blue-tinted, grey mass of thyme. The mountain, mauve in the distance, blanketed by scrubland with a fuzzy fleece, hues of stormy sky, crimson, lavender. Simon likes these stubby desert plants. Their clawlike branches entangle and twist. His desire is to be like a snake tortured by a bird of prey's talons. A confrontation of nerves, instincts, sissing belligerence. The bushes convulse their reptilian stems. Sharp or massive rocks encumber the way. He must cross over whole slabs, chaoses. A tiny pinewood forest spreads its shadow over his shoulders. Simon stops. In the heart of the furnace, this miraculous nest. This time Simon is streaming with sweat. Temples throbbing. He sits down for a few minutes in the ashen recess. The veil that serves to protect him from the sun is so fragile it constantly threatens dissolution.

The shade, no sooner settled, flies off like a tulle headdress, consigning the entire scene to the conflagration. Simon doesn't know why his thoughts are filled with so many light words in this haven . . . hopscotch, blueberry, titmouse, parasol . . . His raft trembles on the sea of light. His heart gives way in his chest. To faint, dissolve into soft down . . .

One last incline bristling with enormous stones. The sunlight strikes full face. A gong of fire. The incandescent wall trembles under the skin of rock. Strenuously he heaves himself up, eyes clouded with huge tears of sweat. He emerges onto the terrace and before him looms the gaping cave, the gloomy porch. Opening ten yards wide, this maw appears even deeper. A crew is working in the cool shade, with no regard for this sunstorm raging outside. The scent of a large cellar, the odor of clay, death . . . The terror of caves. Inside, several layers of soil, each with slight variations. Sediments that running water has infiltrated through cracks in the vault, debris that the wind has insinuated through the opening. Ten, eleven yards of matter accumulated through the course of the millennia, archives making legible five hundred thousand geologic years. The excavations have practiced a cross section cut through these formidable deposits. And every fraction of an inch you can stumble upon the vestiges of Man. For this excavation mound is rife with bones. Simon feels astonishment faced with such an abundance of fragments, shards, segments, nuggets. As if some monstrous feast, some cannibal fury had been unleashed in the cave through the ages, leading to this swarm of skeletons. In certain spots the splinters riddling the ground make it look like a rice pudding with its myriads of welded grains. Ditches disembowel this macabre slab, galleries allowing researchers to examine the layers in intimate detail. A meticulous string-grid divides up these millennia into square yards. The transversal and longitudinal sections convert time into space, a passing flux into a solid, analyzable pyramid. Thus each parcel is dated, numbered, labeled. A labor of mathematical ants pulverizes the deposit into intelligible fractions of inches. The wall becomes a mirror. Reflecting, whispering. The cliff speaks the immemorial secret. Fossiliferous clay and sand utter a long murmur of revelations. The excavators also dig burrowlike holes, open vesicles within the cave allowing for the sediment platform to be bored, making possible unobstructed movement within its innards, making visible its living heart. A lucid, multiple net catches and dissects the mass of soils. An invasion of logical gazes.

A group of ten or so young people slowly toil away on footbridges and in niches of glebe. With awls, brushes, they scratch at the dust, decorticate each lump, dismember every little grain. Their gestures are maternal. They exhibit archangelic precautions. A commando of imponderable surgeons whose lancets isolate and work free masses of atoms. They graze the enormous mummy of the ages . . . They listen to this flesh of the centuries, take its pulse, untangle its nerves, drill every cube of mystery with their dexterous needles.

Simon already knows at first glance that the cave possesses him. His innards tremble. His brain undergoes a complete hallucination . . . seeing these teenagers of all races, in jeans and short-sleeves, dressed like rock dancers, hippies high on grass, students and bohemians suddenly slowed and spiritualized by this subterranean exploration. This animating rapture of the deep guides their very gentle gestures, their loving caresses. Simon thinks he's in the heart of a sanctuary where priests and worshipers as unobtrusively as ghosts slip in and fall to their knees. Peace of altars, of monstrances . . . clouds of incense . . .

A host of questions press into his head. This superabundance of bones baffles and frightens him. Why did the ravenous cave chew, grind up so many living beings? A celestial ogre shrouded in invisible sunlight, crouched in the cool fertile blackness, digesting his booty of cadavers, of simianesque generations, prehuman, human, emptying the chain of the species . . . Visionary mouth, speech of the abysses.

Simon could question the researchers. He'd rather preserve a little longer the magic of his ignorance and surprise. The first shock liberates images, wild associations, undercurrents of thought, unruly ramifications, swells of terror, bursts of desire. It's his very own body that's shaken to the core, his memory, his roots. He feels the deep foundations stirring, buried territories, ancestral chapels. The mountain is the mere reflection of his being. At the summit of this pyre of bones sits Simon, enthroned, a tottering king. In the cave he feels that his destiny is being played out, an epic of knowledge. He'll go down, sink away into the thick crust of alluvium and strata, drop from sight into this infinite well. He'll rediscover the footsteps of ancient man, the remnants of their shelters, their hunts, their butcheries, their remorseless crimes. All this will have been long before Adam and Eve . . . before the clarity of both the conception and defiance of the gods, even long before Saturn in the epoch of origin and obscurity . . . when the beast's thousand impulses become organized, structured, and engender an inexpressible animal, when brain and hand—that old paw freed from walking for over ten million years already—begin a dialogue, building open syntheses that are kinetic, creative . . . Simon's imagination is dominated by this cliché of a monkey-man seated in the middle of the cave. Outside, day breaks and a beam barely illumines the ancestor's shape . . . the caveman gazing at his hand.

Simon didn't speak to the workers. He took to his heels, leaving them to their contemplation. While going out onto the terrace he spots a girl. She must have climbed up after he did. She's positioned at the edge of the void, in the shadow of a jutting rock. She's drawing . . . Black, very beautiful, in Levis and a brightly colored blouse. Simon walks over to her . . . On large leaves of white paper, several sketches in succession, a variety of monkeys, men, animals . . . Outlines emerge, disappear, correct and complicate each other . . . Simon watches this black female demiurge portray the first men. She works at a leisurely pace. This site seems to rule out haste. The journalist, Simon will be initiated into the magic spells effecting a radical slowdown . . . Failing in his resolve to remain silent, he asks her what she's doing. Without a pause she answers, her voice slightly mechanical, betraying her forced politeness. Later, Simon will realize that these youths have also been assigned to provide visitors with information, tourists winded from the climb, eager to learn . . . The excavation is affiliated with the village museum, with a project for education and popularization. Thus the black woman delivers her instructive spiel. Based on data furnished by paleontologists—skeletal examinations, established measurements, a web of hypotheses—her task is to reconstitute the real-life appearance of the era's fauna and hominids. Imagination plays no role in this effort which entails reproducing the body, physiognomy, stance and gestures of the creatures from those days. The bones, crushed and scattered in the night of the cave, are re-soldered by her, completed, riveted to muscular arches, surrounded by organs, flesh-cloaked and coated with hair and skin . . . She unifies what the excavation pulverizes. She incarnates, breathes in life . . . Her scientific exactitude is combined with an artist's sense of touch and contours. She invents the truth. Under the African woman's hands the relics multiply, metamorphose. There exist myths and age-old beliefs telling of certain gods who likewise possess the power to recreate a being from a single bone, a sacrum, a vertebra, that once belonged to it. The flesh grows again through divine magic. The skeleton is a tree whose branches become laden with new leaves. The black woman is springtime itself at work in this icy cavern.

He asks her name. This time she looks at him squarely. She hesitates at this request to step out of her pedagogical role. Simon puts on a childlike, imploring expression. Amused, she confesses: "My name's Myriam." . . . Simon doesn't dare go any further. He contemplates her Nubian-princess profile, her slightly hooked nose, her large almond-shaped eyes, and that fleshy mouth tilted down toward the sketches, that jumble of lines in which the face of Man takes shape, fluctuates.

Before going back down Simon overlooks the limestone theater surrounding the valley. He's overwhelmed by the primitive character of these stones, stripped and bleached by the heat, articulated in crests and plateaus. He loves these glabrous fortresses, these bastions of sterility. He spots slits, loopholes, clinging bushes, hanging scree, birds of prey in flight. *Troglodyte* . . . this word summons him, fills him with wonder like an echo of something dry, hollow. Night dwells in the multiple crevices, black lairs of mystery, primordial habitats, limestone igloos . . . And still farther off, certain reliefs reveal strange carvings, the rocks seem crenellated . . . Ruins of Cathar castles whose alphabet barely pokes above the mineral walls. The elect group of the Pure installed their dens on these summits. Mountain heights and walls merged. The nests were hollowed right out of the peaks. These arid horizons foster fanaticism, the ascetic life. The Perfecti, from the tops of their citadels, could see the mounting batallions of the Inquisition, and the promise of flames swelled their souls.

A castle of sorts rises on a lone knoll opposite the cave. The hotelier has already described to him the tower of El Far, dating from the tenth century. Fires were lit in the enclosing wall, signals announcing attacks from the Barbary Coast. For the sea is close by, the pure blue Mediterranean separating them from Africa. The coasts of Spain, cut into the crimson granite, begin a few miles away. Simon is enthusiastic about this contact. He'd like to open windows in the mountain looking out over these brilliant waves, and lead Myriam toward the beaches. On the sand she'd draw the torsos of the first men . . . Did they fear the sea and its gigantic fin? . . .

Lynne is waiting on some tourists, their faces roasted, long flakes of skin floating on their shoulders. Red, gaudy monsters, excited by the cave's proximity and its historic revelations. The family's still young, excruciatingly impish. A feeling of anguish grazes Simon. An insidious disgust before this little affective gaggle. Their unity is a knowing performance. So you can play at being a family . . . Such a shameless display by this blood-kin patrol, this multiheaded egocentricity whose obsessive insularity, farcical autarky are betrayed by a sealed car, private property and, most especially, the family dinner table. Lynne ought to slip some vitriol into their breakfast. The sight of the family suddenly falling into ruins. Such a great pathos, dad on his hands and knees, mom vomiting up her guts, the kids, more fragile, pass away first . . . Horror in Alphonse's bistro. Touristicide.

Lynne is wearing harem pants, wide on top and narrow at the bottom. Her rump bounces around in the loose-fitting fabric. Her T-shirt, however, is a limpid sheath.

When the family clears off, Simon sits near Lynne. The baby is napping at the foot of the bar. Alphonse dozes at the register. He's gathering his strength for his sunshine jaunt: his mistress is voracious, she needs a refreshed Alphonse, an old man on his toes. Simon makes a fuss over the baby, stream of little smiles, the infant chatters and his mom beams. How affectionate the man is! Strange, but indeed sensitive. Simon conquered Lynne's heart with one trick. Exploiting the advantage, he removes the child from the cradle . . . Ecstasy of the sweet little face regurgitating milk, blissfully babbling, babooning, pooping. Lynne admires the tableau. Arthur and Simon . . . She embraces the two with a common love. Simon strokes Arthur's cheek and his mother's neck in turn. Kind, very paternal hugs. Then his fingers slip, gravitate with gradual surreptitious touches toward her round breast. She bats her eyelashes, blushes slightly, simpers. He doesn't believe his eyes, it's just like a Charlie Chaplin movie, displaying the full range of virginal response. Then, he darts her a swift kiss. She doesn't have the time to pull her mouth back. She shies away with a bewitching click of her tongue: "Tsk . . . tsk . . . tsk"—rebuking him, feigning a thousand suspicions, customary protests, her remorse in a lace of sounds. But this music suggests the veiled presence of ten thousand promises, liberties, caprices, final indulgences, capitulations in extremis. The only thing Simon valued about love was its beginnings. The entirely stereotyped but spontaneous ritual that stirs the heart, enlarges the soul, liquidates memory, dilutes past failures, kills the shadows . . . the self shines, that radiant beam . . .

A small woman just entered, dry, swarthy. Seventy years old, maybe more. But her presence is extraordinary. She has piercing pupils, perpetually moving. She sees Lynne, she sees Simon. She's already understood. She spots Alphonse asleep. She senses Paula's presence out in her kitchen. Her eyes edge in, ferret about, then strike their target. Lynne says: "Hello, Agathe." Simon studies this arid cricket, this slim, fantastically curious weasel. "I'm very thirsty," she announces, "you wouldn't happen to have a glass of water, a simple glass of cold water?" Lynne brings over the glass. Agathe is refused nothing; she's part of the furniture, the necessities, the fatalities of the village. She performs a thousand favors, transmits messages, runs errands for the disabled, old handicapped people . . . She has no peer when it comes to old-time medicine, plants that cure the intestines and the liver, unblock the brain, get the arteries flowing, pep up the cells . . . Skin diseases are her speciality. Warts, allergies, scabies and pruritus. She lives in a small house just outside the village, behind the museum. A good half-mile separates her from the town center. For ages, early in the morning she's been slamming shut her door and trotting off in the light of the rising sun, up the small road, moving along the shoulder, her footsteps crunching the gravel. A trifle stooped, all in black, wrinkled, carrying a big bag that beats against her half-starved thigh. Her pupil guides her, that pointy beauty spot, drawing her forward, detecting the most minor events, the most minute novelty. She picks up every signal, shadowing, sweeping both sides at once with her head swaying from left to right. Agathe, the village gossipmonger. This power reaches a peak of unprecedented perfection in her. Every resource of her thought, her entrails, her every atom contribute to this vocation of eavesdropping and spying. She walks cheerfully through the countryside, telling herself the tittle-tattle, the unhoped-for discoveries. Her lips emit a shrill laughter. She emerges upon the village, starts down the street. She's stopped laughing, she's concentrating, nothing escapes her, she knows all. The housefronts file past, she knows the rooms, the pieces of furniture, the people huddled within. Her eye sees through glass panes and curtains alike, flushes out countless details. The slightest disturbance alarms her, triggers a current of cogitations that corrects her vision of reality and completes her conception of the truth. Her mind is a colossal file that never gets muddled. She collects indiscretions, elopements, confessions, tiny bits of information on the toxicosis of the latest baby, Leon going bald at twenty, Gertrude's chilblains, old Ludovic's eczema, the parish priest's extremely painful hemorrhoids. A roof tile is missing, she enters it into the record, spreads the word . . . Hard, nimble Agathe opens out the net of her gaze along the streets, on the main square, tirelessly infiltrating shops, pushing into houses on one pretext or another. Who'd dare put her out? She's obliging, a saintly woman. She inquires after people's health, pours out advice, resolves stalemates, gets spirits up. She's both confidant and guest, the census bureau and archives of Aguilar. She knew parents, grandparents. She lugs around documents, forgotten songs, medieval stories. She masters lineages, marriage ties, all the complicated ins and outs of blood relationships.

The dazzling light suffuses the doorway where dark Agathe is silhouetted, a lucid wisp of straw.

Lynne served the glass of water. Agathe swallows. But it's Simon she covets. Summer is a thankless period for her. Tourists, vacationers, the whole ephemeral population puts her synthetic and analytic abilities to the test. Life in the past was more peaceful. A person had to take into account only a few births, infrequent moves, some newcomers settling in. Agathe managed her memory in complete serenity. But time speeds up, village dwellers become mobile, unfaithful and capricious. So Agathe keeps watch, adopts a more flexible strategy, accommodates her tactics to a world in flux. Simon stands before her. Agathe senses that he's a prime morsel. The type of man who keeps mum about his past, enamored with the immediate moment. A thick wall. Agathe searches, inspects, she'll find the crack . . .

. . . And then there are those kids up at the cave, the crew of excavators, sixty or so teenagers from various countries. Fortunately some come back year after year. Agathe recognizes that she knows next to nothing about these intruders. The village is her business. But that doesn't keep her from gleaning in the outskirts out of sheer pleasure. For a few months Agathe has been harboring a dream: to go up to the cave. By picking a very cool day, and having some sturdy adult to shoulder her over the rocks, she's convinced she'd succeed. A field of anguishing and boundless discoveries would stretch out at the top. They were waiting for her, those immemorial inhabitants . . . Agathe moaned in lust and fright at the thought of those generations of archaic hunters . . . She tried to make herself see reason, swore the village would be enough for her. But in fact the cave ancestor's name was Aguilar Man! Agathe's knowledge was illusory indeed if these very structural roots were concealed from her. Of course, she's read the brochures, visited the museum. But nothing matched direct experience, Agathe's eye sifting through the shadows, scrutinizing the bones, maybe bearing witness, and such a miracle that would be, unearthing a new skull or entire skeleton. She wanted to go into the cave, this thirst tortured her, her throat was racked.

While sipping the faucet water, she simply exchanged a few words with Simon, slipped in some innocent questions . . . Lynne came to the rescue. Very proud, she revealed that Simon was a journalist from Paris who was doing a story on the cave. No doubt about it now, Agathe liked Simon! A reporter! . . . A cosmopolitan gossip! The grapevine on a planetary scale, cosmic curiosity. She'd become the traveler's friend. He'd really have to tell her all about the world, and maybe take her up there . . . from which point you can see everything, the first man and the whole village in one single glance.

The museum is modern, a stone and glass framework erected on mountain-drawn slabs, blending harmoniously into the landscape reflected in its picture windows. The village is proud of this sanctuary dedicated to science. The Romanesque church has lost its glamour, the old Christ and worm-eaten Madonna supplanted by the horde of pithecanthropi. The new god is *homo erectus.* The building dedication was a local event. A minister had come from Paris, General de Gaulle even sent a telegram of congratulations. The hero's framed autograph is on display in the town hall beside a statue of Marianne, wearing her Phrygian cap. . . . Upon entering, the visitor —whether tourist, schoolkid, university student from Perpignan, a scholar hastened from abroad, or someone simply curious—is impressed by a large vertical panel recapitulating the origins of life and of Man. The saga retraces the whole evolution: from virus to Victor Hugo! At seventy million years Purgatorius suddenly appears: a sort of shrew from which will arise the ancestors of the monkey on one side, and those of Man on the other. At ten million years comes the Ramapithecus, the first protohuman link. Then, between six and three million years, a motley crew already dexterous with their hands, *australopithecus afarensis, australopithecus africanus, australopithecus robustus* . . . Striking sketches reproduce the silhouettes of the ancestors whose spines gradually straighten along the genealogical tree. The small monkeys at the base get heftier, taller, their heads bigger, with a more regular shape. At the very top is the great Cro-Magnon, our peer, our brother, the finally mature flowering of Mankind. Another far more complicated painted panel reconstructs the important geologic and climatic zones. Every phase presents samples of the flora and fauna. The terminology is barbarous. Densely packed tourists eat up this display of knowledge with their eyes. Simon is surprised by such voracity for information and details. Some can be seen learning by heart names and dates. Their children ask questions, thunderstruck, perched on their fathers' shoulders. In the

Romanesque church, their first stop, they were fascinated by the candles, bunched like bushes; they wanted to blow them out as if they were on some sumptuous birthday cake, one belonging to the Maker Himself. But here, bathed in light, the kids get excited over the ladder of the species, graduated monkeys, dubious chimpanzees and shrewd gorillas. The colossal time frame sets the visitors' heads spinning. They get the numbers wrong, mix up billions, millions, millennia . . . yet still come flocking, pop-eyed, their brains aching. The museum is a shore, allowing the expanse of the oceanic ages to be scrutinized. Each wave, in fact, comprises an immense sea and the maze vanishes into an overwhelming distance. Abruptly yanked from their carefree vacations, massed together between glass walls, short of breath, the sweating visitors undergo this flood of time, take measure of the chasm, midgets gawking at the abyss.

Display windows present an array of carved rocks. Round stones set out in all shapes and sizes, schist, flint, quartz or limestone. Some show only imperceptible changes in their contours, others clearly lopped-off sections. There are large obtuse pebbles, rough tools, but also bifaces whose symmetry awakens a new sense in the heart of the first man, the glimmer of a sensibility . . . Two perfectly corresponding notches around a sharp-edged bone. From material such as this there leads an untold path toward what shimmering, multifaceted beauty. The stones are classified according to mineral composition and the degree they've been worked on. Scientists proliferate a vocabulary whose range of nuances would be lost upon any ordinary observer, indicating every sort of modification: fringe markings, thick or flaky strokes, scalariform, raised, denticulated, encroaching . . . Thus the slightest sign impacting upon the mineral surface is at once named, labeled, and every minute gesture of the ancestor inventoried. What was once only instinctive craftsmanship, the splutterings of industry, are transformed into scientific artifacts. The rocks, cast out of their state of innocence, are aligned in solemn archives. Scrapers, chisels, perforators, choppers, chopping tools, polyhedrons, bifaces, hatchets, flint hammers, spearheads, Clactonian notches, beaks, denticles are hauled up to the same level of importance as planes, computers, electronics. All essentially identical. The hand modifies, implements, fashions, works in the thick of things, fleshes out projects, opens paths. That's why tourists are moved, listening as they do to this inaudible murmur, history's whisper within a fragile furrow. They lean forward, fall silent. Signs flourish on the stones' crust. And suddenly Simon thinks about the erstwhile present as something current, tangible, once as obvious as our own . . . Dawn broke somewhere in the mountains. The sunlight flooded the riverbanks. A bustling man, alive, lucid, hand clutched upon a chunk of rock that he banged repeatedly against a rigid edge. The solid stone burst to pieces, shards flying. This din of meditation gave birth to unique, original objects, seeds of intelligibility, splinters of thought, mirrors of an inordinate ambition, of a thirst for conquest and domination, nimble assistants, slaves of matter: tools.

The museum also has on exhibit impressive casts, masses of reconstituted soils with the exact location of each bone. Excavating destroys the different cave sediments which can however be reproduced at any moment based on photographs and sketches. Thus slabs of prehistoric clay wait under glass far from the original mountain. Geological samples interbedded with fossils, encrusted fragments, hard bits, skeleton seeds . . . Archaeology inflicts a strange alchemy upon the past, simultaneously isolating it even as it brings it into being, exposing, labeling and defusing it. On the one hand, the damp cave, a gloomy den with its maw crammed full of inviolate soils and secrets; on the other, the bright compartmentalized museum where, in layered rows, the barbarous earths and tools of slaughter are arranged. Submitting them to processes of inventory and fastidious naming strips them of their magic. They live out an artificial existence like bush animals in a zoo. Touristic voyeurism scours off their bestial charm. The pithecanthropus' grunting, his angers, his bloodthirsty hunter's drives, the hierarchical revolts of his clans, his sexual furies and vital obsessions are emptied by these lucid shelves. Modern man extracts the grumpy, visceral ancestor from his rocky burrow only to sterilize his power, number his ribs . . . Reassuring sleight-of-hand by which scientists skim over the reptilian creature within themselves. The monsters are muzzled by these mathematical heroes. Siegfried perpetually lays low the dragon.

But in the center of the museum reigns an item resisting any intellectual taming. The stream of visitors forms a large circle around this frightening archive. Curious people flock together: the most whimsical vacationers, casual visitors, those out for a laugh, the uneducated, all showing signs of a profound perplexity. Eyebrows knit, gazes cloud over. The vision shakes Simon, furrows his features. The silence broadens. Long face-to-face encounter. Mute dialogue . . . Gazing out at him is the skull of the first man, discovered in '71 beside a lion's mandible, crowned with a jumble of broken bones and tools. Under the prominent forehead ridge open two eye-sockets, the nasal cavity. Black gaps in the paleness of bone . . . This skull is the evidence of Man. This specter with the undershot jaw and receding forehead, long ago housed in flesh, sheathed in nerves and muscles, once was alive. Today, motionless, scoured, fissured, composed of glued bits and pieces, he bears witness. He means nothing, everything. One of death's objects, a box, a hollow bone. Each visitor, himself bearing a comparable skullcap, wants to remain in darkness about his kinship. Who dares recognize his image in this macabre stone? The upper jawbone equipped with a few teeth stands alone, with no counterpart. Bereft of a foundation, the face bites into pure nothing. Mouthless, the gagged ancestor remains fixed in his state of suspension, his stupor. The full jaw apparatus would detract from the essential, bringing to mind anecdotes, appetites, crushed flesh. Reduced to skull and sockets, the man relinquishes his existence as an individual who desired, ate; his meaning is both purified and narrowed. He is no more than seeing orifices within the hardness of bone. For see he does. Where once eyes glimmered, the fresh water of glances, there are now these haunting holes, impeccably cleansed cavities brimming with another vision, a deeper, darker questioning . . . tunnel openings upon what mysteries of the origins? These sockets are now passages leading into the infinite night. They are also graves and tombs . . . Cruelty and death are inscribed in their craters. This absence of eyes deepens sight. Each person can fill the void with his own. Billions of curiosities stir in these gaps . . . A spontaneous, unfocused terror seizes the children in front of this smashed face, the laconic grimace, the impassive torture of the skull.

Just outside the museum, Simon saw a tall, pallid woman under a fig tree. She had long white hair. Enormous blue eyes, motionlessly staring out from her face of death. Alphonse will later reveal that this is Iza the Madwoman. She hates tourists and the cave. Simon comments upon his museum visit. Alphonse has a surprise in store for him: "You know, the skull's a mask!"

Simon shows surprise.

"Yes, yes, they don't emphasize the fact up at the museum . . . But the skull was discovered without the occiput. Plus, a flint fragment was spotted inside the skull cavity. The teeth were also found a few yards away, proving the skull was used, carried around the cave . . .

"And do you know why they broke the skull? . . . To extract the brain and eat it! Then, with the front part they got up to their old tricks. Can you imagine? They say that in the South Seas there are still fellows who gobble up their enemies' grey matter and use the skull like a mask!"

"But you can't compare tribes of present-day men to a tribe of pithecanthropi!" Simon exclaims.

"Sure you can! You really think that stops anybody? I can tell you that the cave doesn't hold much interest for me anymore. Back in the beginning it intrigued me, twenty years ago, when they started the excavations. Still, if you find some fun in it . . . Aguilar Man was an arrant cannibal. Our ancestors devoured each other. They ground up the bones of man and beast, gorged themselves on the marrow inside—a top-notch pick-me-up! They managed better than we do! No tooth decay! Their carnivorous diet preserved their molars! Their grub was raw meat. You can tell by the vertical grooves on their teeth. I'm an old hand at that. I was younger then . . . more curious. But anyway, mustn't exaggerate, those guys didn't live to be old. They found a mandible belonging to a fifty-year-old woman. That's the absolute maximum.

They died on the average at twenty-one, just a little more than dogs and cats nowadays. Time enough for them to invent tools, collect memories, and to focus the first feelings . . . You know, the cave is still practically unexplored. Still thirty yards of untouched deposits! Decades of research . . . A gullet that's probably got some nice surprises in store for us. Take Iza the Madwoman, for example. This is exactly the stuff that's working on her. Her delirium is fixated upon it. It's what she lives on! Bones, skulls, cannibals—they plague her. She says the hole's got to be blocked up, the open mouth closed. She's afraid the Aguilar guy's going to wake up one fine day and come down from the mountain to strangle us all. The girl's a sad case. Nobody listens to her. However the old villagers don't like the cave very much, tourists, noisy buses. They're planning to build a motel on the hill behind the museum. In a small valley, very near here, a campground was set up. As for me, it enriches my clientele. But there are robbers, criminal activity, commotion, uproar, drunken binges some nights. It's progress, it's the pithecanthropus!"

The cannibal mountain captivated Simon. The village was sleeping in its pool of sunlight at the base of the bloody pyramid. The enigma of the skull blazed in the cave's black mouth.

Lynne had brought Simon to the shore of a dried-up stream. They both walked in the bed scattered with gravel and pebbles. A bright channel bordered with stubby thornbushes. They felt a keen pleasure, slipping like this into the heart of the landscape. A small sand basin opened out after a long meander. A slab of smooth, blue-tinted schist occupied the center. They paused on this raft. Lynne took off her sandals, burying her feet in the burning sand. Simon bared his torso. He spoke of the museum, the cave's skull to the young girl who told him that it was just a latex imitation. The original had been stored in a safe place . . . Simon reacted with disappointment. The mask that had overwhelmed him was only a vulgar replica. At the museum they took care not to announce to the crowd of visitors that they were faced with nothing more than an artificial cast. In what sterilized refuge, bolted vault, had the skull been deposited? A few scientists in the know were keeping watch over the authentic fossil. This secret perturbed Simon. The skull was the necessary center of a landscape laden with memory. Deprived of this genuine axis, mountains, village and cave capsized into an unformed floating world. Simon wanted to find out where the original mask was hidden. Locating it might deliver him from this sensation of inner dispersion in which he was suddenly foundering. The truth had been exhumed only to be immediately buried by the initiated, with no uncertain pride and malice, far removed from the profane populace. The museum was merely a jumble of contrivances. Simon thought of the Lascaux cave paintings, themselves hidden from the public, enclosed in a sterile sanctuary, the visitors having to make do with a skillful reconstruction in a neighboring museum. This dualism of the simulacrum and the real fascinated Simon. He imagined a future world where the planet's still-intact, rare treasures would survive in unknown hiding places. And so for the pyramids, Notre Dame, the Mona Lisa, the Pantheon, humanity would be entitled only to pompous duplicates. A handful of the elect would be invited once a year to come and see the originals. In the heart of a vast desert, surrounded by watchtowers, walls, radar stations, they would be able to contemplate the Gothic cathedral, the pharaohs' tombs, the Greek temples and da Vinci's painting, reunited in a fantastic assemblage. A heaven of archetypes, shielded from the staring multitude and reserved for princes, demigods, the exceptionally gifted, superstars, space heroes, purebreds, champions, maestros, dazzling geniuses, conquistadors of the stars and, once every other year, opened to a half-dozen beastly poor creatures, beggars from ghettos promoted to the rank of saints!

Lynne was seduced by the weird ideas Simon was formulating out loud. She'd rested back against the schist slab. Her cotton dress rose over the thighs she was tanning . . . just a little, her skin was so sensitive. Simon was now completely undressed. His sun worship left no room for modest reserve. Both intimidated and amused, Lynne turned her face away and giggled . . . Simon suggested she follow his example. She refused. The sun would scorch her, mar her delicate complexion. Simon's desire was sharpened by the thought of this torture. His sex was gradually stiffened by contact with the rocks as if he had tapped into their rigid heat. He drew close to Lynne and wrapped his arms around her. His mouth already latched upon the girl's fine lips, plumped by a fleshy central ridge. He nibbled this bud. His mouth opened and his tongue explored this avid cavity. His hands slipped under her skirt, stroking her thighs. She freed herself and undressed, then stretched out at the foot of the boulder on the stream sand. Simon contemplated Lynne's body, fragile and supple, her complexion mother-of-pearl. But her breasts and buttocks seemed to have gathered additional strength and flesh. Simon lay down next to her and gently ran sand over her legs and sides. Lynne turned over, rolling in the warm wadi. Her body became sheathed in a grainy net. Her skin took on a flush from the friction. Simon coveted Lynne's silica-draped nakedness. With his nail tip he bared beaches of virgin flesh through the web, rending wider along her thighs, uncovering her nipples, unveiling the twin roundnesses of her rump. Simon's torso was also plated with large mineral scales. Their bodies grazed each other's. Zones fused. His member sought a breach in the scabbard of dust and crystal. The sunlight bleached the stone skeleton, this brook where evaporated water had left behind its imprint of nerves, its excavations, its moving belts that encircled the rocks. A fossil stream, a tortured ghost of crevasses. Simon at last pierced the crystalline armor, penetrating her flesh.

They rose and walked in the streambed. A paving of pebbles spread out its pathway of reflections and flames across the scrubland, between the mountains, heading toward the ruined castles.

When they got back they passed in front of the old men's bench. Lynne and Simon quenched their thirst at the fountain, their two mouths coming together in the spray's coolness. The old folk admired the girl's streaming hair and delicately shimmering legs. On the ground at the lovers' feet the sand left marks.

Shortly afterward, Agathe met them, darting glances as sharp as banderillas. She was carrying a bagful of apricots and she offered them some. Her scrawny fingers rooted out the downy red-speckled fruit. She exhibited them under the lovers' mouths like jewels, then watched them bite into the brilliant pulp, a deep orange under the duller skin. "Real good, right? Right? . . ." She eyed their greedy chops, their sticky-sweet lips, took in Lynne's crumpled dress, Simon's soiled trousers. The couple was dazed with exhaustion, beads of water drying in their hair . . .

"You know the latest?" Agathe blurted out. "I bet you're just on your way back from a nice stroll out in the scrub, right? . . . Well, I for one wouldn't take the chance, they just let out a lynx, a male. And they'll add a female sometime in February-March, so I hear, during mating season . . . because those animals go into heat during the winter . . . That's a fact."

Agathe paused a second. She liked firing off extraordinary news. She savored the effect of her words, enjoyed the expressions of surprise, prepared for the stream of questions to follow.

"Yes, a lynx, a wild beast . . . a species that still lives in Spain, one that ecologists are trying to reacclimatize to our mountains and pine forests . . ."

Agathe sounded the word "ecologist," isolating each syllable. The word was to her liking, brand-new, with a scholarly touch.

"They say lynxes never attack human beings. But who knows for sure? After all, they're like panthers. The only thing missing now is for them to let loose some wolves and bears to make things more natural. We're not back in the Middle Ages. A lynx! In the age of the space shuttle . . ."

Agathe loved saying "space shuttle." Whereas she slowly separated each syllable of the word *ecologist,* meticulously dissecting it, she swiftly pronounced her "space shuttle," her tongue nimbly sissing out the *s*'s. The voluptuous quality she found in speech was contained in a range of registers, in a slow analytical articulation, or in swift accelerations varying her phonic ecstasies.

Agathe then reached the old men's bench. She stayed on her feet, looking down upon the line of drowsy grandfathers. More or less restive prey, depending on the days. She asked after their wives, their health. She was especially gifted when it came to health, the soft spot of the elderly. They didn't hold out for long before opening up about their petty ailments. Agathe listened, reflected, compared one case to another she knew, dispensed concrete advice. She never wearied of this medical drivel. Her power stemmed from an awesome ability to listen and suggest. After she'd made good with so much altruistic kindness, the old men had no choice but to answer the questions she brought to bear on various subjects, family events, joys and misfortunes. Finally she told them about the lynx, her finishing blow that took them by surprise. And one day while they were snoozing in the plane tree's shade, their brains attuned to the fountain's gurgling, what if the wild beast slinked through the streets, leapt up on the bench and clawed to pieces their hoary heads, their cluster of wattles? The red stoplight blinking, and the tinkling water punctuating the forefathers' martyrdom. A torture site tourists, years later, will visit, a sacrificial bench where eight old men were said to have been devoured by a wild animal come down from the mountain. Thus the village of Aguilar would boast, alongside General de Gaulle's autograph and the first man's skeleton, this ultimate badge of horror.

The lynx, a granite word with claws, had inscribed itself in Simon's imagination. Lynx or Sphinx. Syllables concentrated in a lapidary sign . . . A whip lacerates the skin, marking it with what cipher? What fatal stamp? He'd gone over to the library in Perpignan to consult bestiaries and books on felines. He was fond of the cities of summer. Simmering billows of dust sweep through the narrow streets, the gashes of the squares. Automobiles, fewer and farther between. An enormous listlessness. The ceremonial library opens its reading rooms, as mute as sacristies. The elderly, the self-educated, the brainy, introverts and unctuous maniacs circulate amid the card catalogs. A female student crosses her harmonious thighs while leafing through an encyclopedia. Simon really would like to know what she's searching for. Being drawn to a tomb like this rather than to beaches strikes him as both attractive and monstrous. What suffering has she come here to muzzle by hiding deep in the death of books? Small corpses hardened in their word, squeezed into bindings, lined up in monotonous columns along interminable shelves. Coffins of thought. Ossuaries, catacombs of chimeras. Simon grows fond of this macabre place where the lynx's undulating outline is silhouetted. Everything he reads about the creature excites and enchants him. The photos, the measurements, the various species' habitats, habits, biology . . . He spends a whole day among more and more specialized manuals. Most alluring is an old myth found in the works of Pliny the Elder. The Roman writer attributes to the lynx the power to engender precious stones in its entrails. The animal's urine petrifies in the form of rubies, ambers, carbuncles . . . The lynx's stones—or ligures, ligurius—strew the beast's rocky, forested terrain. The belief haunts the centuries. Simon rediscovers it in the Middle Ages . . . On the other hand the lynx doesn't appear to be endowed with a more powerfully keen sight than other felids. Simon imagines the lynx in the mountain and those large limestone caves, those swallow-holes crosshatched with shrubs and pine forests. He's going to buy a pair of binoculars in a shop by a river gone virtually dry. Huge swarms of insects whirl above the desiccated mud. He's decided to find the lynx, to observe it, to follow it. Certainly, no direct account connects the animal to the Aguilar cave. Simon is getting sidetracked from his investigation. But it seems to him that invisible affinities, imperceptible correspondences, mirror reflections, are weaving together the different elements of a puzzle composed of minerals, sunlight, half-animals, gloomy maws and ancestral skeletons. A chessboard where the red and the black starkly alternate. He's going to decipher this illegible scrawl written in an alphabet of claws, flames, shadows and rocks. Why does Agathe's silhouette occupy the center of these deserts? Is she herself the wise-eyed lynx, hoarding the archives of the cosmic village?

Simon did not go back to Aguilar. He parked in the scrub. Now he's walking. He knows he has no chance of surprising the lynx. The animal's territory stretches over four thousand acres. But a new wildness has laid hold of these lands. Antique and rejuvenated, they are watchful under the feline's dominion. With his binoculars he scrutinizes horizons, peaks, steep cliffs, explores the valley hollows, crevasses surrounded by bramble bushes. He observes the migratory circaetus, the sparrow hawks and harriers hovering above field mice. The eagle and the lynx are brothers; but the eagles have died. The only survivors are the birds of prey, less lofty but more tenacious. He walks on a long while, without sweating or feeling thirsty, tormented by his desire for the lynx. At stream banks. along gravel pits, he sets himself searching for the brilliance of sacred stones come from the belly of the beast. Off a short distance, a moving trickle slips between greener banks into the gully. Simon draws near. He soaks his face in the icy current. The water shimmers, carved out of glass, angles and facets of freshness. Simon marvels at this vein, palpitating at the foot of retables and platforms. Water is beautiful only when it eschews clouding the scenery, blurring lines. In rainy Le Havre or Antwerp he despises the weather, the impressionism of water's halo, its shadings, its mists, softening and rotting. Here the liquid springs are miraculous, no result of rainfall or tepid Breton drizzles. They simply appear. Their limpid stingers, like those of asps, emerge from the rock, and their venom refreshes. Simon follows the stream and its sandbed. Someone abruptly rises in front of him, a tall dry man with an immaculate flowing mane. In linen trousers and shirt. The man hesitates and smiles. Utensils strew the ground, sieves, tubs. The current has been diverted, with screens barring the new artery. Simon thought this skill was long since extinct, relegated to the touching mythologies of Western movies. The man is a prospector, searching for gold. A believer who doesn't believe in the apparent muteness of things. A superstitious soul who scratches at surfaces, chips off crusts, cleanses silts, inspects micas and flints. He labors in total solitude. Simon admires his scrawniness and strength . . . He'd like to question him, drag out some secrets about the mountain. By dint of bending over sands and stones this way, has he seen the soul of the first men poking through? Does he know that the lynx inhabits this desolate territory along with him? Simon brings up the feline's existence.

"Yes, yes, I'm aware," the man answers knowingly.

"You've seen him?"

"I spotted him at dawn, a little while ago, he'd come to drink at the stream bank . . . A beautiful creature, squat, reddish fur, with the oddest little face, sweet and aggressive. I knew they'd just let him go. I was happy he came to visit me."

"Did you find any nuggets?"

"Here and there, gold dust. It's an obsession that doesn't put food in your belly. There're still a few crazy men like me left in France, you know. I'm not the only one. People aren't aware of such things. But I'm acquainted with some prospectors. I don't like cities or crowds. To tell the truth I don't expect to fish up anything. I don't care about being rich, I keep going at it out of friendly feeling for the streams."

"Could you show me some gold?" Simon asks with such a naive expression that the man puts aside all suspicions.

The fellow goes into his tent, opens a small bag, pours the contents into his hand and comes back out into the broad sunshine. Tiny flakes sparkle in the crux of his palm. Simon studies this native gold. His heart thumps. He laughs. Suddenly the landscape is transfigured. These walls scoured by wind and light, these smoothly polished heights conceal a luminous pollen. Nuggets, beetle eggs, snakes, wasps of sunlight, bright bilberries, lynx tears. The prospector's face betrays a hint of irony. These mountains, these miles of masses and profane reliefs have meaning only in relation to this ludicrous gold. An infinitesimal truth and precious carpet in the sheath of waters. Simon's joy plunges him back into his childhood . . . Aguilar Man had no concern for gold. And yet, all that glitters—the shimmering spawn of the stars, the copper of the setting sun, embers of dying blazes, the eyes of nocturnal beasts—must have magnetized his gaze. The magic of what glints. If prehistoric man had found this bright metal while gathering stones from streambeds, would he have taken it up in his palm, shown it to the tribe? The gold of the origins in an ape's hand. Still in ignorance about value and profit. The pure pleasure of looking upon matter beaming. Maybe a feeling of fear or indifference? But Simon believes in the first man's surprise upon confronting the eye of gold. He believes in his joy. For youth is what illuminates, youth is the fear-instilling shadows or the furious flames. The shy gold glows. It simply hints at its promise. Hope is mirrored in its shine. Man once played in this light.

He undertakes his second cave climb early in the morning. He wants to reach the top with a sharp mind. The path appears shorter, easier, but his first sight of that shadow-gorged den, those frescoes of bones, still has an impact. At once he went over to greet Myriam. She seems happy to see him again. She has begun drawing. She's speaking with a young blond man. Simon strolls into the cave between the strings, strides over the ditches, crosses the footbridges. He leans down, daring to touch the bone edges breaking the surface. Already the adolescents are foraging through the earth. In lined notepads some record sketches that reproduce the contours of precisely located objects. Letters and numbers in complicated combinations allow for the cataloging of the most minute finds, a rodent's tooth, a molar fragment . . .

Simon questions Myriam about the nature of the soils. She explains how the layers of sand and clay alternate through the millennia. Dry or wet periods, cold or hot, resulting in variations in consistency and appearance. The ensemble is flanked by two stalagmite floors. This deposit was formed between 550,000 and 400,000 years ago, in the course of the Mendelian complex, during the first part of the Pleistocene epoch. Simon can't situate these bits of information on a precise scale, but the learned vocabulary, far from discouraging him, serves as a framework for his curiosity. The words *Mendelian* and *Pleistocene* fall prettily from the black woman's lips. Simon longs for a detailed truth and authentic terminology. He listens to Myriam in the shadow of the cave. Her face projects an air of power, of inviolability, both effects of her immaculate corneas coupled with the enamel of her teeth. Her smooth, dark flesh blossoms around this mother-of-pearl sheen. Myriam is wearing a blouse that opens up over her firm, swollen chest. Never has Simon seen breasts as hard and heavy. A glistening furrow sinks between the curves. He'd like to see Myriam naked in the cave, amid the bones, behind the grid of string. Her long, muscular thighs bulge in her jeans.

Her ankles are extraordinarily delicate. Her thinly shanked leg rises and disappears in the fabric.

She tells about the cave, sorts out the strata, the accidents of its history. A sizable flexure of the sediments occurred, followed by a truncation of the whole formation, the result being that today the layers override each other, disheveled, interspersing their eras. Geologists reconstitute the genealogy of the veins through these superimpositions, these breaks, these writings that intermingle memories. The cave isn't the limpid mirror that Simon had first imagined with its horizontal landings, both visible and dated. The cave twists, curves . . . Chemical reactions lay siege, metamorphosing the solid matter which dissolves, recomposes. A voluminous mass of guano excreted by colonies of bats through the course of the ages has triggered a series of mutations. Seepage through the karstic vault has complicated the phenomenon. Vesicles open here and there, in places where crystals grow. Precipitations are at work, circulations, concretions germinate, oxides spread. Heavy minerals, amphiboles and garnets, become debased. Acids attack the limestones.

Myriam moves nimbly through this panorama of matter. She brings the slow evolution of the laboring earth into existence. Each technical word she uses, far from obscuring her talk, articulates it, sparks a hunger for knowledge in Simon. The cave is embellished with so many details. Geology is a long poem in which minerals live and change. Smectite, kaolinite, the aluminum phosphates, the ribboned apatites are the bricks of a concrete mobile structure. Simon drinks up these angular words, smooth, dull or sticky. The cave is no more than a hole saturated with conglomerates. Now the cave acquires nuances, branches out. Simon embraces the luxuriance of its genesis, creative adventures, phases of annihilation, underground anecdotes and battles. He doesn't know why he thinks again about the whitish deposit of guano whose traces appear in the cross sections of soils . . . the bats lined up in the cave, those flying rats, those furry night mammals in tight swarms, huddled against the walls. They amassed these excrements whose action profoundly transformed the substance and architecture of the sediments. Trapped in these convulsions, the bones and tools changed. The large jaw of the cave swallowed the water laden with residues, windswept debris, its belly engulfing and manipulating this thick chyme. The cavern masticated, secreted. Our memory depended on this enormous digestion. Myriam elaborated her epic with a musical loquaciousness that carried Simon along. African roulades, cattle bells, then deep sequences where her cavernous voice proceeds tonelessly. Her speech also possessed its platforms, volumes, seepages and condensations. Myriam's mouth was a cave of mucus tissue. Saliva and teeth, tongue, uvula, cords and breaths governed her timbres, her silent breaths and exploding vowels. Geology of the Word.

Black Myriam held between her lips the backbone of sentences, the thorax of terms, the dust of syllables and vocabularies. She spoke and her voice was an echo of the origins, the primal cry. Speech in the language of the cave. Gentle black woman, carnal in the rock cavity.

Before leaving her he asked if she'd agree to spend an afternoon with him. She hesitated slightly, then revealed her free day. He accepted. Sped along by elation he dashes down the path, sharp turns, rearing bends, bumps, patches; the small ravine flows, his body slips out of control. He catches himself on the branches of a fennel bush and the blue manes of thyme. Fragrances bake in the sunlight, gusts caress him as he falls. Below, behind a row of black dense cypresses, the crew's camp has been set up. Six large tents provide shelter for forty or so youths. They are seated outside in the open air around long tables. The bags, arriving from the cavern, are emptied by some, sifted, the sands and clays washed. Others pick out knucklebones, vertebrae, metacarpus, tibia fragments, jaw sections caked with limestone. They clean off every last bit of scoria. The perforators that human beings once used for opening skins or a certain Clactonian notch carved on a piece of quartz debris for a lance slowly emerge from their outer coating. The adolescents work along in unruffled calm. They rarely speak. The sun drifts across the sky. Large shadows fall on the camp when the mountain begins to serve as a screen against the rays. In the English girl Sue's white hand is an awl encrusted in a compact accretion. The girl in shorts and a wide-open, sleeveless blouse concentrates on her task. She looks like she's involved in extracting a winkle from its shell. She pummels this resistant hide, peels off particles, careful to keep intact the fossil's surface. Hours pass this way. The crew gives no impression of wearying. Once in a while someone arrives to relieve a worker. Pier, the tall blond Swede, goes for a dive in the lake, takes a few broad breaststrokes, swims underwater, pops up, continues on. He frolics about freely, forgets the excavation, those tiny gnawings, ancient droppings, the whole macabre compost. Long liquid swirls run along his backbone. Pier's body is as white as a candle. The black water drapes in mourning his Madonna-like epidermis. The director and his wife, both overseeing the entire group of activities, are well-known researchers. He's rather stern-looking, bearded, laconic. She, more absentminded. Her thoughtless blunders, roving glances. A smooth angular face. They move to-and-fro, ranging from work site to museum to cave, participate in the soil cleaning, give advance to the adolescents. A Boy Scout way of life and cannibalism are in perfect sync at the foot of the mountain. The mandibles that once chewed man's brain are the object of exacting, almost tender attentions. A tight-knit gang of healthy kids bend over a sorry pack of gut-spilling pithecanthropi.

Sue's conduct may be the worst of the lot. Lynne and Agathe told Simon about the English girl's licentious behavior. The kid's depraved, cultivating just one kind of pleasure: virgin country boys. This is in keeping with the purpose of the excavations: her task is to extract from a churlish envelope of impulses and utmost prudery the delicate bonework of desires and erotic tactics. With brush and awl she carves and polishes her virgins . . .

Simon watches the row of workers. Ants sucking the bones, scrutinizing the mummies. Pawing little corpses. An enormous disequilibrium entrenches itself between their present existence hanging from a mouse's canine tooth and the immense universe of sunlight and limestone where the lynx hunts, with beaches beyond the hills upon which other teenagers exhibit themselves, flirt and carry on, heedless of these immemorial stiffs.

Every Saturday there's a dance at the city campground, where they dance to rock music. The reckless rhythms knock them loose from their greedy, motionless spy work. They whirl and leap, shake their hips, trace arabesques, butterflying arms, swift beams, and their flesh is liberated from the skeletons' spell.

Two in the afternoon. The hamlet is in flames. Paula went to bed up in her room. She closed shutters and curtains. It's dark. Outside, a hail of sunlight. The vise of fire clamps down on the village. Gradually a paleness emanates from the window frame. A ghost day, the far-away memory of things. Paula likes this spectral rest in which she hears her irregular heartbeats. She sees nothing. She listens. She has a vague fear of dying. She survives. Fat and melancholic, without bra or girdle, wearing a simple lace slip, stretched out on the sheets. She knows she's ugly. Ridiculous and pudgy. A paunchy dolly. She's resigned. She daydreams, hears Alphonse closing the door. At once Lynne starts up the jukebox. A record of chanting rhythms and shrieks. Paula never scolds the girl. A miracle the baby doesn't wake up. Arthur's deaf to the world. His nap wipes him out. Alphonse pedals along the steaming, sizzling road . . . Paula fears he'll fall ill at his age. She knows he's off to meet the grocery woman, his mistress. Paula's a little jealous of Yvette. But her feeling is free of any anger. Hers is an aching revolt. Let Alphonse take advantage of it. Last chimes. All the same, that Alphonse is selfish. Leaving her there in the shadows with her fragile heart. What if he found her dead around five o'clock . . . Paula listens to the sounds of the village. A car horn . . . Clinking . . . Not much commotion in this early afternoon. The sunlight drives off the noises. So when a busload of tourists rolls up the street, it's like a storm breaking, an apocalyptic thunder, the walls vibrate. Paula's heart begins to race. Aguilar has turned into the Lourdes of archaeologists. Silence once more. A quiet pool. Lynne stopped her record. She's sleeping beside the baby. Mother and son. Twenty years, adding up their ages. Simon the traveler is a strange but likable man. He ogles Lynne's breasts. Paula noticed . . . A fly buzzes, darts along, lands. Everything falls silent. Children laugh suddenly, rippling drops, their heels click. They're not taking a nap because their mother, the deliveryman's wife, cleans houses every Monday. The kids use the opportunity to run off. Paula enjoys identifying the invisible passersby. Countless crackling sounds, minute rackets, shrill lancets nevertheless escape her. There are footsteps she knows nothing about. In the evening she's fond of the clicking heels of the secretary from the winegrowers' cooperative. The young woman walks up the street heading for her bus stop just outside the city. At the same time, there's the characteristic voice of Marthe Praslin, the jeweler's widow, with that merry lover's trill. The tramontane makes the waterspout across the way whine. It's sad, moaning all alone. She's gotten used to this sobbing that signifies dry wind, fierce heat, passing time with its stomach rumblings and medications, the slow hours . . . Alphonse on his bike, Agathe catching a quick nap, Iza posted behind her curtain, the pastor slumbering, the shopkeepers also dozing in their kitchens, TVs off. Birds in cages hop about, surprised by the silence, eyes wide open. The fountain splashes the emptiness . . . The red, green light almost useless. A bike crunches along, the village gives off a low buzz, an acoustic illusion, maybe it's Paula's ears, the wax inside? Long rustle of sunlight sissing across the rocks . . . The cave gazes at the village.

No, it's not a bus. It begins like the sound of huge insects humming, swift bumblebees. The noise swells, accelerates into a roar, the street lifted by the spasm of passing motorcycles. In their wake, inside houses, can be heard shouts and questions sown by the tornado. Clear-sounding words betray the presence of heads surely popping out of nearby windows. People are indignant. Lynne's baby caterwauls. A rude awakening. The old men on the bench are dumbstruck. The lightning-like mob of machines surged past right under their noses. A large brilliant braid, rigged out with reflectors. And then it starts all over again. Paula hears the swarm of booming beetles, the whole pack heading down the street once more. The engines howl, accelerators at full throttle, the exhaust pipes doctored up. Every head at a window. In doorways small children use the occasion to cut short their naps. They line up by their mothers. A little scared but delighted by the spectacle. The old men on the bench rose to their feet this time. A garland of gnarled silhouettes. The brutes rear up on their metal mounts. Their helmets sparkle, their leather-sheathed thighs gleam. They extend greetings, the finger, hurl insults . . . A dreadfully shocking torrent sweeps Aguilar. The pithecanthropi are mere lambs compared to this armada in heat.

Emerging from their houses, people gather in groups. Paula got out of bed, waddled over to the curtain, cracked open the shutters, and takes a peek . . . People want to call the police station in the neighboring town. Agathe appears at the end of the street, she dashes along, black, aroused . . . In the distance she shouts something incomprehensible. She catches up with the gathered villagers. "I know who it is! I know who it is!" she eagerly repeats.

People are all ears.

"Wildcat campers, a gang that set up outside the city limits, at the foot of the El Far tower, in a ravine! The mailman spotted them on the road on his way to make deliveries at the farms . . . A whole tribe of hooligans, filthy bums with manes, and girls too, slutty little bitches with hair dyed bright red!"

The kids on the sidewalk, set off by that "dyed bright red," open their mouths as wide as stew pots. Agathe jabbers on, jubilant. Ghostly Iza arrives with the pastor. The old man is stuttering. Iza raises her skinny arm toward the cave. Agathe shrugs.

"It's not the cave, they're bikers, a gang in the El Far ravine, the mailman . . ."

Iza isn't listening. Her large eyes light her up: "I always said so, I always said so! See what happens when you tempt the devil!"

She's tall, gnarled . . . sinews protruding under her skin. The priest seeks to calm her. She pushes him away. She strides across the road, a fatal vine shoot.

"I always said so, see what happens . . ."

People give up reasoning with Iza. She won't let go. Pithecanthropi and bikers are co-conspirators in her mind. The gush of machines has sprung from the cave's porchway. The earth's entrails concocted this cruel, shimmering herd. Beautiful bikes, thundering cavalry, living in underground stables, awaiting only the demon's signal before surging upon Aguilar and sacking its sunlit tranquillity.

Lynne, between two kisses, informs Simon of what happened. She's obviously seduced by the scandal. She likes the motorcyclists. She'd love for Simon to wrap his arms around her, take her off into some dark corner. He is quite happy just to give her pecks. Superstitious, he's afraid of losing his chance with Myriam by playing two fields. In order to prepare himself for the pleasure he likes clearing some space, eyes and ears poised . . .

He took his car, heads for El Far. He slows down, stopping a good distance from the ravine, and continues on foot. The dense scrubland conceals him. In this region the boulders are large, with few surrounding rocks, like arching mastodons with barrel chests, legless Quasimodos, crawling Saturns. Simon strokes the stone curves. He gets lost, then finds his way again, slips, scares off a snake. He reaches the outskirts of the ravine, becomes furtive, Sioux-like. He took up a position in a crenel between two boulders. He has a view of the bikers' camp one hundred yards below. His binoculars sweep the narrow valley. A stream flows at the foot of a shady embankment. The guys and women hover in the vicinity of the sickly rivulet. Some are totally naked. A very tall, slender redheaded girl, with a large bottom, is antagonizing two guys who are drinking straight from a bottle. Others, on their knees, are repairing their bikes. A fire is crackling, clothes are drying. Cans of food are piled up under a parasol pine. Spread-eagled bodies let the sunlight pour down on them. A silhouette is galloping along in the stream, water splashing its sides and quivering rear end. Farther on, behind a bush, somebody's taking a shit. Simon sees the head, the squatting curve of the spine. Then two boys start roughhousing, their muscles knot, backs arch, they roll on the ground, come to a sudden stop one on top of the other, and start kissing. A girl goes up to them, stamps her heel against the coiling bodies . . .

They don't give a damn about the cave, Aguilar Man's one big drag. A load of bull about apes and skeletons. They'd love to catch a glimpse of that lynx though. A big fellow crosses the camp, scrawny, hairy, carrying a rifle. He takes aim at the imaginary feline. He'd like to drape himself in the spotted pelt and smear the savage scent all over. The others may be against murdering wild beasts. They'd find it more loyal to attack paunchy villagers and narrow-minded old men. An animal is something noble, especially a flesh-eater out hunting early in the morning. If the lynx came for a drink at the stream, the naked adolescents would honor the dawn visit of this brother predator with a mystic silence.

Simon can hear music. They have their radios on, go through a few dance moves, stark naked, sporting their genitals. Then a group gathers in the shade of a copse. They lie down, catch a few winks. They look like corpses. The camp settles into a stillness . . . A stone breaks loose, tumbles down the steep rock face, trails a stream of gravel in its wake, strikes a ledge and flies off into the void. Simon doesn't see where it falls. Nobody appears to take note of this minute event. Maybe they grumbled in their sleep. They have no fear of intruders. Only the redheaded girl is out strolling by herself. Simon admires her lofty, gawky gait. She's smoking. She's walking along the boulder. The lenses keep track of the torso's maneuvers, elongated breasts, curly locks in the crook of her belly. She stops and scratches her hip. She looks at the surrounding mountains. Wreaths of cigarette smoke swirl above her and dissolve. She stretches out, her thighs light-skinned, enormous. Her red hair hems in her catlike face, eyes creased shut. Simon adjusts his binoculars to fully frame her chest. At last she slowly sits down in the sunlit center of the camp. Whimsically exposing her white skin. Her head falls forward. Her back curves, limpid, mineral. She's grown perfectly still. If it wasn't for her bloody bush of hair, she could be mistaken for an oval rock. Her sex parts open, an invisible fissure in the marble.

Since eight o'clock in the morning Agathe had been waiting for the mailman at the post office exit. Hippolyte couldn't refuse to take her along to the Galamus farm, deep in the back country. She had a niece out there who wanted to see her. Agathe quivered with happiness at dawn. The temperature was still pleasant. Hippolyte emerged with his bag crammed with letters, tossed it in the back of his minivan. Agathe took a seat beside him. They crossed through Aguilar. Lynne was opening the hotel shutters. While a co-worker delivered to the village, Hippolyte took care of the isolated farms, the highway inns, the campgrounds and out-of-the-way hamlets. During the first hours the van didn't cover much distance at all, simply tracing a circle along the periphery of the village. Now and then the mailman stopped and carried off his packet of letters. A door would open, a dog begin barking, bleating sheep would scurry away, goats leap. Generally a woman appeared, took the missive, gazing upon it with an almost religious attention, trying to guess its contents. Often she'd announce her correspondent's identity based on the handwriting or an address penned on the back. And she spoke to the mailman about a son in the army, a brother out at sea, a sister living in Namur where the weather was so cold, what a sad place Namur is, dear Hippolyte, the factories and the coal . . . Namur. Hippolyte knew the Namur sister by heart. He himself asked for the latest news. Agathe listened, titillated. She really would have liked to visit Namur, that dark, ugly city; her curiosity would have brightened it up, oh Namur! during a strike, with marches, police charges, tragedies, flowing blood, the rage for victory, fists raised . . . Agathe in a front row at the show . . .

The minivan bounces along in the ruts bordered by monotonous grape vines. At times a gully opens between two hills. Agathe casts a glance reaching as far as the view allows, scours the obscure recesses. There are small puddles of sunlight where her eye edges in. The van moves through desolate scenery. A fire last spring ravaged thousands of acres. Only a black expanse is left, charred trees, soot-clad mounds. One tiny house was spared. A family lives amid the ashes. While Hippolyte is delivering a newspaper,

Agathe turns to the swollen sack of letters behind her. A paunch stretched tight with gossip and secrets. It wouldn't have taken much for Agathe to swipe a few envelopes with the greatest pleasure. Unseal them at home, after dinner, for dessert. And discover things! Plunging into the maze of private lives, secret dialogues, sealed confessions, capital decisions, ultimatums and pleas . . . Families, lovers, fathers, mothers . . . Agathe, mistress of destinies, harnessing life at its source, stuffing herself full on their tears, their hopes and their short-lived joys. Love letters teeming with affectionate filth. The large bag simmers with its thousands of sentences written in a steady or trembling hand, hordes of messages, pieces of life, of death, lies, blackmail, break-ups, betrayals . . . Agathe drools over them greedily. Say, what about stitching together a dress made out of nothing but letters, a patchwork of gaudy words, sentences full of misspellings, oaths, trivialities . . . Short of raking in a letter, she superstitiously strokes the pudgy canvas, feels the hard edges of the envelopes under her fingers, a rustling comes from within, the sound of words like so many reptiles. But Hippolyte returns and the van races off, climbs the mountain. The heat has intensified. Her window opened, Agathe jiggles in her seat, hums, darts about her flylike eyes, contorts her weasel-wrists, peers to the bottom of the precipice: in the narrow valleys lilliputian men are kayaking up a torrent. Agathe likes gaining altitude, each turn lifts her skyward. She sees more sharply, like those large circaetus flying in the clouds whose piercing gazes reach the ends of the universe.

A long stretch of pine forest was beginning. The light shade offers relief to travelers. The solid red soil had a velvetlike consistency. The regularly spaced trees accentuated this feeling of harmony. And suddenly Agathe let out a cry: there, at the end of the road, seated on the shoulder were the black woman and the stranger. Side by side, awfully close together. The van passed by them and Agathe scrutinized their faces, clothes, postures, expressions. The beautiful woman from Cameroon and that journalist in the heart of the shady pine forest. That rogue didn't waste a second; after Lynne, Myriam. A womanizer. She had a soft spot for the sins of single men. Thanks to them, scandals broke out, there arose complications, tragic adventures, suicide attempts, abortions, flights, revenge taken at gunpoint, faces slapped right in the middle of the street . . . things everybody talked about for days afterward. Simon belonged to the benign race of visitors that cause disturbances. "Now how about that, now how about that!" Agathe repeated to herself. Doesn't Lynne look foolish! I really knew Simon wasn't her kind of guy. The journalist needs to prey upon rare, more complicated game. Lynne did her best to be nice but she didn't mean a thing. Lynne or lint, comes to the same thing.

Simon and Myriam came out of the pine forest. Now the countryside is crackling. Myriam leads Simon onto the high terraces where streams once flowed. She promised him a view of a carved stone. In disbelief Simon follows the woman from Cameroon in a yellow T-shirt and jeans. The sky has lightly clouded over as if for a storm. The rock looks purple . . . The world shrinks down and closes in on itself. A magnetic field emanates from this leaden, compact space. The air is shaken by thunder that seems to be pealing from the mountain itself. Are there such things as thunderstones, Jupiter's minerals that shoot bolts? Myriam's beauty intensifies this heavy sky. Her flesh glows ebony. Her body moves with utmost ease through the humidity. The mother-of-pearl sheen to her teeth dazzles with even the least smile. He made a limp effort to get her to talk about herself, her past, Africa. She proved stingy with information. What's more, he's hardly told her any more about himself. They don't need to know each other yet. These deserts obstruct memory. The rock chokes off nostalgia. This is what Simon sought when he came into this country. He gathers that Myriam's is a more subtle case. The young woman may well be powerful, immediate, yet often her face betrays moments of absentmindedness, a self-absorbed distraction. It is something utterly different from daydreaming or being oblivious to outward things. She is in communication with a real thought, even though her attitude doesn't stem from an act of reflection. Rather she enters a lucid period of emptiness, gazing upon something that concerns her alone and that all others would be unable to see. Simon is seduced by this conscious vacuity separating her from the exterior surroundings and himself, circumscribing her in her personal territory. Myriam exists, deeply present, the sediments of her life superimposed, unknown deposits, muddled, remote. Simon is astonished at being able to read only the surface of her body, only the appearance of her beauty. A short while ago this thrilled him, but now it suddenly is a source of pain. An anguish intrudes upon his heart as if their relationship were inauthentic. Two mirrors face to face, reflecting nothing. Superficial gloss, outward displays . . . Quietly the storm breaks. Large drops splatter on the rocks. Greedy pearls trickling down cheeks. Myriam's skin is lacquered with trails. She smells good, a wild aroma. The water glazes the stones, fuses the dust into a semolina as delicate as silt. The sarsaparilla, the rosemary hued, a sharp emerald. Big yellow thistles blaze, the storms' candelabras. The T-shirt clings to Myriam's breasts, a delicate skin pointed by her very hard buds. He doesn't dare make a pass at her, take her hand, kiss her neck. These easy tactics strike him as being quite out of the question. Myriam is close by but her nearness acts strangely to conceal her. She gives what she wants to give. Consequently she is a perfect mistress of her gestures and feelings. An invisible wall protects her. Friendliness takes on a terrible dimension when it becomes so slippery. And yet with his eyes Simon possesses her breasts pressing through the wet mesh. Myriam didn't want to show them. He steals them from her. He dominates her against her wishes. But this involuntary indiscretion in no way modifies the girl's calm. He gets the impression that the more naked she became the more serene she'd grow. Unveiled, she is forbidden. Simon senses that possessing Myriam is best not accomplished by sight. She stops glances, knocks them to her feet. He wouldn't dare compliment her on her breasts moving under the cotton weave. She hides what's essential even while exhibiting her beauty.

On a ridge of crests Peyrepertus Castle, a stretch of ruined husks . . . Rock and rampart fragments blend. The worn crenels, the diminished turrets are submerged in the mountain, engulfed by this solid swell. In places, however, a wall survives intact, riddled with well-defined loopholes. Simon has rarely seen remnants more striking, more tenacious in their collapse. A slow, dry dissolution. The pride and resistance of these bones of heaven. Burnt at the stake, martyred, the decimated Cathars held fast at Queyribus and Peyrepertus. The last Perfecti, the sacred cast of the Pure hoisted to the rocky heights. The eagles in the sunlight circled around these strongholds of asceticism . . . Myriam scales the peak. Her magnificent, muscular body bounds through the envelope of ruins. Only with great difficulty do the dilapidated vestiges check the black woman's momentum. Suddenly she looms above a low wall, strides over a crumbled rampart walk, stands tall, a sentinel on a tower section. Her flesh is demoniacal, those panther muscles defy the visionaries' haven. Simon considers how right the Cathars were to keep at a distance the body's lures, life's sensual claims. Myriam's beauty devours the ruins, eclipses their magic. Any harmony between the young African woman and the nest of Cathars is impossible. The two realities clash and kill each other. The wall whose vertebrae stretch out along the mountain is the backbone of a hydra lying wounded under Myriam's feet. Everything could dissolve away into dust. Myriam alone would reign, dark and dazzling, animal and clairvoyant, crushing the castles' powder under her heels.

They went back down toward the terraces. Simon doesn't know how to tell natural breakage from human workmanship. Myriam taunts him in his blindness.

"Keep at it! Look hard!" she says to him mockingly.

For her part she inspects the ground, picks out countless details Simon is unable to discover. He's jealous of her, secretly enjoys being inflicted with her superiority. He sulks like a child. At times she kneels and takes up the stones one by one, observes them, slowly replaces them like fragile objects. Simon is overwhelmed by the woman bending over the disorder of the slabs. Her face lit up with knowledge. Fingers as cautious as if she were playing chess, moving the pawns wisely. Simon struck with desire by this rock juggling, a levelheaded performance with calm hands that seem to be protecting, venerating. She who treads upon the Cathar relics is now creating large halos of meaning in the most confusing piles of stones.

The sun pierces the clouds. A violent burst of brightness. Myriam exhales a fragrance of wool and suint. She asks Simon to come over to her. He bends down at her side. "Look! . . ." He sees several smooth, round stones, but one in particular displays a long blade around the edge. He points toward it. She smiles, encourages him to pick up the stone. He raises it to his eyes. She reveals that it's a polyhedron. He's seduced by this word which evokes hard matter and its multiplicity. It's a piece of quartz still clad in storm-dew, gleaming in the sunlight. Its wounds are four hundred thousand years old. But its memory is virginal. The stone remembers the hand of Man.

It would take something more than this to fluster Alphonse. The motorcycles had stopped in front of the hotel without too much racket. The villagers were already alerted. Alphonse, standing behind his bar, welcomed the horde. Lynne was trembling. They ordered Pernod. Their helmets were set on the tables, metallic skulls with felt padding. They were wearing one-piece leather overalls open over their coppery torsos. Others had on short-sleeved shirts baring arms tattooed with hearts, swastikas, winged phalluses, sunflowers, eagles on naked sirens. Without being aggressive they chatted, exchanged a few boasts. Lynne interested them with her fine calves under her very short skirt, her sticklike waist and her eyes wide with trepidation. But they stuck to the customary jokes . . . A group got up to play baby-foot. The infant had opened his eyes in his cradle. The bikers looked at the kid. Five or six bean-poles vaguely troubled by the child. Arthur smiled, jabbered. The guys burst out laughing and walked away from the cradle to go play their game. But a tall, very beautiful redheaded woman, her white skin forming a stark contrast with her black leather, seemed fascinated by the child. She kept glancing over at him. Her face displayed no tenderness, but rather an inexpressive, insistent curiosity. Lynne went over to cajole Arthur; his baubles tinkled from their strings hitched to the cradle's edge. The pretty redhead contemplated Lynne with her slender bust, her angelic profile. She walked over, asked the kid's name. Lynne answered, blushing. This blood-rush moved the redhead. She rocked Arthur gently. Lynne smiled. The redhead leaned a little against Lynne's side and slowly, with her fingertips, stroked her blond, downy forearm.

Simon appeared. Still unshaven. He recognized the redhead whom he had spotted through his binoculars. Lynne lowered her eyes. In front of the hotel a car had come to a stop with a gentle hiss of tires. Four policemen sprang out. They dashed into the room. The bikers flashed expressions of defiance. The cops demanded to see the IDs of the teenagers, who complied with a ritual slowness. But the redhead didn't have hers. The cops decided to take her to the station in the neighboring town to run a check. The boys screwed up their faces, with a disapproving glare. Before going off, the cops warned the gang that camping in the wild was forbidden and that they had to clear out of the ravine. Otherwise, force would be called in to evacuate them. The gang fell silent. The cops advised the bikers not to start their commotion again.

They left with the redhead, the gang following behind. On the sidewalk Iza the Madwoman was waiting. As the bikers passed, she shouted after them: "Vermin!" Thunderstruck by this pure-eyed witch, they didn't react to the insult.

Inside, Lynne was removing the empty glasses. She'd been given quite a turn by the commando of pirates. Sinuous good-for-nothings in their eel-colored tabards. And that redhead's fingers brushing against her arm . . . She served Simon his breakfast. Scalding hot tea, toast. She'd already gotten wind of his stroll with Myriam. Jealousy gnawed at her. This Simon was a pimp with style, hunting little lambs and African women. She was hoping that he would make a move toward her, some sort of peck on the neck, a hand touching her breast, signs of affection she'd then disdainfully reject. But Simon was nice, nothing more. Frustrated, Lynne popped the toast right under his nose. Simon didn't register the movement of anger. He was absorbed in his meditation, juxtaposed images of the redhead and the black woman. The one, very white, and the other, dark and powerful. The archaeologist and the delinquent. The redhead whom the cops had led off reminded him of a scene from his past. What primordial and fabulous vision, flushed crimson with dawn?

Instead of racing up the street, the gang slowly cruised through the village. Their low thrum was anything but reassuring; both shopkeepers and onlookers would have preferred a more boisterous provocation. On their doorsteps they could examine the young people at their leisure. The bikers were barely moving ten miles per hour. What invisible funeral procession were the teenagers following? From time to time they fixed their stares on the inhabitants, their eyes betraying a cold hatred. The houses filed past, the villagers kept silent. Iza opened wide her immense blue eyes. Agathe experienced the thrill of these rare moments. Her lips quivered in fright and voluptuousness while watching the slow convoy of mournful teenagers mounted on their steel beasts.

When the gang disappeared, tongues loosened at once. Everyone understood that the procession constituted a supreme warning, as if the bikers had just marked the street with a long demoniacal autograph.

Simon let Paula know that he wouldn't be having lunch at the hotel. She fixed him something to eat. And he was off. The wind lashed the torrid blue sky. Scrawny bunches were already visible in the vines, skimpy, pure green agglomerates of seeds. It was cause for wonder by what miracle grapes could swell with juice in such a dry climate. Simon became passionately enamored of the scrubland. Miles with no houses. Insects, snakes, beaks of birds. He explored the limestone, collected the quartz, the veinleted marble, the zircon nubs gathering moss in the riverbeds. The legend of the lynx's stones haunted him. Treasures conceived in the hot belly of the beast and hatched under its yellow eyes. The fennel tufts bent under the mad wind. Simon sat in the shelter of some craters. The tramontane howled around him without mussing a single hair. Next he reached a totally unprotected plateau. The wind whistled against the edge of the boulders. Simon staggered under the tornado's muscular waves. He advanced, with body braced, huddled. The wind hurled about countless grains of dust, biting into his face. This dry tempest delighted him. Long whipcracks of wind, nerves of sunlight. He flushed out a rabbit that fled. He stopped for lunch in a hole. He found the garlic sausages and rye bread delicious. He ate greedily, darting swift glances above the cavity. He saw the cave in the distance. Myriam was supposed to be drawing on the terrace. Maybe she had a boyfriend among the guys on the excavation. Who knows whether now and then, forgetting about the rigors of reconstituting mankind, she didn't sketch this familiar lover's portrait? She escaped her obsession with underhung jaws and retreating brows by following the teenager's more delicate contours. Simon would have liked to see her appear on this plateau, naked torso against the wind. The blue stems of the lavenders brush against her thigh. Myriam, a lonely wanderer, breathes in the fragrance of the Etruscan wolf, remembers the aurochs galloping. So many animals lived in these parts at one time. Opulent herds. Bellowing stampedes, beasts in heat. The ancient elephant loomed in all its stature over the herds at bay. Above all else she preferred drawing the pachyderms of the plains whose giant bones filled the cavern. Aguilar Man didn't hesitate to confront these colossi. Traps and superb wiles in a surrounding stand of birch and pine trees. The climate was cold. The cave's eye lost nothing of this hunt. Bear and lion were awaiting their turn in the shadow of the rock ledges.

Simon was walking again. The wind had fallen. He went down into a deserted valley. Here the stones were redder, more polished. A rather lush stream was flowing, bordered with a row of copses. With his binoculars he inspected the banks and saw nothing. No movement. Motionless tufts of bushes. He waited, again scrutinized the valley, moved forward. He climbed the hillock overlooking the scene. Sweat and dust covered his naked chest. His heart thumped loudly. Dizzy, he stumbled. Weariness assailed him. He had run for a mile or so, observed immense desolate zones without discovering anything. He sat at the top of the mound. His lenses swept the deep space, in vain. He rested under a rock spur. He woke up, grabbed his binoculars, began scanning once more. Nothing . . . He dreamed a long while. From this point the cave was out of sight. The bare mountains were free of debris. Even the Cathars had fled the region. Yet a footpath zigzagged through the valley, not far from the stream. Perhaps shepherds followed it in certain seasons. His desire was to see the gang of bikers materialize. A noisy garland of meteors. Gamboling metal and leather. The redhead's hair flying in the wind. The tall scrawny guy out in front, rifle slung across his back. All gathered to set up camp far away from the cops. These hoodlums struck his fancy. He liked the immediacy of their breed, their raw existence lived at top speed. His thoughts turned to them as he mechanically explored the foot of the opposite hills with his binoculars. Surprised, he backtracked. He had spotted an anomaly, something alien to the rock. Over there, on a slab, too distant to be sure. He had to come down from the hillock, cross the valley. But this time his fatigue had vanished. Alert and concentrating hard, Simon slipped between the copses. For two hundred yards he lost sight of the slab. Then, peering on tiptoe over the side of a boulder, he noticed it much nearer. His binoculars distinctly revealed an animal lying in the sunlight. The lynx. He got as close as possible, very slowly, slinking along the thorns and pebbles. At last, stationed behind a large bleached-dry root, he was able to study his prey at leisure. The animal was gazing toward the stream. His cheeks adorned with quiffs, his ears bristling with long brushes of black fur. A Dionysian mask, vile, fascinating. The lynx didn't possess the naturally noble beauty of a panther or leopard. He was squat and ugly. But this ugliness was clad with a strength, a prodigious specificity. Indeed, true beauty consisted in this untamed animality. His coat was red, speckled with dark ocelli. He remained absolutely motionless. Watching without seeing. Perhaps dozing as he gazed. A sphinx on the rock slab. An interrogation in the silence. Muscles, blood, instincts alert under the calm fur. The empty country concealed these two living points. Simon and the lynx. For a long while the man lying in the sand contemplated the animal. Come evening, the lynx stirred. Simon hunched down at the base of the root. The creature stood up, took a few listless steps, then went down toward the valley. The rocks masked him. Simon was hidden halfway between the hills and stream. He waited, scrutinizing the open areas. The lynx must be approaching. Simon perceived nothing. Not the least movement. He turned around toward the stream whose banks he examined. All at once the feline's backbone sprang on a narrow beach. Night was falling. The valley was dark. The mountains stood out against a paler background. The lynx drank. He left the water's edge and disappeared. The black sky proffered a large bramble of stars.

Myriam's crawl stroke was supple, barely breaking the lake's surface. Long liquid crests rolled along her backbone before melting into the mass. Black skin and gloomy pool combined to form a denser, more animate patch. Their dip at the foot of the cave didn't last long. Myriam showed Simon the rocky constriction blocking the far end of the lakes, separating the latter from a fault sunk between the mountains. She invited him to enter the Gueleyrous gorges. Simon wondered how the scree barring access could be negotiated. She revealed the underwater route. A natural tunnel opened at the base of the platform allowing passage to the other side. Myriam showed the way: after inhaling a large dose of oxygen she vanished to the bottom of the lake. Simon followed. The opening was broad. In a few strokes they were back in open air. Simon was surprised by the beauty of the gorges. The high smooth walls gently curved streamward. At times a pediment thrust out like a torso, made up of polished matter. The clay-hued limestone was shot through with paler stripes, and veins as white as milk. Enormous, blunt-edged boulders were ensconced in the water. The total impression was one of awesome power. Colossi in places appeared to be leaning on their elbows, massive backs arching level with the stone. Round napes of quartz. Swallow-holes bored the rock. Opaque, bottomless maws. The current, however, often trickled thinly, transparently. This juxtaposition of bright segments and unfathomable abysses offered the swimmers multiple surprises. At times their stomachs scraped the rocky surface. There wasn't enough water left to go forward. Their movements got fouled up. Knees and elbows hit against solid parts. They felt amazingly ridiculous, like fish forsaken beyond the low-water mark. At other times they swam above impenetrable holes, teeming with shadows and liquid rings, but the banks were so close together that their strokes couldn't move along unobstructed. Then wider pools opened up, totally liberating them. The gorges interconnected a series of cisterns and basins in one continuous rivulet. Links and smooth overlays.

They hoisted themselves upon a rock ledge exposed to the sunlight. Myriam was wearing a brown two-piece suit matching her skin. Simon admired the columns of her long thighs. Her nipples, hardened by contact with the water, stuck to the thin layer of her bra. Her immense back arched, gleaming like an eel's. The light fabric of her trunks became embedded in the furrow of her buttocks, hugging their fleshy crescents. She was naked, on exhibit in her cavities, roundness and vitality. The cloth veiled nothing more than pubis and sex under melded weave. The sun at its zenith poured down on the rock thrones and into the rubbed-smooth circles of the cisterns. Myriam stretched out along the curve of a large blue stone. Her flesh looked like a black almond in a limestone shell. She moved and the intermeshing mechanism of her glistening limbs shifted and fell into place, discovered a new harmony. Her full mauve lips cracked open in a slightly sated smile. The curling rim, endowing her face with a look of sensual abandon, bared her teeth, keys of dazzling enamel moistened by a delicate layer of saliva. Simon desired to touch the black woman's hip, the bone jutting under her dogfishlike epidermis. He reached out; Myriam remained motionless. But when Simon wanted to slide his finger slowly toward the ebony belly, she pushed it away.

She got up, reached the top of a peak in one burst, raised herself on tiptoe. The shaft of her flesh, suspended above the abyss, quivered. Her body plunged downward, a stiff, brilliant bolt. The dark water shattered. The foam splashed in this glassy gash; large shards, fluid and marbled, careened over Myriam's sunken flesh. Breathing hard, the young woman emerged and went over to lie down along a sandy rim. Simon was separated from her. He saw her below in a new angle. Simultaneously offered, yet remote. A black siren in sharp contrast with the silica. He liked thinking that her skin belonged to some sticky aquatic creature. As a child on circus nights in the glittering ring, he trembled at the sight of the slick, inky bodies of seals. That animal blackness, those oiled flexings of muscles, throat and flippers stirred his desire for a duplicitous embrace, a salacious oceanic seduction, climaxing with the seal's cold torso plastered against his chest.

He rejoined her on the sand, after the obligatory acrobatic feats along the terraces and bluffs. She playfully escaped in the stream. She entered more deeply into the gorges. He followed her. They swam on leisurely, thighs nimbly churning. The sunlight didn't flood all the flowing meanders. They had to cross zones of shadow that gave them gooseflesh. The fanning rocks reared up in the emptiness above them. The crack of the sky zigzagged, a rivulet of inaccessible azure. At times the defile widened into an amphitheater, sloping affectionately toward them. Thyme bushes dotted the walls, mounds of fleece in the stony brightness. Trout as narrow as swords darted past. The giant eels in the depths must be dreaming about lightning-struck birds of prey tumbling down into crypts where they could be devoured. Maybe they're seeing Myriam's stomach and the play of her sides slinking along the surface, a more powerful and shadowy sister, a woman-eyed twin, escorted by a pallid imitation Triton.

Myriam led him into a wide, luminous cove surrounded by a beach where she walked. And suddenly the open sky and the backset rocks drove off her last shred of modesty. But was it indeed modesty? Myriam took care to hide her body. Simon sensed an absolute mastery of nudity, completely unrelated to any defiance or invitation. She removed her trunks and bra and ran along the sand with steady strides. She didn't look at Simon. She'd stripped naked for herself, to listen clearly to her own being, the rhythms of her flesh. There was to be nothing rubbing against her epidermis anymore, no foreign material was to irritate the crux of her thighs. Simon contemplated Myriam . . . Dense curly pubic tuft bushed up in the angle of her belly. Her pear-shaped breasts raised their bumpy purple tips. Her sleek, opulent buttocks bounced as she ran. Around her muscles, busked by the slightest stops, there curved clay-hued planes. Myriam was the work of a demiurge potter. You could feel the love of a great hand which had calibrated her thighs and the ring of her waist, fashioned her swollen throat, drew out her neck, perfected her ankles, her delicate ears, filled out the flesh of her lips, elongated her fantastic back, molded and split the rump into twin globes, blackened the crack.

They continued on, penetrating the mountain hollow. The gorge gradually closed. Only a cord of daylight was left between the summits. Here and there an enormous boulder was lodged in the chimney. Vaults completely concealed the sky. It got very dark. The wet stone was covered with a brackish lichen. A scent of saltpeter filled their nostrils. They slipped into the faults. Their sides barely fit between the icy tomblike walls. Simon saw Myriam's flesh and her tender fuselage caught in the jaws of sarcophagi. She grazed her nipples against the sharp edges. Simon would have liked to touch her, paralyzed as she was in this vise. Born in the conch of the boulders. The gorge opened a little and the passage got easier. A bright ray pierced the shadows. Myriam advanced into the heart of a cathedral upon a paved floor of light. Her body gleamed, dark water-spawned fucus. Dawns like snowflakes dropped from the open arch. Then the bronze of her flesh became violently manifest. She looked like a great wandering diorite. And Myriam walked deeper into the maze of anthropophagous mountains . . . After a gully so constricted that it squeezed the woman's hips, they came out into a solar valley. The fiery star washed their stiffened limbs. The saltpeter had left its white plush on the African's skin. She smelled of ether and death. It took an hour for her body's tones to soften and shimmer. A veil of sweat polished her back like a flow of amber.

Agathe likes getting up in the morning. The pleasure hasn't grown any less keen these past seventy years. She comes down the stairs nimbly, opens the window. The nippy air gets her tiny mouse-head going. Her house stands at a roadside. A few cars pass by before disappearing into the Corbières region. Agathe watches them, catches sight of couples and families, at times lone travelers. Several accidents already occurred near her place. There are knocks at her door in the middle of the night. She draws near, stationed behind the shutter, suspicious, then eagerly opens up. Tragic moments are her specialty. Injured people, blood flowing in the middle of a vacation. She has a weakness for faces in shock and all sorts of horrors. The air is pure this morning, the breeze frisky. Agathe feels fine. Her nerves are hopping about. The mailman brings the newspaper. She pumps him on two or three topics. Then her friend leaves to make his rounds. She'd never tire of accompanying him. The weather's going to be nice up in the hills. A thousand things are going to happen . . . adventures that she surmises. She's got a sixth sense, her hopes are high. She places the newspaper on the dining room table, turns on the radio for the latest. She heats up the coffee, listens to the forecasts, the most recent political events. Unemployment is what she prefers, the rising curve. Soon to hit three million. France on retirement, an impotent nation, revolution or psychosis. The pot whistles. She pours her coffee, takes a sip, bites into some cookies and unfolds the paper. A moment of perfect voluptuousness. Life begins. Acute, promising. It's April all year round in Agathe's heart. Flowers can be felt breaking into bloom. She hates roses, adores only crocuses. Their curious beaks piercing the ground, genuine penknives of greenery. The coffee is scalding, lashes her scrawny thorax. Her arteries beat. A brief shiver nips her lower back. It's a good sign. She reads the headlines. Assassinations. Hunger strikes in Northern Ireland. IRA members dropping like flies. Agathe is deeply impressed by these libertarian suicides. And then a Mafia massacre, the queen of England's leukemia, a break-in in Honolulu, a heart transplant or the birth of twin gorillas in the zoo at Basel, the scandal of orgies with young boys in Pont-l'Évêque are all pretexts for her to barge through a door, start up a dialogue and weave in a few indiscreet questions. There is little Agathe doesn't know about the infinite possibilities of the art of conversation. Starting off with the pope's botched assassination, you wind up at the rising price of kidneys. What an adventure! And the vast universe furnishes its inexhaustible, multicolored material against a background of genocides, exoduses, continental drifting, fantastic cavalcades, quests for the Grail, struggling peoples, electronics, Berlioz symphonies and death-rays.

The regional and local news are real goodies. The politician's visit to Vingrau, Tuchan's fishing contest, the indoor plumbing installed in Lindoux, the birth of a five-footed pig, the winegrowers' march on Perpignan, the price of plums, the holdup at the Esso station and the mysterious death of Madame Verdouble, the wife of the secretary general at the prefecture.

Then she spotted the discreet, banal paragraph. She never would have believed it held in store such a glaring surprise. The newspaper had minimized the news so as not to sow panic. But a Basque terrorist had just escaped from a Spanish prison, crossed the Pyrenees and probably vanished into the Corbières region.

Agathe squinted at the innocent column: fit for a king, ideal for starting up, fueling and multiplying hundreds of hours of thrilling gossip . . . She remembered the case well, all about this terrorist who had exploded a bomb on the beach in Valencia at four o'clock one August afternoon. A slaughter that had shaken the collective consciousness . . . Perfectly innocent souls one and all, working people on vacation. Six Frenchmen, twelve Germans, three Belgians, two Spaniards, a Montenegrin immigrant. Mincemeat in broad daylight. Beaches in mourning. For days running, the little sluts flaunting their bare breasts were deemed sacrilegious, rebuked, requested to get dressed at once. They would have deserved a nice charge of plastic explosives all to themselves, their tits sent flying miles off, food for sea gulls and herrings out at sea. Agathe has a clear memory of the time when the first woman dared take off her bra. It was strictly forbidden. Snapshots of the insolent creatures turned up in all the newspapers, naked bosoms, being led off by cops to the stations. Then the fashion spread. Agathe had wanted to witness the spectacle. She'd taken the bus to Perpignan and another to the beach at Canet . . . All in black, dry, clucking dolefully, she had strolled along the sand. Breasts proliferated: big ones, small ones, tired dugs, tiny pimples, clods, bells, light bulbs, soccer balls, boomerangs, crescent rolls, spindles, pears, apples, wrinkly things, real thoroughbreds, stumps, twisted, swollen, weasels, indistinguishable lumps, hybrid and monstrous, one-eyed, stiff, visionary, limp noodles, rats' maws, pigs' groins, fat rabbits, ingots, egg-shells, radishes, curvaceous cantaloupes, scored like pieces of flint, plus certain oddballs, plump as hair curlers . . .

Agathe talked about them for months, giving details in each home, bending the ear of the stunned priest, who was nevertheless attentive to the descriptions and sizes: mimosa, cherry, walnut, plum, potato, kitten, puppy . . . And some, yes, Father, puffed up like turkeys . . .

"And the color, Agathe? Tell me about the color . . ."

The terrorist had fled. He was now roaming somewhere in the mountains. An assassin for future causes. Agathe swallowed the rest of her coffee, refolded her paper, sprayed a few squirts of lavender water under her arms, tightened her pointy hairbun, ran her tongue over her purple lips, closed the door, put her key in her pocket, and left. A tar-sweat broke along the surface of the roadway. Black blood of summer. Agathe liked this odor of bleeding and baking. Her last erotic emotion went back ten years to the time when, in front of her house, foreign laborers, with naked torsos, tat-tooed, torpedoed with sunlight, had poured out along the road heaps of molten tar peppered with gravel. Like devils they sank their pitchforks and rakes into the smoking, swarming matter. Piles of blackberries, goat droppings or caviar. What a wonderful smell! Their glazed chests sizzling, those beautiful slaves expiring from the heat . . . And the tar glittered, jewels of death, black eggs spread like seeds.

A hermit dwelled in the mountain. He lived in a ninth-century church that had been built by Visigoth masons. This simple word, *hermit*, excited travelers' imaginations. For professional reasons dedicated to the mobility and allure of the current moment, Simon thirsted for what was atemporal, permanent, what petrified time. The hermit and the gold prospector were wedded in his thoughts. The search for God and gold. Prayers or sieves. Churches or streams . . . Loners astonished him, their slowness, their absence of desire. Plus this fleeting terrorist whom Agathe mentioned. A relationship woven of the ascetic life, violent attacks and the scarcity of gold.

Simon drove through the center of the gravelly hills. The sea was nearby, glimpsed through gaps opened by salt marshes on the horizon. Plots of white houses adorned large arrows of pond-encircled land. He sighted taller buildings, raised by the vacation industry along the coastline.

When he arrived at the small stone church, the sea was no longer in view. However, it was in close range behind the barrier of the mountains. The church had the proportions of a rustic cabin. The stones were barely cemented together, a shapeless frame, tiny and crude, supporting a wooden edifice resembling a stable or barn. The hermit would explain that it was a former leper house. Simon rang a small bell whose tinkling alerted the occupant. He arrived slowly, opened a door and welcomed the traveler with an expression showing none of the benevolence expected from a holy man. Yet there was no hostility in his gaze. Simon wouldn't have been able to say what it did contain exactly: a paradoxical amalgam of curiosity, patience, harshness . . . He was clothed in a dirty cowl, his skull wasn't tonsured, his hair fell to his shoulders in greyish locks. Tall, rather potbellied for an ascetic, he had the mug of a drunkard, a bohemian, a Verlaine tormented by the Devil and the Word. He showed Simon into a small courtyard decorated in the center by a well coping. Then he brought him into the church. He was preceding him and, when Simon jerked forward to see over his shoulder, with a calm but peremptory gesture he made the journalist understand that he must yield to his authority. The visit followed a long, established ritual. Simon meekly stepped back. The hermit was a blend of obsessive and contemplative elements. The chapel, sunk in the shadows, betrayed no hint of its intimacy. The hermit guided Simon toward a wooden bench where he ordered him to sit. Simon obeyed complacently. The man lit simple candles and the interior came into view. Bare stones, with neither plaster nor decorations. The ceiling was low, the surrounding wall cramped like the hull of a small boat. There was nothing. On his bench sat Simon to witness this spectacle of nothingness. He made a motion to rise, to scrutinize more closely the walls' appearance, but the hermit indicated with a glance that he should remain seated. The man then succinctly summarized the chapel's history, he commented on the work of the Visigoth masons, spanned the centuries, made a few remarks on the architecture and fell silent. His speech hadn't even lasted five minutes. Simon was allowed to rise. The hermit led him off into a sort of niche carved into the side of the church. A statue of the Virgin stood on a stone ledge. It looked very old, sculpted in wood, eaten away in places; a blue pigment signaled the veil of her robe. There were also traces of red. The face had few markings, vanishing contours. A blank expression. Still this statue captivated Simon. The hermit noticed this and smiled ever so faintly. The traveler's admiration had apparently been anticipated. It was part of the ritual, the crowning moment. The poor statue was the surprise stashed away in this rock canopy. An utterly worthless treasure. Between the Virgin and the hermit a link must have existed, very strong, stubborn, despotic and malicious. Simon felt invited to look, to marvel, yet he was kept at a distance. At the slightest gesture the hermit would order him to step back and follow the rules. In contrast, the guide was free. His attitude exuded an impression of strength and familiarity as if he alone were equal to his immemorial Madonna. Visitors were condemned to this humiliating role of impotent voyeurs. And the hermit secretly enjoyed their paralysis. A childish idea began to take root in Simon's mind: stealing the statue.

The hermit left the niche and Simon followed him. He was next invited to contemplate a large sacred book placed on a table. The hermit announced that this volume was both precious and ancient. Simon, of course, was very careful not to touch the leather binding. He nevertheless would have liked to look inside. But already the hermit was drawing him onward into the small courtyard, then the leper house where, far back, a room had been set up. Grime coated the walls but all was in perfect order. A wooden bed without sheets, draped with an old piece of linen, took up one side. The hermit paused before a stool where a pack of postcards had been placed. Simon recognized the statue of the Virgin alongside a plate on which a few coins were arranged. Simon added a five-franc piece and took a card. Then the hermit conducted him to the door. Simon was back in the bright sunlight with his photo of the Madonna. He had the impression that he had been a victim of a hoax. He'd glimpsed a truth whose access was strictly forbidden. The hermit had led him by the end of his nose, sat him down by force, got him up, walked him around in a ball and chain, then sent him on his way furnished with this cardboard simulacrum. And yet those few instants spent on the bench in that thoraxlike chapel riddled his flesh with huge, spiraling shadows. The terror, the hermit's footsteps in the heart of that silence, the candles, the stony hut arched upon its sides, the wooden Madonna, the thick untouchable book. The hermit had a sense for bare-boned, archaic theater where a con man's hustling vied with the sacred. For a long while, out on the road the traveler thought of this despot in his mystic cave. He would have liked for the escapee to kill him . . . He was haunted by the old man's obesity and faith, having expected some elderly creature, hypnotic and emaciated. In Simon's mind the ascetic life was linked to the purity of bone, yet that man exhibited his enormous potbelly and layers of dirt. Vermin must be flourishing in his greasy hair. Weighed down this way, how could he ever pass into the supreme state of deprivation? But Simon sensed a hidden connection between obesity and meditation, as if deep thoughts in order to develop required an expanded girth, a slow maturation. The swelling attested to an aptitude for dilation and ecstasy. In addition, grime concealed the flesh, hardened it like an eggshell stuffed with life. An effervescence simmered under this outer coating. The ascetic's paunch had the roundness of a terrestrial crust wrapping a fiery core. God was germinating in that reeking cask . . .

When Simon entered Aguilar, the shops and streets were being thrown into an uproar. He spotted Iza the Madwoman striding down the village's main thoroughfare. She looked drunk, jerkily thrusting out her scrawny arms. People vainly stepped up to calm her. Iza shouted and her monologue swept everything along. The terrorist's escape had overstimulated her delirium. She accused the cave of drawing down the curse, of magnetizing drifters and impure creatures. The cavern was the devil's cackling, an eye of malice boring into souls, corrupting memory. The inhabitants were accustomed to Iza's excesses. Today, however, the madwoman's convulsions tormented them. After all, the bikers' invasion and the terrorist's escape constituted two tangible threats. That cave where the dead were being unearthed snapped up noisy hordes of tourists and foreigners driven by unknown motives. The old people complained about the disorder. The village was no longer a refuge nestled in the foothills. The cave saw, spoke, and created concentric rings of anguish and panicky desire. Was it wise to exhume the secret of Man and his true face? The children watch Iza. She doesn't make them laugh anymore because she's beautiful in her madness, strained by her visions to the breaking point, her large eyes riveted on the eternal porchway, up there, in the sunlight. This voice surfacing from the abyss in order to declaim all under the open sky . . . The cannibalism and rage of the ancestors, and their animal slaughter, their fear of the world. Iza shouts louder and louder, flailing about. Paula up in her room is the only one who stays calm. Her heart worn out by the daily monotony no longer reacts. Paula, in the darkness of her confinement, likes Iza's madness, savors the scathing kris of her speech. A seeming complicity exists between the modest woman and the lunatic. The paroxysm soothes Alphonse's spouse. This monstrosity is her revenge and makes her accept death. Let Iza stamp Aguilar's heart with fantastical thumpings, pulverizing pulsations! Paula feels mysteriously protected. This frenzy surrounds her with a wall within which she reposes, intact.

Simon dreads that Iza will see him. Swooping upon him, she'd heap on deadly accusations, saying: "What are you up to here, what did you come to see, why did you come to see yourself through us, what did you come to forget, to lust after, to seduce, to betray . . . and what about how you slipped a peek into the beggar's pouch of the cave and went fingering the ancestors' bones and touching the skeletons of the big primitive animals and foraging around, ransacking our memories to escape your own, disguised in different faces? Simon, why are you after the lynx, the prospector and the hermit? Those loners obsess you, predators devoted to gold, slaughter or the gods. You track them, envy their savage composure . . . Why rove around rocks, bone-dry mastodons and flint profiles? . . . What spell upon your flesh has changed you into a limestone bean-pole? . . . You'd like to stand at the village entrance, divine and petrified, so that people will say, 'That's Simon the traveler, the one who slept with Lynne in the stream and grabbed the African woman out in the Cathar ruins, that's Simon, the voyeur of the dead. Selfishly he came to pillage. We all had the task of assuaging his ravenous hunger.' "

But at present Iza is howling the word *skull*—"The skull! . . . The skull! . . ." And Aguilar tenses under Iza's tooth.

Agathe was in her roadside house when Iza lost her head. The next day she had all the details of the crisis relating to her, the trip through the streets, the people watching, who wasn't there, who came in at the middle or the end, who was at the windows, their expressions, surprise, the kids' faces, the sudden watchfulness of the old men, Simon arriving, his low profile, slinking along the walls, dodging glances. Agathe doesn't shun secondhand accounts, she pieces together the puzzle. First, there's the joy of being on the spot, of seeing, feasting on the immediate thing, undergoing its impact in a violent orgasm of curiosity. There then follows the happiness of reconstituting the facts afterwards, having them told again, confronting, correcting, spinning them out in turn with other tales . . . "And Simon?" Agathe repeated from door to door . . . "And Simon?" . . . She liked the biblical name, hoping a piece of information might spring from the simple repetition of the word. Her lust swelled as she made the echo resound, dull, smooth, oblong. This mute term, in French "See-mon," shiny as a tie clasp, nevertheless concealed the delectable hypothesis of "seeing": a burning vision that related to "my own." Was it the enigma of the self that Agathe wanted to pierce by saying "Simon," by closing her mouth lovingly upon the name's pronunciation?

That evening Alphonse tells Simon all about Iza . . . She went mad after a miscarriage caused by a strange incident. Iza was on her way to meet her lover out in the scrub when she stepped into the jaws of a trap set by hunters. Iza tumbled onto the rocks and lost her baby in those fiery teeth. Afterwards she endlessly repeated that she'd seen the fetus burst between her thighs fitted with the monstrous head of a fish. Little by little, people gave up trying to make her relinquish this demented conviction. When the cave excavation began, Iza's insanity flared up with renewed vigor.

Simon likes watching Sue and Pier work around the long tables. They wash the mud samples, sort the straw from the bones. Protected from the sun by hats, they apply themselves without exchanging a word. The mirror of the lake reflects the cave. The valley is encircled by rocks. She cleans a phalanx fragment from a Mosbach horse. A powerful creature, over five feet wide at the withers. Large herds ran over this region. Aguilar Man especially prized the meat of these Equidae. Innumerable remains have been found. Simon is still fascinated by the vigilance of the silence surrounding the cave. Shouting would be impious when the past diffuses its revelations in such a manner. Chatting prohibits patience and attentive listening. Boisterousness is contrary to the spirit of an experimental sounding. The wind strokes the limestone walls, sweeps a stretch of pine forest, rumples the waters, backsurge. You embrace its breath, become one with its sound, a voice speaking of the earth, its echo unveiling the mystery. A beneficent presence envelops the teenagers . . . This trembling light that circulates, subsides and is reborn, those deep flowing pulsations communicate a rhythm to this feeling of immediacy and happiness. A soul breathes as this pneuma lives and dies . . . Aguilar Man between two hunts, during his moments of dreams, feeling the fluid hand of the wind along his backbone, must have loved the world and sensed its essence.

Simon is waiting for Myriam. She leaves her perch. Her calf muscles thrust up along the steep slopes. Under her arm she's carrying the ancestors' latest portraits. Her thighs quiver, ingots of brilliance, when she takes small steps, braking her downward progress. Her arms swing. The pebbles stream. She finds her balance on intangible edges and dashes down toward him damp with sweat. She'll smell of her effort, scents of rosemary, the copper of sunlight and the dust of the dead. The brightness splatters her body, weaves gold halters at her heels, straps in her breasts.

She stands before him, so lofty, so dense . . . Large mineral trails are imprinted on her limbs. Her sides seem whitewashed with sand. She takes a long while bathing, at her own pace, slipping through the secret, low-hanging foliage of the banks. She vanishes, brushes past stumps, a long tube of roots, barely disturbs the swarm of insects. She parts the liquid surface with her eel back. Her head with its cropped, plastered hair seems sleek; poking up, an obsidian ball. The head of a pond goddess slices through the cave of heaven's mirror. Simon doesn't know why the vigor of Mosbach horses comes to mind, aggressive mouflons, cavern lynx, aurochs and bison. By dint of painting them, mimicking their leaps, Myriam has captured a share of their power. The creatures gallop under the hump of her lower back, bite her nape, tug at her breasts. Her body is forged by their jolts, their brutal, loving frictions. Traces of muzzles and chests hammer her sides, her skin is slick with their slaver.

She emerges, runs, renewed, lighthearted. Her bathing suit is little more than a crumpled remnant speared outward by her breasts, glued to the rounded turf of her bush. She laughs, frolics. She dries off in the sunlight magnified by the rocks. Then she slips on knee-length shorts and a khaki shirt. She rides off with him. The village appears. They drink at the fountain while the old men ogle the African woman. So then, every race is present up there in the cavern? . . . daughters of Africa, half-breeds, Chinese women, who knows? Women from Malaysia, Mexico, Japan, an Englishwoman . . . strange mixture, German women blond as war. Youth from all lands, fearing neither God nor man, but nice, better than the bikers, not the same breed although this one here, you never know, this woman from Cameroon in the saddle would bolt ahead of those choppers . . . the beautiful oil-slicked creatures, black as a butt-crack. None of them ever slept with a black woman, except Alphonse in Morocco, so people said, they only want to touch . . . The fountain sprinkles slabs of flesh, beautiful chunks of mica, the kind you find on beaches, washed in by the sea . . . smooth all over, polished . . . their crowlike blackness. In imagination the African is tide-born, spawned by sharks, her jet belly palpitates in the white silica shell.

They're going over to have something to drink at Alphonse's bistro. It's Lynne's day off. Paula just got up. Soft, damp. She serves them lemonade. She smiles at the black woman. She finds them sluggish, unusual, beautiful, these unknown foreigners, come for the bones of our origins. A macabre curiosity. Huge dogs greedy for the earth's marrow. As much cannibals as that first Man, old pithecanthropus going around clubbing his brothers, then gobbling them up . . . They're all interested in these monstrous appetites. They observed the mask in the museum. For hours on end. Interrogating a skull. How awful. Deformed, hardly human. Simian . . . Simian. It grows emaciated, insinuates itself. The mischievousness of the ape in which the Other's profile shows through. Callused window from which mankind darts a first glance. The village should have kept on sleeping like all hamlets, all these people coming and going, TVs at night replacing front-door chats.

Changes would be welcomed gladly, even noise, a factory, but why does it have to be these finds from such a far-off time, buried in the night? . . . In the long run it turned out to be disturbing. People spoke of rooms for dismembering, with heaped-up corpses, where animal bones were mixed up with human remains. Did such atrocious truths need to be known, subjacent, stirring underground? How far would those excavations extend—into our wine cellars, under the church paving, graves, the old men's bench? . . . Scrutinizing their traces, their tracks, their least marks. Marveling over a carved stone . . . they were animals anyway. Without fire. Herds. Hunger, thirst. Packs. A beginning . . . unaware that they'd started the whole mess going. If they'd known, poor creatures, they would have been paralyzed with dread. If they'd seen their descendants! Man bustling about, trafficking. If today they saw on this very spot the helicopter from the police station passing by in its search for the escapee, that gang of growling monkeys would tremble. Comical, outmoded. Plus jet planes, Mirages hacking the skies with a scar of thunder. Then Aguilar Man, scrawny, cowering, would crawl back into his hole . . . They could only concoct a crude anvil, a makeshift hunting spear. And think of the pithecanthropus plopped in front of a TV set, just like that, the whole family in place! Look, there we are, your great-great-grandchildren. Peekaboo! What would the cavern herd do in front of the cave full of images? It would act like the chimps you see at the circus looking behind mirrors to see who's hiding. Clownish, simpleminded. Such cruel yet childish cannibals! They'd shit themselves in terror during a simple car ride. What would we do with them? Pen them up in a humanized zoo, provided with veterinarians and psychiatrists. People would get tired of them. No longer in fashion. Ingenuous creatures arriving from too remote climes. They would be left to die in the end. Overly cumbersome fossils, distorted faces of ourselves, like wolf-children. We'd feel so odd and anxious standing in front of them. Caught between two states: anguish and dream. Probably devoid of love. Moved by momentary pity.

Simon and the black woman made the climb. Now they're in the middle of making love. That's all people think about. Alphonse on top of Yvette. Lynne, jealous, has hooked up with a new boyfriend. Bones and kisses. That's their hobby. Orgies, sepulchers. Archaeology and caresses. Like animals, doing it from behind anthropoid-style. Planes, TVs haven't changed techniques. Of course: carrying on, preliminary sentiments, overcourteous politeness, poetic step-by-step approaches. All well and good! And then interlocking like goats, rams, horses, mouflons, wildcats and bulls, even hummingbirds, one atop the other . . . fucking. It's the immemorial task, reaching orgasms and multiplying. Simon on top of the black woman. Beautiful voyagers. Unknown, maybe dangerous. Linked to those Basque terrorists, the Spanish police, informers . . . not to mention so many other liberation fronts, underground revolutionary brigades from Italy and elsewhere, fanning through the countryside—conspirators, wait-and-see fellow travelers, big-hearted assassins, visionaries, presidents of future republics. Outlaws soon to be legalized, honored, sharing the repasts of princes at the Palais de l'Élysée.

Paula contemplates the empty street. Barge of sunlight. The blazing molecules vibrate. Nobody. Thirst gone. The pinball machines glint. Dead, multicolored shells. Good aroma of coffee. Thoughts of dry grains, a thread trickling between palms. Forbidden because of her heart. Now she knows she could care less about her arteries. She feels like rebelling, walking away, leaving.

Simon knows next to nothing about the beautiful woman from Cameroon—except for this dark heavy word, *Cameroon,* knocking about in his head like a gong, a tom-tom, a plush fragrant pelt, from deep in the brush rallying the hordes of desire. Cameroon . . . she is that flesh from the heart of the world, that purple mahogany from the equator.

Coming together as a couple, they are enveloped by the village bedroom's worn-out wallpaper transformed through the years by dampness, dryness, and gusts of wind. Having undergone drenchings, chemical reactions, exposure to the discoloring sun, today the paper has the look of lime or tea leaves being shriveled and dulled by a patient dehydration. Yellowed, ochered and rainbow-hued. Streaks baked on during summer afternoons. Surfaces pyrographed by countless bursts of hard dust, textures dyed and re-dyed, rolled in large spider webs, among dead moths, powdered with heaps of houseflies, soiled with insect and flea droppings. The paper mimics the fragile elytra concealed under black shells of beetles, lucanids or maybugs. The look of old newspapers from bygone days used for wiping yourself inside country latrines built on piles over streams. Bedroom or attic, the color of frost-gnawed winter bark, beleaguered by the first asps of sunshine. But this effect of withered herbal leaves from some sickly brew overjoys Simon when it drapes Myriam's body. A black woman whose muscles are adorned with antiquated provincial rags, garbed in old Balzacian tatters. A savage vigor caught in a cone of ghostly paperwork. Simon tells her:

"Get undressed."

Myriam removes her blouse. Her breasts rise, slightly diverging, smooth swollen torpedoes. The tips extend under the harder hallmark of the aureoles, pierced by large grainy buttons, pink-tipped, chapped with cracks. Simon contemplates these amply curved gourds, reared up before her torso, inert and animated, floating earthenware jugs, blind and bewitching. His hands touch, stroke, graze, grab the breasts. Her flesh sinks inward, soft clay, bulges between his fingers. He digs, twists, hurts her gently, but she watches his expert palm, his scratching nail and the pressure of his thumb. He kneads, massages, as if his hand wanted to discover, to flush out the secrets of this fertility on display, exhibiting itself. Shieldlike breasts, puffed-up sentinels, proud janissaries, a harem's lion cubs, birds with fully fanned breasts . . . He punishes them for their haughtiness, torturing them, enlacing them. Myriam laughs.

"Take off everything."

She peels off her jeans, makes her skimpy panties disappear. Naked. Simon is struck by the formidable miracle of this word. He's seized by terror. *Naked* . . . The universe has unveiled this giant almond like a round rock surmounted by the breasts of the waters. Myriam naked. Everything in view. A new power reveals itself, sprung from the buried depth, the more opaque layers. The world has lost its forests, its seas, its prairies, its clouds, its atmosphere. Suddenly shorn itself of countless luxuriant details, opening its womb in the earth. Myriam is its naked fruit, an athlete of the origins, a great black androgyne, its colossal fetus. Both a virgin and experienced like the beginning of all beginnings. The earliest offering of woman. There is her belly beveled inward, polished, set in the brilliant vise of her hips and her abundant fur, knotting its black gorilla curls, nested in its den of vines. Simon plunges his fingers into the branching mane. He approaches her mouth. His nostrils inhale the scent of musk, suint, roots, sap and poison. His fingers spread the lips of her vagina, sink in, his tongue extends delicately, sharply, to dislodge the clitoris, circumscribe it like a vague serpent burrowing at the foot of a rock. He coats it with saliva, grazing laps, rhythmic sucking around the core. He pinches the base between his teeth, the ball swells, smoothes to a roundness. He traps it and his freed tongue moves to and fro, rubbing it down, listening, enwrapping, sliding off, understanding, discovering. Suddenly the woman comes. A stream soaks her pubis. Simon unzips his trousers, pulls out his member. The black woman drops to her knees, then lies down. He sinks into the hair-moistened crown. The cave scalds him, a bath of come. Welded, oiled, intermingled hairs. The black woman's breasts roll in his palms. He embraces them, trusts them. Massed, cradled globes. He bites their spurs, licks their cracks, sucks their blossomed buds while furrowing in the cavern, swimming in its stream. His balls, with each thrust, knock against the soaked curls. She moans, pants. He answers with hoarser breaths, forging grumbles, rough bits of words. He talks to her like an animal, a cave lion, a lynx of the rocks. He grunts to his female, whispered aggression and affection. Now and then, fully formed speech springs to the forefront of an assault. He gives birth to short repetitive words, spasm-sentences, grammarless, basic phrases, impulsive clichés like: "You're making me come! You're exciting me! . . . You're making me come, you're exciting me! . . . You're making me—, exciting me," musical whiplashes . . . Neither words nor sentences, but accents, jolts, echoes of frenzy. And she utters cries, squeals, a mouse squeaking under the foliage of tropical forests, snakes, lizards, marsupials, tiny felines . . . Small, quivering cries rising from her magnificent mouth whose protuberant lips bare the immaculate harrow of her teeth. Mother-of-pearl. Tusks, reefs of snow, ivory booty. She chatters her teeth, bites her lip, opens them wide, clamps them shut, roars, surrenders them, full and mauve like riverbanks, ridges of silt. A song rises within her like a drill, fitfully bursting out, looping, cooing, her throat's cavity tendered to intone the nuptial hymns, to allow the notes to flow, a waterfall of "Yes! Yes! Yes!", myriads of "Oh yeses!", flutelike, raspy, murmured . . . strewn with beaded "yeses," of torture or orgasm, muted or sharp. She juggles . . . Tom Thumbs of "yeses," thus she blazes her trail through the jungle, everywhere planting "yeses" . . . Apaches and Sioux . . . yes-tomahawks. And the panting returns, war hisses . . . "Turn over!" And, sailor of her nape, he governs her, again biting into her curls, the soft part, membrane and tendons at the top of her neck. He traps the latter firmly on the side, between his jaws. Gentle strangled totem. Then she says to him: "Hurt me, hurt me real hard." He wounds her. And her buttocks arch up, enormous and slender, a mare's curves. Conch buttocks, obsidian forges, steered by muscles now relaxed, now tense. The immense black back, a petroleum jetty, undulates. Her buttocks voracious as the belly of a huge fish surfacing, diving, ebony fins, the hump of a dolphin, a sperm whale, black polished seal's buttocks . . . "Oh yes, your ass!" And repeating "Yes, your ass!" swelling, feeding the word, shaping its curve, filling up this beautiful ass of a carina and unicorn. "I'm pounding you! I'm pounding you! Spurring you and splitting you! . . . Cramming you, cramming you!" . . . And she: "Yes, screw me! Screw me hard! . . . Go all the way in, hard . . . I feel your balls! I feel your balls! Your balls swarming, purses, bags of gold . . . Spurt! Oh yes, spurt! . . . And work at my cunt, my anus, down in the hold!" The supple solid buttocks, insatiable, parted in two slabs, ensconced around his member, thrust forward, keeping pace, racing along, thoroughbreds, black Siamese . . . And the gaping furrow contracts and palpitates. He doesn't know where the cunt is anymore, the ass . . . Where am I? Where? Annulus, sluice, vagina, rectum exchange their wells, tunnels, networks . . . stream out their secretions, maze of fluids, circuits of mire, of hard things, velvety, ample . . . radiating faults . . . Capricious rivers of skin, thighs, hair . . . "I want you to . . . Slut! Slut! Slut!" And then: "Whore! Beautiful whore! My whore, whore!" A hundred times, immemorial, miraculous curses . . . wallopings, galaxies . . . And gently, gradually, in a slow whispering ebb . . . "You're my angel . . . My snow . . . My Madonna . . . my hold and my felucca, my gold and my peasant, my crystal and my plow, my black galley ship laden with stars, my tunic of sweat and my Punic torch . . ." And she: "My sweet bastard! My sweet bastard . . . Oh yes! Oh come! Oh spurt! . . ." "And fornicate in your cunt, your rump, my antelope, down to your bone, sift your surge, darling, my very own . . . my hovel, my precious stable . . . harpoon you, ransom you . . . You'll shit out of love for me!" And the sentence recurs, recurs: "You'll shit!" setting in rhythm "native forest" and "chaos of love for me." "You smell good, pepper, dung, and happiness . . . Pierce you, clean you out . . . A song casts us on the Ganges' shore . . . Strip you clean . . ." "Yes! Yes! Yes! Hurt me, again, harder, give it all you got and slap me hard, slap and spit! Let loose! . . . impale yourself, skewer yourself . . ." Taken to Cameroon by hammering balls . . . "My jug, my cataract . . . my bank, my lance is in your cunt . . . my hunting ground, my cossack, my mahogany Cosette . . . my burning filth, my churning rut . . . Hermione's ass! Bloody torso! . . . You smell like a loved woman! You reek of joy! . . . Constellation, you reek of an abominable ecstasy . . . Fleece, house, ejaculated trailer . . . A thousand suns in your shit! A thousand times . . ." And in his ear she whispered: "My cock, my beautiful cock, my big bursting, burning prick . . . my fat, shiny purple prick . . . Your bouncing balls full to bursting battering my ass and in my cunt, my mouth . . . My mauve lips swell up, dilate around your member swallowing all the blood, come, saliva, flecks of excrement." The two bodies are mouths, soaked rods, web of anus and cunt, made of sweating fleshes, woven, oceanic, interpenetrating muscles, and trees of the shipwreck . . . And desires panic, drum: simian herds and surly fury. Holes, cocks, Milky Ways, cave, humus, long flaming tongues, split bellies, cliffs, two, four, eight, buttocks, furrows side by side, hook into each other, cunt climbing the prick, prick scooping into the cunt, two four eight ten breasts . . . He black, she white . . . both black, red cries . . . And cocks, chasms of darkness, shivering sprays . . . jam-packed barges, pitching ark . . . "Firmamenting you with shorn lambs, teeming roadstead . . . my clove, my crane, my camel! My beautiful licorice galleon . . ." And now both howl at the end of their strength, clinging yells, throwing themselves upon each other's throats, bristling hyenas . . . They howl . . . "My . . ! My . . !" gloomier, rages. Lightning bolts. A thousand warriors loom up, in close ranks, armed with picks, arrows crackle behind the large portal . . . a thousand belligerent wasps buzz, casques and stingers twinkle . . . Swarms thunder past when the copper urn at last opens and spills out the thousand billion suns.

Iza entered the church at early dawn. The door had been forced open. Traces of booze soil the altar. Vomit is spread through the oak stalls. Iza falls to her knees: the Madonna has been decapitated. The Virgin stands in her white dress. Headless. The gaping, crumbly plaster emerges under a scale of paint. On the ground a pool of white dust is visible. The head has disappeared, that sweet beseeching face . . .

This time the villagers have been struck to the heart. The evil eye has singled out Aguilar. The demons settle like owls on the roofs and gaze down.

It was only a Virgin, an artless statue. But she was what people came to see; furtively . . . She, what each person carried away stashed in his memory. The beheading severs from each and every villager his share of the immaculate.

The cops are not accustomed to such crimes. They'd prefer some sort of concrete plundering or a fresh corpse. In military uniforms facing the wounded Virgin, they strike a bizarre pose. They seem guilty. "The work of hoodlums, vandals . . ." they repeat, shrugging. No tangible motives, therefore no clues. The cops leave in their night-blue car. The village stands alone around this enormous vacuum.

The police conduct an investigation in the bikers' camp. Once again they are ordered to clear out. They furnish alibis and phlegmatic justifications. The beautiful redhead bursts out laughing at the idea that people think they're stupid enough to chop off Mary's head. "Maybe it's some worms that ate away the plaster, one of the devil's thefts, a maniac with a thing for pious faces, somebody with a morbid fondness for purity . . ." The cops linger at the campsite, explore without much conviction, leave a car parked for hours in the proximity of the bikers, come back, interrogate again. The teenagers are long familiar with this tyrannical sham, this farcical seriousness. But there is no evidence. The impeccable motorcycles are in order. Boys and girls delight in a placid innocence. They tan themselves while the cops examine the insides of the tents. Black mechanical parasites, without faith or ideals, here to ogle intimate details, enormous voyeurs barred from the spells and schemes of gangs. Their miserable little uniforms are puritanical girdles. Underneath, soft bellies, pale skin, cramped hearts. The teenagers stretch out in the sunshine. One couple flirts. The big bike-toys shine like idols. The cops come back, inspect the foul, fabulous outfits. This shit-shimmer disgusts them all the while secretly exciting them. Soiled under-shorts, sweat-brown bras, studded uniform belts, amulets, copper bracelets, narrow black suede trousers, the surprise of an intact nightgown, white as snow. The cops take a step backward before the apparition, circle around it suspiciously, as if the angelic garment might explode—dynamite silk, an atomic hymen.

The priest returns to his presbytery. He wraps the plaster debris in a lace hankie, which he locks away in a closet. The priest is senile, his prayers flounder about. A fitful lucidity in which he rehashes the same crazes. His flatfooted housekeeper serves him two sausages and a sweet pea mash for lunch. The amputated Madonna leaves the priest speechless. He gapes, drools . . . his mind at a dead stop. After his meal, he goes hobbling off to his armchair and sleeps . . . He dreams, mutters. The housekeeper sweeps the parquet floor. A fragrance of lavender water intensifies at the window. Sounds arrive . . . crickets, cars . . . in diminishing dins. The priest snores. The housekeeper settles into the neighboring armchair and also snoozes, broom in hand. The sound of their breathing intermeshes, rattling timbres, hissing nostrils. They are engaged in dialogue.

The priest has always harbored a deep-rooted hostility toward the cave excavations. His superiors tried in vain to calm him, but knowledge in his view went hand in hand with the devil. People should admire the world, the house of the Lord, not ask it indiscreet questions. Unearthing all those bones, digging, rummaging around, exhuming those dead strangers and sketching portraits of the monsters constituted an impious act. Finding out what happened five hundred thousand years ago was madness. Illusions, aberrations stalked all proud creatures. The museum waged an outlandish competition with the church. The statues of the saints soothed consciences. The macabre display of skeletons sparked unhealthy anxieties. The church was Jesus' cave, that thing up there was Satan's shack. The museum: a baleful dump. The priest made do with Adam and Eve. Mankind descended from this harmonious couple. Evolution was some bad adventure unfolding, blurring physiognomies, creating hybrid beings, giving rise to demonic mixes, everything got all entangled, confused in the hodgepodge of beasts and men. There was no good to be garnered from these weird gestations. This was perfectly clear to the old men on the bench. They preferred the church and its serene statues to those sketches of matter, those jumbles of misshapen skulls. The past didn't reside underground in the cold humus, that seat of corruption, of mutations and of treason, it lay in books, respectable tradition . . . What an abyss separated the refined relics of the saints from a pithecanthropic tibia! Yet that joke of a museum presented itself as a new and authentic reliquary. The priest, agreeing with poor Iza on this, would have liked to see the cave closed, thus reducing to silence those sordid grumblings, those flesh-eating deliriums, the whole ignominious gorilla grub.

At present his revolt has petered out. The priest splutters. A vestige of protest haunts these litanies of decrepitude. His flaccid eyes see the hole of the cave amid the limpid sky. His mind is now empty. The Enemy's threat has fallen limp. God himself is becoming soft, crumbling to pieces. The priest presents a surly frown. His thick lower lip dangles. He no longer loves. His wrinkled carcass quivers on his bones. He parades around frockless. His mind is all in a muddle: cave, museum, man all dissolve away. His armchair: the broom grazes past like a rat. The priest awakens with a start. The filthy creature devoured the Virgin's head. The Madonna is ugly. Sad face at the end of the tunnel. Looks like Agathe's gaping maw. The Grasshopper and the Aunt. Ugly . . . Sausage-burps. Pithecanthropus on the cross. Miracle of Lourdes. Clean blue cavern . . . He desired Iza, very long ago, when she first went mad. She was young, beautiful, ennobled by her visions. White flesh, long sinews. Her loins in the cemetery. She gave off a fragrance of cat and sweat. Dark dresses. Forest of hair. She always came to see him and he blessed her, heard her confession, contemplated her. That unwed mother miscarrying among the boulders and the legend of the fish-boy. They'd grown old together. That strength, intact, tempestuous, now exhausts him. He was afraid of her fits, large arms strangling the wind. Iza. In days past he uttered her name very softly. Iza, Iza . . . She was on her knees, he stroked her hair a long while, all the way down as far as her nape and its gentle warmth.

Paula grows tense in her room, a bad dream . . . That beheaded Madonna. Who could ever have done it? Alphonse rarely has anything to say about the latest news. It's as if there weren't any goings-on. But quite the contrary! The old Madonna . . . The escapee? The lynx? Why not the pithecanthropus? Disguised, wearing his own mask stolen from the museum. Agathe. Iza. Simon the voyager. Or the priest, himself in the grip of madness. Bikers, babies, paleontologists or tourists. All guilty. Nevertheless the night seemed so calm, so innocent. And Paula sensed in a very remote region of her mind that this barbarous act could fit right into the world's tranquil train, flatten out, relinquish its sharp-edged, outrageous relief. The hoodlums' aggression was only an illusion, an appearance. In reality they too were moved by the serene weight of the universe. Nothing had troubled the immense organization. The Madonna had lost her head. But the statue holds up very well all the same. Even if they'd hack away at it all over again, smash it into a thousand pieces, and the debris were scattered all about, quietly settled in the plaster dust. Beautiful matter. Powdered sand. One second after the crime, peace reigned; someone could have said a prayer. Even while being sacked, church and surrounding sky didn't quake. Paula glimpsed a truth, she was so close to waking Alphonse in order to announce the big news. But suddenly, in an unpredictable reversal, she was struck by the horror of the infamy. The sacrilege loomed perpendicularly once more. Was it Simon, Alphonse's friend, the stranger? Why should strangers always be the culprits? Or else one of the village regulars, so regular you could never guess who? Or possibly. . . ? The portal opened, the moonglow paled the floor paving, the man entered, or a woman . . . Yes, very beautiful, determined, maybe two or them . . . women. A handful of vandals. No, it was a man, some loner, depraved, hairy, wolfish . . . Alphonse had a smooth torso. Small, underhung jaw. That's it. Masked, ugly. With a large rock in his hand. He went up the center aisle through the stream of moonlight, in his wake the scent of lavender, the cicadas' hymn. The rustling night stole in; a cascade of stars, the plumage of the trees, the sound of the mountains entered through the portal. He was ugly. He was handsome, strong, sturdy, thick-set. Clutching the carved rock. He reached the choir. Large honeycomb cell of silence. He spotted the statue. Shy, tilted face, with its vein-blue tint. He didn't kneel. Made no sign of the cross. He was wicked, blind, an atheist. Maybe he was taller, skinnier, more supple. A noble feline biker. Slaughtering the Madonna properly, for his own honor, to atone for wrongs against his tribe. Hairy then, simian, a leather-clad Apollo, stark naked underneath. Or a woman? Redheaded girlfriends . . . The decapitated Madonna. Stone picked up from some streambed. A natural ax, hill weapon. The Madonna was struck. No cry. Plaster and paint. Fragile debris. Dust and fragments. And he, she, they, everybody, the whole gang or herd, the shaggy prowler, the marble-bust dandy, all turned on their heels. The gaping portal bared a patch of shadows strewn with stars and cicadas. Back-first they went out, with no remorse, or shaken by a feverish joy, or sad, crying perhaps . . . The girls, the escapee, the lynx, the voyager, the king of the bikers, decked out in black leather, brilliant, his prick hard in the Madonna's mouth . . . Or else him, bandy-legged, with an undershot jaw, the archaic hunter . . . The church, calm and intact, hid in its depths this minute scree, dispersed plaster, paint chips. Lesser Madonna. And he ran perhaps, singing, the pithecanthropus on his bike, or galloped up the slope to the cave, the naked redheaded girl, beautiful big-bottomed black woman, twins, a female clan or some blood brotherhood . . . Happy in the blue unsullied night. The expanse of scrub where the wind whistles, caught between the gorges and the cave. Open valleys, highway heading to the sea. Infinite swells. Profound happiness.

The lynx has sprung onto a boulder's ledge. Gazing. The milky glow of dawn washes the pierced, fractured limestone crusts, flickering with deeper mauve filaments. The first sunlight seeps like blood into the rock pores, a network of veins, gentle placental links masking the belligerence of the sheer slopes, crevasses, trunnions undermined by the white cutlass of the fresh water springs. The lynx observes the world off in the distance. This creature, the "stag-wolf," the diabolical predator that immemorial tribes and hordes have hated above all others. Reviled lynx. With his simpleton's mug, his carnivorous Bacchus mask. Old rogue. He's free. He likes the great desert horizons. He hasn't killed any game in two days. This morning he's going to hunt. He feels his muscles tensed under his supple skin, his beautiful fur sheathing the javelins of his poised sinews. He sports his red crimson coat. A sunbeam ripples in his ambered eye, lodges in a ruby of slaughter. His territory extends around him. Four thousand acres of primitive rocks, holes, ravines, dry echoing scree where the bushes grip down, absinthe or arbutus in complicated paragraphs. The air is pink, fluid . . . This phosphorescence seems to rise from the center of the mountain. The mineral takes on a sealike hue. A lapping of rocks. The lynx is mauve in this water. Prow of a Viking ship. A large red bush. Killer gargoyle. Everywhere his excrement on display, offered to the eyes of other animals, strewing the countryside jealous of his reign. He perfumes his field with laurels of stench. The solitary lynx was just born at dawn, his maw dazzled with sunlight. Rapacious baby-face. He looks mean, he's hungry. And his gallop begins. Stone turns to velvet under his light paws. He halts, is off again. He circles around a peak, follows the course of a dry stream. What is running through his mind? Perhaps that hidden somewhere is the hermit, the prospector, the escapee, the journalist? The lynx fascinates so many people. Bestial and baleful. Nimble, cruel. He dances on the edges of marbles and micas. He moves along an unpredictable path, obeying the logics of thirst and murder. He knows where he's going. Following an invitation. A power in the morning when the sky brightens, pure as a trapezoid.

But the heat is present, settled on the reliefs, crouched in the hollows, nested in the shrubs, stretching out, ready to pounce also, to race along with its dragon tongue, the torches of its eyes. It's going to bite into the tender bread of the rocks. The lynx comes upon a sheet of water, a mere mirror in which the feline's shadow scatters, and takes fright among countless quivers of sunlight. His bristling fur of luminous glass shards, banderillas of water and fire, casts him in the guise of a blazing chimera . . . Part lion, part goat, part snake. Sheathed by scales, in an enveloping mane . . . The water trembles around the monster who escapes with one bound. He reattains the heights and suddenly stops, quivers, huddles next to the ground. A danger . . . a presence, something moves or watches keenly in the rigid setting. He waits. He can observe this way for hours on end. The long brushes prolonging his ears are pricked up, capturing the slightest stray sounds. He sorts, sifts myriad noises. Far more than a piercing gaze, the lynx is an obsessive, selective ear. He hears everything, that's why he knows everything, sees everything. His eyes are merely a fabulous sense of echo. He made out those footsteps, that animal tread somehow mingled with a human scent. The gravel is barely disturbed by soles accustomed to the course. A hunter . . . a beast . . . a naked huntress, light, musk-wreathed. And then in this pine forest, green verging on yellow, in this islet of delicacy, of tapering slats, he saw the lofty silhouette, the black skin. She advances, heading steadfastly forward along a familiar path. The lynx senses he is not the target of this splendid monster. He breathes in this odor, richer, lusher than other men's. He momentarily covets this unusual animal's flesh. He'd like to seize that somber antelope by the nape, feel her sides struggling, and her sweat would enrage the lynx to a peak of happiness. But her high waist, her heft frightens him . . . She scales a schist slope. Her skin merges with the rock surface. The lynx continues his hunt, nervous now, agitated by the sudden appearance of this unknown game . . . scent of human bitch, of she-goat.

The lynx, perched on a quartz slab, pivots, listens. Over there he spots her again, very far off, the magnificent beast, like a large black serpent, snatched up by its goal. Unfalteringly she cuts through the bushes, spanning more difficult obstacles. And when she disappeared again, he keeps watch a while longer, fascinated, trembling as if everywhere imperiled by the infiltration of some more powerful, more mysterious wild creature. Located nowhere in particular, out in the limpid wind, in the sissing grass, in all those sounds of scratching, creaking, in the rustling of plants and living stones. The earth cracks and ferrets about, the water forms, bubbles burst in the vesicles, roots clench down, molecules of light explode, gasses whisper, elytra flutter, snouts poke through the sand, columns of ants skitter along, transporting a cadaver iridescent with flies. And the herd screeches, squeals . . . Not to mention the circaetus' cry like clipping shears, the greasy clacking of wings on the dead tree.

The lynx dashes along, and in his flight this wonder, a hare, flushed from cover. It shoots along the ground in a concentrated whirlwind, a cylinder of tawny fur. The lynx dashes forward. The hare picks up speed. The lynx hits his swiftest hunting stride. He senses that he's taken off on a blind, endless race. Flawlessly his muscles churn, the tireless turbine of his breath . . . his feverish fury engulfs him in something like night. The hare is this prize prey running wild at the end of the tunnel. The lynx and the hare are the two poles of a meteoric thread. Knowing nothing, they know everything, both flying along, one fearful, the other ferocious. The difference in terms is abolished. Hunger is a fear. Anguish is a desire. They are equals in this death-challenge. Lynx Lepus, Lepus lynx. Metamorphosing. The lynx has such desire for the hare that he becomes it, the hare such terror of the lynx that it feels the beast enveloping it entirely. They run but it is no longer them: a power holds sway, commands the distance separating them, interlinks the trajectory of the meteors. This game doesn't belong to them. The mountains and the streams witness this struggle without seeing it. Interlocked in their festoons, their limestone arabesques, another task absorbs them, one they also perform unawares, unseeing, blindly driven by the chemistries of air, sun and water. Eroded, reformed, they are obstinate in their mineral labor. There exists neither hunt nor wild landscape. Neither hare nor lynx nor rocks. Only forces, ever more turbulent tensions, relationships, symmetries, a to-and-fro of volatile molecules, knots of atoms, of objects in motion, pawns of the cosmos that catch each other, defeat and devour each other, change into each other. Puzzle of air, of matter. Nothing thinks. A rigorous activity magnetizes each element. A merry-go-round, more or less slow, more or less lively. Mineral or fur. Ants gravel. Roots snakes. Thorns claws. Blood water. Bone-spurs stones. Each with its goal, its target, its crenel. Things have always happened this way. Before as it was later. The present is a mere illusion, the instantaneous image capturing eternity. The other hares, other lynxes run, those from antique peasantry spinning legends of "stag-wolves," of eyes seeing through walls, anuses laying gems. Every lynx, never a lynx. And the cave lynx tracked by the other, that feebleminded creature, the ancestor, the simian hunter, the old grumbler from the origins, the canine-toothed biped, the future thinker. Lynx, lynx, lynx and hares, generations of hares . . . pursuing each other so as to imitate life, to rehash the living. Images. Images of images. A genealogy of images. For the lynx is no more than a frenzied robot. The hare frenzied, the mountains also in a frenzy . . . Dead things imitating life. Vast inertia, automatons copying this miracle: a moment of unique life.

The lynx knows that he comes up the loser in this hare hunt every other try. But it seems that the lynx is imperceptibly gaining on the hare. The stubborn prey is unrelenting, gathers its last resources, delves into its guts, tendrils of darkness, mist of blood. The wild beast is ever closer. The hare forks off, comes up against a steep rise, hurtles up a slippery incline, stumbles, rolls, rights itself, but the lynx seizes it by the nape and smashes its backbone. Pinned to the ground, the hare cries, eyes bulging from their sockets, mouth agape. Wedged down this way, the head appears enormous. The lynx knocks the skull once with its fangs and devours his prey's brains. Breasts of fatty snow. The brain . . . From the pithecanthropus to the lynx, the same skull-feast can be witnessed. First, stuffing your face with this good delicious rice. Eating the power of the head, of the eyes, the jaw, the nose, the ears, swallowing it all down. Crunching into the sticky semolina where a thousand reflexes lie dormant, a thousand drives, thought itself at rest. What chicken feed! What a fish fry! A cassoulet of ideas. Next comes the liver, the bowels. Red matter now, hot innards pissing blood, the bountiful guts, intestines in sugary laces. And the lynx seizes the remains, drags them off toward some shelter where he'll savor them more deeply, in peace. Perhaps he suddenly dreaded the shadow of the roving beast, the black giant . . . rival or absconder? He goes to the foot of a stump in a warm sand-lined hollow to eat the rest of the hare. They were running, both hare and lynx, running forever. Neither he alone nor the other. Both together. The hare at present within the lynx. The lynx sated on the hare. The hare's blood showering the lynx's arteries. He's falling asleep in the coolness while noon glares wide-eyed. The lynx is abolished. The limestone formations solidify their base, rear up in the blue vacuum. They roll their hips, trace their tormented grandiloquent alphabets: châteaus, keeps, stone ledges . . . The rock sleeps or surveys, simmers, spies. Perhaps after his steaming repast the legendary lynx will lay his precious ligures in some rock casket. A limestone moneybag collects his treasure. Jewels for the black woman on the prowl.

Paula awoke in the middle of the night. Heart ground down. Short of breath. A feeling of suffocation overwhelms her, blocks her chest. She's been long familiar with such troubles. But this time the pain is stronger, tentacular. Paula's afraid, smothering. Slowly she rises, pushes apart the curtains, opens the window. Alphonse is asleep. She doesn't hear him snoring. Silently he's dozing, mute, unobtrusive. An angel. The deserted street slithers in the rippling moonlight. A checkered pattern of black diamonds and very pale squares. Hopscotch. A ghost could skip along the boxes, a very white visitor, or some black lady. An owl-woman. Paula puffs hard. This geometry of night darkens her mind. She sees figures advancing along the sequences of shadow and brightness. Processions. Half human, half animal. A bestiary of magi. She's delirious. She sees weather vanes, the cock on the church steeple, lightning rods like living beings crossing the stages of this lunar journey. And then maybe Myriam, Simon . . . Paula's pain subsides. Dead village set in this astral brilliance. She understands all at once that these ordinary adjoining houses stand exposed in the sky, the starry abyss. Night is everywhere, the Milky Way has invaded the street. The village seems on exhibit, presented like a target to flying meteorites. Daylight created an impression of a safe shelter against the anguish of infinity. The village was shut in, familiar as a large collective hut. And now, suddenly it no longer harbored human beings, shrinking so small, crouched, scooped out everywhere, consigned to the immaculate night. And in Paula's heart this great darkness opened a slow ecstasy, a thirst for peace. She was less afraid of death. She would have liked to dissolve into this starry tide, to spread outward, to leave behind her wreck of a harrowing carcass and swell into all this milk, this blueness, to swim deep into this immense gulf. She said to herself: "They're asleep." She imagined them tiny, curled up, twisted in the familial sheets. Oldsters, youngsters, every member of the village, having choked back their hostilities, diluted their petty spite. She felt stronger than they, her illness made her powerful. She reigned because she had accepted voyage or absence. She aspired to the vast silence, a calmer, darker ocean with no shores. She wanted to drift like a piece of flotsam, a water lily, an Ophelia . . . to be off, die, escape through the window. A definitive Melusina . . . to rejoin and lose herself . . . and float.

But the pain flared up. A tingling in her fingers. Tightening arm. Breathing cut off. She's going to lie back down. The window has been left open. The air palpitates, grazes her mouth with fragrances, whiffs. Things pass into the room. Impalpable shimmering traces. Invisible entities that bustle about, move off or settle in. All around her she senses presences in the guise of glimmers, meanders, dark specks, slow black curves. The night breathes inside the bedroom, silver-tinted like a fish, with a bird's neck. And then the agitation recurs, but patient, light, whispering tendrils, slippages. Paula sees fragile architectures being constructed, then dashed, beaded atomic webs. Blades, needles displaced, altered or demolished. She witnesses a queer ballet of lilliputian objects, imponderable but brilliant, lovely, graceful. Gold work, lace spun by miraculous legions. Paula can't get over it. Helpless to describe this impression of delicacy, of perfection. Without shining it glows, radiating a feeble, intimate sparkle. Chirping of lights, straw wisps, minnows. Paula would like for these expert goblins to decompose her body under their fairy lancets. Her corpse, cell by cell, molecules, drop by drop, like a kind of sand or salt, grain by grain, emptied by these delicate hands and strewn through the sky, spread to infinity. That's how she prefers to die: to be sown among the stars.

But the pain ensconces itself like a slab, an acute, tough cramp clamping down, biting deeply into its terrain. Paula imagines some wonder that might give her immediate relief, freeze her battered flesh, her gnarled muscles. Magic. Then her fluid body would be pacified like the glowing light of the moon.

She woke up Alphonse. She explained her anguish. He turned on the bedside lamp and wants to call the doctor. She refuses: "Take my hand." He holds her palm, plump, damp. She looks at him. His face is affectionate, worried. But his expression strikes Paula as superficial, its features set. Alphonse feels no real dread. He doesn't subscribe to her personal suffering. He only wishes to, mimics her anxiety, with middling success. And this impossibility frightens her. Even while watching her die, he'll display this overly gentle pity, this perplexity. His face has a hint of stupidity, idiocy. He'll wait on the other side with the living. She, a stranger, having already tumbled into the unnameable, the abyss; he, embarrassed, bereaved, perhaps crying but with no horror or revolt. She'd have liked for him to howl, clutch her in his arms.

She takes some pills from a drawer. He gets up, fills a glass with water. "Drink . . . drink." He holds the glass. She swallows, a bitter taste. She remembers her childhood illnesses. Her throbbing skull. Feelings of nausea. And her mother holding the glass: "Drink . . . Drink." Alphonse sets down the glass, kisses Paula on the forehead. She starts crying. Sobbing. She's never indulged in such outbursts. Alphonse repeats: "You mustn't . . . You mustn't." She hears the words like cats, rats, gloomy doleful creatures, all in a row, shivery, shifty, omens of dread, extinction . . . tolling the bell.

"I'm going to die . . ."

She was expecting him to protest, coddle her. He falls silent, surprised. He's closed off in a huge hole of muteness. Perhaps he's trying to pull something out of his throat, just the right word. Nothing emerges. Doesn't even make a gesture. He remains motionless, sitting up in bed. She doesn't dare look at him. She regrets what she said. She reproaches herself, she thinks she's been too pompous, pitiable. A monstrous indiscretion. Why torment him, lay it on so thick, make him ashamed . . . This time she's the one who takes his hand.

The idea had germinated in Agathe's brain. Simply a premonition. A keen intuition while thinking about Myriam, the beautiful woman from Cameroon. Agathe had gone over to the excavation camp. She'd waited for Myriam to come down from the cave with her large portfolio. Agathe amused the youngsters with her questions, her curiosity while ogling the skeletal fragments, fiddling with the ossicles in her palms like beetles, small animalcules, untamed, cunning. Agathe even joked around, pushing a macabre bit with her finger in her cupped hand. She really fancied these sorts of off-color antics. It looked like she was tickling tiny creatures . . . slugs, lizards. From time to time she darted a glance toward the cavern edge. At last Myriam came down. Seamed shorts, a dirty rag around her breasts. Agathe found her to be slutty and secretive, clandestine. She had a weakness for that word: *clandestine.* She'd gladly have made it into a first name. In her mind's eye she saw someone who was svelte, daring, disguised, slinking with muffled tread across the rooftops, a nimble noiseless thief . . . Myriam. Agathe surmised something. This Myriam wasn't like the others. She barely had a role in the excavations, she didn't sift soils, she drew half-human, half-ape faces, touching and retouching. Her breasts swelled under the crumpling cloth. A beautiful girl. Too black maybe. But well made. Agathe had never been beautiful, tall, put together. Skinny in her mirror. Not feminine. More like a weasel, a shrew. Men liked feeling round brazen breasts, firm curving asses, pulpy buttocks . . . pulpy! Agathe had no pulp to her. A soot dress. Agathe would have gladly touched Myriam. Behind and breasts, just to see. And her vagina . . . what color was it? Teenagers were swimming in the lake, taking dives, splashing about, making threats, if I catch you I'll dunk you under. Youth! Agathe had no regrets. She didn't know how to swim. She'd never worn a bathing suit. This Myriam and her drawings constituted Agathe's second youth, an awesome rush of desire . . . Simon the journalist, the escapee, the bikers, the lynx, Myriam and the pithecanthropi . . . Agathe was searching, smelling out trails, relationships, possible parallels. It was her private feast. All at once she turned cheerful. She kidded with the young people, took playful slaps at them. A spry, old girl, horsing around. Amid naked teenagers, undershorts, the crawl stroke, tussling and a lot of other things: a mouse sorting through the Swiss cheese of bones. Unconventional kids, but decent. No troublemakers among them, no weirdos. Except for . . . that Sue! The English girl, one terrific trollop. The stories going around about her! Agathe had personal proof—out in the pine forests, on the boulders she'd caught by surprise such things, but such things . . . Oh Sue! But at least it was clear what she was all about, she was in a very definite category. Whereas Myriam put on such airs—her mystery, her warlike, gawky gait. And now this friend of hers, Simon. Plus . . . Plus . . . The mailman couldn't be positive but Myriam went roving, he'd supposedly seen her . . . far from the campsite. OK, she wasn't the only person who went out exploring, or for a stroll. These kids weren't afraid of anything. Hunting butterflies, carved rocks, thistles, saxifrage. You came across them in the valleys, meticulous, detecting flora, fauna, photographing. Ecology-minded . . . very much so. But Myriam also went roaming at night. A black woman at night. The beauty of it gave you goosebumps. Myriam from Africa. At times Agathe's mind turned to Africa. Cameroon. Going up a river in a pirogue and seeing the animals, birds, tom-toms, naked muscular men, their flesh glistening, women's breasts with their greedy kids clinging to their nipples. Wild beasts, jungle vines. Tom-toms. War dances. Totems. Tomahawks . . . giant tarantulas, the whole topsy-turvy tropics. Agathe wouldn't be afraid. She'd be the one who'd scare the hell out of them. Stubborn, very black, her gaze glinting with cunning. But neither her health or her means would allow her such a tour. And then too many things would submerge her. She'd never be able to sort out, note, store up. She'd get lost in a fabulous hodge-podge. She'd be overcome with lush profusion and cries. And the poverty, the paupers she'd seen on TV over at Marthe Praslin's . . . Baby martyrs. Was there anything sadder than throwing bread away, finding untouched food in trash cans? She was more comfortable in Aguilar, in her own microscopically scrutinized milieu. Limits had to be set, you shouldn't spread yourself too thin, you had to hover in one spot like a circling sparrow hawk. You had to know what you know. And know it well, probe deeply, warily allow in new things. The rest—Africa, the world, enormities—wasn't her business. A bunch of messy, illegible stuff. A territory for God Himself. Each to his own fiefdom.

Simon was very moved, as though receiving communion in church. Hands trembling. Ashamed of, yet savoring his weakness. Enshrouded by the black chapel. The teenagers worked at a leisurely pace, their gestures precise and measured. He was amazed by the way they invested their labor with no transcendence. They wouldn't have betrayed any greater intensity of devotion had they been laying a simple brick wall. He too was devout. As if at Mass. He'd been authorized to participate in the excavation. He'd been assigned a position in the grid of strings and soils. He fit in like a rabbit down its hole. An incense bearer facing the altar. His heart was in his boots. In front of him the edge of a bone broke the surface. The crew leader informed him that it was the mandible of an Etruscan wolf. What luck! They threw around these magic words without seeming to touch them. But this archaic qualifier opened a wider sense of the sacred within him. Everywhere there was earth, sandy or sticky clay, concretions of welded grains, the soft white innards of the centuries. Because the image of bread entered his thoughts; and in this floury slab, the dead were wedged in narrow sheaths of reminiscences, paltry detritus, cores, crusts. With nose down against the sediment the earth struck him as enormous. Such a prodigious spawn deposited by water seepage, wind, guano and erosions. The tumulus overflowed upon him. He'd have liked to dig out his gallery, establishing a nest all the way down among the relics. Yes, going into this mountain of millennial excrements, moving about amid the flint, the schists, the chiseled quartzes, brushing up against the skeletons, skulls, femurs, tibiae, teeth . . . sinking down, disappearing into a center of sorts: the insides of an immense giant's skull, a Himalayan ogre in which he would have lit the first fire. The earth produced bumps, bulk, protrusions, and slopes. This density flabbergasted him. So many inner secrets that the excavation mazes of the future would be exploring! What would they discover in one hundred years? And here within this circumscribed parcel at the base of a powdery embankment, this mandible of an Etruscan wolf. Two teeth protruding along a bone border, matching in color the compost in which it had been encrusted. Earth and bone fusing in the course of time . . . An identical yellow-brown, the color of the origins. A mash of clay and skeletons. Armed with brush and awl he dusted scrupulously, decorticated. He felt himself to be tiny, shrunk to the dimensions of a foraging ant. His eyes contracted, needles picking up minute seeds. Suddenly the idea of the Etruscan wolf loomed up out of the remains, the idea of five hundred thousand years that separated man from beast. Then the dimensions capsized, were inverted. So all became grandiose, imposing. The very clamor of the cosmos, of a formidable machinery of instincts, life forces, cycles, circuits, evolutions and devourings emerged from the wolf's jaw. And Simon was transformed into a muscled gladiator, braced against the formidable creature. He struggled against the brute, animalistic attack. Coated with clay, ochered, daubed with ancestral waste, he seized hold of the wolf. He felt that he had gradually turned into the design of a funeral fresco. A primitive epic buried in the depths of the pyramid. Man confronting wolf. Wolf skeleton combating hunter's flesh. And the others, levelheaded and meticulous, bustled about, carting around heaps of dust, photographing, molding, marking, labeling, as if it were nothing. Didn't they have souls? What had they done with their memories? Simon wanted to shout out insults, warnings. Wake up! Remember! Don't be so Boy-Scoutish, so buddy-buddy, so all-in-this-thing-together, guitars and campfires, open your eyes, you're treading upon the sand of the origins. The soils are carpeted with traps, filters, ravaging talismans. A bone might explode at any moment. Sacrilege! Pray! Kneel down, don ritual chasubles. Invent cabalistic formulas. Only the priests will be allowed to invest these sites. Catacombs, ossuary, sepulchers. The dead are watching us, a swarm of animals, men, ancestors, demigods, dwarfs, giants, hybrid monsters. They are present here. Their eyeballs poke through the earth's cartilage, spying upon us the way fish watched Moses along the walls of the parted Red Sea.

He chopped away at his wolf. A dentist tackling canines. And this term, *Etruscan wolf,* was so beautiful. *Etruscan*—hard and gleaming as bronze. The statue stood over him, noble wolf, virile, sinewy, pure-blooded. A mathematical block, hewn, polished. Upon an imaginary square or in the heart of a temple. The perfect wolf. Basaltic, astronomical. Etruscan. This architecture, this musculature. The dentalium in a column and portico; the last escaping syllable, too smooth, slippery, shimmers, seeping blackly down deep into the most ancient dwellings of the earth . . .

He grew calm. Obsessions and hallucinations receded. He became banal, craftsmanlike. He worked as they did, nibbling, hacking holes. The jaw was emerging. He touched it with his fingertips. Dark, almost cold, smelling of saltpeter, night, a grave in the workshop of the dead. And the traces of guano bleached the schists and clays like salt, droppings that had changed into snow. He thought of Myriam, who was out drawing in front of the porchway, opposite the sun. She could contemplate the landscape, the sky, the vines, the peaks, the pine forests, and the sea between the notches of the mountains. Perhaps she was drawing the wolf at this very moment, a bear, a reindeer, a beaver, an elephant, a lion . . . A pithecanthropus was being brought to birth under her pencil, becoming real, beginning to walk, entering the cavern, grabbing from behind his pale offspring of adolescents, rosy-cheeked, with chubby hands.

Simon was somewhat concerned about his mental slippages that ran over all possible paths in every direction. At times the process exhausted him. He dreamed of a perception that was motionless, in which every object would occupy a place to itself as in the museum down below in the valley. Each bone, each skeleton, each statue rigid on its pedestal, labeled, photographed by the troop of tourists. He envied this destiny of fixed stars. Essences confined in their circles.

His thoughts turned to himself, his forgotten, disguised life. Voluntary amnesia. Cut off. From Her. From the Others. From the abysses in which he had thrown himself of his own accord, dashed to bits as if upon boulders. The Etruscan wolf snapped up his memory. The cave's gaping maw kept turning over tragic memories. Simon wondered what he was doing there, in this godforsaken little village, like some dotard manhandling this die-sized chip of putrified earth. When there was the sea out there, the shores, naked girls all along the coast as far as Spain. All races come running. German girls, Swedes, Danes, English girls . . . Bodies as far as your desire might reach, choices, vices, marriages, and love's lucky finds. Excavating women with your hands, your sex in the soft mass of muscles, the network of fleshes, the water of gazes, the forest of hairs, pubis-sheath, breasts-thighs, would such not lead him on his way toward his authentic destination, his genuine habitat?

But the religious silence of the caverns casts a spell over Simon. He'd have liked to ask them to leave him alone, to go down the mountainside. He'd have kept watch over the colossal past. Minute and vulnerable and mortal before the world, his weight, his graduated layers of landings, down to the primordial bricks.

Toward evening Sue called over to Gilles, the crew leader: a rumor was going around the cave. The chief director and his wife arrived. Along with the others Simon followed Sue's finger pointing toward the bone shard. Under the thin layer of crumbled clay, an antler tip could be seen protruding. The director announced that it would take twenty or so days to free these human remains undamaged, cautiously. They were hoping for more than a trunk, a thorax—their imaginations were already at work, extrapolating. The teenagers' faces lost their slaves-of-routine expressions. Seized by a curiosity, shaken by emotion. With eyes like children's on Christmas Eve, the cave was the tree surrounded by presents. Guesses sprang up, a flood of happy hypotheses, of promises. Perhaps they were on the brink of a great discovery. Since 1971, the date the skull was unearthed, nothing extraordinary had occurred. Today, in the cradle, something, someone was drawing near. The slut Sue stroked the delicate vegetation of bones with her beautiful hands.

The day before, the valley crew that cleansed and marked the remains had sent several pounds of bones to the laboratory in Marseilles. The truck transporting the relics in its safe crossed paths with the caravans of tourists. Tanned crowds. Mobs of the exodus toward the beaches. It was a rather nondescript minivan, its suitcases crammed with skeletons. Graveyard tourism. On the one hand, life heading down toward Spain, daylight herds. On the other, the dead going up toward Marseilles, the tribes of yesteryear. In case of accident Germans and Dutch crashing into the van would have intermingled their flesh with fragments of lions, lynx and simian forbearers. Dreaming of some invisible splinter from an archaic hunter driven by the impact into a driver's torso. Recovered from his injuries, such a man would spend the rest of his life carrying around the ancestor's imprint lodged deep inside his chest... Simon! Simon! Don't start drifting again, spinning out this string of images that lead you into the abyss or else perhaps to paradise, when you reach the end of your rope!

The laboratory, clean as marble, sanitary, sterilized. The bones show up in bags like tulip bulbs destined for the flower beds of a public garden ... How does that legend go, the one about an animal's, or is it a god's sacrum, Dionysius, Osiris no doubt, which, when planted in the ground, regrew, engendering a new flesh? The scientists, dressed in white like surgeons, lean over the skeletons. They are going to submit them to complex dating tests, measuring amino acids, studying radioactive chains. They all juggle with thousands, hundreds of thousands of years. Sagacious specialists. Passionless technicians. Correct, efficient as those who diagnose. Interested but bereft of lyricism, steam, metaphors. Inspectors of the centuries. Astronauts of oubliettes. Bathyscape lancets. Animals that ran in the antique present, hunting, biting, breathing in the wind; tools that landed blows, flying through the air, shattering members—all now scrutinized in their atoms, their uranium, their potassium, their radiations, their fissions. No more fur, nor flesh, nor bone nor stone, but relationships and symbols. Instinct becomes number. Life pressed, sponged, reduced to the ascetic state of ciphers. The pithecanthropus hunted in turn by a mathematical eye, tumbled into a chemical trap. This distance was necessary, this placid, electronic conquest, before the first man finally cast his eye upon us, before the ancestor came back to life in his environs, his exact span of time; a prodigious to-and-fro movement, from obscure vitality to atomic physics, from this latter to the feasts of origin. The night of blood, the clinical whiteness of science and the broad daylight of time . . . The bones will come back to the museum to exhibit their tears, their incomplete puzzles before the ingenuous eyes of tourists.

Sue had made a great discovery. Somewhat agitated by the ghostly apparition. But she was up to confronting any skeleton. All the same she preferred the beautiful upholstery of the flesh, the glaze of sweat, the arabesques of hairy tufts, the toughness of animal napes.

On Saturdays, as usual, Sue goes out hunting for virgin farm boys. Her game emerges, large gangly bean-poles, all kneecaps and round elbows. In her pockets she slipped a little dust of the dead. Pithecanthropus powder, perfect for virgin lads. She likes it when they have Joan of Arc or Beatles haircuts, hairless chests, as chaste as shepherds from the Middle Ages. She likes carving their first pipe. She's a real sucker for rustic glandes. Their cocks turn as purple as storms, the milk spurts out in long streams. Sue finds that her own skin stays virginal thanks to the country sperm. The semen from mountain springs purifies it. She could give a damn about the gossip, the cheap talk of old biddies stigmatizing her. Sue is nothing out of the ordinary, when all is said. Like her girlfriends, she does a decent job of excavation, puts in her time at the cave, shares meals at the canteens. Sleeps soundly. Rather well balanced. Healthy looking. Nothing raises her to the ranks of Messalinas, Agrippinas, obsessed with sex. Nevertheless, bucolic pricks are her hobby. She knows all the nubile boys in the area. She gathers information, hangs around the cafés where guys play pinball, drink Pernods and lambaste each other with smutty jokes. All alone she'll install herself at a table. Out toward Rivesaltes, Estagel, Tuchan—all villages rich with game. The boys ogle the English girl, who begins by observing them very discreetly. But they dare not approach her. She smells them out, sizes up their thighs, the bulge of their zippers. She prefers them in tight jeans like girls. Most of all, impossibly clumsy, blushing and pudgy. She's rather keen on braggarts who lay it on thick in order to camouflage an even vaster vulnerability. With special fondness for a scant vocabulary. She loathes words and still speaks French badly. She hates tans above all else—she likes her boys to be immaculate. Yet she's got a weakness for the imprint of sweater weaves on sheepish torsos. She'll follow the guy of her choosing when he leaves the joint. As soon as they're away from their gang of buddies, some boys lose their self-assurance and get scared, dashing along the embankments under the olive trees. She catches them, whispers to them . . . These Corbières winegrowers are big babies, well built. It's up to her to go three-quarters of the way. They're ashamed of some things. She takes them young, it's true, as soon as childhood is behind them. They stammer. They've got porcelain balls.

Tonight's Saturday. Sue's almost Sioux . . . when the skin of well-sucked boys breaks into a sweat. Their moist loins and their primrose hairs. Fern-guys. Shepherds of guileless rocks. With their airs of peaceful sheep. She is Cybele, Isis, Dionysius . . . they're going to catch on now. Because the night's beginning. Oh their mommies! . . . Oh their youth! . . . Because now there's this dreamt-of voyage, out upon the sea . . .

Agathe would have loved to travel around in the police helicopter. A tiny toy sweeping over the imbroglio of the hills. It gains altitude, then swoops, hugging the ground, edging in, descending into certain gorges. It wouldn't take much for that propellered bug to take a peek into the hideaway of the caves. Circular glass as in a lorgnette, a beveled magnifying glass, it scrutinizes the expanse in its search for the escapee. Every day it can be heard going, coming, grazing the pine forests, making the limestone quake. Its racket becomes familiar, reassuring, it stamps a rhythm upon the passing hours like the Angelus. Agathe imagines herself beside the pilot, a whole other world than the mailman's minivan. That flying vista would furnish her with a pair of glasses ideal for inspecting space in its entirety, in every least detail. God's gaze in all its splendid diversity and unity. Agathe: a black insect in the drop of glass. Carbonized Cartesian diver trapped in a bubble of jelly, condemned to horizontal explorations, a mob of scenes, secret views escape her. From above she'd chance upon the terrorist and the lynx, Simon's forays, Myriam's suspicious rambles, the stampede of bikers, their new tricks. Mind-boggling maneuvers, hedgehopping like during wartime, she'd see Apaches on the attack, kamikazes dive-bombing, serpents darting across the floor of boulders. The big, venomous girls, Isis with her bandaged neck, would siss as they watched the big, brilliant maybug flash past. She'd see the adulterous couples making love in the scrub. Small backsides like pneumatic drills. Machines for stitching the flesh of sinning women. The helicopter would hover motionlessly above certain narrow chasms which she'd scrutinize at leisure, down to their very bottoms. The gaze of Melusina in the hollow of these black wells would meet Agathe's eyes. Beneath her she'd spot sparrow hawks, buzzards, she'd triumph with her own piercing stare over the birds of prey. The helicopter and its speed, blast of wind, vibrating metal, like a saber singing in samurai loops. Assault helmet. In the craters Agathe would see fissures, ditches, forests of rowed trees. And the escapee flushed out like a deer, running, galloping naked, pursued by mechanized pruning shears. Yoo-hoo!

Yippee! Agathe with her terrorist lasso, I'm Buffalo Bill out tracking ferocious game . . . Come to think of it, why not some sputnik, a satellite orbiting around the planet and empowering Agathe's eyes with a cosmic vision? The whole earth at her disposal—seas, dented continents, populations on marijuana, tattered megalopolises, exoduses of wild beasts, sagas of puppets, topped forests and cement-sealed volcanos. The world in Agathe's mirror, a cricket of heaven!

But crawling around presents an obvious advantage. Infiltrating, scampering, eyes riveting the slightest shift in the terrain. You see what's hiding under the branches, in the hollows, the small mushrooms of life, parasites, concealed twigs. The danger of flight is the type of view it imposes: too bird's-eye, too synthetic. A genuine gaze is one that's analytical, pupils posted, eyelashes like multiple detectors, quivering antennae, sensitive to microns. Agathe does better on the ground, on all fours, nothing gets by . . .

For example, no observation deck is superior to the town sidewalk when Lynne and her new friend stroll down the main street pushing baby Arthur's carriage. Agathe's in the front row. The helicopter and its din upset the scene, warn the protagonists. Too far removed from the actors, it wipes out expressions, the shameless blush of the skin, the stray locks of mussed hair, the hole in the boy's elbow . . . Lynne, betrayed by Simon, set herself to pulling off a flashy stunt. She dug up a serious, considerate guy. A university student! More cultivated than Simon perhaps. He understands unwed mothers, explains them, provides commentaries. A sociology major. She saunters up the street with her fiancé. Bearded, glasses, an intelligent face, pale pink, enormous fragile eyes. Sky-blue pupils. Simon, sitting at a table outside Alphonse's café, views the procession. The journalist is a bit miffed! He preferred Lynne in her role as ingenuous maid at his feet. So much the worse for him. Let him get back to his pithecanthropus hunt, to his traffic in black women, that obnoxious Myriam with her coal breasts. That ebony bitch! That mica camel . . . Lynn's got herself a fiancé, she flaunts him, introduces him to the entire village, town hall, museum, campground. I'm the nice little maidservant perhaps, the girl whose ass gets slapped, the one laid up in the attic. Oh, really, think so? A student protects me now, a thinker who loves me. A man who respects my rights, ones he knows by heart. He reflects beforehand, during, and after intercourse. Takes notes and recopies them. I feel important. He asks me if he can sodomize me, apologizes, proceeds in polite stages, is sorry, withdraws, repents openly. Simon sitting at the table . . . This'll shake him up. The student's younger. I'm passing by . . . I straighten up, give just a little wriggle, a quiver of my behind to stir up the rotten journalist's regrets. Who cares! Let him get a full sense of all that he's lost, the acres of smooth skin, sweet suave delights, a cuddly mommy suckling greedy Arthur. How he used to love watching her feedings . . .

melting in affection and depravity. Arthur pocketing the nipple. Breathing in, suckling. Squirts of milk. The delicate network of veins marking the swollen breasts. White, blue. Greediness, roundness. She didn't mind him looking on. Because Simon was mysterious, melancholy. Better in bed than her student. Well, tough! Never asked permission. Bluntly wheedling. One or two tricks, sinuous ploys, tongues and pricks as acrobatic as apes streaming through the branches. Simon greets her. She answers with a curt nod. She feels like a university graduate herself, married, proper and settled . . . When she spoke to him about Simon, the student listened with concern. No anger, jealousy, petty possessiveness. On the contrary, enlightened, full of esteem . . . You could tell him everything, never a bitter comment. Sort of like a worker priest, a young communist. A generous intellectual. Pure heart. A real whiz at dialogue. Red Cross and Catholic Charities Appeal. Listening, never cutting you off . . . a clean soul, levelheaded, guitar player and pacifist, squeaky clean anus. Whereas Simon's one sly devil, cruising every which way, draped in that phony loner look of his. That pig with his caves, eyeing holes, nosing around everything that stinks, bones, orifices, lynx turds, well, tough! He knew how to get Arthur babbling, the old bastard! Effortlessly . . . A real gift as far as charm goes, little tickles under the chin, cute smiles with a flick of the finger, using his artist's flimflam magic sleight-of-hand and he got what he was after from her . . . Unhappy men are moving. They call out to you from their bitter sofa. Their sullen fire. Their silhouette of nothingness lying in the ashes. They manipulate you like chess experts. And that's how they succeed, irresistible because incredulous, somewhere else, unpredictable, blazing, starving but slinking away with a show of indifference, an absentminded kindness. A race of assholes. Lynne, the student and his pullover knit together like his theories. She walks on by. Simon watches. Agathe. The whole village. The helicopter combs the area in the event the terrorist, perched on the rooftops, might also be watching. Lynne would like to fly off in such a helicopter on her wedding day, wearing a white gown with an elaborate train, veil and Swiss muslin, all taken up in the air. Open sky. Escape. The adventure of life. The others below, shops, loaves of bread, sidewalks, sewers. While she floated on high with her student prince. They'd never come down. A boundless voyage among soaring birds, famous mountain tops, the Empire State Building and Mount Fuji. Love on a cloud! The student will explain the meteorological phenomena. The tides tilting back and forth under their eyes in the moonlight, the Gulf Stream, Hercynian caterpillars, the eyes of cyclones, the golden fire of the epicenter under the earth's crust. He really knew how to give an explanation, using simple words, patiently, ejaculating a bit too quickly. Simon never ejaculated or only at the very end, beyond the mazes, ramifications, caresses, positions—on all fours, on one leg, "hot air balloon," "camelback," standing, "leapfrog," on sofas, chairs, staircases, grandfather clocks, after he'd exhausted everything, his zinging ruses, his wild-eyed stunts, he ejaculated but never by way of finishing up. More as if he had seen as far as possible. He took his pleasure in a distant land, so hazy, beyond borders and frontiers, after every landscape had rushed past, trees, animals. He'd have been perfectly capable of not ejaculating. Like suspension points, a parenthesis he'd close later, at the end of an asymptote . . . It seemed he wanted to make love without letup, the way you breathe, live . . . A monster. A sick man in love with skeletons and animals. The student was too quick about it. He flopped back on his belly in five seconds flat. She stroked his hair, indulgent. She walks on by, Simon watches her. Agathe. Perhaps Paula behind her curtain. Iza, the priest . . . the whole of society. The kids playing marbles quickly touch themselves. And Marthe Praslin in her garden. Then three cycles suddenly appear. At first the uproar sounded like the helicopter's. But no: the racket belongs to the bikers. The redheaded girl out in the lead. She slows down, stops in front of Lynne. Tender-souled assassins. Hold nothing but contempt for the smug villagers on their doorsteps. Simon the reporter. Crappy newspapers. Rotten articles, shitty tittle-tattle. A voyeur of the dead. And one, two, off they go, bolting swiftly. Lynne feels a long tweak of nostalgia. Would like to take off on Paloma's bike . . . For Agathe revealed her name, by way of the mailman: Paloma the redhead. Paloma, green-eyed sun. A chieftainess. A siren-breasted scout. It's stronger than she, Lynne must confess to her penchant for those who dominate, carry off, abduct . . . kidnappers, thieves, starry outlaws who live in rocky valleys like cowboys, Cheyenne, buccaneers, oh the Court of Miracles, that den of thieves, Turtle Island, Harlem, the Mexicans' camp, bone-dry gnawers of jackal muscles . . . Holding out in the heart of the desert by drinking cactus sweat. The student required one nice big quart of milk every single day.

Myriam, barefoot, jeans rolled up to her knees, holding a long stalk, a dry blade of grain, draws arabesques on the sidewalk, where she's seated next to Simon. The reporter studies her sinewy chestnut feet, the delicate bone structure of a shell or beach pebble. The dust bleaches them in a patchwork of salt-colored scales. Man and woman barely exchange a word. Simon desires her. But he knows she hesitates to go up to the room. She prefers dawdling on the sidewalk, her eyes on passersby, villagers, tourists. Myriam experiences long spells when her mind goes empty like an innocent child's in a trance. Her mouth agape, she engulfs the spectacle of people. Simon observes this abandon. This woman, so powerful, vigilant in her muscles, with a painter's eyes, lives upon the swarm of surrounding impressions. Her existence is sustained by nothing but a thousand fleeting sensations, brief contacts, echoes, encounters, sounds. Simon lusts for this flesh with no transcendence, purely animal, assailed, possessed by the noises, colors, movements and fibrils of the air and dust. The world gleans and pillages her. She's the whore of this daily street that comes to touch her skin, feel her up, utterly slack, soft lofty African woman, penetrating her black female indolence. A misty cave where the village scatters, sounds of crunching, of sissing, jolts, thin shards of life. The kid on his bike who passes with a whistle seems to have just crossed through Myriam's sleek tunnel: shadowy chapel from which he emerges coated, oiled, licking caramel and dew from his chops. Air, wind, hillside smells deposit within her their seed and their down. She refuses Simon's too restrictive embrace, she's fucking the confusion of things . . .

About twenty yards away, on the other side: the fountain and the old men's bench. They're all looking in the same direction toward the couple sprawled on the sidewalk, feet in the stream, they're her fans, flighty butterflies. The old men remain on their bench, each on his specially assigned seat. Sitting upright on the ship of the dead, moored to the street.

Myriam and Simon as a couple exhibit too great an extravagance and casualness. They might as well go ahead and bed down right in the middle of the street as has been witnessed, at times, on certain nights. Young people nowadays coupling right under the windows, teenagers from Paris on vacation, spoiled, depraved, shitting right on doorsteps out of spite, whim or bravado . . . But it's always a good thing having those two at hand, few cars at this time of day, little traffic . . . So Myriam and Simon offer a choice morsel. They barely move. She with her little intrigues: the stalk and bare feet. Mystery. Simon, his sheep eyes. Looking more severe than the girl. Like a TV reporter.

The retired winegrower, the most lecherous of the old hands, remarks that she's got one terrific pair of tits, that Myriam does. Jugs from Cameroon. Oil-black breasts under her flimsy shirt. With tips like animal snouts. The whole bench laughs, except those too on in their years, too tired, frozen, their minds walnut shells. Meditating on their arthritis, their burning bellies. The winegrower likes to keep track of Simon and his girlfriend's face-to-face encounter as it evolves. Hanging around there like lazy kids, so beautiful, so young, they ought to be up in the hills where you find green narrow valleys branching with springs, nested amid the rocks. Simon's hand strokes her thigh, displayed on its side, musketeer style. She's a large, slovenly girl. Her thigh rocks under Simon's nose. A firm cylinder. His hand touching. Her thigh swaying. Myriam places her hand on the reporter's. Two hands superimposed upon the balanced thigh, which pitches and rolls, a powerful oar, a scull in an eddy of muscles. Her worn jeans stretch over her round bulging flesh. Cracking on top. A runner's thighs, fantastic mechanisms of springs good for leaping, motor belts of pleasure. Hubs, levers in the velvet, the soft membranes under the beautiful sheath of black flesh. It must be brand new inside, all aluminum tubing... bright chain links, automatic gear shifts, smart-looking parts, axles nickel-plated the way they are for beautiful bicycles, mopeds, stamped *made in Japan,* never a breakdown. Obsessed by the excavations, all Simon would need to do is dig under the thick integument of flesh in order to free the pure white bone frame. Dazzling metal skeleton. Its bones must be like teeth, arranged in some secret geography, hard, immaculate, crisscrossing the deep night of its body with ivory . . .

Simon asks her questions about Cameroon. Stingy answers. She laughs evasively. He reacts in similar fashion when she wants to question him. Yet he guesses that Myriam is imitating him just for fun, as well as out of politeness, whereas deep down she could care less about Simon's past. Lynne was so different, curious, attentive, consumed by a desire to discover, to dream, to find a place for each revelation along the shelves of her memory, like jars of jam she'd savor on winter nights after Simon had gone. They play at hiding the truth from each other. They make do with this exposed life, confined to the shimmer of the present, the arrow shafts of desire. Depth is prohibited. The little underhanded games of their personal stories. There is no other horizon but this sunny street, facades, benches, fountain, bistro. The dark black shade, straight as a die, marks a contrast with brilliant rectangles of light. Myriam's bare foot hops from one side to the other, scorched or cooled. She'd gladly do likewise with the rest of her body. Breasts in darkness, sex in fire. Simon begs for a hopelessly ordinary hug. She hasn't the least desire to budge one inch. The sidewalk is her ecstasy. Mineral tambourine. Her joints stiffen in the warmth . . . Air molecules, flower seeds, bubbles, whorls, phosphenes. She basks in the immediate. A sleepy lioness. Look at Simon becoming more and more harried by his craving for hugs, ploughshare turning over clods of earth; he wants to assail this African fur. She knows this. But without really seeking to defy him, she exaggerates her thinglike, animallike passivity in a way that comes to her with perfect naturalness. Her body, a gift to the street, hussar thighs spread, jean zipper swollen by her pubis, sturdy ass firmly propped on the paving stones. Just deal with it, Simon and you old geezers, while I laze in the serenity of my richly oiled machinery, sliding frameworks, outfitted with intimate rims of flesh, carpeted with hot silks, enveloped with feathery ruffs. Nothingness swallows me up. My being blossoms in a deep, delicious mud . . . oh my moist cushy organs . . . all these shivery thrills of love.

The time for the tourist buses rolled around. In the middle of the afternoon the street shook with their racket. The old men complained about the noise all the while enjoying the lavish, renewed spectacle. The museum filled with all sorts of people, self-educated, innocent, vacationers, mature adolescents come for a dose of culture, foreigners, especially senior citizens, Dutch, grey-haired Norwegians in greenish clothes, with cardboard skin . . . the women fat, curly-headed, in glasses. The men taller, skinnier, large soft candles, waxy palm trees. The whole group flabby, corpulent, loaded with cameras. In greyish hues and pale materials with a greenish-yellow tint. The bus gawkers ogled the black woman's slender bony foot. So skinny of toe and heel, so opulent of chest. How beautiful, those assagai limbs, bush wrists, consumptive ankles set against the rich harvest of her buttocks, the horn of plenty of her breasts . . .

Several buses. Glass and light. Massive but flexible coachwork, aerodynamic. Multicolored galleons sailing up the street, quickening along the straight stretch before slowing at the upcoming turn.

Simon and the black woman eye the invaders. She held aloft the long stalk, that spike at the end of her arm. The tourists' eyes settle on the woman from Cameroon at attention, brandishing her yellow saber of wheat. A Cybele from the tropics. Hoodlum and gold plant. A slut of the cosmic cycles and seasons.

At intervals the old men reappear, hidden by the procession of buses. In the crenels: the bench. Their faces fixated on the triumphal chariots. Barbarous motors and shining chrome.

Abruptly Simon saw the bouncing, that ball of rags. White. In the space of a second. The bus's brakes shrieked along the straight run. A death hiss. The vehicle, heavy and motionless, splattered with sunlight, windows aglow, metal shooting glints of blue, gold. A pure colossal vessel. The rag vanishes. A hush descends. Simon, stupefied. Myriam drops the blond stalk. An old man cried out along with many others. From the opposite side they had a better view. A chorus of yapping voices, a raucous clamor. The halted bus hides the bench. Simon and Myriam hear only the flood of horrible, bawling shouts. Doors of houses open. People flock into the street. He fell under the bus, his whole body under the wheels crushed by the big tires. Some people are kneeling, bending down, turning their faces away, falling silent or screaming, reaching out their hands. Somebody jostles her way through. The distraught mother, on her feet, stares at the front of the bus. She makes no motions. She simply is riveted to the spot. Her hand partially raised, suspended in front of her. Without trembling, stunned by this instant, this thunder. Simon and Myriam stayed seated. Bare feet, the so very blond stalk tossed in the dust. Alphonse comes back from Yvette's on his bicycle, which he rests against the bus. He sees the mother's face. He stands up straight, one leg before the other like a tightrope walker, a dumbstruck funambulist. Simon looks on, devoid of pity. He shakes himself inwardly. He'd like to feel his heart beating. The people are like puppets. Stage marionettes. The tragic facial expressions and jerking about of silent movies, melodramatic poses. A woman, bent forward, presses her two hands against her face. Another holds her sides as if disemboweled. Simon gazes at the magnificent bus. An ocean liner of burning embers, an enormous diamond. The apparition is hypnotic. Lynne, thunderstruck, a very little girl made even slighter by these tragic dimensions. The bearded student sags at the knees. The machine gleams. Behind the windows, the heads of travelers forbidden to move by the driver. But their faces are animated, crane forward in a comical tumult. Inside the shimmering carriage. The police van's siren resounds. The cops rush out... Uniform caps, belts. A red van suddenly appears with guys in white. They hunch down on one hand, on all fours, looking for the kid. Imitating crabs, crawling like athletes in training or clowns before the king... Choreography of horror. The men in white slip under the bus. And nothing is visible, the shredded rag can only be imagined, the once affectionate little boy . . . and then such a vision is driven away. The mother, paralyzed, flanked by two neighbors holding her arms. Agathe is there in the gathering. Her mouth strangely closed, jutting out. The profile of an ape, a fish. She has trouble swallowing. She scrutinizes the large, carnivalesque bus. The travelers inside talking, moving in their seats. Rather old folks, wrinkled, with fat, flabby cheeks. All you can see is the row of jiggling heads, white curls, big noses, pointy honkers, hooked beaks. They look like they're sheltered from the catastrophe. Their armored cage contains them, cutting them off from the pitiful village. They do nothing but make faces, legless cripples, bewildered but not frightened, not panicky. In their protected district. They know that they'll all be leaving, that they'll forget. Seated one behind the other, with their luggage, their cameras, their family memories, broken down in the thick of a tragedy that doesn't belong to them. Their hotel awaits them. Rug and gadgets. The swimming pool will cool them off. Ice-cold lemonade. But no! We didn't see a thing, we weren't allowed to get off. The driver forbade us. They say it was a child. He crossed without looking. But we didn't see anything. That's the way we like it. It's not worth the trouble . . . What good would it have done us . . . It's sad, of course! But when you don't know firsthand, when you haven't seen anything (so thinks an executive from a large Dutch company) except that beautiful barefooted black woman on the sidewalk, a long ear of wheat lying against her thigh. She was beautiful, she looked on, her legs open, superb, shapely. A brazen, protruding chest... while the child who was run over... So beautiful, and since the victim was out of sight, we didn't even know at that precise moment what was happening... how good it felt contemplating her, svelte, plump. Her skin, so hot, deep, over her whole body, the beautiful color... looking at her a long while, hearing the sound of the rescuers, the ambulance siren, while imagining the terrible incident with difficulty, glimpses of an injured youth perhaps, torn clothes, flowing blood . . . but especially she, planted on the sidewalk, back arched in surprise, high, forged breasts. Wide-open urchin's thighs. Black, dense, velvety . . . that the sunlight caressed like honey. For just one chance to bite into her fleece!

The street was cleared. Splotched brown on the side. The old men left the bench and gathered at the bistro. There was Agathe, the notary, his sister Lison, Paula, Hippolyte the mailman, Lynne, the student and Marthe Praslin. And everybody was thinking: "This can't go on, this time's the limit, it was bound to happen, fate at work, decreed in advance, and how very predictable, ever since we asked over at the police station for tour buses to use a bypass. Those huge things. You saw it take off again, that racket of motors, glowing glass, sumptuous chrome, disappearing at the bottom of the straight run, on the other side of the turn. It looked like some illuminated monster, a sun chariot, a minotaur in flames . . . the museum, the cave are all well and good! Just fine! But there was no reason to carry things so far. They should have moved in small stages . . . rather than . . . the invasion of these buses, all in a row, hundreds of tourists thirsting for pithecanthropi squeezed in front of the mask. In a panic before the genealogical tree of the species. And the scatterbrained kid crosses . . . Why? What was on the other side? But why? A kid's goofy idea, a sudden whim in the middle of playing . . . A forgotten marble in the gutter across the way. Simple as that! They like playing, kids do . . . an impulse, running, crossing the street, gamboling . . . for a bit of fun, for no reason, for laughs. A bet, a flash, a burst of joy no doubt, the body bounds forward at age seven, just like that, it's something animal, a twirl of happiness, a hop, you run, sing, a dirty trick, you go to the other side, toward the brightly lit facade, a pirouette, telling yourself a story out loud. This abrupt battering ram of light. Paradise. Fairy magic, a fall. . . !"

And that cave . . . to excavate, unearth . . . The priest babbles, repeats his litany, the sacrilege. After all he's right. Iza the Madwoman too. We're not strict enough. Not on our guard, we let things go on, it's the times, the modern way. So it's called pa-le-on-tology! Fine . . . the young people like it, their teachers take them up there. We were proud of the museum, but the mechanism ran crazy . . . broke down . . . the whole mesh of gears . . . a snowball, buses, a perpetual merry-go-round of buses, jam-packed with tourists, Dutch, Germans, Swedes, Danes, Belgians . . . races and nations, tower of Babel. A UN, a NATO . . . We had nothing to do with . . . it's too much, too much . . . But of course! But of course! . . . absurd, absurd! . . . had to happen, had to! . . . all this for what? Tell me! Bones . . . That's all . . . poof! bones . . . Old stuff! . . . Oh that's one thing for sure . . . rotten, stinking stuff . . . unhealthy, who knows? piling up so many skeletons in the macabre museum. A person can't live with the dead all the same, with all those putrid mountain-macerated memories, flesh-eaters, monkeyshines, slaughters, prehistoric monsters, gigantic lions, a mess of tigers, don't even mention the elephants . . . So then, people come along and dislodge the whole thing, wake it all up . . . attracting Parisians, tourists, the whole damn lot. It's not our village anymore, it's a museum, a window full of corpses. In a word, a grave . . . We turned into a grave, nothing more or less . . . Pouring out bone fragments, whole heaps, enough to last for years, full of queer geezers, apish hoodlums, half-thinking, toothless, one-legged, blasted gorillas strewn together with the wolves, beavers, sparrows and pollen they study! . . . Nothing better to do! And then that Sue, whoring after virgin lads, who just made a big discovery, uncovering a new rascal with angelic care, a fraction of an inch at a time, yet another one! Not only the skull this time, but maybe a whole fellow . . . What'll he have to say to us, that ghost! What's he got in store for us, tell me! . . . But the child . . . what about him? The child running, singing, the darling bird, all in a daze, hopping, sprinkled with sunshine. "And the child! The child!" they repeated in constant chorus . . . "The child!" echo Alphonse and Paula, "The child!" . . . the words ricochet in Simon's empty mind, are tapped out on Myriam's lips . . . "Oh the child!" . . . and Simon still feels no emotion.

Let the cave be closed in mourning! Some think that's going too far. The cave's only partly to blame. It could just as well have been the bikers who drive so fast . . . It might have been . . . A simple idea, he just crossed. All it takes is one dancing ray of sunlight, one butterfly on the other side, a blond ear of wheat in the black woman's hand . . . hey, Miss, can you give me the flower . . . and pow! The slightly built body, frail nerves, a feather! leaps . . . And the other, a dragon of glass, dazzled ogre. No end of racket. All those Jonases, all those Judases watching the show from inside the belly of their glass Moby Dick.

Toward evening they'd arranged to meet on a hilltop. There was a fountain just outside a very old hamlet. Myriam was seated on the coping and Simon in front of her on a carpet of moss. The water tinkled, clear, luminous, the gush trickled away into the depths of the stone basin. At first violent, tightly coiled, the aquatic serpent broke apart, dissolving in softer segments that blended with the mass of water. A few coins had been tossed in by superstitious strollers. Before them they saw a maze of valleys in scorched, ashen hues, dotted by the spiky islets of pine forests and green, shrub-strewn patches upon clay sienna slopes.

And Simon asked Myriam playfully: "Who are you? Where do you come from? What are you hiding?"

They liked parodying the dialogue of normal lovers, imitating their banal, anxious queries. Then Simon continued along the same line of questioning: "Who are you? What are you hiding from me?" But this time his expression was more serious, intense, he seemed to have stopped playing. Yet Myriam still felt that he was. She answered: "Who are you, Simon? Where do you come from? What are you hiding from me?" They both laughed. But their laughter had a sad, nervous edge to it, as if when all was said, these questions did matter even though they didn't dare ask them in the requisite tones of pathos. The truest situations struck them as false. On the other hand, they felt more genuine in their parody, their double-dealing, sidestepping, the manipulation of masks. But Simon guessed that their secrets were of different natures. What Myriam was hiding from him had little relation to what he himself was repressing in his memory. Myriam seemed poised at the edge of her secret, separated by a thin screen. Her truth was right at her side, behind this narrow but impenetrable wall. She drew on her face as upon a transparent curtain. This attitude was something new. For at the start Myriam's character revealed itself to Simon as a succession of scattered secrets reaching from the surface of her face to the depths of her self, proceeding in regular landings, a gradual descent into denser and more remote shadows. Yet this harmonious journey entailed no break. Today, on the other hand, she held a glass rectangle against her features, an imperceptible glaze of frankness which paradoxically blocked the way, reflecting an empty brightness. It's exactly like a form of courtesy, of politeness that she was extending to him. He also perceived a seed of aggression, a nuance of provocation, of contempt, as if Myriam belonged to a universe forever inaccessible to him. As if a fundamental difference existed between them. She dissimulated something alive, a presence . . .

Myriam's black hand plunged in the fountain, swam, darted in whirls, mobile or stiffly extended, suddenly cut the water as if through a more resistant substance, a cake divided up. She sliced through this parted pureness, these swaying segments. Simon grabbed her hand and began sucking the streaming fingers, her skin embossed with a patchwork of blisters. Shiny scorch marks. Fresh grazes.

"What's the child's name?"

"He was six years old . . . His father's a fireman, his mother, a housewife. Agathe spoke to me about him . . . He's just a little boy, nothing special about his personality, an average pupil, pretty good at spelling, not violent, liked by his pals, capable of thoughtless acts, rather easy to get along with, a regular appetite, fond of watching animal movies on TV . . . playing marbles, dice, a good swimmer, a little pampered by his dad, in fair health. Neither skinny nor fat, a satisfactory nature . . ." Agathe was standing at Alphonse's bar when she reported this information, very slowly and meticulously, but with no sign of eagerness. One by one she listed the details of this slender biography, emphasizing that the child was unremarkable, but nice, almost never naughty. He went to bed without carrying on. He read a small picture book, then shut off the light after ten minutes, faced the wall, heard the sound of the TV, which lulled him to sleep. He got washed, had his breakfast, learned his lessons, met his friends on the sidewalk . . . Now and then you see these little folk stop and congregate, discussing things like grown-ups. You don't know what they're talking about. Well behaved. They don't laugh. They exchange a few words about their tastes, their homework. They do a little boasting. They're slightly jealous of each other. Six, seven years old, a tiny memory, no concepts, just instants, joys, woes, sudden impulses. Christmas is around the corner. I put in for a bike. I'm going to spend a week at my aunt's who lives on a farm! There'll be lots of animals . . . Hey! Tonight I'll be allowed to watch that Western on TV . . . they say it's a good one. What are they telling each other? Small, slender, without a past, in the street, chattering on calmly, smiling as they envy their buddy's beautiful brand-new cap . . . What do you like to eat? I like rice pudding . . . Well, I like raspberries in cream. Over at my uncle's you can pick as much as you want, I go over on Saturdays with my parents. My uncle's too fat, Mom says his heart's going to kill him . . .

Agathe had collected a load of insignificant details. Ordinarily she licked her lips over gossip and spicy revelations. But she didn't seem one bit disappointed by the skimpiness of the accounts. Quite the contrary. Her delivery, steadier than usual, and her lesser degree of excitement conferred upon her words a more gripping rigor . . . While Simon was listening in front of Alphonse's bar, with Paula present, along with a few others . . . Agathe was saying that the child's mother had just bought him a new pair of shoes. Death lent a strange weight to this minute, intimate detail. As if the new, unused shoes would be waiting at the foot of the little lad's bed for all eternity. Beige, intact leather, new laces, thick blond crepe soles. The immense shoes of the dead child. Agathe said the father was an upright man who never touched a drop and loved his little boy. The child had had an older sister who was nine. The two children got along well. Lending each other their toys. Sitting side by side at Mass . . . Going off together for summer camp in Brittany. And Agathe clearly pronounced the word *Brittany* in such a way that you could almost imagine the two kids up there in the iodized creeks, swimming amid purple blocks of granite. Agathe had accumulated a multitude of information apparently of no interest and yet mysterious, fascinating. The more she stressed the child's good behavior, his banality, the uniformity of his life, the more she developed a feeling of fascination. He had gone into death with his marbles, his sister, his new shoes, his carefully done homework, his Brittany, his fireman dad. Peacefully, with no sudden starts, he had crossed over. And his tattered body belonged to another world. It was no longer his, it was a broken thing, a wretched object.

"It didn't have any effect on me at all when I realized he was under the bus . . . A total emptiness inside."

Myriam fell silent, studied Simon, twilight was sweeping through the valley; the lone fountain just outside the hamlet was enveloped in a great silence. Stars were being born in the serrations of slender clouds.

"I got very scared, I almost screamed," Myriam revealed . . .

But then Agathe was really reciting those things in that tone of hers, precise, low-key, without melodrama, and everybody in the bar listened to how the boy had already put in for a bike for Christmas, that he liked rice pudding and was good at spelling with an innate sense of the French language . . . his teacher complimented him. He jumped for joy when school was over, I got an A+ in spelling, he looked at the swallows jabbering on the electrical wires beside the town hall's wisteria. He and his sister fed a hamster in a box. Agathe revealed the orphan-animal's name: Titoune . . . Alphonse, Paula, Simon, Lynne looked at each other . . . What a queer name, Titoune. The kids' hamster, their creature of love. Agathe captivated the assembly. People wondered when she'd run out of steam, creating with ordinary words pulled from thin air this awesome impression of monstrosity and fate.

Myriam asked Simon the child's name. Simon answered: "His name was Aurèle."

A little later on Myriam indicated that she wanted to go for a swim in the fountain. The sleeping villagers wouldn't suspect a thing. She got undressed and crouched in the basin. Simon joined her. The water was icy. Myriam shivered, her muscles hardening all over. The sound of the spray distorted by the intrusion of these foreign bodies had lost its compact resonance and became diffused in a high-pitched pattering, a streaming fan. Myriam and Simon remained side by side, their hands leaning on the fountain's coping, faces turned toward the nocturnal valleys. They felt the coins slipping under their feet. The water had a mystic savor. Its coldness bruised, burned. Their contracted flesh filled with horror. A voluptuous sensation gave Simon an erection which he pointed toward the black woman's back. He entered her gaping anus while her hands clung to the edge of the basin. Their superimposed faces watched the stars opening in the shadowy far reaches of the valleys. Welded together. They let out howls of pleasure, of coldness, of death, of pain. While ejaculating, Simon drew blood from the black woman. Myriam squeezed the drenched stone of the coping.

The church was jam-packed, decked out in flowers, flooded with music and candles. A vast aviary of reflections, of gold. In the first row the company captain and the fire chief flanked the father, very simply dressed, his wife and the little sister: the girl in white, tight-lipped, large greenish circles under her eyes. Very beautiful. Nine years old. Everyone looked at her. Two rows of schoolchildren occupied the choir side. They intoned hymns in their shrill, unpolished voices. Sometimes the straight line of a girl's timbre rose above the rest, very pure, made of glass. Iza was there, her head bowed, muttering her prayers. Agathe in a black belted suit. Limpid skin. Serene wrinkles. Bright eyes. The director and directress of the excavations. He in a dark jacket, she slender, delicate, wearing a black net over her hair. Agathe looked at them often. Distinguished people, almost aristocrats. How weird, this predilection of theirs for skeletons. Gilles, the crew leader. Sue, the English girl, also present, kneeling with her little angelic face stretched altarward. Lynne, trembling, and her puny student. Simon, Alphonse, Paula and Yvette in the back. Hippolyte in his mailman's uniform, the notary, his sister Lison, Dr. Chany, the old men from the bench: Ludovic, Raoul . . . Marthe Praslin and Myriam amid the lights. The priest jabbers prayers. His jaw lolled the whole service long. He scurried about, a bag of bones, soft dangling lower lip, behind the incense bearers, as blond and chubby-cheeked as the sun.

The father couldn't hold up anymore, burst into tears, collapsed. The fire chief patted him on the shoulder. A baby-cleric slipped on a carpet and spilled masses of incense in his friends' faces. Some laughed hysterically despite the tiny, preposterous coffin in the center of the choir. Colossal candles stood around the box draped in a black veil embroidered with fleur-de-lys. Underneath could be made out the panel of light-colored wood. Everyone took communion. Except Simon and Myriam. A long line of children, of villagers swallowing the host. Some secretly revolted when they spotted Sue tilt her head back and display her throat, that well of delight, and extend a pink supple tongue where the priest deposited dear Jesus. Kids could be seen struggling to get down the papery wafer. Their faces displayed panic, shame. In single file they went back to their chairs. Their thoughts were on Aurèle in his crate, under the broad black sheet, the silver-spangled cloth. A bit shy, their minds empty. They looked like kids who'd had a bad night's sleep. Wide eyes. No tears. They watched the adults manipulating the handkerchiefs, cheeks streaming, blowing their noses, flushed faces, as if they had colds, stuffing them back, a flood of weeping. Some had swollen noses, honkers bursting with juice being crushed in squares of soaked cloth. Cheeks trembled, it was contagious, a mess of pissing, chomping, exploding, that created an impression of spasms, of bulimia, a vast, gluttonous ecstasy, a big blow-out, a feasting tragedy in which the tumescent mugs wallowed . . . The stiff, uncomfortable kids, choked up, holding back nervous giggles, witnessed the grand debauchery of their parents. Sometimes a small, rounded bead slid down the satin of a cheek that a kid wiped furtively with his hand. A delicate, fragile sorrow. A tiny, heartbroken chickadee pecking at death. Then when the organ swelled, thoughts turned to the beheaded statue of the Virgin, to all those misfortunes, to the bad world, fires, epidemics, famines, entrenched wars, poor harvests, highway pileups . . . to the dead, parents, family lines, ancestors, the innocent. The blubbering ballooned, billowed, frothing chiffons, handkerchiefs. The mugs gazed at each other shamelessly, puffy, obscene nakedness. People grew uglier under these unchecked gallons of tears. Now and then, a little embarrassed, with a shifty, voluptuous delight in displaying their flaccid face-flesh, their crimsony jowls. They undressed, breasts bared to all eyes, in their seamy distress, in raptures of happiness actually, as if inebriated with grief. Aurèle in the middle of this ocean. Stitched together as well as could be, invisible, unimaginable, his corpse very tiny in the cute skiff under the large black sail. The enormous candles: masts, lanterns. The crowd, all the firemen, officers, families, uncles and cousins, aunts down from Paris, even from Brussels, and one from Ireland. He. Alone. Small, ice cold. Stone dead. Upon the immaculate pillow. Invisible in the darkness. His new shoes, leather, solid, will last for many a school year. And the coffin, carpentry, wood shavings. The plane passes, passes again over the beautiful oak. The father kisses what remains of the little boy, refuses to allow the lid to be shut. The mother harder, her mouth strained . . . the gentlemen from the funeral parlors are accustomed, patient, slow with a perfectly assimilated slowness that they learned over the years. No brusque gestures, trained to be in the service of the dead, in stride with the rhythms of misfortune. But their children were also passing into death. The priest's prayers, his final blessings. The family members continued flooding in from every direction, mountain villages, small seaside cities, border towns. A young aunt, a beautiful widow, sincere in her pain, held Aurèle's sister by the hand. The child was astonished by this almost unknown woman, a mythical city dweller who was said to travel widely and to have lovers from all races, even Argentinians. She'd given the girl a splendid present: a statue of an immaculate angel for her bedroom, with two blue wings.

Simon, upon leaving the church, saw the big chopper alongside the sacristy's venerable walls. She could have parked it somewhere else . . . But the contrast between the religious stone and the chrome-plated vehicle was beautiful. Paloma had come, by herself. Her long red hair wrapped her white face. She was wearing a dark dress. You could only wonder where she'd dug up such severe attire. Booty brought back from some raid? Had the bikers launched a special expedition to a villa abandoned for the summer to steal Paloma's dress? . . . She went over to Lynne, who felt herself quiver from head to toe when a lock of her friend's hair stroked her cheek. The only person missing now was the escapee, or even the pithecanthropus draped in a black coat . . . Children with active imaginations thought that the terrorist and the ape were there too, slipped into the crowd to follow Aurèle's funeral procession. Those fragments in the coffin, coveted by the lynx. The procession advanced into the cemetery at the edge of the pine forest. A distance of half a mile. Clear sunshine. Cheerful brightness, rustling fragrances. Oh those lavenders! Sue eyes the bellies of the handsome boys, virgins of rustic tribes. The procession stretches out with these gaily decked children in white, those rows of black, impeccable firemen in red stripes. Agathe moves forward, solid, dry, a great moment. She looks at all these distant cousins, uncles, brothers, she picks out points of reference, refreshes her memory, revives genealogical chains, fills in blanks, discovers new affiliations. She masters her impatience, her fervor. So many things, so many names, so many faces in such a concentrated lapse of time. She mustn't get fouled up. She'll find a place for everybody in the end. The whole ceremony is still ahead of them. At the cemetery she'll have a better view, they'll be in a circle all around her. She'll identify the recalcitrants, the collaterals, the remote branches, the strangers. Agathe lucid, pure. She slept six hours. A strong cup of coffee. Two crackers with jam for glucose, vigilance. She notes, records, classifies. She recognizes, interrelates, now and then asks for a female relation's first name, the age of the young widow with lovers from around the globe. She puts on finishing touches. When she pockets her piece of information, what satisfaction she feels, what a sensation of plenitude, of strength, of wisdom . . . She enjoys walking in the sunshine, heading toward the marble stones and the grave and all those deceased souls, each history. Tragedies, laws of things. She reigns supreme. Her active eyes scrutinize in total calm. No trace of desperation. Self-confident. No panic. She has the time. Right after the accident she paid a customary call at the child's home, began to make inquiries about the imminent arrivals of family members. She continues. She knows nothing will escape her this time. The helicopter from Perpignan, unaware of the local tragedy, crosses the sky. A racket. The procession pulls up short, covers its ears. The escapee still on the run. That's another matter. Assassins, terrorists. An epic gust sweeps the crowd. Lynne studies Paloma's profile. Pure domed forehead, fleshy lips. Paloma's hand slips toward Lynne's hip, brushes alongside, caresses it. Lynne is aroused, stung to the quick, a rush . . . The student doesn't notice a thing. The beautiful bike gleams against the church wall. Lynne is brimming over with a sudden happiness. A dizzy spell. Paloma's red curls toss in the breeze, her fiery tresses snapping. Her torso undulates, breasts erect under her funeral dress. Lynne doesn't get over her own reaction, her gesture escapes her: she thrusts her hand toward the young woman's thigh, climbs, seizes the firm cheek of her butt. Paloma smiles, staring straight ahead. Lynne feels Paloma's wind-whipped hair, beaming. The funeral procession reaches the cemetery in a thunder of sunlight. Tolling bell, chimes of the flesh. Aurèle, an emperor's name, from Italy, triumphant. Laurels, myrtle. The gold plating of sunlight.

Furies grumble away inside Iza's brain, convulsions, shapeless images of black fetuses, howling children, small fishy bodies, one-legged birds. Her mind hits vague peaks of cackling and sudden paleness. She's entered the cemetery. She often frequents this territory, faithful to the dead like a basin in which motionless boats are moored for all eternity. She knows each of the graves; with her hand she touches the docile herd. Iza has an intuition for skeletons. Agathe rules over the biography of the living. Iza's gift is restricted to ghosts. She watches them lying assuaged under the tombstones. Warriors and suicide victims, the murdered, the stillborn. They are clearly marked out in the crystal of the stones. Beautiful, unruffled slabs. The lanes as straight as a die and carpeted with gravel. Flower pots, golden chrysanthemums. The crucifixes, statues of virgins, private chapels, sometimes a simple mound of bare earth. Aurèle's grave is very fresh, innocent. Aurèle smells good. Iza is the shepherdess of the deceased. They must be fond of this tall, skinny woman's silhouette, this sad village madwoman. She sits right among them, on a low wall. She keeps watch, speaks to them. These are the true dead, the noble ones, those from families with firmly rooted bloodlines. Their dignity exists in stark contrast to the barbarity of the cave's cadavers. Real corpses sleep under carved rock, reclining in their oak coffins, six feet under. She feels no horror when imaging them, more or less emaciated, swollen, purple, dry and yellowed, bones puncturing their rotted skin, bleached skeletons, sacks emptied of their innards, seedy under ringlets of thin, tanned leather. Hideous but well behaved. She takes pity on them. Her madness sets them out in calm rows, a harvest of honest carcasses. Decomposition is a slow, variable process, rich in nuances and contrasts. Bituminous bodies, sticky pockets, arid barks, bumps and crevices overrun with vermin. Iza ponders this swell under the graveyard slab. Aurèle . . . Iza remembers nothing, maybe she once loved the pastor. She did desire him. He did cast his eyes upon her, caress her. It was long ago at the beginning of time, at the edge of things. She glimpsed a bright period, full of laughter, then a great portal slamming shut, dark and guilty. A slab rolled over the evil. The angelus and matins, burials in the countryside drunken with vines. She had followed each and every one. She had aged rapidly. Darkened, thinned. The dead had slowly come back to life, existing again in the rural cemetery. With their names, their epitaphs, their decorum. They'd become her kith and kin. She cleaned the very old abandoned tombstones, skeletons with no descendants, trees without branches, ashen stumps. Orphans forever. She kept her ghosts from falling into nothingness. The priest had forbidden her to visit the cemetery at night. Such things weren't done. She'd obeyed, then gradually sidestepped his orders. She'd come back at twilight when shadows slide across the graves. Iza shivers, she believes in immense powers like long dark hands unfolding. Then she falls to her knees, enveloped by the phantoms, their whisperings of owls, bats. She is motionless. Ashamed, she waits. She delights in her shame, her abasement. They are watching her. She asks for forgiveness. They mutter reprovingly. Children, old people, girls, mothers with their wan hair, their moonlike faces . . . Now this shame no longer torments her. This murky voluptuousness of her youth, a rite during which she discovered herself naked under the large watchful eyes of the dead, utterly transparent, condemned. She was passionate before their anger. When they overturned the gravestones and slipped out in their white magus gowns, Iza had her very own nights of love. The dead crossed their hands over their chests like inquisitors. How she loved this tribunal, relished their sepulchral voices. Her gravel-bruised knees throbbed exquisitely.

At times the dead went mad; they took off their gowns and walked along diaphanously, formed swaying circles, distinguished, obsequious. She discerned the extravagant busts of the skeletons. They swelled up nuptially, royally, whirling around, bowing before each other like wise men from the East, slow, courteous . . . And then they left off cursing her. The masters had little by little changed into children. The older she grew, the more the dead dwindled in size, craved her presence. She was now the one who sent shivers through them when she came up the lanes, grumbling, skeletal. They shrank down like children in their tiny coffin-beds when she came to wish them good night, mete out rewards and punishments. They felt watched over. Saved or damned.

Aurèle was no little boy in her eyes. She didn't differentiate these fragile dead creatures from the others. He touched her no more than the old men who had died a natural death. The children didn't bring a smile of tenderness to her lips anymore. She showed them no kindness. Aurèle was one of the dead, a new inhabitant she watched over with no inner turmoil or pity. She didn't recollect the episodes of this childish life, tenuous miracles, venial sins, ignorant of any anecdotes. She did see again Aurèle's calm, handsome face beside his sister's at Mass. She no longer remembered having shed tears over a dead boy. Unless it was way back in the beginning, at that threshold of her life when she may have felt a sorrow stronger than all others, a terrible agony. A great saber of pain. She stood there, implacable, mumbling beside Aurèle. She prevented the cemetery souls and the cave spirits from intermingling. She blocked the way, haughty and vigilant. Bustling. Stars, cicadas, the rustling of privets, cries in the night and lavender fragrances all failed to seduce her. This flashy display held no interest. Only the invisible, solitary dead, lying in the gloomy bowels of the earth, existed in her eyes. She listened to them. The sound of the wind died away. She heard them. It was a sound that she alone perceived, not an echo striking the ears but a solid sound, dull, mineral. A sound she could see, that congealed inside her, as sharply defined as a series of stones. The voice of the dead was material, opaque. A hammering of bricks that she alone understood, a sound of winter clogs. She could almost touch these ancestral tom-toms, taken in her hands these dense voices, set them along the lanes, just outside the cemetery, in the pathways between the vines. She could have walked across them . . . Heels, paving stones. Voices opening the way. She'd mentioned these visions to no one. She alone easefully manipulated this testimony, this paving of ghostly voices. Aurèle had his brick like the others, neither larger nor smaller. His voice was the same as the adults'. A steady, multiple anonymity drumming here under the earth for mother Iza's heart. Aurèle had his chance, his instrument, as vocal and mineral as that of all the dead. Suddenly she trembled. Aurèle had emerged from his shadow. He was turning into a child's silhouette, pale, doubtful. In his hand he carried his voice solidified into a brick. He moved forward, set the stone down, walked on top, picked it up, advanced, carrying it once again. He went off toward the cave. Her nerves rattled, Iza prayed vehemently, conjuring the dead to intervene, to prevent the frail boy from ruining their kingdom. But they allowed him to leave, their bricks no longer resounded, they listened to Aurèle's. Which was so beautiful . . . A flat, lonely sound, pearl-grey. But clear, with a hint of lightness. It's this minute lightness that was so moving, ears drawn by this spell to the musical stone, a perfect, balanced echo, a delicate yes . . . star-fragment. Chunk of light and frost. The dead in their graves formed only the flattest of shadows, blind rectangles, so completely were they eclipsed by Aurèle's divine hammering.

Arthur gets on his nerves, sitting up in his stroller, very straight, legless, his big baby bust, pudgy cheeks. He jabbers, laughs, gurgles, fidgets, fusses about . . . simpers. Lynne is in ecstasy, bowled over by the baby-bump. Alphonse has taken off for Yvette's. Paula is asleep. Alone. Tough for her. She's going to die. Simon isn't a bit affectionate. The little tyke bursting with energy, swelled up, shows off. A ham from the cradle, a wily guy full of funny faces and totally overdone babbling, delights in the effect. Lynne wallows in the idiocy of happiness . . . That kid of yours is ugly, retarded, mongoloid, already a nitwit, absolutely harebrained . . . He'd like to blurt it all out straight to her face. A blow to the belly! Lynne, caught in the solar plexus . . . Just stop that brat from jabbering!

"He's completely stupid."

The sentence shot out in the cozy, intimate, almost complicit atmosphere. Lynne froze. Stiffly. Struck to the quick. The hunting spear lodged in the maternal breast. Straight to the heart. The milk curdles inside her, hyena piss.

"Bastard!"

"Lynne, please! I didn't say it in anger, planning to get you all excited. In all calmness I think your boy's stupid . . . slightly imbecilic. He makes faces, gurgles like some unbearable histrion . . . 'Histrion' means a buffoon . . . a two-bit comic actor, a goofy clown . . . The child's a zero, a dum-dum . . . I'm letting you know in all sincerity, equanimity, passionlessly, I swear to you in the name of all that united us . . ."

"You're sick and pathetic! . . . Sex fiend . . . Attacking a kid! Coward . . . I won't bring you any lunch. You make me ashamed. You shit! Sex fiend!"

"Sex fiend! Sex fiend! . . . You're not so innocent yourself, if my memory serves me correctly, out on the stream bank, remember . . . You came out with things you'd never have let go with in front of your student. I'm sure he wouldn't appreciate obscene chatter of that kind. You're one hell of a little lecher. We got on great as far as that goes. It's all one and the same . . . At the moment you were . . . at that very exact moment it took guts, it was almost vile to suggest for me to . . . in those breathless tones, that whorey voice losing control, enamored . . ."

"No! Just cut it out . . . What's your problem? You really are sick. That black woman's gone to your head. You're a sad case, a . . . psychotic!"

Arthur, bust thrust forward, perky, comes out with short rippling coos, spasms of cheerfulness. He multiplies his loony gestures, his rascally expressions. He looks like Winston Churchill, with a vague touch of Rubinstein. Doddering, drooling. Quivering rolls of flesh. Double chin. Cheerful! Cheerful! An infectious wave, swept by a fit of giggles! He puffs up, digs in his heels, flaunts his paunch . . . a womanizing little joker while Lynne and Simon hurl saber-sharp words at each other.

"Your student's a good fuck then? . . . It's his goatee that turns my stomach, that cuckold's rim of hair . . . Now show me a real beard, a comical pagan billy goat mane. Wild abundant fur, musky, bogeymanish . . . But that skimpy fake brush, pah! . . . How goofy both of you look, pushing that damn lump along in his stroller. Hey, you'd be better off fucking. Come to think of it, why not out on the stream bank, in the same spot, we could go another round?"

"Sick . . ."

"Tut tut tut! We'd leave the student behind, you can be sure of that!"

"This student's really getting to you!"

"Oh come off it, now you're a psychologist . . . Huh! . . . Who knows? Go figure out why I'm attacking you. Actually it's the first time in weeks that I've lashed into anybody. Admit it, that's not like me at all, this loss of saliva, this salve of bile! . . . Funny, huh? . . . Normally the kind of guy who's so courteous, so indifferent . . ."

"You! You! You! Always you! Enough already! Can't you talk about anything else?"

"Yes . . . Yes . . . There's you too, you mustn't think . . . there's you. I like you a lot, Lynne, I still desire you. Delicate and silky. Your backside's so round, firm, hot, soft . . . cute and colossal! Paloma would share my opinion. That redhead's been ogling you like some mouthwatering prey. You attract all the filthy pigs, Lynne, what can I say? With your shepherdess air, your cheap, hot-to-trot sluttiness, titillating titmouse . . . Hey! Give me a shot of rum! Get to work, Lynne! Serve me, maid!"

"Don't get carried away! It doesn't work anymore . . . You're going too far, honey . . ."

"Oh, what's this now? You're getting . . . getting more . . . But I insist, serve me a rum or I'll wake up Paula and tell her you're slacking off."

"I'm getting it . . . I'm getting it . . ."

Lynne heads toward the bar, takes a bottle, fills a glass, brings it over to Simon on a tray. He pinches her bottom. She starts giggling.

"I've always wondered what sort of pleasure a man gets out of pinching a maid's ass," Simon confesses ingenuously while pinching her a second time. "No, I see it now—none at all! Hugging, yes! Fingering, jerking off against it, slipping into it, oh and how! Here's to the early hour, to your health! But pinching it, Lynne, what interest does that have? What does your student tell you about your bottom? Does he come out with lyric couplets, an intimate eroticism, his own kind of hymns, cunning obsessions . . . or does he keep his mouth shut, discreet, pillaging his pleasure without a word, with apologies, a true ecologist, clean, wipes himself, knocks before entering, doesn't eat with his fingers, doesn't burp at the table, but civilized, one terrific guy, into conversation and all that, puts on his glasses, folds his napkin, helps clear the table, does the dishes, vacuums afterward."

"You're completely wacko!"

"My advice is to go for Paloma, zoom, zoom! Paloma on her bike . . . What a gorgeous sorrel, a gorgon of tropical vines, beautiful python with penis, a sky-blue Himalayan, a brazen sultana, a guzzling muzzle of love, an alluring Zulu . . . a Lulu of Austerlitz . . ."

"Great . . . You really get off on words!"

"They're useful in love too, when I whispered them into the hollow of your ear, adapted to the perfect moment, the appropriate discoveries, uttered, named when the time's just right . . . the word that sets things off again! Makes you pant. Ingrate! You kept asking for more of my sweet, filthy words . . ."

"Don't be too proud of yourself!"

Then Lynne, anxious and suddenly calm, asks, begs: "Arthur's really ugly?"

"But no, honey . . . of course not! The little guy's adorable. The sweetest kid. I only said that to give you a taste of the whip. Bam! In the belly! Lynne caught by an uppercut! First off, Arthur's a pal. Sometimes in the morning I've seen how you work; you're so confident in me that you leave him in my care and go run your errands. I write. Arthur's under my eye until you get back. I really like working on my story with Arthur listening! Because he doesn't sleep or cry. He watches, eyes wide open, listens to the music of my pen on paper, he likes it, Arthur's a music lover . . . sensitive to the faintest sounds, to sinuous writing . . . to the fine scratches of my gold-tipped pen. We really get on great."

"You were ferocious just a little while ago."

"Suffering's good, it primes you for real pleasure."

"Don't start again . . ."

"But it does, really . . . we're two of a kind, nothing like an ocean of tears to get the juices flowing."

"That's sadistic!"

"You're awfully funny when you say the word *sadistic,* the word dumbfounds and secretly seduces you. You act like you're asking my permission to like it or for a justification to think about it. Yes: sadistic. And if it works for us? We're not forcing anything on anybody . . . We're past the age for being ashamed. And I don't have the time. Who cares about their general ideas, you get a good fuck only from very personal drives ascribed to an individual partner. Your vices got to fit together. That's what a really keen pleasure's all about. Don't you agree? The student's big failing is that he's forcing you into a democratic deal that doesn't suit you one bit! Think I'm wrong? He's a tyrant of goodness . . . You need a violent daddy, not a kind brother . . . Shit! Each to his own rituals, weaknesses. No rules . . . Can't do anything about it . . ."

"Yes, but I love him."

"Fine, all well and good, you'll go far with that."

"What you're saying is sad."

"It's . . ."

"No, don't start up again."

"That's the second time you've told me that—even though you're the one who keeps starting."

He went up to the cave in the late afternoon when the heat clamped down on the mountainside in thick sheets, a burning crust. A solid heat you can tap on like a crocodile's hide. The arbutus and thorns buckle beneath a fiery greyness. He tells himself his own body is also quaking, wobbling like the things around him, dislodged by sunlight, flown off in a blaze. A mirage! Simon . . . Ghost eaten by the flames. This ascension: what happiness! Sweat envelops him, he is afloat. He feels liberated. Muscles underwater. A rower. He is swimming toward the mountain. Transformed by an energy that doesn't come from himself. He has no consciousness of expending effort. The landscape is adrift. The surrounding ruins of hills. The peaks sway. Dancing stone. And Myriam, at the summit, calmly draws. Set upon the threshold of the void, her back to the cave. Simon's heart thumps madly. His temples like snakes caught in a noose. Her tranquil gaze upon him. He sees the shadowy depth of the cave. A veil masks his eyes. The cavern is astir with black things, pale objects. A confusion of lines, of somber volumes and glimmers. He sits down. He makes out Sue first, grappling with the precious fossil . . . which she's slowly devirginating, strip by strip, a fraction of an inch at a time, peeling off the thin layer of clay and welded grains. In slow motion new ossicles emerge, outlines of a skeleton being born. Sue is astonished. The whore looks to be praying. The others let her toil on. Nobody better than she respects the fabric of the soils, the architecture of substances, their foliated folded layers. Her long, masturbatory fingers rake without altering. They listen, hug contours. Antennae . . . Only a terrifically sensual woman is capable of uncoiling this string of fine bones. The directress suddenly appears from the back of the cave. With her skinny Madonna airs. Beautiful, lofty, aristocratic. A general's daughter type, from an important family. Honor. Nation. Purity. Mass on Sunday. Hereditary tennis. She treats the pithecanthropi with the same rectitude that nuns used to display when evangelizing tribes of natives. Hygienically, Red Cross, Catholic nurse, an earnest, overgrown girl . . . Now and then she's absentminded. She watches the visitors, this pretty, panting female tourist, dress hugging her body after the heroic ascent. No ambiguity in this gaze. No . . . with curiosity she admires the flimsy dress she'd never dare to wear herself, the latest fashion, fluttering all around. She gazes with interest, perhaps just a bit too much interest. That's how she escapes her milieu, her archaeologist's work . . . Through these glances drawn by the clothes of young women, affected hummingbird types, Botticellian and Leonor Fini models. Very slightly stunned. She gazes. Simon gazes at this gaze of the Madonna of the rocks, a gaze cast upon these Madeleines, beautiful Judiths, titillating Lucretias, shapely, smiling Salomes. Free of envy or animosity. A beautiful gaze of interest. She disappears once again into the shadows where in the remote recesses she supervises the taking of pollen and guano samples.

Myriam is drawing. Slightly pug-nosed, lighter along the very round wings, insect-bite swellings. High, domed forehead. Braids clinging to her skull. A long neck . . . antelope, giraffe . . . vigilant, fragile animals. Her blouse concealing breasts that her bowed posture both curves and deforms. Suddenly shifty, glowering, capable of anything, of leaving her bust like the muzzles of animals, of sniffing all about, alive, heads yanking on their elastic necks. Tendentious nipples which grow bored, dawdle, risk doing something stupid, Myriam all the while unaware. And then her hips, ass, thighs . . . What a pedestal! Smooth under her shorts. Her legs, narrow ankles. Flat feet, a touch of the macabre. It's the first time Simon notices this. Bony, whitened by dust, as delicate as death.

She is drawing a profile that she erases, dissolves. Another is sketched out, becomes confused. Three or four hesitate in tones of grey. Simian and superb. Simon has never measured the beauty of these immemorial skulls. Stubborn, less harmonious than our own, constricted in a sort of terrible, cantankerous worry. Haughty. Not the beauty of intelligence, but one that is brutal, unpolished . . . the charm of beasts, monsters and gods. The glamour of all these creatures unaware of the fascination they exert, their shapes break through, the pencil-work envelops, clouds, delivers them. Myriam holding, releasing, reviving . . . In the hazy layer of lines: two, three, four profiles, ignoble undershot jaws of cannibals, rapists, enraged murderers. In mists, subtle shadings, shifty, receding foreheads belonging to shrewd, frightened, rudimentary men. Who must have bitten, cried out, with neither hearth nor . . . They moved forward through the somber welter of strokes, an ashen-hued forest. Next, polishing their limestone objects, carving branches into stakes. Then they became more gentle under Myriam's caressing hand, bowed over their stone or their sculpted bone . . . What were they thinking about? What thirsts? What worries? What joys? . . . While polishing, slivering . . . Myriam seemed to know. Questions burn on Simon's lips. If Myriam would only discover some answers! They'd respond to her. While drawing she trapped them, captured them, could surprise their thoughts. You sensed that she was communicating with these ancient brains, these mutterings of the origins. The ancestral herd obeyed her. She was the witch of the apes. Their wet nurse, their priestess. They buckled under her gaze. Let her ask them everything! So many questions about sex, death, hunting, their anguish and their desires . . . What were they thinking about when grinding their flint tools? When skinning elephants or lynx, building walls against the wind? Their skillful, precise hands, the beauty of their gestures carving out the cheeks of rocks, sharpening the edge of a stone for splitting animal flesh . . . they make matter talk. What are they saying? Tightly wedged into tribal hierarchies, punctilious and aggressive as baboons, dominating and dominated, a rigid ritual group, a clear savage protocol. The least gestures labeled. Rare bursts of imagination. Let's not get any ideas about nice little Rousseauist characters full of good cheer flitting about the happy vines of our genesis. But rather obtuse, hardheaded, sectarian characters. The laws of instinct cannot be infringed. The pithecanthropic label. Each assigned to his place, his role. Beware of cranks. No poets or bohemians in this coterie of greedy hunters. Chiefs, females. Embryos of magic. Barely beginning. Peeking through. They're learning to change the order of things. Scratching at masses, contours. Imprinting their timid signs. Whispering at the edge of the woods . . . Very slow, ponderous . . . What do they prefer? Hunting, the horde pouncing upon bristling, quivering wild beasts, or this calm, precise craftsmanship of those with leisure time on their hands. Their wives and their gang of brats? Are they loved? The affectionate father, proud of his offspring? Father? Mother? The words have no meaning. They are torments to come. But the child plays, he has always been left to play. He's not yet been caught up in the network of rules, constraints, showy ceremonies, homages, imperious, comical and bloody customs.

Myriam is now drawing a complete, precise profile. She erases the useless strokes, reabsorbs the false starts. The man looks at the stone he's working on. He's handsome, violent, he cleaves firmly to his gesture, his whole being concentrated in this effort toward the rock. Myriam's face leans over the man's profile. She's serious, beautiful, violent, cleaving to her gesture. Her gaze tenses. Her lips open, tremble . . . The two faces bend toward the stone and Simon watches them, grows attached to their faces. The directress comes out of the shadows, carrying a bag of dirt samples. She watches Simon, Myriam, who also are watching. The sky is a thin, infinitely hollow blue. The limpid azure set upon the socket of the mountains like a pure immense eye watching the lady, Simon, Myriam and the ape watching his stone that speaks.

Alphonse brought over a goatskin, explaining that a young Berber girl gave it to him long ago in Morocco. Simon found himself confronted with Alphonse's past. Was he already a roadside innkeeper back then? Alphonse didn't say. He didn't like talking about his youth. He'd traveled. You felt he had engaged in certain things he wasn't happy about. The flexible leather gourd sprang up from a forgotten time. Simon asked him if this Berber girl had been his mistress. Alphonse acquiesced. He'd been violently in love with her. Never had a body captivated him to such a degree, the color of her skin: noble, smooth, homogeneous, clay, tile . . . he can't find the words . . . polite, noble . . . the word came back: a thoroughbred.

"She was delicate, Simon, a fine bone structure like a gold-work weapon, a piece of cutlery. Her beige skin. I was struck dumb by its continuous hue along her slender limbs. Her narrow hips, almost pointy, gleamed on either side of her dark sunken belly. Sometimes I touched her with my fingertips, barely grazing her, contemplating her . . ."

Simon listened to this unexpected stream of confidences. A little disturbed by these admissions. He was afraid that Alphonse would regret doing this, divulge a detail or revelation that later on he'd hold against himself. Until now a certain quality of muteness had joined them. They prized their vigor and their silence. They liked each other for their sense of propriety, this hand closed upon their secret.

"Yet I didn't find this girl attractive, I liked round flesh . . . And then she . . . Emaciated, javelin-waisted, a masklike profile. Beautiful as a totem. But with an unsuspected force when she was in her clothes. She seemed a little lifeless, with a hint of hyena, indistinct, mingled with other girls, furtive in the wind, spirals of sand. I'd undressed her spinelessly, absentmindedly. And my heart was struck by a brutal, poignant anguish, the blade of a desire, yes, almost religious. When I saw the softness, that smooth surface, words fail me, Simon, a ceramic body, angular contours here and there, but exquisite, graceful, long shoulder blades, a musical fingering in her neck, ankles, wrists. I never paid any attention to these details. The finely chiseled perfection. Gracile and yellow, brown, warm, fragrant. But with firm, creamy, soft breasts, plump slender buttocks, a discreet, barely contained opulence, most apparent in her palm against my stiffened prick. Everything about her was hallucinatory, emanating from a visionary process. She showed nothing, she gave a hundredfold in a region between dream and reality. I discovered her while making love with depths, horrors, sweetnesses. I dug into her, I plied her endlessly. I never wearied of her. She resembled a statue that may never have been sculpted, or sculpted by a genuinely artistic tribe, a touch mad, an unknown, hysterical tribe, desert-dwelling, in Sudan, Nubia, in the land of the Nuers where women are as beautiful as Isis. She had the beauty of a young pharaoh, fawn . . . Sororal, Egyptian . . . Ethiopia, young queen—I'm looking for the perfect word—daughter of the magi, desert-born and protected by it, burnished by the sand, wind, water of the oasis. Imponderable, miraculous. I stood horrified before her, my mouth agape . . . just touching her; each of her limbs, each fraction of an inch of her skin was a jewel, a fetish . . . Yes, she had the magic grace of ebony terra-cotta goddesses that had yet to be discovered. Lying vigilant, deep in the pyramids, new in the labyrinthine depths, she would be brought to light only at the end of an immense quest."

Simon went off with the goatskin that he'd filled with water, also taking his pair of binoculars, a knife, a few provisions. He was leaving for two days out in the scrub. He wanted to catch a glimpse of the lynx, watch it and perhaps see the escapee, witness other scenes, admire the arc of boulders and sun . . . He wanted to spend time by himself. Without Myriam. The black woman would be everywhere, a shadow cast over the aridity of things. He was happy. He raced off as fast as his legs could take him. The farther the village receded into the distance, the keener his happiness grew. He thirsted for these dead places, this great lithic paradise.

He knew that his chances of seeing the lynx again were minimal. The escapee tempted him. He was alone, yet space itself was infiltrated with a presence and ominous messages. He walked a long while, scaled slopes, dashed down to the rocky floors of valleys, followed wadis, crossed rugged plateaus, cracked chaotic stretches of ground where the stone seemed to have burst apart under the relentless heat. He was burning up. He savored his scorchings. Salt of his sweats. Desert sugar. He felt free, tightly woven out of muscles, exertions, breaths. He consumed himself without depleting any of his energy. He halted in the middle of his hike. He stood motionless. He listened to the silence. He inscribed himself wholly within it. His brain emptied. The creaking rustle of the pebbles and his bones intermingled. His eyelashes had the sensitivity of inert antennae. A stiffness came over him, a voluptuous sensation in not moving, in blending with his surroundings, mimicking matter, the world's dryness. He too was going to burst apart like the marbles and limestones. Each fragment of his body would be a shard, a mineral grain trampled by the escapee and the lynx, those prisoners of passing time and the flesh. Slaves of their fear. Both thirsting, sick . . . He, pulverized into shimmering mica bits, particles of zircon, porphyria studs. The abandoned pair of binoculars gazed into the void.

He ate. He drank from the Berber gourd. He stroked the supple side a long while, rippling the volume of water. He remembered Alphonse's words, that long, strange poem of the desert innkeeper. Who was that old traveler? Now sedentary, his memory a treasure crypt. The icy stream squirted from the leather pouch and refreshed his throat and lips. It was as if the sterile setting had been holding an unexpected flood in store for him. A crystalline spring for his mouth and body. He felt that he was the object of beneficent demons at work. A devil, dark and beautiful as the shadow profiled along the boulders, offered him this cool, luminous ray.

He sat down with this taste of water still on his tongue, water bronzed in the beast's pouch, black goat's teat. The drop was within him, islet of life, moist, enduring, edging its way inside, trickling through the vegetation of mucus membrane, drenching them with multiple rhizomes, fine threads, arrows . . . A spidery liquidity wove its net, opened its petals in his gullet. Then he contemplated his surroundings, armed with his binoculars. Shrubs, green bushes, puny plants, or those in bouquets of hard leaves. Thistles, cacti, stumps, wind-eroded tubes. A cracked limestone mass, heaps and chimney stacks, porticoes, gullies, crossroads of mazes, amphitheaters, basins, unusual vineyards that cut through the middle of these thorny shambles, opening a cultivated patch perfectly curled with stocks and tendrils. Like a clear tattoo marking, a comic alphabet . . . To tattoo: the word often recurred, and its image imprinted his flesh. Tattooing connoted barbarity wedded to precision. Savage, meticulous. But above all the idea emphasized the sensation of the flesh, vulnerable, marked, scorched, initialed by some mad shepherd, semidivine faun. Tattooing was also associated in his head with ferns, with plant patterns like those on fossils recorded in stone. He dreamed of a woman, but it wasn't Myriam, tattooed with a fern design on her pale left hip. He sought out the face, this woman's name . . . He asked why Myriam was barred from this sensual stamping. This sign fascinated him, a verbal expression upon the flesh in the form of a fern or beetle, scorpion. His binoculars, hoisted above the horizon, revealed two virgin circles. He scanned the lens over this limpid surface. Soon a bird created a clear notch, a claw, an outline of an insect in the transparent sky. And the azure metamorphosed into a pure, immense animal that a lascivious god tattooed with black.

He'd have loved to see the lynx but not during the course of some patient, avaricious surveillance like last time. He'd have preferred a fleeting vision, a stampede toward the peaks, a will-o'-the-wisp between the arbutus. An uncertain glimpse, after a sip from the gourd, like a dream in a half-drunken state, greeting it as if a distant, furtive messenger, Hermes or some spy, a frail sentinel slipping between the boulders. He'd have liked for the lynx to be the escapee's accomplice. The only dog worthy of the man who murdered on beaches in broad sunlight. Brotherhood of the terrorist and the feline. The thought of them regenerated Simon, revivified his body and mind. Rejuvenated, he advanced through a violent, palpable, legendary landscape. Then Myriam came back to mind, spontaneously generated by the idea of the escapee and the lynx. He remembered her body, the idiosyncrasies of their embraces. He would have liked to see her, surprise her, but close up, without her knowledge . . . Suddenly, before him, not the flying ghost of the lynx, but the brown-scented side of a black woman. She, between two boulders, curves, muscles, huntress breasts, without quiver or arrows, belt or mark, leaping, nimble, in close-up, with no other sign but her flesh. In profile: the smooth, swollen arc of her buttocks, the immense arched back free as a rope, the laziness and vigor of her lioness's haunches in which black desires are being hatched.

Coming out of a canyon sealed by shadows, he entered a plain swept immaculate by the light. Flat circular boulders strewed the surface. They looked like large mineral wheels. Simon moved forward, fascinated by these disks, funeral slabs, eyes of matter, hubs of some gigantic, fantastical chariots that once transported half-human, half-dragon ancestors, gods, great androgynes garbed in clay, speaking trees, sea monsters with female breasts . . . Were wells hidden under each of these stones: a gaping hole, a stairway, a maze? Were they still the lids for a colony of underground hermit dwellings, grouchy misanthropes, tiny, squat, bearded beings burrowing in the earth whenever a stranger passes by, disappearing deep down in their dens after yanking the slabs over their heads? . . . Simon would have liked to be a giant so he could cross the plain in enormous strides, his foot landing or springing forward upon these round, rigid trail markers.

He halted in the center of the plain. He sat in the middle of the thorns and flints. Thistles of sand speckled the ground with blue elegiac touches. The color seemed unreal, uprooted, hovering in his gaze, disappearing farther off like an impalpable aquatic being . . . Simon stroked a stone lying flush against him, smaller than the rest, no doubt lighter. This is the one he chose. He desired this arousing, barbarous rock. At first, leaning over, he swayed it between his outstretched arms. Then with a push, he budged it a yard along the ground. The stone, all the while seriously resisting him, proved to be relatively easy to manipulate. Simon lay on the ground and brought the beautiful limestone wheel over his chest and belly. Wedged between the burning sand and the stone, he first felt his heart thumping fiercely toward the breaking point. He was afraid his aorta might burst, and his torso too, within the sheath squeezing him. Then his breathing relaxed. His sweat-drenched head grew accustomed to the heat. He waited. He felt comfortable, well-situated, suspended above the world between two lapidary palms. Riveted, stifled, but gradually diluted, escaping inwardly, swimming as if in a sea cave. Long moments passed. Flights of birds, sparrow hawks, buzzards traced circles in the azure, moved in divinatory orbits. Simon's hearing was phenomenal. He listened to each fragment of the setting, each particle from east to west; a secret, resonant web converged in his direction like glass rods. Matter in its monstrous folds, ridges, crusts, rugged slopes, crevasses, articulated all around him dense but intelligent, almost musical configurations. His thoughts were on his own rock. He couldn't wrap it entirely in his embrace for his shoulders and a part of his arms were pinned to the ground. Only his forearms remained free, allowing him short, awkward movements. However, between his hands he felt the roundness of the slab, its lesions, its grain, its fractures, its fibrous vegetations. He moved, slid, drifted under this limestone sucker that revealed itself to be mysteriously inflatable. Cannonball or life preserver. Meteoric submarine. His brain clouded. A porousness hollowed his tissues, his muscles, his skeleton. The periphery of his body, clutched downward in pain, was set against this fluid, liberated inwardness. At times he had the feeling that a giant scarab had settled over his heart, that the sun itself, transformed into a lynx or boulder, sat enthroned upon his thorax. Then the rock changed back into rock, whole, noble, interlinking its molecules like crystals, pieces of coral. A madreporian vessel resting on his chest. Other images emerged . . . the rock like a loaf of bread with its crust and nodes of inner whiteness, the rock like a statue's breast, also like a church chime, a great cathedral bell, huge bronze clapper stilled upon his sides. Images, chains of images . . . And then the rock was like a mirror and a balm. He dreamed. The sand gently whirled under his loins, a void opened, vibratile, and he spiraled into the depths. This void contained no hidden menace, but was filled by a great looping wind, a violent soundless cyclone free of cruelty. And the rock flew to the peak of this aeolian dance. It stayed afloat all by itself. Simon contemplated it far above him like a great mineral sparrow hawk. Then he saw things, heard others. Neither objects nor words. Simon listened, looked. His face a bit distraught, pitiable. Moments of former happiness resurfaced, old sufferings of his soul. But no faces as yet, but emotional states submerging him in successive waves. Then there were episodes, brief blurry sequences, sharply etched scenes in no setting with no characters, like landscapes of pure vision with no light or shadow. He was awash in a wild ferment. A horrible affliction. All his wounds reopened, all the scourges of his past. And it was her face he was awaiting in this procession of images. The anguish of not seeing it again tormented him. His beloved woman's face . . . Parasitical layers interposed themselves, sediments from other epochs, other ghosts, other skeletons. Anecdotes loomed up sometimes, picturesque and almost happy, but they were suddenly engulfed by a black swell, obscured with fears, with hopeless loneliness. Simon was awaiting her . . . He only wanted to see her again so that she would forgive him for having betrayed, hurt, wounded, and scorned her, for having destroyed her. Humiliations, affronts, havoc, love itself filthied and trampled underfoot. In the gloomiest ignominies he had cast their legend. Corrupting their truth. He had stabbed his beloved with more than one blow, reattacking during truces. Remorse like a nest of swarming asps under the rock assailed him, bit him. Faces flashed past, crowds, homely creatures and stunning specimens, men, mythic old people, childhood friends, and then women appeared, all those he hadn't loved but desired, possessed, betrayed, seduced, worried, wounded. He looked at them, and their gaze remained impassive in the wind's turbulence and the motionless flight of the mineral disk. Did they see him at least, did they know that they were filing past their guilty lover? There were animals he'd raised or hunted on snowy days, fabulous birds, fieldfares and golden plovers. A puppy he'd adored, lost, found again, a rabbit, an over-pious grandmother, tiny, touching things like toys, children's books, toy soldiers and some even smaller, out there, far off on the parquet floor of the home where he was born: colored marbles, blades of straw, thorns of light: nativity scene, Christmas tree, ecstasies. A brilliant blue bicycle . . . Candles, stars, those immense, visionary, gaudy nights, coming down the staircase wonderstruck. And his mind bounded through time, other gusts unfurled bearing other messages . . . first loves, flirtations and presents, a very small spray bottle of cologne decorated with pink flowery designs, paid for out of his own pocket, given to a girl whom he was to abandon and whose hurt still made him suffer. That was the beginning of his fall. Other moments, other forgotten memories.

He kept waiting amid the wind, the sown seeds of sand, the sad blue thistles under the angel of hovering stone. Simon must have wept during this journey, cried out . . . For the lynx fled when it heard the rock howl. The terrorist stood out in black profile against the sun, rifle in hand, to gaze upon the verbose wheel. Then Simon saw nothing more in this blind zone, his hope still persisting that he would see her again, and tell her . . .

It was brief . . . modulated in a lightning flash whose waves endlessly propagated within. Sweetness, bliss. There were his eyes, his mouth, his smile . . . his harmony visibly transparent, indistinct, without color or contour. His beloved had appeared and cast her eyes upon him. He had but a blinking glimpse of her, yet it sufficed to restore his wholeness. His entire being swelled, swaying in awe, the inexhaustible grace. He was inhabited by her smile, an infinite melody. Darkness had fallen. The rock illuminated Simon.

Agathe had set her armchair before the open window. She saw the sky above the limestone ranges. She was sitting bolt upright. In her formal dress. It was four in the afternoon . . . She was reminiscing, repeating:

"Aurèle was stung by two bees when he was five. In the neck. Fever. Flustered. The bees had slipped into the sun-dappled bedroom. Aurèle, at six, placed on the train to Dijon, was entrusted to the care of a lovely young woman, vigilant, with a cat meowing in a basket. His grandmother came to fetch him at the station. Aurèle had remembered this trip. The following weeks he imitated the racket of the cars, the whistling of the locomotive. He described the slide in the garden where his grandmother brought him every afternoon. His rear end landed on the pile of sand after each exhilarating trip down. Aurèle, every summer, spent two weeks with his parents in Royan. He dreaded the waves' violence, wobbling transparent walls, collapsing on the beach and bleeding their streams of white foam. Aurèle dug holes which he jealously protected from the approach of other children. His sister was given the right to come and visit the ditch only after obtaining very ceremonious permissions. They both sat, serious as pontiffs, deep inside their moist hole. It smelled of crabs and coldness. Their flesh was splotched with broad patches of sand like fresh cement. They heard the sounds of the world, the shrieks of joy, the continuous squealing of summer afternoons when the purring of the state security patrol boat rends the web of countless shouts, interwoven screeches, splashes ringing out amid the galloping stampede of bathers, barkings of a frenzied dog frightened by the formidable water machinery, the tireless babbling of mothers knitting, the refrain of the ice cream man, showers of sharp cries piercing the humming mass of sounds. Aurèle and his sister, proud, wild-eyed at the bottom of their dark den crowned with sparks, splendors, a solar shimmering . . . Aurèle won two big precious gaily streaked marbles under the plane tree at school from a classmate on the verge of tears. Aurèle walked up the street clenching his booty in his pocket, terrified at the idea that it could be snatched from him before he could show it to his father."

Agathe muttered her mumbo jumbo about Aurèle, tenuous episodes . . . Fascinated by this minute biography, she discovered an almost demiurgic sensation of voluptuousness in pouring out the briefest anecdotes, precise links. A beaded string of solid facts as self-contained as crystals. She spoke out loud. A clear shrill voice, avid but with a drop of slightly hypocritical sadness. There always was a plaintive hum in Agathe's words. She took shelter behind this vaguely elegiac tone that was nevertheless lovely, tenacious, cheerful upon closer listening. The infinite litany of sadness was merely a slender envelope wrapping strength and wild-eyed curiosity. The old woman listened to herself reciting Aurèle's life. She savored this power of narrating in front of the open window, in the open air, under the pure sky, the rippling brightness, the soaring mountains nearby where the gods, metamorphosed into sparrow hawks, scrutinized the world.

Agathe had gotten into the habit of making Aurèle's sister talk, an orphan in her own way, marked at a tender age . . . His sister was secretive, made herself interesting . . . She was stunned and genuinely grieved, poorly understood what had happened, attracted by this misfortune that everybody was making such a fuss over. Aurèle was dead, run over by a bus. More than anything, the circumstances of the accident shouldn't be spelled out in detail before her. But a little boy came right out and told her. Under the bus, Aurèle, a bloody rag. Agathe repeated his sister's revelations, her memories, her fabrications that added a nice touch, with a sisterly novelist's flair. The girl eluded her strange grief by embroidering Aurèle's biography with imaginary events, even, for example, that Aurèle walked in his sleep every single night, moved through the hallways counting up to two hundred without once making a mistake.

And Agathe, undaunted, her voice clear:

"Aurèle even walked in his sleep . . . He peed in bed at night and his mother scolded him, he loved—yes—rice pudding, absolutely crazy about it, eating his sister's serving when she wasn't hungry anymore, gobbling the fat sweet grains in their milky coating . . . ruff of creamy velvet . . . Since people said he adored rice, he engulfed masses of it, far beyond his real appetite because he had to uphold his reputation for being an ogre of rice pudding."

Agathe marked a pause. She waited. Her face displayed a surprising blend of dryness and deference. She continued, on a slower note:

"On October 8, 1981, his mother remembered that Aurèle gave her a surprise. She'd come in to wake him as she had every morning. The evening before, after his parents had kissed and tucked him in, he'd taken off his pajamas, got back into his clothes and fallen asleep, all ready for the next day. He wanted to spare his mother some trouble. She was very touched and everybody spread the story of Aurèle's tender thoughtfulness . . . 'Oh, he's so thoughtful! he's so thoughtful!' repeated the moved neighborhood chorus.

" 'Oh, he's so thoughtful! So thoughtful!' " Agathe utters, her voice cheerful but severe. "Getting dressed the night before to spare his mother the trouble to . . . It was on October 8, 1981 . . . He was conceived one August night, a night of love, in Royan, his mother will never forget it, after an exquisite evening when her husband took her dining and dancing. [She confessed this to Marthe Praslin who'd repeated it to Agathe.] He was conceived one August night, in Royan, at the edge of the ocean, the sky teeming with stars as big as . . . They danced an old-fashioned tango without one false step, they had dinner by candlelight and even ordered crayfish, it was the first time, no taste at all but she'd never eaten anything so good . . . Aurèle had been conceived . . . Aurèle . . . Aurèle . . ."

Agathe repeats, listens to the word and its frail syllables. She experiences no sorrow. Death no longer moves her. But the kid's story obsesses her, she declaims it to the sky in an ever-more metallic voice, with neither honey nor any hint of that affectation with which she is wont to envelop her sentences. But instead with a joy so concentrated that it comes across as sternness. An intense, profound, mystical pleasure. She had a premonition of something unfathomable while telling of Aurèle's destiny. She's afraid of no longer being able to do anything but repeat . . . that he captured an injured swallow one June morning and wanted to raise it in a cage like a canary, with large black satin wings, that he cut out from a newspaper a photo of his father published on the occasion of a fireman's banquet, he'd saved the snapshot in a Tintin storybook, *Tintin Goes to America,* his favorite of the series because of the Sioux. He'd reread it at least ten times. He liked reading, "Oh how he reads!" his mother would spontaneously exclaim, proud, serious, almost religious before such an unusual tendency.

"Oh how he reads! Oh how he reads . . ." Agathe continued her limpid, urgent litany. "He's ruining his poor eyes, he'd do better to get some fresh air . . . He's the one who reads the most in the family. His grandmother does some reading too, at night before falling asleep, a page from a photo-illustrated novel. Maybe he gets it from her, who knows, from her . . . Aurèle," repeats Agathe, "rice pudding, a swallow . . . and two bees for the fire captain . . ."

By dint of reciting Aurèle, Agathe feels stronger, purer, serene. It draws her together, intensifies her. She's brand new. Clear. Morning fresh . . . semidivine, starry and almost immortal.

Simon suddenly pulled free from under the rock. Standing in the light. He feels virginal, pristine. His body is born from a long river of sweat which strips him of his obsessive fears and blemishes. An intimate truth now armors him. His eyes glow. He has an urge to laugh. He walks toward Aguilar. On his path rises a knoll that he climbs. Reaching the summit, Simon instinctively drops down, crouches. A stream is slinking along at the foot of a hill.

Someone is bending over toward the slender, shimmering trickle. The man displays his skinny back. He's wearing nothing but a torn, brownish pair of trousers. A revolver hooked to his belt. There's a rifle lying beside the bandit. The man has knelt. His back bows, glistens in the sunlight. The man drinks by cupping his palms together . . . driven by an animal thirst, with a virile, wolflike nobility. He drinks a second time, slowly, he savors . . . And Simon full of terror and pity contemplates the escapee. He's handsome, alone, on his knees before the cold spring. Simon focuses his binoculars and observes the escapee close up. Long, fragile back, sun-blackened. Thick crop of dark hair. His face, carved flint, a birdlike profile, sunken cheeks, eaten away by a beard. Feverish eyes. "It's him," Simon repeats to himself, as if he were talking about the rarest game, an almost sacred prey: the very last okapi, African manatee, the last example of a race in its death throes. He drank. And all that water trickled, tinkled in his parched throat. His cracked lips, encrusted with grains of sand, grew moist, came back to life. The man remained fixed to the stream. His arms dangled on each side of his hips. Palms open . . . the terrorist gazed at his face in the mirror of waters.

Paloma stopped her cycle right in front of Alphonse's bistro. Noon on the dot. Wearing denim shorts, a white blouse loose over her bare skin, she swaggered inside right up to Lynne. Seized by surprise, moved by the redhead's gawky yet supple gait, her audacity.

"I'm taking you somewhere! We're off for the weekend . . ."

Paloma had found out all she needed to know. Lynne got off at twelve. She had a day and a half to herself, free until Tuesday morning.

"Not one word, don't even mention that student! Don't tell me you've made plans for who knows what . . . Cancel! That's an order, you're coming with me, I can be nasty, so if Arthur means anything to you, obey!"

But Paloma's smile belied these threats, qualified her authority with a wily, mischievous kindness.

"Who'll watch Arthur?" Lynne stammered.

"Your student, naturally! And that guy over there, right?" Paloma exclaimed, eyeing Alphonse behind his bar, who showed great interest. "He'll watch the kid, right? . . . Or else, look out for my biker buddies!"

But this blackmail was softened by her wheedling expressions. Alphonse looked at the brazen girl. He was happy to be taken to task by this redheaded intruder.

"Let your bikers come, dear, let them ransack my bar, I don't give a damn . . . No, really, I couldn't care less! Let them guzzle down all my booze, get plastered and puke all over, I don't give a shit. I'm looking at you, that's enough for me, you got hair that hurts because of all those curls, sunny locks.

Where'd you find that mop of sparks . . . You're bushy, golden like a daughter of Mars. Vesuvius is your twin or I don't know anything!"

"So you'll watch the kid then?"

"I'll watch him, if only because of your shorts and your mane."

"Maybe I should take some things along?" Lynne asked, frightened.

"Not a thing! Come as you are . . . The weather's nice. We don't need anything, we're out of here, no more blues, we're going to fly over the roads, right down to the sea!"

Lynne snugly straddled the big black shiny motorcycle behind Paloma. The redhead basked in Lynne's warmth, the delicate chain of her arms. She felt the points of her breasts pressing against her back. Lynne looked at Paloma's two thighs, long and full and muscled, spread wide just in front of her own. With her knees Lynne brushed their blond, sun-ripened flesh. The motorcycle backfired, started up, crossed the village, passed in front of the old men's bench, and they all followed it with their perfectly synchronized eyes. A comet's golden hair would not have made a keener impact than this motor-rocket straddled by two girls. The old men, with mouths agape before so much beauty and racket. How they would have loved for them to come by again, for them to stop . . . for the girls to surrender themselves to their patient observation. First, the raging bike with those thick twisted guts, those nickel organs, and then the two riders. This Hell's Paloma, hoodlum bitch, queen of all the bashes, buttons undone, and cocky under that thatch of red straw. She would have stuck her tongue out at them in contempt. And with their eyes they would have devoured that pink and serpentine whiptip, great for licking their wattles and wrinkles. And then the other one, little Lynne, Alphonse's girl, slender, a blade of wheat, a reed curving against the sultan's back, her cornflower eyes, her trembling mouth. With her schoolgirl's pleated skirt and starched blouse. Let them stay here, the whole day long, posing for the men, something for their old age, such fireworks, people never gave them the presents they wanted! Let the Municipal Council hire the motorcycle twins for them, for the whole day long, until night comes, so that they could feast on their arrogance, their daring, their brand-new, bucking bodies . . . If only they'd stop still, and the village disappear, and the noisy pack of the other bikers fade away. These girls are plenty and make you forget many a scandal and such disgraceful wild living. Let them stay here, frozen, sculptural, arched on their motorcycle, warlike and twinned as in a mirror, puffed up, cobras of desire . . . The fountain stretches out its spray and sprinkles them . . . drenched tomboys, let them dry off in the bright sunshine, slowly bake until they're crusty. They want to see their skin smoke and the copper of their hair. The wet motorcycle, whiffs of gas, how it's boiling up, it may be dangerous. Water and fire, those things explode. The bench destroyed by the blast... Too bad! Let the maidens kill us, the Valkyries carry us off to heaven. These gorgeous hipsters, these musketeerish starry-eyed girls . . . Don't go! Don't go! Change into an inviolable pedestal, become statues for all eternity. Asylum guard-girls. Sirens across from the bench. Oars of your thighs, such leggy gals, tendoned with tenderness, rein in our raft of the dead. Sturdy life preservers. Yank us in from the shipwreck. Be an eternal dawn.

They raced, gliding along the winding roads, laces among the vines, under the skewered stare of the Cathar fortresses, bushy-browed ruins. The finger for those suicidal puritans, and fuck the cavemen too. The motor dances. The wheels gallop... paths narrowing, zigzagging, meandering, the exhilaration rocks their hips, tickles tummies, digs in between their legs... They rocket, spinning, the mountains veer, and assaulting gusts, the water of desire. It's Paloma singing . . . The sea! It rises up in blocks of purple granite, violet inlets. So pure like a multifaceted metal. Gems held in caskets of rock. A thousand watery sheaths in the crenels: pupil of the ocean, keen as a cat's. The gold quivers, and the sudden vistas of the blue valleys, within magical recesses. Going down is impossible because the slope is steep . . . Paloma bellows that they're heading for Canet to make fun of the hicks collapsed on the sand, tourists piled up one on top of the other, a big mob scene for laughs, it was on a day exactly like this that the assassin exploded his bomb, a bikini-carnage, and for what reason? Irish, Basque or Palestinian, you tell me the reason a sunbathing beach goes boom . . .

"I don't want to, I'm scared!" Lynne cries.

"I'll watch out for you, my pet," Paloma hollers. "You'll see, it'll be hysterical! Right... Fuck that student! And the cave! And fuck your job! And fuck that village! And my cannibal buddies! . . . Time for a rest! . . . Time for an orgy!"

And Paloma jolts her head back. And her hair froths up and perfumes Lynne's face. This head of hair's a shield, a mirror of fire. Lynne's not afraid anymore. Let Paloma show her the way. She bursts out laughing, squeezes her arms more tightly around the young girl's torso. And she, disheveled by the wind, her face distorted by the speed, lets go one handle, takes Lynne's right hand and plants it higher up, over her breast... Then she returns her hand to the bar, and goes through the same motion with her left hand. Lynne trembles. It's so swollen, so solid, but it's moving, it's pointy. In her palms beautiful pears are knocking about. Breasts so much fuller than her own... Lynne's cherries, puny plums, Paloma's grapefruits, fresh swelling melons . . . Ill at ease, Lynne quivers. The speed rockets them into vast, flamboyant regions, a red cope swallows them up, it's as if God was pouring sunlight upon them. Sometimes a gust lifts up dust which lashes their faces, tiny dry pellets, riddled cheeks. But their wounds make them ecstatic. And during the vicious veerings, when the machine is almost prone upon the embankment, Lynne grabs onto Paloma's breasts. Sometimes, she gets a better grip, loosening her hand a little, and then seizing hold of the tit again. The open bust crumples the blouse along the edges and hides them, the hand navigates between flesh and material. Roundness. Very gentle bounce. And with one jerk of her hand Paloma throws back the flaps of the blouse so far that Lynne latches onto the two jutting breasts bared to the wind. And that's the way they cross through the small town. Lynne flushed with shame. Paloma orders her not to change position . . . Without slowing down! The villagers watch this breathtaking prow with the two crazy ladies glued to each other. The blouse flying in all directions over the naked sides and with her two hands Lynne holding onto the magnificent breasts. Mammiferous monster, torch of red hair, roaring of the motorized thoroughbred . . . What fairy magic! What horror? . . . The bike has already disappeared, raped another hick town where the ritual bench of mummies receives the radiant blur, a bouquet of girls, an iron horse, a ship's red flag, the jubilation of pirates. Another castle. Decapitated ruins. And their maniacal vines lined up along the hills, like identical sentences. The same words stretching to infinity. The satiation of bunches. Rip through this leprosy as dottering as hair curlers, ringlets and vegetal frills! Let's bring back the chaotic scrubland, lavender and thyme and the absinthe bushes so that Paloma will carry Lynne off, and lay her down upon the sharp scree and the aromatic bramble of the country of the lynx.

They have been moving along for hardly an hour when Paloma stops in front of an inn. They're going to have lunch there. Feast with the stolen money. "Loaded with dough, my dear," Paloma singsongs, "I'll treat you to a bourgeois banquet . . . a blowout of goodies."

They seat them around a small table, across from each other. Paloma prefers a side-by-side. She moves her chair and sets it right up against Lynne's. The polite waiter bows before this whim. First, the oysters flat as beach pebbles, very beige within, walnutty, shades of silex. The lemon oozes on the collar of the dipped mollusk. Paloma tenderly brushes Lynne's thigh. Thigh against thigh. Silk rustling. Warm and secret. Chummy ankles. With her short fork Paloma pries off the gelatinous mass from the bottom of the shell. How beautiful mother-of-pearl is! She gently fingers the opalescent cavity. Perfectly smooth, perfectly white . . . brilliance. Her long, very red nail scratches the smooth inner walls. And one, two, she downs the juicy iodized oyster . . . so good for the eyes, oh yes it is! the eyes, the skin, oysters rejuvenate everything sensitive and delicate. An oyster bath for the inner thighs, for shapely ankles and satiny buttocks . . . Lynne blushes, laughs . . . Paloma moves her moist finger across the scarlet cheek. "I like it when you blush. I want you to be real ashamed. Say it, get it out... Say it: no! no! no!... I don't want to, I don't dare ... If my mommy saw us, running away, stuffing our faces on ripped-off loot."

Then come the crayfish, fistfuls of them, plump, stubby and red. Served lukewarm on a bed of various green and violet leaves, chubby and curling. Paloma picked at a leaf or two, into which she sank her teeth. The champagne in the ice bucket had finally grown cool. The waiter wanted to pour it. Paloma grabbed the bottle away and poured Lynne a very blond, sparkling glassful. "Have a taste of that, my angel. That's fine gold, that's heaven's piss. Holy Mary's juice couldn't be more limpid." Paloma plunges her mouth in after Lynne, at the same place so that the taste of the liquid mingles with the flavor of her friend's lips. A double impression of lipstick stains the edge of the glass. A bite drawing blood.

And then the pheasant with cabbage. Creamy, tender, suffused with an aromatic sauce. Wild game hunted down and shot in the summer's growth. The multicolored bird surrendered its musky flesh.

"Pour me some champagne," Paloma asked.

Lynne took up the bottle with a professional twist of her hand which Paloma's intent stare made tremble. Huge, coveting eyes, full of mischief and repressed giggles. A prodigious mirth ran along her bust and prickled her spine when she observed Lynne's embarrassed gesture, tipping the enormous bottle into her glass. Paloma's mouth watering... "Go ahead! Go ahead! Keep it coming, Lynne. No holds barred—girl, let it bubble till it can't no more." And she downed the whole glass. And forced Lynne to do likewise. "We're getting smashed! A thousand little flames are nibbling at my stomach, my ideas are like diamonds and my thoughts like hummingbirds. My Lynne." Paloma leans over and kisses the cheek, the neck of her friend.

Then the cheese, goat droppings, product of our local farms, stiff turds of precious matter, covered with greenish molds, spotted with black dots. It's nanny goat dung, powerful and biting to the tongue. It's hard, bitter, billy goat shit in a choice stench, ligula of rot. A vacherin for dessert, meringued and frosted with chocolate, strawberries, and festooned with Chantilly... More champagne, a bottle drained to the very last drop, shy and slow, which oozes onto the bottle rim, sparkles, and stretching out, falls into Paloma's throat, ecstatic, "Married within the year, with you, Lynne, two white dresses, side by side in church ... Tulle and bouquets. Naked underneath, titillated by the organ, hymns and choirs. Who laughs last laughs ... Why not a wedding of Lesbos, great immaculate veils upon married sisters. Sisters and Siamese twins."

"Lesbos, Lesbos ... what's that?" Lynne asked.

"The country of my desire," Paloma answered. "We're flying there on our bike."

And the motorcycle took off with a full tank into the maze of the hills. Dry pine forest, vibrant sprays of flowers. This pale green clothing the granite. Balloon-firs, bubbles in the sea winds. The world lighthearted, detouring downward. The colors stopped clashing in the circumscribed and rabidly defended territories. They go hurtling down, climbing up, little girls fluttering, cockades in the belly of the mountains. Even the rocks tottered. The bike rumbled, clattered and climaxed between their thighs, with the sun directly above, a din of ions, a fiery top. Lynne clings to howling Paloma, who speeds up as if spurring a thoroughbred. A champagne burp, a crayfish fart. Amazons at the top of their lungs. The ridges twist on themselves. The cavemen scurry off, seized with panic. A waterfall freezes in midflow, stopped short by the two wild women springing into sight. They lay siege to the valley of vineyards. Paloma puts on the brakes and gets off for a piss. She picks out a dry embankment. It hasn't rained for two months. Come on! let me water you, withered soil, faded pebbles. Shamelessly she pulls down her shorts and panties. Lynne takes in her milky ass, firm and round, with curves fit for an empress. Standing, with her legs spread. And the stream squirts out. A fountain shimmers. Music. The thirsty earth opens its mouth and savors. An endless feast. The sun makes shimmering flecks in the urine. Paloma pisses out a golden net. It's the champagne, a string of vices in fine mail. And in profile, her marble haunches solidly set, a fine-bred mare's curves. Then Lynne feels dizzy, spots of light dance on her pupils. Angels fly up in her breast, a host of petals and hosannas of the heart. It's the desire to feel, to fondle the hoodlum's ass.

"Aren't you having a piss?" her friend shouts to her.

So Lynne motions with her chin, steals over to the first trunk, a scrawny almond tree. Squatting, hidden, modest, so she can piss a graceful trickle in short nervous bursts, a lace of spindrift. And it's very hot around her sex, her pubis in open air, the stones refracting the heat. Whiffs of lavender drift under her nose, the crickets glide their long and strident bows between her thighs, up against the crack. It's sweet to piss here between the vines and the languorous snakes, sleeping pebbles. Skittish lizards. To piss while watching this fertile, unstoppable river gush from Paloma's buttocks. Fermenting the champagne and other exhalations, caresses and memories, seeing insects float past in the wave, little bugs sparkling in the crevices of the rock, a sliding, moving sand, hourglass of the seasons, dust of life. Limestone fangs, hot steamy droppings of the lynx. Your eyes grow misty with happiness. White Paloma in two plump halves. So beautiful, deep and powerful. And this warm milk, champagne or piss, flows through Lynne's brain, floods her breast, streams around her neck, waters her back. Beautiful flow. Scalding envelope. Paloma's pee in a sweet-smelling dress. Piss on me, beautiful, piss on me. Lynne tells her orgy to herself, a dream of wings and fins in which Paloma, a fish, a bird catches her in her lines, utterly sluggish and blissful . . . She could almost fall asleep there against the trunk of dead wood, a stiff and burning bark, ants on top, red as copper, tiny spiders, midges, life which burrows and multiplies in secret crannies, the pupils of grasshoppers or shrews peering at you, all around, twigs, thistles, ashes of things and seeds . . . Come, Paloma, I'm asleep, asleep . . . the universe is rocking me, the great sweet-smelling gusts, in the hammock of your buttocks gorged with the flesh of oysters and pheasant with cabbage.

And the bike takes off toward Canet. Lynne snug against Paloma's back dreams on at full speed. Prunes with whipped cream. Zipping through a boarding school of crayfish bearing poor boxes. Girls making their first communion, on bended knees, giving up their hard-saved pennies, and praying that the two brides dressed in white love each other and have lots of children.

The enormous beach, swarming with bodies, a mosaic of ultraviolet limbs, broiling, inextricably entangled. The sluggishness of a short fat sea. Glistening shell of a somber crustacean. The tide digests. The mob sweats. The stillness oozes. All races intermeshed. *Pax orbi.* Yesterday's enemies, hostile camps, as far as the eye can see are rubbing up against each other, bellies bulging with beer. Jews, Muslims, Germans, mixing together, soldering their cellulite. From time to time, in the jumbled heap, Paloma spies a pretty foreigner, points her out to Lynne: "Take a look over there! That jewel in the casket of oafs, how darling, how elusive, her button breasts, her pimple-tits. Her belly sinking in like a bowl. With little curls on top. Her skin pearling with smooth drops. I'd gladly drink that natural Sprite. She has a fever. Sacrificed on the wheel of the sun. Masochistic, exquisite, pleasure ripping her to splinters, she's going to groan!"

Then, a young man curled around his belly as if he had been stabbed, whose shorts, pulled down three-quarters of the way, show two swarthy buttocks, bricks touching on each side of the crack. It moves you when you uncover such treasures in the middle of so much waste. Like hunting for rare butterflies in a jungle full of mammoths. Lynne unearths a very young girl, blond, Danish, her bathing suit thin as a rubber band, two stiff amber pigtails. Swollen breasts with coarse brownish tips, you'd think they were dyed. And such long, long legs, thighs that go on and on, a gymnast's body who leaps on the parallel bars, or a desert messenger's. Immaculate Masai warrior. With assagai's paws . . . Long . . . She must wobble about on top of them when she walks, as if upon fragile stilts. Such smoochy legs. Stand up and show how your chubby nymphet breasts are set off against the endless stretch of those masts.

"It was on a day like this that he intervened," Paloma whispers in Lynne's ear to give her a scare. "Bomb in hand, then camouflaged under a fine layer of sand. Did he pick out where? Would he have been put off by the sight of teenagers, forced to go elsewhere in his search for less innocent victims? No doubt you don't hesitate in these matters. The bomb planted blindly. Kids, old people, adults, all mixed up. The explosives in position under the hump of sand. The surf dies, spitting up its foam. And they're dozing. A mother from where she's sitting motions to her infant who is crawling on all fours at the rim of the surf. A father is taking a picture of his wife and son. They are smiling. Naked, healthy, happy. Full-cheeked, tanned, with sparkling eyes. A dog is panting. The vast ocean, a mirror. Sails gliding along, slicing the surface. Motorboats crisscrossing, canoes, movie stars. The familiar din. Large patches of silence during which you make out the faraway shouts of the bathers on the horizon of the beach. Abstract hubbub, a joy which has been summed up, already a vague memory. The unreality of the present which has crumbled, dissipated by the chirping and warbling of people playing close together, in the distance. The bomb is spying. The terrorist is in a bathing suit so he won't stick out. A shoulder bag. Good-looking guy. Thin. Tan, without any oil. Dry. Rock-hard torso. Shoulders like stones. He walks along politely, stepping between the bodies, apologizes when he sprays a bit of sand. Nobody looks at him. Or only a teenage girl here and there. A young thing who pulls her nose up out of a photo-novel, bored, glancing around, dreaming about males like him, feline and secretive. Solitary creatures of the sun . . . He walks along, very limber, smiles at the girl, who reimmerses herself in her novel. The beach is brushing up against death. Peaceful, stunned with light, bursting with laziness. In one leap they would be on their feet if they knew. A swelling panic would lift them, like you see during fires at discos and movie houses. The savage ebb and flow of a terrified crowd. Each one selfishly pummeling his neighbor, trampling him. Scrambling over each other, climbing on top of each other, crushing each other, smothering. Hoarse from shouting, in tears . . . asphyxiated. They sleep on, they're dreaming. Their flesh breathes, coated in cream. Slow, gentle, stupid. Lovers whose arms and legs are intertwined. A child sprawled on its mother's belly, mouth open, a round spool under a linen hat. And he has withdrawn, has calculated the distance, has gone over to lie down a hundred meters away. Tick tick tick tick. Somebody asks him: 'What time is it?' He answers and the person says to him, 'Thanks, mister.' Courteous, helpful. Stretching out. Waiting. Hearing the muddle of sounds muted in the same nebulous, faraway demolition, something abstract, from a previous life in which the sea would be rumbling, the flash of a crest, moving sands . . . Over there, death, a hundred meters away, the same bodies, the same subtle and exhausted symphony. The bomb . . . what does he feel? Fear, anger, pity, an icy lucidity. Does his heart beat faster than the sleepers'? All of a sudden the bomb."

"Shut up, shut up!" Lynne pleads. "Shut up . . . You're such a monster, you know, you scare me when you go on like that."

Paloma breaks off, she wraps Lynne in her arms and kisses her on the temple.

"I'm shutting up . . . Let's go in the water."

Unless, after stashing the bomb in a sand castle, he had not decided to go into the water himself, to swim toward the open sea. In the cool air, the velvet of the ocean. Long muscles at their ease. Floating on his back, or doing a slow butterfly, passing happy swimmers, women, kids, old people . . . all at their own pace. Frogs, tadpoles checker the ocean floor. Only his head sticks out of the water, pointed toward the beach. In the distance he makes out the mound of sand, children's castle, crude towers. He waits. He is going to see everything. He is out where it's brisk and cold. The pure water beats against his thighs. Glinting blade, the light sparkles. Coffin of glass. And his soul shimmers. The bomb has lost its meaning. It belongs to another time, entered into a game of foreign schemes. His consciousness becomes one with the diamonds, the cubes, these bright liquid geometries, when suddenly the bomb . . .

"Shut up! Shut up! But you're really so rotten, what's got into you?"

Am I really as rotten as all that? there when my mouth brushes against your mouth, your little lips chapped with salt and sun, and dotted with grains of sand. A marine mouth. A thin bud rubbed with algae and jellyfish. The sand has come to rest on top of them, they have been touched by the breeze of the wide open sea. They're almost red, bleeding slightly, swollen with greed. All those bodies coveted throughout the afternoon. By your mouth, your whole body . . . you are swarming with visions, obsessions. Myriads of tanned, golden skins. Calligraphies. Naked alphabets. The supple hollows of arching backs, playing in the light, twisting, assuming the photogenic and obliging poses of stars, of whores, of pouting little girls. It's all gathering up within you, poignant, parched with desires, your mouth betrays the savor and the secret. Your flesh . . .

Upon the large bed of the blue room. The tough bike dozes at the back of a spacious garage. Metal, motor, enigma. Machine dream in a parking space. They went up to bed after downing two coffees. Lynne shy. Paloma amused but tense. Be a bit shyer, Lynne . . . Plead, protest . . . bat your eyelashes, blush, hands over your pubis. Not Lolita, but Alice . . . Sophie Ségur. Get undressed . . . No, you first. Not at the same time, such a waste. Each in turn watching the other. No, I'm embarrassed. But that's exactly where all pleasure is. Awkwardness, leg stumbling on its way out of panties. Shiver of light-complexioned skin. I'm ashamed, don't look at me that way, and if I turn around it's worse, you ogle my fleshy bottom, you devour it . . . The room is blue, blandly girlish and Madonnaesque. But their berth is immense, with a silk fleur-de-lis embroidered spread. Soft, royal silk. Golden lilies in staggered rows. Brilliance. A large mirror directly opposite, which Lynne shuns and Paloma craves. Mirror, mingling. A cold pool in which they'll be reborn. The sea, nearby, beyond the very black beach, empty at present. Come nightfall the ocean is nasty, angry, bristling with horned whitecaps. No longer this lake of lazy summer light, but shifty, dark, deep, digging the sand with its beaks, moaning and softly coughing, shaking its war feathers. Its black cunning presence can be sensed out there, crouching. A Cheyenne. The mark of human beings on the sandy slope, scraps, lost trinkets. Forgotten watches. Coins. Tubes of tanning cream. Small chains sparkling in the cold. Blue, stupid . . . so angelic with its little girl's furniture . . . The hotel whispers, noises . . . small waves, sounds, faucets spurt, full bathtubs lap. Women take showers, wash up. The sand browns the white or pink marble. Spots and stains, it's disgusting, germs, a sticky amber pitch. The sinks slowly belch. Furtive beats, heels striking carpets. All of this muffled, dreamlike, a family of echoes, mice everywhere. The life of people in the evening preparing for dinner, the city's distractions. Lynne and Paloma tucked themselves in by eight. Like punished children, grandmothers, sick people. Let the city accost the crowd with its jugglers, ice cream men, fire-eaters, rock singers, howling platforms and PA systems. The city so hollow at night in its spangles of spotlights and its flashy bird-seller's rubbish. The women supine upon the broad bundle of feathers. A firmament of caresses. A very blond shadow-swaddled lamp. The hotel softly hisses, a heavy machine on its axles. A ship crammed with posh galley slaves, chic fans of nightclubs and discos. Let them all leave, flee the schooner. Paloma Lynne, the sole survivors of the twilight shipwreck. Soon the rooms will be perfectly empty. The streets aswarm. Back alleys on a binge. A junk orgy. Paloma Lynne, two orphans on a wide pallet. Two female Robinsons. Vulgar visages in the city, a mob of people sprinkled with flashbulbs, mugs gleaming, gilded fakes, run-of-the-mill good looks. Pizza pusses. Tight-fitting pants, tip-top, immaculate. Tawdry jewels. Sunburns in disrepair, crimson kissers. The whole crowd chubby-cheeked, vermilion, gregarious. Evening streets, all you can stomach . . . What if the terrorist threw a wrench into that jumble? The bomb, a beautiful crater. The avenues cleared out. Debris propelled seaward. A city in ruins at the water's edge. Sodom beside the flood. The two, surviving in the baroque, luxurious hotel, rampant with climbing green plants and exotic lilies. They've all gone away. The last keys forage about. Hurrying footsteps. The ship floats in the emptiness. The sea and the vessel.

The city simmering, a meringue of flashes. The lynx sat on the sand. He contemplates the brilliant sea.

Paloma took off her clothes first without looking at Lynne, but all the while calculating her every movement reflected by the old, very pure mirror. Paloma studies, imbues even her least gesture with an affected slowness, and then jerks, loses her cool when a button resists, regains her composure, shams and modulates her movements. Paloma wields her cunning. Lynne watches her in the mirror. Thickset rump and breasts. Her hair ravishingly red. A devil-may-care Sabine. Strong, prominent. But with delicate ankles in bracelets, wrists of a Saint Blandina bound to the stake. Such is Paloma's fortune. Awesome chest and haunches. Opulent, arched. Milky and hard. But so light in her limbs: a marten's calves, a warbler's arms. Long. White. Artemis of the forests. A crenellated citadel made of water lilies and moonlight. Venus? Yes, vain, prodigiously female, pulpy with muscles. Cast in the very image of a movie star, a prow, wrought in iron. Monroe, Hayworth. Lynne, slender. Curly-headed brat. Lynne gets undressed without looking at her reflection, but brave, staring into Paloma's eyes. Paloma quivers. Lynne takes off her T-shirt, spindly arms scattered with fuzz, taut breasts. Her shorts, a little slowly, while swaying from left to right. In the mirror Paloma saw the perfect ass, apricot-shaped, round, halved. Delicate, prudish. And her lamb's fleece, her Venetian titmouse pubis. Lynne lay down on her belly, displaying the two buttocks that her light, narrow muscles tightened in reflex. The lamp flooded her golden backbone. Paloma turned out the light. She gets up and opens the curtain, allowing the moonlit brightness and the brilliant mass of the sea to stream in. This will be as mysterious as snow in darkness. An atmosphere of plunder, hour of the she-wolf. Hair suddenly comes up more abundant, bushy, bulging in the shadows, flanked by the shafts of white thighs. Pale females. Furs. The moon governs the heavy nave of the waters, swarms of fish, wakes, milt powder. The sands shift in the heart of the liquid gloom. The stars fixed. The vessel-hotel. And the sirens on their silken fleur-de-lis rock. Paloma runs her finger from her twin's nape down to her loins. When her waist dips, what happiness . . . taut tendons, shimmering back. Shield, lance. Long trickle of kisses. At first, along the shoulder blades, pullulating in tiny, grazing pecks. Rising toward the sweetnesses of the neck, the nape curls, nimbly sliding all of a sudden down to the ass. Buttocks coddled with greedy, open-mouthed kisses, tongue sticking out. Buttocks bitten, eaten. Lynne moans, squeals, booby-trapped smile. Paloma a feline. Her tongue, supple and pointy, darts into the furrow, edges in, now a plume, now a stiletto . . . licks the ring, the small pleats, goes back into the hole, comes out, springs lower, languishes, lingers long, roves along the groin from underneath, grazes the lips of her vagina, then suddenly climbs at the call of

Lynne's desire. On purpose. Strategic tongue. Very hypocritical. Her kisses along the back begin again, along the shoulders. The bitten neck. Conger, you're in my grasp. And Paloma's belly flattens itself against the round, narrow rump. The white thighs hem in her hips and Paloma jerks off on the silken buttocks. And her finger roves underneath, sets Lynne on edge without really touching her. Masturbates gently, then violently. PaloMan, phallic lesbian. The bike shines in the naked cave. Slab of shimmering sea. Night. Parking lot of stars. Express-Milky Way. Paloma turns her over, presents her white powerful breasts against Lynne's mimosas. First the very tips, to make her tipsy. Excited snouts, tits folding upon each other, and then the white ambered globes side by side like the bellies of fish, supple sea lions, Gulf Stream seals. Round breasts, voracious, massed against each other. Silk against silk, then crushed. Full flesh. Both embraced. Lynne gives way to rage. She grabs the hoodlum's clusters. She squeezes, yanks them, full palm, strangles them at the base, molds them into sheaves swelling at the summit. Her fingers sink in, burrow the velvet, tip the gland over like a stone into a purse of soft skin. Paloma's breast erect. Hard thimbles of the aureoles. Lynne smears them with saliva, sucks them up. She swallows half of a breast, expels it, gobbles it, coats it with slaver and orgasmic pleasure. And Paloma lodges her belly in place, wedges in one thigh, raises the other, straddles Lynne, spurs her, hair against hair, lips against lips, welded clitorises. Lynne burns, finds the angle tight, the point of contact sleek, sharp. Smooth, rock-hard cores, where water murmurs. And then their mad knotted hands working witchcraft, clinging to hair, plunging, skinflints, buried in vulvas, flattering, fissuring, forcing the rumps up to the open anus, foraging them in their wetness, heat . . . the sheets flying off, kissing, clawed, rended, interlaced with fleur-de-lis and mirror shards . . . The ocean whispers, the stars siss. The hotel of leather and wood sets sail toward the open sea. Its stairways take flight. Its elevators rocket toward infinite attics mingling with the stars. Its cellars gut the foundations of moist clay and fossils. Ossuaries and catacombs. The surge shoots like a saber. Resilience of the holds. Snoring of the kitchens. The swimming pool heats up. The ovens slog away. The velvet banisters, garnet curtains, thick tassels. Exotic plants tracing heavy arabesques in the foyer, emerald festoons. The green world. The padded hallways furrow the building, then move into the earth and under the ocean. Rooms brightened by chandeliers. Sea, sky. Shooting stars and schools of fish. Paloma Lynne knotted at the center. Leech sex. Lips snatched up. Braided throats. Hair intertangled until it hurts. Viselike thighs. Paloma swallows Lynne up, distraught in the watery deep, enraptured by the white dogfish from far below the surface. Lynne cries out, spits, pisses, shakes her head at a furious velocity, and Paloma digests her whole, chanting obscenities, filthy words chiseled on their cunts, asses, farts and secretions, urine and come, shit, drops of blood, diamond guts of the lynx, cutlery of pleasure. She enwraps Lynne with crude syllables, studs her with gems of curses. Lynne shimmers in the heart of the sea under layers, clans of stars, mirrors where great black plants flourish, serene branches heavy with stars and shadows.

Sheepish, the poor student, the cuckolded ecologist . . . a dumb lump. Simon observed him pitilessly. Seated at the table, always the same one. He'd carved out his territory inside the bistro. The traveler's table, the journalist come to spy. Arthur in his cradle tinkling his tiny bells. An irritating concert that jangled your nerves. The student patiently bearing his difficulty. A peaceable, understanding boy, conversation and all that, a good listener . . . who always placed himself in the other person's shoes, a young saint in short, bearded like the apostles. So he told himself Lynne needed to go all the way with this fling of hers, that he ought to respect this unpredictable escapade with the . . . He had trouble naming the redhead. His tact forbade him the offensive term "slut." "Lesbian" was too literary. "Dyke": almost racist . . . He gave her no name. She was the other, the beautiful rival on her fleshy bike. The student, despite his infinite tolerance, had his heart struck speechless. His scatterbrained Lynne had hit the road. He was suffering. He didn't blame her in any way. Made an effort to understand. He vaguely sensed that this tendency to analyze had been his downfall. Lynne wasn't fond of fair-minded men. Justice bored her. Simon at his table, sardonic and malicious, could care less about just rights. He was a man who took, with no arguments . . . an abductor like Paloma, a vicious pillager . . . Lynne fragile, with an active imagination, was nevertheless far too uneducated to fully fathom the fine points of the heart's affections. Violence attracted her, the glamour of lies, the razzle-dazzle of love at first sight, the piracy of rape. Simon gloated, his nose buried in the gossip of the local rag. It was as if he were reading about the two girls' jaunt under the "News in Brief" column. Then there was Arthur. Father unknown. Lynne, a weak, infantile Manon. Arthur fatherless but watched over by three men: Alphonse, the student, and Simon. The latter straightforwardly aggressive, in favor of exposing the kid, as the Greeks did with androgynes or Oedipus, consigned to the savage beasts and eagles of the wilderness. Alphonse, beyond hate and paternal feelings. Indifferent to the boy, hardly touched by his comical expressions. Has seen too much to put great store in such feelings. And he, abandoned, humiliated, encumbered with the child who tinkles his chimes, wriggles and giggles, rather diabolical, could give a damn about his mother, the bastard, reassured by the thick goatee leaning above his cradle. The student coddles the child, a way of cajoling his own pain. He'd prefer not thinking about it. But the question secretly pierces him. Has Lynne ever desired him? Myriam arrives. Simon looks at her and surmises the young woman is hiding everything from him. An anguish seeps from the black woman's gaze. A sudden hunted look. The superb tramp seems on the verge of trembling. Something plaintive within. Simon is speechless. He's a little afraid of this fear. In a while they're going to fuck, without knowing each other, treat each other roughly, burrowing within each other to emerge upon what heavens? That look she gets sometimes in mid-embrace as if she were thinking about something unusual, a hypothesis, as if she were interrogating her own pleasure, eyes wide open, white-encircled black. Before being seized by rage, she appears surprised, she listens, looks inward, she questions her female body. He loves her at such moments. He senses that he means nothing to her, matters no more than a springboard, a kind of revelatory presence, allowing Myriam to enter her own happiness. Afterward she gets along perfectly well without him. He, wholly surrendered to smooth, undulating sides, renders the same to the black woman. Side by side in orgasm, they penetrate only their flesh. And perhaps that's the reason they cry out sometimes, mistaking for orgasm this thirst, this insistence . . . Panic of their absence. Impossibility of attaining each other. They know they're engaged in a mutual lie. Their immediacy is merely a mirage. Their bodies are hollow tom-toms. Both turned to face emptiness and death. That's why they shout all the louder. Their orgasm is a song of loneliness. Who ever spoke about the fusion of bodies?

So then Simon falls back on the archaic hunters. He puts the finishing touches on his story. He takes pleasure in polishing his style. Open window. Peaceful village. Steady light around Aurèle's ghost. Black Agathe posted at the crossroads. He works, corrects, develops. He feels as conscientious as a schoolboy while Iza decries strangers and the funny business up at the cave. He copies while Sue slowly unveils the sacred remnant. Each to his own hobby, his stubborn repetition . . . He glimpses the pithecanthropi behind the curtain of words. The sentences bring them to the fore. All at once he is struck by a mad desire to see them, watch them closely. He'd give anything for one chance to catch them by surprise on their way down to hunt in the valley, while the sky grows pure again after a storm. A haze rises from the primitive earth. The scales of fish skimming under the lake surface cast electric reflections. Animals hiss deep in their lairs, bristling with terror at the living being of the storm. Purple glimmers still hover in the silver birch forest, flickering water. The mud of the tide exhales an odor of lightning and bracken. The eye of a great green plant lights up in the mountain's side. Behind, there is the octopus of the sea.

The scene up there on the rock's ledge is empty like the rim of a forest. The wind free, the gusts of the summits lash the limestone facades. Like a theater at curtain-rise. Time roars, an enormous blast knotting, rumbling, plunging to the bottom of the chasm. Immemorial memories lie sleeping under the lake's waters. The old mirror once reflected their image. It now holds its silence, black and brilliant, an African woman's skin. The wind, mindful of the centuries, pummeling the rocks, strives to give voice to what it saw one day at the very bottom of the abyss in a ghostly cleft; shadows as if in the wake of some storm, rather clumsy silhouettes . . . The remembering wind repeats it often in squalls, its sound alive with very remote scenes, horizons . . . So small, the cave at the very beginning, brand new like at Christmas, dark and round in the hollow of the mountain. No one on the rock ledge. An eagle lands, flies off again, circles above the plains. No one looks at the world. Bare things, unseen. The quivering thrill of first objects.

A theater in the air. Backstages of rock. Powerful spotlight of the dawn sun. A man on the lookout perhaps, a god keeps watch over the cave. A demiurge from those days, extralucid, scrutinizing this window with its bright, immense eyes . . . It waits. A giant, or a tiny transparent creature. Lying in ambush in the lake, its fish eye blends with the transparent water. The cave in the god's gaze. This is the genesis. They are going to be born. Puppets of rough-hewn clay . . . Elementary marionettes. Awkward, limping like men disguised as apes, divine commedia dell'arte. God photographs the clowns of the origins. A demiurge reclines in the valley. Beautiful, blond. His eyes devour his face. Luminous mirrors, solar disks. He films the apparition of the first men.

Silence, night. Nothing. Dawn, the mist conceals the rocks. Nothing. Day. Lovely sunlight. Splendor. The valley opens broadly where the animals graze. Game. Lures. They are going to go out. The cave setting. The painter need only draw, color in their gnomelike silhouettes. All lies in readiness. The trap set. The jaw open. It's a two million-year-old cave. Dug out by erosion. This gallery in the Urgonian limestone. A lair, a hollow, a hole in matter. When the whole planet is movement, molded reliefs, sculpted mountains, terraced plains. The scenery has been fluctuating for thirty million years, seeks stable ground, varies from sea to hills. Alluvium, rivers. Thick silts. The cave, drop of silence, listens . . . skull or belly in this awesome digestion of the beginnings. With both hands the gods knead the dough of the riverbanks and the rocky ranges. The torsos heavy with sweat, mud, sunlight. The cave very small, a pupil, a shell . . . an emptiness . . . The wind's music. Spirit filtering into the notch.

Why this day . . . Free of clouds, storms. Precisely at dawn. Free of mist. After a fleeting shower. Light. The cave's porchway stirring. Then they appeared: brand new. Two at first, then two more, and the others almost at the same time. All in a row on the edge. No one below to surprise them. The god has gone to sleep, his backbone merges with a river's meanders. Simon is alone, virginal, voyeuristic. His heart beats. Convinced this excess of beauty will kill him. They are the ones. They gaze out over the plain. Not big, still hairy, with the mugs of good-for-nothings, of innocent killers. With each passing day they gain status unawares. They flaunt themselves in a natural way. They know nothing. They live a commonplace existence. A Monday from five hundred thousand years ago. A tranquil day. The weather's nice. They know this. There are herds moving through the plain. Out there, that swarming of elephants. They take counsel, armed with hunting spears. A chief calms them. Tribe, clan of knock-kneed beings, sublime beggars. Their humanness stammers on their lips. They are beautiful, beaming. Simon is ashamed to observe these events from before paradise. God comes later. Simon betrays the millennia. Posted, lying sentry long before Eden. Adam and Eve have neither bodies nor odors. With their mother-of-pearl luster, artificial replicas. But these creatures here ruminate, shit, reek of flesh and musk. Crawling with fleas, vermin. Covered with bite-marks and dried blood. Long before Cro-Magnon, before Neanderthal, before, before . . . Everything that's been said, imagined, shown on screens, told in books, proud Simon has wedged at the outset of the lineage. He's ashamed. Through the keyhole of the ages he sees the very first parents. Side by side, surly, disheveled, aggressive. A pack of scruffy characters. They nibble away, they're nervous. Out there, the elephants.

Weak pithecanthropi. Hot-tempered and fragile. Craven. They're going to attack the ancient elephant. This was long before mammoths. Beasts before beasts. Tall, enormous . . . And they, pathetic, puny with their spears . . . Yet bold. They start out. They confront the largest, the strongest animals. Ambitious themselves, megalomaniacal midgets. They could browse on plants, suck berries, chew on beavers. But no! Elephants! Dissolute, dissatisfied, debauched beings: men already, equipped with rockets, space satellites and star voyages. Atavistic malcontents. They eye the proboscideans. But they have nothing more than a grumble to designate the tusked juggernauts coming down the plain. Chariots, citadels of leather. Lumbering carriages saturated with meat.

Scholars of today depict a region rich in game. "The fauna was exceptionally plentiful and well preserved on the various habitat deposits of the

Arago *Caune* . . . Originating in polar regions during the Ice Age, from Asia or Africa during warming periods, the animals that lived in the plains of Aguilar or Tautavel did not all survive the dramatic climactic changes which occurred during the last five hundred thousand years. In Aguilar, one no longer finds arctic foxes, Siberian 'hissing' hares, Alaskan musk-oxen, ancient elephants, black panthers or cave lions . . ."

What a menagerie, what a procession! . . . arctic, "hissing," panther . . . vividly colored dreamwork, contours of a very pure zoo. Parade past, my lambs. Howl, growl, gallop, my darlings. As gentle, as beautiful as can be . . . Black panthers, gold lions. Noah's Ark. Archaic hunters have only to choose hues and fleeces from this thawing tide. Bouquets of odors. They descend along a path in the rockface. Cunning, slow. The light smiles. Simon is afraid. He ought to flee. He is committing the sacrilege of spying before the gods. But it's so beautiful. A greener landscape. Vigor, profound forms. And these creatures, grouchy, narrow-minded eaters. They're going out to hunt. That's their job. A mist rises from the savanna. Gentle, fragrant. The sides of the ancient elephants are awash in warm pools of sunlight. The long, diverging, almost straight tusks follow each other, or huddle together. The hunters disappear amid the rocks. Out of sight. They whisper, exchange signs. They concoct their plan. All the while hidden behind limestone slabs. They think, speak, are afraid. They've promised to bring back a supply of fresh meat. They're hungry. Their children have big hopeful belly rumbles. They are joyful, excited. They obey the chief, a mean-spirited male, a wily hound.

They sniff the wind. Out in the grasses their presence is sensed. Skimming through the savanna, shadows slipping past. Hair and blades of straw intermingled. Grassy expanses, apes. The sturdy elephants sway. Vessels upon the swell of stems. Paunches of apotheosis.

The hunters have passed out of view. The plain sparkles in the sunlight. Plants, tusked beasts. Time. A day like any other. Monday, five hundred thousand years ago. Suddenly the hunters let out a shout, a racket. The elephants trumpet, rumps knocking together, pressed side by side, the whole herd regroups and dashes forward. The small hunters, unseen but howling. The elephants flee ahead of them. The race through the plain is off to a start. A long journey with halts, detours, islets of hesitating animals, others zigzagging. The round horde. Splendid game. Violence of bulging bellies. The huffing hunters. They have their plan. The sun revolves. The eye of the cave watches over the great opera of the hunt. A gorge plunges from sight between two mountains. The elephants have rushed into the crevice. Densely packed flood, tumult. Abraded stomachs. Invisible and hopping, the string of pithecanthropi squawking in their wake. Dreaming of the huge booty of meat. Full of desires, fears. On the other side begins a rocky plateau. The elephants now gallop starkly between the slabs. The hunters bawl out. The herd hesitates before turning right or left. A sheer slope smack in their path blocks the way. The lead elephant charges leftward. But new shouts resound, a hellish jabbering, stones roll down the slope toward the passage on the left. Other hunters were waiting, in league with the first. The plan falls into place. The elephants checked, thrown into a panic by the din of the falling stones, make an about-face, move to the right. The hunters are happy, crouched behind undulations of the terrain. They look at each other. Victory will be theirs. Mysterious is their joy. Simon can neither measure nor express it. Viscera swelling, a yelping happiness. The hunt continues. The two groups of hunters have joined up and the squawking intensifies. The animals, blind. Males, females, offspring. Trumpeting, jolts, thunder in the echoing space. The ground abruptly gives way, the plateau without warning topples straight down. The lead animals rear up, draw back, pushed by the mass behind, the enormous herd coiling, arched, trunks upright, tusks clashing, and some animals tumble into the void driven by the momentum, the terror, the horror of the crush. Five, six toppled elephants tumbling headlong into the void, windbags pierced by jutting rocks, paunches spiraling down, muscleless bulks, carnivalesque barrels. Six cadavers fifty yards farther down. The survivors stream back along the plateau's slopes. Finally the archaic hunters appear. No longer in hiding. They dash to the edge of the precipice. At first watching motionlessly. Then stamping their feet. Their joy is magical. Then, a ravenous tribal hunger. Their triumphant mugs. Their gleeful drool. They'll make a broad detour, return with tools. They'll come into view below amid the remains. Armed with bone perforators, hatchets, choppers, they split, rend, shatter. Blood spurts from the crevices. Thick rolls of flesh move under the sharp ridge of the implements. It's very hot, steaming. The hunters sit on the animals. Their feet sink into the holes, their hands slip into the bundle of sinews. They yank out packs of muscle. They dismember, carve. The men red, with clawing grips, yanking free scarlet shreds. They bring their mouths up to the springs gushing from the skins, they guzzle savagely. Drunk, wallowing in the mud of fat and meat. One plunges up to his waist in the belly of the prey. He jerks his limbs. The corpse quivers around the gluttonous butcher. The sunlight makes their crimson maws shine. Ruby scrape-marks are mirrored in pools of blood and heaps of guts.

The beasts are taken apart on the spot. Enormous portions remain stuck to the bones, severed limbs, heads. The hunters transport these chunks. The long trek back begins, plagued by flies and birds of prey. Wild beasts follow the victors' return march to the cave. The group scales the slope, straggling out, struggles, towing along fantastical tibiae, Homeric thighbones, Saturn's mandibles. Apish ants bearing loins, flanks, great pink lungs.

Up above they'll crack open the bones and swallow the monsters' marrow. The skulls will be the object of a special feast. Do the strongest and most cunning males have the privilege of taking the first bite from the giants' brains? Overjoyed, the females and children suck the bones, savor the remains of penises, sticky hearts. The cave runs red with blood. All around there is a circle of felines and winged predators fighting over the scraps fallen along the way.

Agathe is shining her kitchen tile floor. It's got to gleam. She drives off the dust. She likes to see a sparkle, she cleanses, slays. Ferociously she tracks down, ferrets out. She listens to the bowl of tea she's just drunk tinkling in her tummy. Her window is open. The light bounces off the red hexagons of her floor. While eye and arm toil, her thoughts are on other matters, sentences float in her head, images come back chaotically from the ocean floor of her memory, cork stoppers and illuminated debris . . . Such is the case with Aurèle . . . who liked breathing in the fragrance of roses . . . in his grandmother's garden. Sometimes he caught by surprise a velvety buzzing bee in a flower's calyx. He went off for a rubber band, stretched and snapped it, beheading the insect in the center of the blossom . . .

Agathe has finished her housework. She sits in a chair, listens to the news. Nothing special. Little change in the current state of affairs. Two swallows bicker atop an electricity pole. A fly died in the pot of geraniums. Her dreams are once more filled by the terrorist. He's very handsome this morning with his exploding bomb. He's dying in the sunshine. Scattered all around him: girls' severed heads, uprooted torsos, glut of slaughtered breasts, child martyrs, Herod, Caligula and the scarlet sea, two stiffs out in a pedal boat. Their tombs ought to have been erected on the sand. Immutable marble grave sites, anchored to the bottom, secured to the bedrock. Tempests would be unable to destroy this genuinely seaside cemetery that each tide would lay bare and then blanket once again. Beautiful, brilliant marble slabs under the restless waves. In the coffins: horrible pieces, dismembered bodies, bits of carnage, shorn bones, split skulls. The terrorist who died with them is mysteriously intact, whole in his black grave that the sea washes and unveils. The tomb of the solar murderer is visible, asleep in its skiff under the sea.

She heard the footsteps on the road. Rather heavy, steady. Unrecognized. Her heart palpitates. Discreetly she glides over to the window. She sees Paula, the impotent, housebound woman, the lady who has been forever dying. Yet here she is walking along. With only a blouse over her pudgy bust, a skirt roundly hugging her rump. Neither her hair nor face fixed up. But not disheveled. No hint of a distraught slattern about her. She walks with seeming delight in the already broad daylight. This excessive heat's no good for her heart. Walking out in the bright sunshine down the middle of the road. Sure of herself. Very determined. Steady. She's heading for a rendezvous of sorts up in the hills. She hasn't set foot up there since marrying Alphonse. Agathe's thunderstruck, her lips dry. Her tongue-tip fluttering, her eyes quivering. Oh my, my! Look at Paula out and about. She's never been so round, so obese. It's bad for her heart, so much belly down there, and those hips of hers. She's walking along. What's got into her, out in that swelling sunshine, so full of itself! The sun's a young madman, all hot to whack the skin of a beautiful woman. Trot along, little lady. Agathe bends slightly on her calves, her nose pointed, her hairbun like an antenna. Paula, Paula, is it possible? . . . Is she going to see a lover deep in the mountains? No . . . She's walking for her heart, a new therapy treatment. No. Fierce sunlight, bad time of day. Agathe watches closely, detects the dumpy body, how gawky, bundled folds of flesh, poor Paula, horned cow. And when she passes under the window, Agathe sees the smiling face, almost radiant. Hunched down, Agathe suddenly feels like farting, she fidgets, black and hoarse, she pants. Paula, Paula . . . Contemplating her along down the road, from behind, her clownish sausage rolls. Skirt and blouse heading scrubward, how awful! The felines, rock-blades, the wild-eyed assassin and hermits, skinflint prospectors, desert monsters. Paula, Paula. What are you doing? Agathe is jealous. She can't follow her. She senses this. The other would see her, chase her away. Agathe's got good intuition. A shrewd female vine shoot. She no longer has Paula in view, lingers at the window, slumped over, thirsting. She could bound outside, race along the main village road, knock on every door, visit every shop, spread the news, maybe in time to save Paula . . . Paula is madly trotting toward the mountain. In an hour the blazing heat will become unbearable. And the ferocious lynx, the frenzied terrorist, the darting snakes, falcons with knives drawn. Paunchy Paula beaked to pieces by the crows. She hasn't moved. She draws back toward her chair, falls into it. Music on the radio. Swing. Anyway that's what she calls it. Whatever she doesn't understand is "swing." Present-day rhythms, jumps and jolts for shameless kids, drugged-out teenagers. But she likes being up-to-date. "Swing," the "jerk," jiggling, swaggering. Asses thrown about, nimble boobs. She ought to go warn Alphonse, the priest, Dr. Chany, the firemen, Aurèle's dad, the police helicopter. Paula's gone, cleared off right into the mouth of the oven. An apocalyptic furnace. The terrorist in heat and the lynx lustful. But she feels an inarticulate complicity with Paula in flight. Let her reach the end of her path. Trot on, Paula, trot on, my girl, go see the world out there, splendid rock, the ravages of dust and heat. In fact, the lynx is at peace and the snakes nonchalant. The terrorist is asleep deep in his cave. Paula, a little girl. Red Riding Hood, age sixty, gone off to gather a stalk of golden rosemary.

Paula hurries along. She no longer feels her breath nor her heart. The sun bites into her white flesh. Perspiring. Painless. She's walking for the first time in at least ten years. She can't get over how easily she's moving. Comfortably, lightly. She'll go far, all the way out. An ecstasy bears her along, buoys her. She forgets her flesh, her weight, her fat, her misery. Upon setting out she drugged herself like some punk. Pep pills, stimulants. High on drugs she dances. At last a cicada. All right, now dance on! The sun is a great samurai with brand-new swaying swords. A lion's mane, phoenix wings. He whirls, his blades thunder. He roars, Redbeard, a good fellow, a bit violent. Paula shows genius, feels she's going out in the prime of her beauty. Proud. Free at last. Her sole remorse is Alphonse. She had no thought of revenge. Today she is taking death as her groom. A great tenderness for Yvette. No jealousy, no regret. Alphonse is a child. Indulgent, she smiles. She's fleeing like some fiancée. The blue, pink mountains, the streams locked in grimaces. She stops, staggers. Her temples pound madly. But no headache. Her heart pain-free, an atomic battery. Beats without injuring. She drinks a trickle of icy water beading between the nettles. The sky. The bolt of blueness lands squarely behind her forehead. She's enduring the azure. She stretches out and the stream touches her with its finger, reptile under her thighs, navel, against her breasts, a razor's sharp metal cutting her. She's going to die there, reclining in the flow of blood, open artery. She gets up, crumpled, wet, soiled like a debauchee. They came out into the scrub, those resourceful couples, springlike striplings, lewd greybeards, offending town dwellers. On the banks of flowering streams, in the shadow of large boulders, on beds of sand or fine gravel, they embrace. Greedy, gluttonous, gobbling each other. Their vinelike bodies intertwine. Especially the very young are beautiful, savage and awkward in their haste, hurl forward, rear up, purebreds, frisky lambs. The urine and sperm of the stream stick to Paula's flesh. Those sparrow hawks, beautiful as lynx. Attacking with beak and claw. Genitals and sinewy thighs. Buttock cheeks hunted down, soft-tipped breasts. No! No! No! . . . Oh yes! Yes! Yes! With Alphonse in the very beginning. She walks. A person can go twelve hours without food after what she's downed. Twelve hours of autonomy if the machine holds up to that point . . . Around her damp, shadowy bedroom, a cloistered recess, this vast theater of rocks and blazing sunbeams opening outward. A setting for conquerors, caravans, pirates, falcons, shimmering assassins, striptease queens, escaped galley slaves, stoned bikers, female Tarzans with cutlasses, corsairs on cocaine. Those who are tall, strong, who got guts, Apaches flying through this desert. She left her doghouse to catch sight of them; amid the plains under the clear immense sky they gallop and covet, carrying off their treasures, their rock dancers bound on the rump of their steeds. Renegades and gladiators, Zorros and Sioux chieftains. Out there, behind the hills, are gulfs, galleons, oases, fruit-laden gardens full of birds and happy slaves. Her childhood books come back to her. She climbed to the summit of a peak. A sentinel, she observes. She sees everything, she is penetrated by all that is around her in every least detail. This harshness, this silence, these dark purplish and mauve hues, these ochers, these chalky spaces dotted with copses. Out there flames have sprung up. It's the season for tragic fires that people track on their radios. Invasion, epic. Ebbing, breaking out. Scorched firemen. Incinerated tourists. Devastated campgrounds. She heard the news deep in her dark room. Those imagined flames, those holidays, those alarm bells, the large shooting streams splattering the infernos. Yes, they were alive, gasping for breath, they lost farms, vineyards, falling into each other's arms in tears, ruined families. What luck! The heroism of the firemen, special brigades. Siegfried with a brass torso confronting Medusa or the dragon. She envied the dead, the injured, the separated lovers, the panicky wives, the maniac arsonists, the campers . . . So many beliefs, superstitions, battle-ready instincts. She in her bedroom. Today she bows and takes leave of the sun and salutes the complicitous blazes.

There's a very small hostel in a ravine. She enters. The owners look at her. They disguise their astonishment. They aren't as surprised as all that. Accustomed to crackpots, wanderers, shaggy lovers, bearded ecologists living on goat cheese, ascetics and satyrs, mercenaries and saints. She asks for a pitcher of white wine. The finishing blow, out of sheer happiness. For ten years she's been forbidden the smallest drop of alcohol. This time, big gulps of strong wine, asp nerves. Let her heart burst, explode, a bomb shattering the shop. The cabaret in flames. So cool this white wine, a waterfall. She savors the liquid. The inn is scraggy, ashen paper. The managers are old dodderers. Cheers, friends! I'm off. The terrorist is waiting for me with his dog, the lynx. We're leaving for a vacation in the land of the Nile. My Robinson of death and Anubis are taking me off to Nubia.

Upon leaving, her thoughts turn to the lynx's stones, ingots, jewels. She inspects the crannies of the rock, this is the trail leading to the felines. Tom Thumb crumbs. A string of nuggets. Lynx are crucibles of ultra-precious gems. Gleaming in her memory. She sees gold, diamonds, rubies, beautiful amethysts, aquamarines along the paths, under the thick mane of the arbutus, their resin seeps in, sparkling seeds . . . Blissful, she follows this wake of stars. So many prowlers have sought the lynx's stones, retired army veterans, half-starved cowboys, mafiosi, ruffians, penniless kids. Unintentionally she set foot on top of some gems. All around, gleaming, shimmering. Ali Baba of the Arabian Nights. In a canyon there's shade, no water. And the stones' brilliant luster dies away. Paula passes a bare-chested man, rifle in hand. He's not suspicious of her, he doesn't seek to avoid her. He stops not far off under a pine. Then she sees a woman she recognizes, Thousand and One Nights, whom she saw once or twice, heard talk about in Alphonse's bistro . . . The couple intertwines, kisses. He's kept his rifle in his hand, the weapon pinned against the girl's naked breast. Their rendezvous in the canyon. Tall. Marked faces. He clings to her mouth, kneads her buttocks under her shorts. She bites his beard, massages his biceps. Paula looks on. They pay her no mind as if they knew she was beyond betrayal, that she'd decided to die. They offer her the final spectacle of their thirst. She sees them as if on a pedestal, a statue, muscular bodies, the daring of a sculpture with stomachs fused together, writhing loins, the woman's breasts under the terrorist's teeth. Joust of the sexes. In the shadow of a canyon. With the saber of the intense azure sky reaching to the mountain peaks. She contemplates them, free of envy. Suddenly worn out. Her euphoria dies away. Her drug drifts into depression. There's still something ecstatic inside her, at the periphery of her being, in her clenched hands, her dilated pupils, her terrible smile. But, in the center, a spreading sensation of death. Destruction, junk heaps of busted organs. Trashcan, failure. To the garbage dump. Black barbed wire. Ecstasy shrunk to an ever-narrower strip, fearful grimace. She goes off, leaves the canyon where they are adoring each other, the word blazes one last time within her, *adore* . . . She would have liked to choose a stone slab in the broad sunlight on which to burst open in death, to beam forth at the very heart of the landscape. But she will not rest until she reaches that sparse copse beyond so that she can hide in the crooked branches, slip underneath, crawl to shelter, where nobody will see her, crouching in her room, back again in the shadowy cell . . . She thinks about Alphonse, without affection . . . An image steals in, her father trying to ride the bike she just got for Christmas. Very big, he topples over. There's a train station behind, black with coal. She's got stuck in the bushes. In pain. Afraid of animals. She'd like a hand, not Alphonse's, but a woman's. Her mother's. Her dress bleeds, clawed with thorns and flint. She's burning up, covered with scratches. She can't see anymore. She lets out a cry. A shrew gazes at her. She throws up the wine.

Arthur keeps silent, mouth open, anxious over the abnormal hush, subdued voices, procession of furtive silhouettes. People are whispering all around the cradle. A network of emotional words, sudden outbursts, streaming tears. Reddened faces, freely dripping mucus. Arthur finds the whole thing fishy. He doesn't know if he's going to start bawling right away or wait and make an effort to understand. Planted on his big ass. A curl plastered against his forehead. He's just taken a shit, drank his milk. He observes the changes, the comings-and-goings, the relays. All those heads hurrying, good people, fine ladies. Mommy brimming over. Lynne . . . Lynne . . . he recognizes her among the groups, moving about slenderly in bright colors, he follows her, a lifesaver.

A grasshopper landed in his cradle. The motionless bug nibbles, raises its leg, chews, large thighs, antennae, green all over with a big lemon-yellow abdomen. Arthur reaches forward his little finger, a pink index smelling nicely of soap and baby lotion. The bug hops, runs, leaps, takes flight. There it is again on the other side of the cradle, closely watching. Arthur giggles, nears his finger and whoops! the grasshopper hops, looping to the right, the left. Arthur, a dimpled dumpling, laughs and laughs, face crumpled up, twisted, beet-red, the playful grasshopper cavorts and capers. There it is in a circle of sunlight on the white sheet. A hot golden circle; Arthur puts his finger inside. His skin warmed, happiness, and the bug-eyed creature ogles him with its big seeing droplets. Arthur waits, a wily one. He has understood. It's going to jump again, clear off like an acrobat, worse than flies, bubbles popping up. He's crouched, the tomcat . . . insect hunter, lying in ambush. And tap! He thrusts out his two big paws at the same time, topples forward, belly and chin. The squashed grasshopper stains the murderer's bib. He looks for the bug, doesn't see it anymore, looks everywhere, sticks out his lower lip, and there, all at once, he sights the yellow splotch, the bits, the fragments. He laughs. He claps as when he's got his tummy full. Hooway! Hooway! . . . His first kiddy crime. Then he leans back, a conquerer, little Nero on his plump pillow. Tickled by the gentle sunlight. The silhouettes are still stirring, in files, single or by twos, a little shameful, noses down, sanctimonious, dry and wizened or delicate flies on the young side. Passing piles. Arthur could cry, but the rustle of the secrets, the wonder of the hush, the miraculous whispering . . . casts a spell over him, rocks him . . .

Upstairs in the attic bedroom Simon is stretched out beside Myriam. Footsteps slipping past, muffled words along the sidewalks. The kids dare not shout. At times a big bus crosses through the indifferent village. It grumbles, provokes. There are packs of gleeful kids on vacation in the cabin on wheels. Colonies. Chieftainesses and camp fires. And the silence takes shape again after the racket, weaves its links of snow, fingers of ash.

The mulattress in her clothes. Khaki trousers and blouse. Buttoned up. Closed. Simon almost straitlaced. They're lying on the bed, floating on the surface of faint sounds, this discreet din, mute rapid molecules dissolving. Simon remembers a dead woman when he was a child. He tells the story to Myriam, who is not so much interested in the facts as she is in Simon narrating them. The event consists of Simon confessing a fragment of his past. Sick, they'd lain down, his sister and he, on the big bed of their parents who had put them together for convenience's sake. Across the street a lady had died. The kids had gotten up, looked out from behind the curtain and saw the large black catafalque in front of the door. The age still kept a feeling for funereal grandiloquence. A river of black velvet sown with lilies, silver tassels. All black. After that surprise glimpse they lay down again. He recalled it now because Paula had been brought back downstairs after a two-day search. The dogs had found her. Under the thicket, wretched and mutilated, a cradle of thorns. Alphonse shaken, a robot carcass. The handsome old fellow wept. A softness blurred his features. Paula was cleaned up, restitched, her injuries painted over. She was at rest in the room below. Three levels then: Arthur at the bottom, Paula in the center, and Simon, Myriam on top, then the roof, weather vane, the sky and maybe the angels and lightning bolts and last of all, the heavenly bodies. Arthur, and under him, the tile floor, concrete, the cellar, the earth, worms, and subterranean streams, the ring of rocks and mantles, lava, fire.

Agathe can't get over it. Paula ran for miles, a fabulous jaunt leading her to the Cathar castles, Montségur perhaps or the outermost reaches of the country, the borders bristling with contraband and revolutions. Breaking loose Paula all but set foot in Spain. Cannonballing along, tireless, she walks on and on, bullfight! . . . Paula poses a problem in Agathe's mental card file. This flight is aggravating, unbalancing. She prefers for people to die at home. She visits them, at times witnesses the extreme unction. That's the ideal. Each in his or her nest. But this flight—she might have totally escaped, fallen into some chasm, been dragged by some animal back into its lair. In which case, no more Paula. This hole in Agathe's archives, the mess of an unbearable blank. She almost holds it against Paula. This debauchery before dying. The flight of some maiden, some hysterical virgin. But here she is now brought back to the fold, wiped clean, powdered. Agathe shows up, all is in order, condolences. Paula will take her place in Agathe's memory. This incident frightens her. All of a sudden she feels her structure threatened. Then as always in such cases, Agathe recapitulates, takes stock, enumerates, classifies the families, couples, children, ancestors by houses, territories, origins and professions, birth dates. A good training routine consists in pouncing upon a name at random and immediately producing predecessors and descendants. Finding the sentence around a word, in a way. Filling in the dotted line like in a grade school vocabulary exercise. She excels at this game. Weaving the chain around a link, nourishing and populating space. Her tale brought crowds to birth, people whom nobody remembers but whom she connects to others who are more familiar by way of matching links, roadmarks. She likes the world, humankind, the dead. One and all, a mass of good shadowy souls aligned in her head like swallows on a wire. Tightly packed, pitch-black, labeled fetuses, compartmentalized insects swarming. She knows the phenomenon well. For the moment Paula takes up the whole space. Enormous Paula, her brand-new death. She alone is visible, stretched out, on exhibit. But she'll join the darker ranks, the remote rows of the dead. Agathe likes them this way, shadows or ciphers existing in her memory. Black Tom Thumbs. Mathematical structures. The village computer has a name: Agathe.

Iza came into Alphonse's bistro while Agathe, sitting at the foot of the bar, was watching Arthur squash the grasshopper. Agathe couldn't repress a laugh as she saw the fat paunch, the terrible trap, topple onto the bug. Agathe neither likes nor understands Iza. Disheveled, muddleheaded, thundering out her mad rants in Pythian sentences disgorged from her diseased throat. At times she's jealous of the madwoman, for the latter possesses a spotty, perilous memory. She erases a whole block of the past for you, but then suddenly sheds light on infinitely remote events, details she abruptly unearths. She comes out with some dead person, somebody inconsequential, tosses him or her right in your face, center stage, as if presenting an essential character whom somehow you've forgotten in your distraction. Agathe is wary of Iza's workings. Iza, with a bit of luck, more self-mastery, some advice, would have made such an excellent magician, village sorceress, priestess or seer. For a long while Agathe dreaded Iza's hallucinatory gift of the dead and her savage spontaneity. But she squandered her possibilities. Foundered in her senility alongside the priest. The bells pealed in their brains, deserted, out of joint.

Agathe went over to Iza. The two old women gazed at each other. Passionate Iza with her loves buried out in the scrubland of the beginnings, her guilt, the aborted child. Fertile Iza, killed in the egg. Sterile Agathe, filled up with other people's lives. Agathe, a casket, a pantry, a refrigerator. Iza, a spittoon, metaphone of obsessive fears and alarm bells. Agathe would prefer for Iza to die. At last immobilized, stripped of all her bumps and rough edges, tentacles of madness that reach too far, unearthing unpredictable things, taking soundings of the future. Bone-dry Iza, a fossil in her presbytery bed. Now that would have suited Agathe just fine. The thought filled her mind, eyes upon Iza. The female who had desired, experienced a mad love, incredible embraces out in the bush, the heavy fragrance of rosemaries, lavenders, the springtime of the world. And fought the devil, lusted after the priest. Bitch! Get lost, whore! Beautiful Iza. As a young girl she had the beauty of an apparition. Madonna and she-wolf, ardent and pure, race of the Cathars. Agathe begrudged her those splendors of love, those magnificent, impure caresses. Iza, Iza the gust, the tempest: when the storm rumbles and fans out, when the dust along the paths rises and the bones crack deep in the graves, when desires run riot under the flesh, and the tide unfurls far along the beaches, when conflagrations spew their sulfurous flames, flood the mountains with their smoke, when you want to flee, burn, do battle—it's Iza's soul that triumphs! Her puritanical curses nowadays are merely a recycling of the mad desires of her youth. Iza had orgasms out in the coppery scrubland ringed with golden sun. Iza had orgasms. She anathematizes and shouts down with the same carnal impulse, the same convulsions of black pleasure. Agathe detests this blast of breath, these leaps, those fluttering waves that bear quarrels and messages, that inflame bodies and dishevel souls. She's the anti-Iza, in a petrified space she orders the data of time. She labels life, collects and places it under glass. Iza disturbs the sediments, upsets them as she yanks out shreds, scours, expulses them. She brings time back to life, reanimates its passage, its spasms, its outbursts. She has the genius of squalls and living things. Her law is chaos. This howling hyena sets ablaze dust and the dead. The cave has changed her into a vociferating mouth, a maw full of curses, a monstrous outpouring of atavistic gossip. The pithecanthropi are sorcerers with vengeful skulls. The mask grimacing in the heart of the museum.

Agathe, the housekeeper of the cosmos. She prepares jars of jam for all eternity. Ancestral blackberries and bilberries. Worker ant of corpses. Secretary of time, which she shuts up under double-lock, takes apart in rigid segments. Iza vomits it up, every minute for her is an untold agony and a cry . . .

And the helicopter passes through the silence and mourning. It's reassuring, opens a vista of joy in the hearts of children and teenagers. Simply because it's in flight, traveling, flashing over gulfs of azure, oceans of sunlight. What fun it must be, perched at the edge of the heavenly toy. Minds idiotically visualize Jesus coming down by plane to greet Paula. Deus ex helicopter. Silly superstition. Maybe it's Paula's soul being carried off by the plane so as to be set free on high and fly off, beating wings above the fires, warlike castles, torturous gorges, caves that are pantries for bones, the idolized lynx, Paloma and Sue, gentlewomen, suckers of the steppes. From up above she'll see the old men's bench, veterans of Verdun, old fogies from the last century. The fountain bathing the thighs of insolent tourists. Paula, up above . . . with neither affection nor regret, above Yvette's garden, hello Alphonse, I forgive you, hail vast village, the journalist is hiding what he's up to, the terrorist has an accomplice. Don't trust appearances. Lynne will visit the world, a phenomenal future is promised her. Watch out for Myriam the mulattress. Who could say where good or bad lay, and what's being hatched . . . In any case the fire has started. Devouring vines and pine forests. A beautiful seasonal fire. Young, still quite lovely, the firemen vainly attempt to slow its progress, look how it rears up, gallops off, mane of burning embers, how it whinnies, glinting spurs. It threatens farms, campgrounds, enveloping and circumventing, slithering. A mad warrior, a poet whose pockets are full of matches and rockets. A torero who tickles, brandishes ten thousand muletas. It plays, dances, drunk on the vines, knocking against rock, crunching into the dry copses. Clappers and flamenco. Dancing on its young dragon's tail. An acrobat's wedding. A dazzling set of teeth and writhing scales. It gets a hard-on, waves its member around like a plume and shoots its semen, gets tipsy, veers. Paula wishes it long life.

Myriam is nicely dressed, like a good little girl. Profane. Whereas nakedness makes her sacred. Her bestial blackness of a goddess. It looks like autumn has arrived despite the sharp blue sky. On the point of taking a trip, or some empty afternoon devoted to reading or mulling over regrets. Constantly these shadows slipping past below. Paula enveloped with gazing eyes and pity. Aurèle's ghost, angel of light, has come to rest on the dead woman's abdomen.

Myriam and Simon are riveted to the bedroom. They could go outside, flee, picnic in nature. Bathe in the gorges, lust in the black ass of the caves, trek through ruins and top-shorn keeps. They remain in the rooms waiting, wasting time, savoring this waste, this sweet boredom. With this discreet chimney-sweeping of the dead below. Portly Paula is coming apart. Her flesh is sparking mutations. Rich chemical reactions attacking muscles and fat. Her skin turns blue, her organs soften. The seams of her body burst, abubble, her flesh restored to the anarchy of corruption. Crevices and holes, squinting with pus. Shorn of its guard railing, matter overflows. A river of lively fermentations. Paula delivered at last, giving birth to every possibility, delighted multiplicities. Firmament of vermin.

Myriam a touch severe, hair smartly fixed, sitting at the table against the window, comes over to ask Simon for a sheet of paper. She wants to write a letter. Stretched out on the bed, Simon dreams about death, the angel Aurèle and Paula's carnal follies. He watches Myriam. She looks all dressed up like just before a journey . . . I'm leaving for Manhattan tomorrow. I'll work in a famous photography studio. A photo album is in the works, featuring my oval face and my firm loins. I'll wear simple, elegant suits. A hint of Chanel visible in Myriam today. An academic Cameroon woman. The lady pirate did her nails, shiny red luster, glinting claws. The village ferrets about. Space, in the distance, with its traps and murders. Its animals stationed under rocks. A pithecanthropus survives out in the remote scrub in a no-man's-land, beyond the castles, mountains, in deserts bristling with cerastes and fennecs. Simon is interested in mosquitoes, swarms of dust hopping in whirlwinds of sunbeams like great perfect visionary tribes, full of a mist of eyes. He'd like to come up with something to say to Alphonse. Or at least a glance. A gesture from the heart. But he hardly knows him. Simon is an intruder, a passing voyager. A reporter of emancipated apes. Is Alphonse full of despair anyway? Rather he feels put out, vaguely remorseful. A profound sense of waste. Paula is his failure, a long decay. A twenty-year degeneration. Myriam is writing: naturally the first question is to whom? Simon has the naive impression that by using his paper she'd be unable to betray him. He takes control and imposes a minimum of propriety upon her. All the same, that Myriam is thinking of other people, other places, constitutes an event. She slips out of this mythic sheath that shaped her in the immediate present. Suddenly civilized, more human, she enters into time, constructs a future and a fragmentary past. She's lost her overalls of a conger eel, black and slick. Dressed like a model young lady, she looks like she's about to board a plane, not to return to the lush wild savannas, but to some tropical bourgeoisie, an idle, rapacious oligarchy. She's the image of some government minister's daughter, an ambassador's wife. Paradoxically he likes her very much in this guise. This duality reinforces her power, the violence of the woman bound by her fashionable clothes lies dormant under the fabric, asleep like a purer ingot. Domesticated lightning bolt. But her appearance evolves. Soon Myriam shares in the decency of her dress. A young woman like any other, with no legendary mystique. Still beautiful, but without arrogance or softness. Stable, balanced. She is writing her letter. Thinking about her life. She's getting organized, foresees, maintains an emotional environment of bridges, rails, intersections. Places spring up about her, established town compasses with added improvements, practical details, customs. This letter integrates her into the city of men. Maybe she's writing to her best woman friend. Simon can't quite imagine Myriam engrossed in girl-talk. Laughter, little secrets. Their heels click rhythmically in the street, window-shopping. Trivial confessions. Off to see a movie. Discussing politics. Right, Left. The sort of thing you see in today's films. The charm and banality. Maybe she's writing to her man, her steady guy, announcing her return. Their life could pick up where it left off. Now she's acquired enough distance to do so. All very animated, not very original, life passing by as the pen glides over the paper, with its hesitations, its deletions, its paragraphs written in one burst. He'd really love to read her letter. In the grip of a jealous curiosity he'd love to get his hands on it. But he accepts his total ignorance. He acquiesces to this unknown realm that hems in his mulattress. She's before him, in his room, but not for long. This present weighs heavily. Suddenly immense. All the rest doesn't matter, an abstract network. She's paused, pen in the air. The blinding sunlight makes a fragment of paper shimmer. He sees the brilliant, dense rows of signs. Words in the fire. Soot of messages. Starlings on the snow. She's searching. He pretends not to observe her. Somewhat turned away, eyes half closed, slow heavy breathing. She writes, links herself to the chain of beings and things while he slips, sinks away into the fuzziness of his musings. The bikers pass in the street without too much bedlam, instinctively they've caught the whiff of a pleasant death. Their cavalry stretches out in proper order. All present. The village interrogates them, poised to explode in hatred. The kids, afraid and envious. The bikes gleam, intermeshing red and black machines. Now they've left the village. They've verified the death. Regards to the drinkable empty. Alphonse is a fine man. Racing between the vines toward the hills and rocks. They are going to bathe in the gorges. Paloma spotted Lynne and the child near the bar. This vision enchants her. Swift, lodged in the mind. A precious vignette. Evidence of a great happiness.

Myriam has finished her letter and slips it into the envelope. Her very pink tongue sharpens, a strand of saliva moistens the sticky strip. She seals her missive. How fatal an enclosed letter is! It condemns you. Decisions taken like so many murders. An envelope glares as whitely as a knife.

More calmly: "I wrote my mother."

He imagined everyone except Myriam's mother. Black woman awaiting her return. Heavy, a bit drab. Her father, some government employee in the prefecture. He could question her gently about her mother, family, profession, dwelling, births and trivial events, deaths, disasters. Perhaps she'd talk since she just ventured "my mother . . ." Go ahead and keep your mother, I'm not saying one word about my parents, ancestors and descendants. Tribes, fatherland, lineages, brat-crammed lairs, phratries. Silence! And yet Simon feels paralyzed by this mother. He surmises that she's laborious, haughty, corpulent. Her skin darker than Myriam's. Not as beautiful. As if she'd paid with a mourning of sorts for her daughter's beauty, liberty, dance.

And brothers and sisters no doubt. A petit bourgeois apartment. The father reads his newspaper while smoking cheap cigarettes. He's skinny, not very handsome. He didn't make much of a success of himself. And the male and female cousins of Cameroon, swarming uncles and aunts, he's heard how African families proliferate. They go right up to the river and the brush, those straw hut villages, right up to the freshly opened clearings, to the large-scale cocoa plantations . . . You see them, slow, bare-breasted, carrying jerricans of water on their heads. A real family encompassing every stage, from paltry agrarian encampments to urban settlements. Every step from primitive nakedness to pleated suits. Cameroon is heavy, deep. Mother, father, brothers, the branching networks share a past in this strong word, round and ample, tom-tom skin, lioness' mane, armpit pepper, bosom of the caves and voluminous brush. Paula's soft white corpse bobs about at the bottom of the totemic cooking pot. A ballet of black men and vultures.

She's just rejoined him on the bed with the feeling of a duty fulfilled. I've finally written my letter. He strokes the blouse and trousers. Well balanced, very well behaved. There are some deaths that give you a hard-on. This isn't the case with Paula. Now the terrorist slain—what a surefire idea to make our coitus keener! Cock upright to salute the hunted killer's corpse. Executioner and prey. A flint dweller. But Paula. He feels certain that Myriam's letter to her mother lends Paula an obscure maternal meaning. He takes good care not to probe deeply into these secret undercurrents.

Myriam turns the radio low. An easygoing melody vamps and coddles them. When all is said, death's a good thing. Reassuring. A warm jam, tasting of apricots. We feel comfortable with Paula, the village's long visit, one and all in the procession. White man and black woman, paleontology and journalism above the funeral march, lovers reigning on the raft of the bed. The water rocks you sweetly. The litany of the midsummer dead. The bed is steeped in an ashen gloom with pieces of burning embers blinking whenever a ray of sunlight perforates the curtain corner. Comfortable in the sheets, amid the dust, dead moths, dry beetles, stiff bugs . . . the smell of charred mice and scorched vine stocks. Wallowing, getting warm in the powder of a felicitous shadow. With Paula white as can be. Alphonse's sorrow. Arthur killing insects. The mailman gets back from his rounds out in the middle of nowhere. The sound of his minivan motor is recognizable. Agathe crunches into cookies, an ossicle snack. Iza prays before the beheaded Virgin's altar. In the cave, the old routine. Everywhere live populations can be sensed, discreetly stirring; weaving their web, adding a design, fabricating, knotting, spinning out life, good spiders. The black woman is beautiful, well dressed, prim and respectable on the journalist's bed. He touches her with his fingertips. Ass in her clean brand-new jeans. A Sunday ass, back from church, that'll shit out hosts, "nun" pastries. Breasts in the cotton bra. Disguised, pickaninnies in bonnets. Simon is infused by a delicious respect. A warming sunbeam reaches his balls. He slowly gets hard. Unfolding at leisure. He feels vast, better . . . The ray of light gropes toward Myriam's breasts . . . Both should also snuggle down, bear cubs under the warm hug, softened, languid, netted cowl over their mauve snouts.

The lord and master of the bench is Ludovic, an ascetic bean-pole whose dominion extends over two yards of green-painted planks. A perimeter of glory. He ran a large hardware shop in Perpignan. Booming business. But tragic loves. He's the chief because he has the quick tongue and sangfroid befitting his duties. He's the one who spends the most time on the bench. Bright and early he installs himself. A short break at noon. Then he doesn't leave until darkness falls. Goes without dinner. The broad shade of a plane tree protects the bench from the sun's claws. The green mass gently moves, a people of rustling and sliding silks that either irritate or soothe. The sound stirs memories. The leaves proliferate like the years. This delicate volume, this sissing commotion, these intermingling shadows, breezes, filtered sunbeams cradle the old men, sweep them off, a good skiff on the river. Traveling along. There are regions of the tree as far off as the remotest zones of the brain. Dark hemispheres. Winding mists and boughs, emerald wisps. The old men drift along, discover and wake the sleeping birds. Ludovic is flanked by a sturdy, big-bellied companion, a local winegrower. Every now and again they bring up the war, black episodes from way back before the world, the muds of their epic. The northern rains, cold, snow. Wet death. Within the tree's foliage these memories are located to the west, on the second tier of a wide-forked branch. There is a knot of shadows in that spot, gnarled interlacing boughs that block up an aerial cave of sorts, a maw scooped out of the bark. Some days, a special conjunction of wind, shade and moonlight contracts this portion of the tree. Ludovic and the winegrower communicate with the horror, the death throes. They don't ever need to raise their heads to look at this awful tunnel in the inky leaves, those eyes riddled with sticky darkness, speckled with skull splinters. A spiral of hell where the gloom agglutinates like hoop nets of blood. It's the recess of war. But the tree possesses other crannies, its lands of loves, its summers, its paradises of desire, located sky-ward when the leaves awash in sunlight shrink to a web so translucent that they resemble luminous tongues, open dancing palms of pleasure, suffused with brightness like angels. The bench is exclusively reserved for elderly men; if you're under seventy, you have no place on the sacred planks. A thorn, a pedestal that must be earned. You must have lived, conquered death a thousand times in order to settle upon the venerable seat and hear the tree's voices. The large plane dreams about the beginning of autumn. The faded leaves cackle, fidget like duennas. In the spring, turning green, there's the rustling of a guipure, supple blossoming of cornets, unfolding buds. A Botticellian skein of hair unlaces itself, displaying its separate curly locks under the shoulders of the ancestors. There are three other old men: Polyte, a drunkard, a good-for-nothing, ex-farmhand, more or less suspected of a rape back in the forties. The old women say that Polyte was really a handsome lad. A rather feminine demeanor. A delicate complexion. He started getting drunk from age twenty onward. He carried his liquor well. It never altered the transparency of his skin. He lazed around all the time, in barns, cellars, mountain sheepfolds where he tumbled clumsy gals, lively lassies. Sickly, he was said to be more or less stricken with tuberculosis. Depraved, craven. Charm to spare. But he'd grown old, survived, his milky cheeks had wrinkled, hardened, got eaten away. At eighty Polyte was a physical wreck vegetating on the bench, a worn-out branch. His eyes came alive again with a yellow gleam whenever a girl came to bathe her calves in the fountain. He straightened up a bit and contemplated the water-splashed limb. Mouth agape, he sought out fresh visions of shepherdesses, he staggered, stuttered in his rags of the past. At times, he found his prey once more. He could be seen poised motionlessly, features stamped with a rapture of innocence and senility. He stroked the ghost. He'd forgotten her first name, but a quiver along the nape, the pubic patch sufficed for his ecstasy. The fountain gurgled, the new water rending itself against the angles of the rock. Curls and long, liquid nerves. Two old men left: Alexandre and Raoul. A retired grocer and a blacksmith. Lives with no special glamour. Destinies of honest cockroaches. Raoul had a gift for doing impersonations that he might have exploited. He'd settled for performing at dances, communions, marriages. He imitated celebrities that nobody knew anymore. Comics from the beginning of time. Original teams like the twins in myths. As for Alexandre, the only thing glorious about him was his first name. He was a tightfisted, swindling grocer, and a malicious gossip. He chronicled his neighbors' adulteries.

Two old men had just left the bench. A heart attack and a hemiplegia had dispatched one off to his bedroom and the other to the hospital. They missed the bench. The unctuous panache of the plane tree. The breaths, the brief showers crackling on the leaves' paunch. The young people strolling from one end of the village to the other. You could see them coming from a distance. Laughing, almost naked, vulgar. They nodded their noggins, condemning so much insolence and defiance. Shorts so skimpy they look like loincloths, dirty pants sewn with initials, disgusting graffiti. Stark naked breasts under blouses. Fifteen years on the bench! Twenty for the champs. They've seen them all parading to the fountain: the cuckolds, the incestuous, unwed mothers, pederasts, those into bestiality, plus nice people too, novices, fathers in their glory, admirable matrons crowned with their brood, noses rigorously wiped clean. The bench survivors give no thought to the recent victims of infarction and paralysis. They say a few words, mumble with a shrug, hypocrites at bottom, unable to fully understand, refusing to picture the truth. Their whole lives long they've seen scores of people pass on their way. So they got wise, faces set in grimaces fit for greeting the death of other people. A hollow, whining pantomime. An empty litany. Scared, huddled in the cowardly and ungrateful hole of their pates . . . Then a swelling gust opens the plane tree's branches. A happy wave plows the beautiful mane, smooths the tufts, capsizes the leave-stacks. Their brains become absorbed in this deluge of winged sounds, of sighs.

But today something happens. Simpleminded Julia, a two hundred-twenty-pound ninny who's spent her whole life doing housework for monied families, walked up to the bench. The old men suspect nothing. They let her approach. She says hello. She looks at the bench, the tree, the geometries of shadow and sunlight, the fountain's lapping. It's more beautiful than a hotel here, a genuine Eden. An awesome desire for the bench seizes her, she wants to sit down, plant herself on the spot. Put down roots under the tree's breast, the twists and turns of this age-old plane, its tough stumps, its Jupiter's pitchforks. There's an empty seat between Polyte and Alexandre. Suddenly she advances, swivels around, shows them her enormous ass, her flabby plow-horse back. She reeks of sweat. Her filth is legendary. She plops right into the open notch. Her rolls of flesh touch the sides of the quondam shepherdess raper and the ribs of the tightfisted grocer. The five old men are petrified. They could stand up, evict the sacrilegious intruder. That idiot, that old cow, that grandmother with the flaccid udder. They didn't move. They squeezed together a fraction of an inch. Inwardly rebelling. They fulminate, on the brink of protesting, of driving off the female. But Julia pacifies them. The invisible influence of her belly, her huge bosom. She reeks, how delicious . . . Like the tree, she hangs over them, swells up, her mass all-enveloping. A group of teenagers passes by, stops, struck dumb by the sheer fact, the unprecedented scandal. All thought of making fun vanishes, of carrying on just to get a rise from the row of old fogies, all thought gone of shaking their pricks conspicuously just to hear them grumble, explode, cheeks scorched with hostility. Simpleminded Julia is ensconced amid the elderly males. The first woman on the sacred bench. A septuagenarian Eve who smells to high heaven. She defies no one.

She doesn't even smile. Spherical, tranquil. The speechless kids stare at the heroine, the one-woman shock squadron. A century has just changed. They've been abruptly propelled into a future age, a revolution accomplished by Julia's rump. All she needed to do was sit down, really desire the bench. Plop! Whoever loves me follows me. The guys didn't let out a peep. The blusterers, the old goats, the biblical penny-pinchers, the mistletoe gatherers, the patriarchs with staid brains, the glandes of immemorial epochs dating back before the discovery of the pithecanthropi. Julia, plop! wedges in her ass. The tree exhales a storm of sounds, the oceanic verve of the plane pitching and tossing. The young, the old heard tumults, grumblings, a surf of whipped leaves, a heaving of awakened chasms. And then this broad, gentle gust, this soft warmth, the hovering branches beautiful in the breeze, the settled mass of mother waters. The ark has just crowned Julia.

This morning Lynne receives her first love letter. Arthur's father never kept in touch. Her other lovers weren't men who took to pen and paper. The mailman held out the letter. With an attentive mysterious air. Agathe already knows that Lynne received a white envelope marked with an energetic and tumultuous handwriting . . . Agathe wonders whether it isn't the father announcing his return just like in soap operas. An adventurer returned from America where he found fortune. Rich and mature, he returns to bring happiness to his offspring. With Alphonse's permission Lynne went up to her room. She opened and read the letter, signed Paloma. Getting your first love letter from a partner of the same sex floods you with a strange emotion. Paloma's signature is all-conquering, an autograph as glorious as the lash of her locks. Lynne has yet to read the letter. The sky is grey in the window. Ten A.M. She steeps herself in the atmosphere, the particularities of the moment. She's happy that the everyday sun hasn't shown its face. She wants exceptional circumstances. Those darker clouds match the half-light underlying all love. Grey as falcon's feathers, the hair of distinguished old men. Grey as a person's complexion sensitive to the cold, a grey shiver, grey with fright and desire. She's going to read, she has read, reread ten times . . . standing, then sitting on her chair, lying on her bed. She doesn't weary of starting over word by word, whole sentences. Read with embarrassment, consumed by vigilance. For Paloma's letter is rife with audacious statements. It's a love letter, written out of genuine erotic appetite. Full of oaths, challenges and bold propositions. Lynne is totally shaken. The downy, cozy greyness. Paloma describes Lynne's body, and the girl sees herself naked, recognizes herself for the first time. Then come caresses, but in writing, detailed with keen, delicate words that can be reread, rolled under her tongue and into her flesh. Aggressive words springing from a gluttonous fever. Words to be repeated, reread, all swaddled inside. She also speaks of the raging fire that simultaneously delights and worries the clan of bikers. Her buddies are accused of lighting camp fires everywhere in the hills on purpose to destroy and alarm the world. It's more likely the terrorist exacting his revenge. At night creeping out in the scrub and lighting fires right under farmers' noses, herds shitting in fear, eyes rolled back in panic, grilled to death in five seconds flat . . . The terrorist disturbs her, supplants her. There's worse out there than the bikers, other jokester-rebels. That killer, for example. The gang is beaten on its own ground by this champion of threats. He draws down cops, investigations and journalists. He constitutes a danger for Paloma and her cronies. He's starting a mad vigilante fury. Then she changes the subject, alludes to Simon and Myriam. She finds the couple shifty and sexy. She uses Simon to get under Lynne's skin. Declares him to be rather ugly but ambiguous, a manner that takes you in, cloaked by his absent airs. A burning coldness. But he hides what he's up to. That journalist is depraved. The pithecanthropi are a pretext for some underground shenanigans. Along with Myriam he's cooking up a few things, each alone or together. Difficult to determine. The scrubland magnetizes them. The desert, plus roving about in it, posting sentinel, trading messages. A sunlight plot. Perhaps he's a traitor . . . Lynne is aggravated by these insinuations. When in Paloma's company, Lynne made no bones about heaping Simon with abuse, attributing to him the worst possible crimes. But these accusations coming from somebody else wasn't much to her liking. Simon is her business. What if Paloma were jealous after all . . . Laying it on Simon as a way of dissolving the last islets of weakness that still might be surviving in Lynne's heart. Paloma is not a bit hostile toward the student. The bearded guy gives her a laugh, she rids herself of him with a flick of her fingers. This attitude hurts Lynne, for Paloma thus indirectly reasserts the other's value, salacious Simon. Then Lynne ponders the hated couple: the reporter and the black woman, their manifest lack of closeness, worse than complicity, confers upon them a mystery, a magic. One wonders what unites them once this ice is shattered, melts in an embrace. Their rage, their flames of Satan. Lynne is wounded, stabbed by jealousy. Yes, he's a coward, a traitor, a maniac, into bestiality, sodomy, a corrupted voyeur, a fetishist, with a thing for skeletons, he steals bones from the cave, worse than a dog, he swipes them from science to stash them under his mattress, sacred ancestral bones that he harvests, a macabre collection. The truth at last! He'd gladly weave together a necklace of ossicles for the black woman so he could fuck her with heightened frenzy. He'd made suggestions along this line to Lynne. Laughing, showing his teeth, the bastard. But was he joking?

The student has just knocked at the bedroom door. She recognizes his discreet, polite timbre. He comes in, sees the letter. No attempt to grab hold of the pages, to betray. He's respectful. As if he were biding his time, awaiting the hour of justice, for a really clear, honest dialogue. He knows nothing of love's voracious glory. A fanatic for peaceful solutions, a maniac in his own way, sick with lies. With his gentle, myopic face, a sheep lost in thought. How can he love this way, without anger, without venom? Taking the worst snubs; after the sadistic reporter, the dyke . . . Never tires of playing the saint. He returns calmly. Self-assured deep down. Without ever doubting his convictions. Lynne prefers cowards, depraved creatures with fear-racked eyes. Their fright intoxicates her, their boldness, and as indirect consequence, their defiance. The guy standing before her is a submissive dog. Noble on all occasions. Perfect. A-Okay. With his pecker and its well rubberized glans. His neatly wiped ass. Simon also stank of the previous night's sperm. Paloma too got drunk on aggressive scents: armpits, dirty holes. This guy's all detergent. So she says to him: "I got a love letter. Full of lightning bolts and filth . . . from Paloma, one terrific slut, an Amazon who sets me on fire. A real tyrannical letter, spellbinding. Packed with poisons, a constellated swamp."

And he shoulders this, accepts it fully. Without ever losing his composure. He understands, explains to himself. A psychologist to the point of impotence, offers the other cheek, his whole body, to the blows. Maybe he likes it, savors the details that she deals out, polishes, quoting Paloma's sentences, her rhythms, the splendid smutty, rotten carryings-on. Lynne would go so far as to masturbate right in front of him on the bed. To get even for everything, to celebrate her new life. Because the student is jarring, knocks loose a vestige of shame, of scruple within her. When all is said, he treats her like a spacey kid, an out-of-control animal, a maid incapable of choosing her own destiny. She shouts at him to get the hell out, she cackles, swears, pulls up her skirt, thumbs her cunt at him. Want more? Want a little more, cuckold, cretin! He's surprised all the same. A little pale. If he spoke, he'd stutter. Touché! . . . Wobbling. No longer up to it. He can't really see how to get back on his feet anymore. Discouraged in his apostolic Boy Scouting. Face mushy. She laughs, wriggles, thumbing her crotch, adding a few comical flourishes. She bursts out laughing. Paloma! Paloma! Paloma! They're both going to take off for Gibraltar! To Gibraltar! She wonders why she blurted out that word, uttered that desire. She doesn't know a thing about Gibraltar other than its bluish calumet sound, a boulder rising above a pure sea with syllables of sculpted marble, of rare animal Africa, of a great exotic flower garden. Giraffe's neck. A mauve flight of turtledoves. Gibraltar makes her come like a large standard planted on a paradisiacal peak.

Myriam leads Simon into landscapes far removed from well-trod paths. She penetrates the skein of the hills with a capricious genius. She zigzags through the bushes, the chaoses. She plays with the world's order, shifts direction with the cosmos. Myriam is cheerful today. She's so secretive, turned inward toward an intimate preoccupation, pursuing a maze of reveries unknown to Simon, suddenly bursting free in mischievous leaps. Myriam's cheerfulness on this particular afternoon, these ludicrous pranks catch him unprepared. Maybe she's been drinking. She's smashed on the firewater of the caves, that alcohol seeping from the centuries. A sloshed black woman. She's going to speak, reveal everything, her real dwelling. Tell all. The alibi of skeletons. I don't give a damn about those grandpas with undershot jaws, here's why I've come. Truth of Cameroon. She trots on the rock, a chamois . . .

And soon, in the heart of this arid region, between two slopes, there opens a very green valley. A torrent gushes from the mountain, a cool profuse waterfall, moistening the earth, flooding the rocks, feeding grass, moss and flowers. A thick layer of green carpets the banks. Rushes, reeds sway amid the ponds where moorhens dart about. This is the spot where Myriam takes her vacation. Simon's very surprised. He thought that he himself had meticulously crisscrossed the landscape. Inspecting, combing, that's just what his profession of voyeur and sleuth is all about. But he'd missed this site cleverly tricked up, an emerald cache reserved for Myriam. She came here to draw for her pleasure. Her cave work imposed an inordinate rigor upon her. There were times she almost suffocated in her task, condemned to defining the pithecanthropi, to reproducing their supposed appearance from their bones. Her hampered freedom suffered from respecting to the letter the researchers' constructions. Certainly, she felt great moments of happiness when she succeeded in capturing an expression, their faces clouded with humanity. She experienced a saintliness of sorts in so fashioning the ancestors. But a whole region of her nature found no outlet in this enslavement to the truth. So she came into the valley, with not only her pencils, her charcoal crayons, her large sheets of paper, but also tubes of paint, a palette, rags, much vaster sketches that freely brought visions to birth.

They picnicked at the edge of the waterfall. Emerging from the soil's crust like some living conveyor belt, with somersaulting loins, corkscrews, ribbons of pureness. Simon imagined the underground sheets feeding the spring. Maybe caves and galleries one hundred yards down. A Jules Vernian setting of crypts, stalagmite cathedrals where islands were anchored in pools. All the accumulated waters, hoarded riches, buried in the desert, in the pocket of gloom. Tears of the future. A deft fistula pierced the deposits, climbed through the sediments. On the surface, this hole in the rock. And

Myriam drank with her fleshy mouth. A shell of heavy lips. She breathed in the spring, gurgling against her mother-of-pearl teeth. Siren spewing her stream. He all but saw the black woman encrusted in the stone slick and brilliant as bronze. Her female sides and face fused with matter. And the funneled water gushed from her petrified body, her fat, polished lips flinging out the liquid prick. For Myriam was sculptural, shared something in the nature of statuary, the race of caryatids arched in the broad sunshine, Neptunean telamones in pagan temples.

She stretched out in the stream. The current slipped along her backbone, reversing flow along the arc of her buttocks. Her head alone emerged. She closed her eyes with an expression of devotion. Sheathed in this jelly of water. She warmed herself afterwards in the sunlight, ate and drank plentifully. A snake now, a viper writhing in pleasure. Glossy with fire. She ran through the dense grass which she yanked up in tufts, chewing the bitter stems. The sap spreading under her tongue filled her with a voluptuous sensation. She squatted, defied him, crude, vulgar, burped out a mince of macerated twigs, asked him to taste. He had adopted an attitude of smiling nonchalance. But he didn't manage to get in tune with her dangerous joy, at times bordering on anger, murderous provocation. She was taking revenge for something. As if cackling, sinking in her teeth, exulting. She might well have grabbed hold of the great metal flow of the stream and twisted it between her strong hands, suddenly snapping off its neck! Revenging herself upon cowards, spineless beings, the excavation crew, villages, bikers, Simon. Lukewarm craven souls, one and all. So Simon surmised. He'd gathered a long while ago that she had taken a risk, was gambling with the devil.

Then upon a grass-encircled slab she spread out a broad section of drawing paper and began sketching outlines and features haphazardly, a confusion of forms, deletions, disheveled manes, her strokes scoffing at rules. In one swoop she composed raging whirlwinds, wild galactic chicaneries, dancing, melding with other spirals. Next Simon saw animal silhouettes emerging, rudimentary dragons, salamanders and gorillas embedded within each other. She spun out monstrous combinations, the pithecanthropus sheathed in reptilian scales. A goat, snared up with a hyena's muzzle. Wolf and lamb welded in one flesh. Horned men with flower-faces, or fins, Cartesian divers. She endowed her bestiary with fantastic sex organs like conger eels, gluttonous boas. Complete autonomous penises endowed with eyes and paws. Personified pricks. Hairy vulvas with sky-blue eyes. Beaked breasts. Buttocks with ears, asses split wide in laughter. She seized the paint tubes, pinching their bellies. Sticky turds oozed out, slinking along, in every color, a vivid array glutting the sketches. Soon she overspilled the boundaries of the paper, began to mottle the boulder itself with huge claws, lubricious masturbators spurting quarts of semen. A thousand tiny beings could be spotted in the torrent of sperm: bear cubs, baby elephants, dwarves and giants, dolls and giraffes, but objects as well, pendulums, radio sets, lilliputian automobiles, computers and satellites. On the limestone she devises centaurs shitting avalanches of shrubs, cottages, trim cumulous clouds, adorable sparrows and mystical cherubs, other creatures vomiting moons, stars, planets, miniature cathedrals, and shrunken, ravishing towers of Babel. And superb females, wasp-waisted Tarzanas and sultanas in panties, spitting from their enormous nipples a confusion of animals, machines, a jumble of statuettes, plants, books, minerals, cocks, cunts, eyeglasses, oysters, and dozens of eggs. Myriam would have daubed the mountains, embroidered the sky with a pandemonium of visions. She would have cut the clouds into wildly silly demons and panicky menageries.

Then she asked Simon to grab the brushes and paint his dreams and fears on her body. Simon, still not caught up in the momentum, apologized for his awkwardness. She kissed him with her greedy mouth, searched him with her tongue. She sucked in, aspirated him. My dear Simon, how sad you make me, you freeze up . . . I'm going to revive you, forge you, create you. I'll transform you into a divine rascal, a transfixed sorcerer, a cosmic athlete. With the thick lock of the brush she tattooed him with signs: mountains, cities, igloos, tepees, factories, submarines with sails and electronic pedals. And Simon, little by little, filched her instrument to paint in turn the big black body of the woman. He gouached her ass, riddled with mad gardens, ebony crescents, sowing oases over her buttocks, her basalt shoulders, smearing her breasts with vermilion, planting along her side a volcano exploding with palm trees whose crater, a rectangle as small as a playing card, disgorged an ocean rigged out with a beach, replete with bathers, posed terrorists, and helicopters crammed with cavemen in cop costumes.

The excremental reek of the rags sticky with paint, heavy with oil and stains, permeated the valley. Myriam emptied tubes into the stream, which spewed up russet, red lead, ultramarine, sienna plumes. She slopped the backs of trees, speckled the loose stones like ladybugs, would have tamed the birds of prey to coat them in gold-yellow. People would have spotted these prophetic eagles with gold nugget beaks hovering over Aguilar.

Finally she rolled with Simon in the rock havoc. The mud of colors was their bower of love. Sioux-painted sex organs. Their asses ridged with scarlet, buttered with periwinkle blue, yellow-hued like Van Gogh haystacks. The valley was incoherent with their brawl and cries. The White Man and the Black Woman interlaced at the water's edge presented an amalgam of star-sprinkled salmon, of obsidian seal, of condor studded with fireflies, of rainbow rams, of dragon with emerald eyes, of fox feathered with jewel droppings, urine, the milt and suints of a Noah's palette.

Have a good time, my darlings, have your fun. Orgy, wallowing in your shit and turbulent sperm. Have fun . . . I'm weaving, ratifying, collecting, browsing on births, bits of biography in Aurèle's light. Jumble together. Misspend your youth. I'm distinguishing, separating, lining up my pawns, my cards, the figurines of the world. A scale model of Aguilar down to the last micron. Splash about in your foul stew. Reek of sex, magma of crap. Plunge, lose your heads over this hodgepodge. Go back to the sludge, the slimy alluvium. I'm drying, hardening, carving the boxwood of the ages while sipping my sugared tea . . . They're out there! I know it, out in some grassy hole, blinding themselves, cicadas jackhammering, madly popping with passion. Lovers, city couples, shopkeepers on a binge, tourists, teenagers on vacation, raving Madame Bovarys, wildly dreaming damsels, ladykilling old fogies, defrocked priests, backstage trade unionists, lady teachers partial to green fruit, razor-sharp sex maniacs and defeated politicians . . . all out in the scrub knocking about. Noon, king of summers . . . Night is coming on, it always ends up by falling. Shadow and cold. Rout! Get your duds together! Wipe yourself off. Pick the twigs from your hair. Redo your pleats, mess of rumpled creatures. How sly you look. The party's over. Bitter herd of disappointments. Without frenzy, I've foreseen it all. My soliloquy is lucid. I see you racing out into the road. You're all passing in front of my house. A stampede of jalopies in heat. Lady hairdressers, secretaries and bosses, salesgirls and department managers. I recognize you. Ridiculous and pomaded. Two-bit lustful and sentimental souls. Latins, Germans. Come night, you pass again, debacle, Waterloo, powdering your cheeks, creaming over the red blotches, the stigmata that beards have rubbed in. Ugly, faded freshness. Shameful, furtive, I know you. The road is empty now. Clean. Asphalt. Snow of silence. I'm going to go to bed after the news. For a half hour I'll recapitulate the day to amuse my memory. All is in order. The horses in the stable. I'm going to sleep. My lofts full of wheat. My cellar crammed with archives. I'm beautiful, oh galaxies. The mountain wind rocks my house. I hear the bats and the pure springs gurgling. I, Agathe.

Irresistibly attracted by these lonely expanses, Simon has begun walking again. Equipped with binoculars and, hitched to his belt, the goatskin, quivering with icy water. He advances into the scree, the wadis, the ravines, the blade-sharp lace of rocks protruding in spots like knives. The awesome gusts blowing from the mountains, the brutal storms. The razor of the sun whittles the rockscape with weasellike incisors. The fractured blue sky whistles, caught by the hook of the arêtes. And then, always, he sees the circaetus circling in the sunlight. The sacred vultures, buzzards. Their wings are transparent at the summit of the sky. They hover, revolve. Imponderable and golden. Simon feels vaguely lyrical as he contemplates them. He likes their violence, their implacable gaze. The frenzy of their beaks rending prey. Bits of stone marten or snake pummeled by the frantic bird. That neck, shaking and perforating muscles, skinning, reveling in the sweet scent of death. That concentration of strength, ire. Lucidly the bird disembowels. Its plumage quivers. And then it takes flight, forgets this feast of innards fought over by flies and worms. It's no more than a feeble shaving. A sign. This spiritual ideogram sums up the ferocity of birds of prey. Simon delights in thinking that these birds are following, keeping watch on him. Killed by the terrorist on a gravel bed, the traveler would expose his remains to nature. A more enviable fate than rotting underground. How he despises those nocturnal tombs. Dank boxes where meat ferments, misshapen, comical. The merit of the cave is that it shrinks to the size of fetuses and grains what's left of the pithecanthropi. The solar rodent understood Simon's true mission . . . He hasn't come to do research on the first men. That's not his kind of work, squeezing out a successful interview with hopes of discovering the killer. No, he's eyeing and tracking him with other goals in mind. But the terrorist saw Simon, as soon as he entered the desert. He snickered while trailing the foolish innocent, the hunter hunted, the tricked sleuth . . . Then, in a defile, he lodged a bullet in the bastard's head. Simon punished, what delight! Delivered from evil and time, spread-eagled on the rocks, awaiting the birds. A golden screw, letters from the sky diving and metamorphosing into devouring animals, wingspans like furious sentences. Bursts of fury, quarrels. They riddle the soft beggar's pouch of his body and tug at his balls and throat. Drink in his oozings. The insects and aridity will cure the remaining shreds. In the end he'll be as pure as their wings. As clean on the stones as the birds up above on the beach of sky. He walks. He knows the landscape has surprises in store for him. The shock of the green valley, Myriam's paradise. He could have foreseen anything but that orgiastic lawn, the insatiable waterfall, the overflowing colors and obscene matter. Undercover shack and cesspool. For Myriam, an equator worthy of her. Tufted pubis, musk, shit. Dense crotch curls. Other secrets are hidden in the heart of the setting. He knows the gorges and caves. Spaces already queer, shaped like cavities, galleries. The shell of the soil is gashed with orifices, faults. You enter the mountain. Then all is cold, black, horrible, so remote from the sun. The other world, the lair of troglodytes and dragons, the cradle of the pithecanthropi. He doesn't know why this word seizes him so deliriously, wide-eyed stare of infantile curiosity. Abruptly spellbound, reduced to the level of hypnosis and childhood. *Pithecanthropi* is more archaic, barbarous, far more bestial than *prehistoric* or

*Neanderthal.* Bestial? Not quite. The point is precisely that they've left the animal state behind but not yet entered into the boredom, the harmony of Mankind. *Pithecanthropus* is rugged. It smells of rocky terrain, torso trunks, the caverns watched over by bears. How can this be expressed, this wonder of a shaggy world, still wet from the genesis? Primeval forests. Backbones of gnarled crests. Water trickles through the moss, blood under the fur. The lion lies in wait for that grumbling novice, man. Simon would like to see them once again... The scene under the heap of the ages, under the arc of sky and rock. At times, around steep slopes, in places where copses cling, where crows nest in Gothic limestone, there hovers an indescribable savagery. Simon gazes, admires, his soul ravaged with superstitions. Eagerly he spots the hump of a bald mountain crowned lower down by shrubs and pine forests. The pithecanthropus is possible. He appears, hunts... The lynx creeps along the vertebrae of the boulder. A stand of beech conceals man and beast. They drink from the same spring. The land is said to have been greener. Savannas flourished where now stone skulls raise their hooked domes.

Simon removes his shirt, his torso burns. Religiously he lowers himself to the ground, dips his hand into the dust strewn with hard insects, thorns and flint shards. He powders his body with the earth's ashes. Then the sun bakes him until his skin hardens like a lizard's scales! Knight of sand, he'll confront the other, the orphan, the errant, the wolf and rebel. The guy who opted for carnage. Vocation of horror. Does Agathe know where he comes from, has she pieced together newspaper fragments to recreate the evidence of a native land? He adopted as his own the revolt of Spanish Basques. But is he a simple mercenary, condottiere of one cause among others, or a fanatic of a unique territory, a unique history? A bandit disguised as a partisan? What is he, this Cro-Magnon lying low in the desert? Would Simon prefer him to be an ardent Cathar, a puritan faithful to his country, or a pirate with no homeland, a carnivorous loner? He hesitates between the two legends. But both no doubt fuse in the runaway's heart. By means of attacks, hatreds, vengeances, a new man is forged, hardened, scabby and sublime. The myth of a free country is the springboard for a savage destiny. The cause falls by the wayside as he heads toward fulfillment. So, the terrorist is out there, in the steep faults, craters, rainless ruts. He's afraid, he desires. He no longer knows why he's condemned to so much solitude. He, a recalcitrant soul, moved to pity over his own fate. He awaits a woman, gentleness. Strange bells chime in those cathedrals chiseled by the wind. He oscillates between hermit and beast. He learns to carve rocks, to light fires by rubbing a stick in a mortise. He goes mad, has visions, sees herds, a stream, musk oxen, Mosbach horses. The ark is full. They stream past, bellow. An opulent swarm. They're beautiful, fat and timid. Milk-laden udders, swollen testicles. Maybe they're migrating. With their horns, triumphal headdresses, their floating withers. The young followed by wild beasts. Old, sick animals that Etruscan wolves hunt down and dismember. He sees this epoch, the gorges teeming with rumps, stomachs, chests. This living corral. He tells himself he's wrong. He hits his head. Basque, Spanish, French, Palestinian, Irish Catholic, Apache or Peul, what difference does it make! The earth obsesses him, its millennial architectures, its telluric turmoil, rushing rivers, patient erosions, glacial eras, warming periods, worn-down platforms, forests, cave-ins, volcanoes. Fire, frost. Boring, folding, filing, bosoms embossed with fertility. Plants pullulate, become scarce. Brushes, ergs . . . Vines of thistles. He doubts. He becomes enamored of a vaster belief. He prays to matter, venerates the rocks. He would like for the birds of prey to come land in his heart. He'd like to meet the lynx, stroke its glossy flank, play with its fangs. Perhaps his thoughts are on them. It's been said that some five hundred thousand-year-old skeletons have been discovered in the region. A cave contained their bones, long before the age of fire, funeral rites, flowers placed on the breasts of the dead. Men without hearth . . . nor law, corpse-eaters. The first men, consequently the most pure, the true tender ones, the outcasts. Those who bear the brunt of evolution. Those whom the gods send to the slaughter, sentence to average lifespans of twenty-one years. Groping, vacillating beings, pawns of a risky plan, a makeshift, murderous stonecraft. They advance. They attempt. Digest, copulate. Their molecules, their genes evolve, weave together, mutate secretly, branch out, an obscure intelligence, a trail blazed with glimmers, accidents, tropisms, a panic whirlwind active deep in their skulls, in the pulsing of their organs and breaths. The terrorist is scared. His convictions stagger. Now he's interested in geography, paleontology. Frozen in meditation for hours on end. He'd like to know the name of the constellations. A thought that's never occurred to him before. Besides the Big and Little Dipper, all the rest eludes him, seedbeds, wakes, perfect geometries, mists, nebulas and galaxies. Shimmering trapezoids and swarms. Summer nights, what else to do but contemplate this great astral screen? Coitus of suns, fired with comets. The blue-tinted abyss . . . He from his hole listens to the Word of the wind. Biblical crap, smooth talk, mystic gossip hounds him, thingamajigs from the Flood and before. Lucretius, Hesiod. A fresco of atoms, swell of clay, imprint of the gods and ferns. He'd like to write, to know how to. A poem perhaps, inscribe words in stone or, with ocher dipped in sap, paint sky and herds upon the walls of his lair.

Simon advances, possessed by a new certainty. This time he'll trap the man. He'll subjugate the killer. Insects and sand, rock shells. Thistle spikes. He'd like to see strewn at his feet large skeletons of animals dead of hunger and thirst. Caravans or beasts migrating toward improbable waters. Thoraxes clinging to the emptiness in their cage of vertebrae. Weird skulls of elephants and bison. Long jaws of fossil horses. Hideous and scoured. A desiccated carnage. There, on the path, on the way to the springs. Croaked, comical. Road markers, milestones, figures. A writing in bone. The earth hardens, an ashen hue. And there, in the scorch-mark, he spotted the footsteps. Clear, well demarcated in the less powdery soil. Bare human feet... the footsteps of the terrorist or the hermit, the prospector... of some pagan god that fed on scorpions and flint shards. The first steps of man. His walk and his presence. There, biting into porous matter. No other tracks but those steps. A ghost slinks through the sands. Pithecanthropus feet, vestiges of the first hunters. A large, divine, human-footed sparrow hawk has hopped through these deserts. An amalgam of lynx and ape-man. A sphinx . . . the footsteps abruptly born, marking regular intervals, then dissolving. Simon retraces the same steps, falls into the passersby's stride. He follows in the wake of the killer, the god, the hybrid, the monster, the saint or old prospector and pithecanthropus. But he knows he's dealing with the terrorist. He takes a drink from the goatskin gourd. An urge to sprinkle the footsteps, water this furrow to make sprout the stump of an ankle, the hump of a calf, to make a man grow like a plant from the seed of his tracks. He walks beyond the footsteps, behind an absinthe bush, into a flowering of needles and yellow blossoms. He sees moving in the opposite direction a scattering of other steps, more slender, supple. Exquisite in the silica crust. No shepherd or nomad she-wolf. Female footsteps off to meet a man. Female sphinx, Lilith, fleet prophetess. She. Accomplice, traitor in the bandit's service. She brings him water, cheese and bread. She feeds the escapee. She soothes his sexual heat. She transmits messages and balm, courage. Their rugged, sand-hardened mouths moisten each other's. She pours felicitous saliva into the cursed creature's throat. She tells him the news of the cities, the revolutions of men, changing religions, crimes, enemy camps, wars, oaths. He mounts her after she's said her full. She gives him her sex and the odor of her rump. Simon surmises this. Does Agathe know? . . . A male ploy, a maneuver of lovers and brigands. Their footsteps, covered, uncovered by the wind's fluid reading. The wind, blond . . . disguising and unmasking, making the footsteps murmur. They came here, whispered, exchanged the truth. Then separated in anguish and happiness. Simon would like to trace a large mystic perimeter around the male and female steps. Approach forbidden. Taboo to all eyes. Here are intermingled the footsteps of wild man and friendly woman. Not for reading, do not open the book. The conviction steers him. The woman has taken the killer's hand. The wind turns the pages and uncovers the underlying texts, baring other footsteps upon each layer of sand, other meetings, other exchanges. A feast of shared game, pits of sucked berries, cooled embers from some secret hearth, the wind lies down upon this evidence.

Simon advances . . . Steered by the conviction. A flash of sunlight both hurts and guides him. He climbs a hillock crested with cork oak. At the foot, in a basin, the naked terrorist is hunting, rifle in arm. He's taking aim at a very pure sparrow hawk. The struck bird of prey spirals groundward. The man continues along his path holding the bird with splayed wings in one hand and his weapon in the other. And Simon follows him, eyes peeled, bounding behind boulders, posting himself behind shrubs. The slightest pebble set rolling will betray the follower. Perhaps the killer knows that he's being observed. He's leading Simon off into some gully. There, between the stone walls, he'll sacrifice the traitor. But Simon is bursting with light-hearted vigilance. The long wings of the bird graze the sand's surface. Blood drips from the head. Flies flit around the feathery throat. The man stoops a moment, drinks the bird of prey's blood. The wine trickles down into his throat. Sap of a killer hawk. Orgiastic, the terrorist looms up in the sunlight, the bird's wings swivel around his loins. The naked man appears bristling all over with drunkenness. His back, weaponed with feathers, an incensed Icarus. Then he sets out walking again. The blood-drained bird bounces against the pirate's black thigh. In a caress of agony the beast's neck crawls against his skin. Everywhere there are other birds' cries. Half-starved buzzards and migratory circaetus. Nature out here is subject to unpredictable excesses: bickering of beasts, tom-toms of storms, squealing of foxes, murders of the oviparous. The sum total ebbs back into the peace of limestone and sand. The scarabs and rodents torture the belly of a dying lizard. The gold scarab shell is radiant in the sunlight, the reptile's green skin gleams. The man returns to his lair. Simon stretched out atop a mound; with his binoculars he can follow him across the long, narrow valley. The man has entered the bushes: at the base of a rocky wall he disappears. Everywhere tenacious, wooly arbutus nestle in vesicles of limestone. Simon has spotted the crucial place. A cave must open up somewhere behind the layer of thorns. He has to wait for the man to leave. Simon takes shelter on his perch behind a belly of rock protected by a patch of shadow. Sand and ants. A grey skinny root writhes under his feet. He drinks, his binoculars glimmer, burning hot. Simon listens to a screeching from the mountains. Unable to identify the call. He imagines some sort of fish of the gorges whose mouth emerges from an icy black gulf. Nothing more. Simon is flooded with images. He likes the apparitions of animals. The signals of violence. This climate of war reigning out in the scrub. These lookouts, screechings. Pointed like a knife, the water keeps watch in the corolla of the rock. The streams slit open their trout. And the fish bleed on the schist tableland. A weasel arrives to hack into their red gills. Simon knows that his wait will be long. The man has to eat the bird in his hideout. He rests. Curled up, meditative, stroking the sparrow hawk's severed wings. Simon dozes. An intuition commands him to sleep. Time is suspended. It's a good feeling to know the other man's trapped in his cavern. The sun has moved. The stone thumps like a heart. It's the silence, an immense calm intermittently tautened by a splinter of wind, a constriction of stones. And what is the other one up to? He's pulled the bird's wings over his torso. He ought to be caught by surprise in his shaman costume. Uniformed cops, a ludicrous squadron capturing this beautiful winged sorcerer reclining in the night of the cave. He'd jump to his feet and spread his wings, his Osiris beak would frighten the city police. Simon falls asleep, the sun sees everything, navigates a gold-laden galley. The hills are black slaves.

At nightfall the terrorist emerged from the bushes. He walks quickly, heading straight eastward. To all appearances it's not to do any hunting. Maybe to drink from a particular spring? Simon follows him with his binoculars. He disappears behind a circle of pines. Then the journalist draws near and searches the passages. Behind a bar of laburnum, the cave hole is visible. Fascinated, Simon slips into the sanctuary. A coolness falls upon his shoulders. He shivers. His eyes must grow accustomed before making out bone fragments, remnants of game, a large fish's skeleton, a bird's wingspan. A revolver, a hatchet, a dagger, dynamite charges, a shovel, two bowls, a sleeping bag, a flashlight, a bundle of paper on a rock, a studded belt, a preposterous, brand-new bathing suit, matches, rope. All strewn about, jumbled together. The terrorist calculates his murders but doesn't keep house. The cave is shallow and low-ceilinged. A cavity, a manger . . . Shelter from the wind, storms. In a small bag Simon discovers a roll of five hundred franc notes. A tidy sum. That's where he's waiting . . . nights, days, except for cautious excursions, quick hunts. On a slab, sheets of paper are spread out, two pens. A few pages of writing whose language eludes Simon. In the bundle of other paper, Simon digs up newspaper clippings about the sunlight attack. Simon holds proof of the Basque terrorist's identity. In the photos his skinny escapee's face can be seen, his beard, his black eyes. Full-face and profile. The man underscored certain sentences in red ballpoint. Horrible details about the victims, the massacre of innocents. With photos of the most typical martyrs as well. Those who ought not to have been there on that famous day. Swedish fiancés. Little twin girls. Others . . . Bits of biography, tricks of destiny, irony charred like black stumps. This is the terrorist's literature, his press clippings, his memories, an album of macabre images. In his eyes these pieces may merely go to make up necessary documents. He preserves them unsadistically, with no voluptuous delight. Does he experience only remorse? This money, these weapons, these faces of death: a hostile booty. He daubed a cave wall with animal frescoes. Bison, buffalo, elephant winding through a broad grassy plain with scarves of stars in the sky intermingled with huge suns. He used blood, clay, sap to compose this daylight vision. An unschooled painter, rustic genius. He conceals immemorial hunts in his cave. The animals possess cosmic paunches. They seem pregnant with round, proliferating worlds and endless herds. In such a way he distracts himself, staves off his hunger. He found himself a hobby, his own personal Sistine Chapel . . . these elephants, these horses bearing heavenly bodies with ape-men in their wake. Every cave conceals a movie screen. The darkness becomes a mirror. A hole transformed into a gaze. He's surmised this, the assassin himself. He's moved from his political cause to this lavish bestiary. He's regressed, as you might say. Simon has a fit of giggling. His indiscretion both frightens and excites him. Stumbling upon him by surprise, the terrorist's only recourse would be to kill him. Easier said than done. Simon's got plenty to fall back on. Secret arguments. He knows this. He's attracted by the wanderer's litter. He opens it wide. It gives off a powerful odor of grime and sweat mingled with a different aroma, a familiar scent . . . more sugary. Simon dreams a long while. There's no more time for reflection. This cradle of smells lulls him. So the woman entered this cave to join her body to the murderer's. The amazon knows no fear! The heap of corpses on the beach didn't dull her lust. Perhaps it adds an extra touch of spice. This rock-edge, these bones, this bird's skeleton form cynical nuptial furnishings. A militant like him, a conspirator, an accomplice to the very end . . . in life, in death. Simon giggles away. Shoulders shaking madly. How beautiful to believe and spill blood to celebrate such a thing. A passionate partisan of destiny. Two people who know where they're going. Tenacious craftsmen, happily sharing the same religion. They liberate the people. An obsession that's very human, very well viewed by history. A good way of making your mark on passing time. The Basques will be Basque, the crucial thing is to be what you are and to stick to it . . . Simon would like to be Basque, Irish Catholic, a black from South Africa, even Corsican or Breton, even . . . He drew his herds in a moment of depression, a puerile impulse. Unless he hopes to advance into the Promised Land, the land of plenty crammed with buffalo bellies. Canaan in every direction. El Dorado within striking range of a plastic explosive. The beautiful girl came into the cave for a snooze upon the criminal's torso. She left behind the odor of her body. A seal of gold sweat. She'll be Basque like him. Both free at last, reigning over a happy people, cultivating their land, trading their goods, multiplying, offering the world their humble example of civil peace and progress. Simon giggles. Now here's an idea: swiping the large fish bone to give the terrorist something to think about. But where did that fish bone of mine get to? . . . Simon trembles. In the grip of fever, a fit of delirium. He's got to clear out if he doesn't want to faint on the spot from exhaustion. He looks at the cave one last time. This wild pause in the man's life. A waiting-lair. A meditation-trap. Simon flees the night. But he's forgotten his binoculars.

Today, Sunday, the blaze is doing fine, just devoured three pine forests, two campers, one house, eight foxes, a dozen hares, three wild boars, one wild-cat, one owl and its offspring, plus a few lovely acres of vineyards. The blaze puffs up its torso, spits its flames, beats its drums, shimmering with biceps. It's a handsome fire, young and greedy, strapping. Merry and murderous. Totally amoral. Galloping along. Sticking out its tongue at six companies of firemen, guys from Perpignan, reinforcements from far off. The Canadairs take over from one another to no purpose. The fire's got balls full of sparks and deafening lungs. It brandishes its pricks like an innumerable Shiva. A touch of the show-off and stuntman, braying, gobbling up hills, transforming small brooks into steam, frying up trout and eels. A rolling barbecue with a giant's appetite. It likes giving a show. Especially Sundays after Mass. Whole families of bumpkins turn up by the cartload. They line up on the peaks, ridges, at the end of valleys to contemplate this jubilant acrobat. They compare it to the great fires of history. This is the biggest. In living memory. The elderly, informed by passersby, swear that this one here breaks all apocalypse records. They ask for details, weigh and compare them with the phenomenal blaze right after the war that had encircled a whole village and roasted seven old men. This fire here could go one better. Off to a stronger start. Numerous widespread seats, solid, impetuous and branching out. Its bases superior to all the others. A champ of the third millennia. All the vices, plagues, decadences of the modern world feed its furnace. A boundless cancer. The old men of the bench both admire and curse it. It's especially the grandchildren who come galloping in troops to inform the old hands: how the blaze carries on, spinning its windmills, devilish curvets, how it juggles like a corsair attacking galleons! Tiptoeing twirls and tomfoolery. A real sense of humor, but worst of all, inexhaustible. The kids adore the bean-pole with the fiery mane. They hope he'll kill everybody but them and the old men who are ugly but nice. Most of all the school will go under, maybe parents along with it, but this is open for discussion. The old men tell about fires, mix them up, those from before, from their grandparents' days, from the age of kings, fires which—such magic!—even came from the sea, crossed the ocean in galleys, passing from one continent to the other . . . in legends . . . blazes born spontaneously in the night of the caves. They stick their sweet lion-cub faces out of the hole, swiftly change into raging beasts, insane hordes. Semidivine blazes crossing the sky in chariots of sunlight, swooping upon towns like the Huns, bronze-armored Attilas all acrackle.

They brought their uncles and aunts, cousins, elders, in small groups or processions. Mayors in the lead, regional councillors, a prefect, officials, men in ribbons and medals, archdukes and grunts from the trenches. Everybody kept at a good distance as a safety precaution. The orders are strict. Agathe, equipped with a telescope, arrived in Hippolyte's car. One and all lament, moved to pity by the ruined farmers, carbonized campers, drawing intense delight from the marvelous disaster. The firemen's trucks stream along the road as in wartime, a concert of sirens sowing anguish and elation. Great events are being hatched out toward Tuchan, Maury. The fall of a village is announced, an exodus of peasants and animals. The fellow attacks, traps the enemy in a pincer move, flares up, wreaks an Austerlitz.

An entire campground went up. A headlong flight of all races. Sodom and Gomorrah. Another Babel . . . People from Holland, Hermany, Hengland Horrified and Howling, wholly tanned, precooked—the people who sought out hot vacation weather got their wildest dreams fulfilled! Sue, who is part of the group of anxious people, ogles the handsome young men, half-naked and terrorized, fleeing along the road whose tar is fermenting. Delicious aroma of simmering, the blond boys from cities in Sweden and Norway naked, with enormous stiltlike legs, at age twelve or thirteen giants already, their sisters naked, moving along the road with their belongings, a few cars cause traffic jams, stands of very handsome Danes, gentle-looking despite the fear, a crop of asparagus nourished by good milk, fresh fruit, greens . . . Young, shy peckers, fleeing, fleeing, from forests and lakes, passing in front of that sucker Sue biting her lips . . . And little stems of breasts jiggle on the girls' swanlike torsos, slender Valkyries, saplings . . . Some are ugly all the same, thinks Agathe, big beer drinkers, roasted bellies, baked like Buddhas. Were handsomer during the war when they had the souls of invaders. Back then, tall, slim, and savage, booted and guttural. The whole female population went quivery all over, even the men got effeminate at the mere sound of the martial din. Their descendants got bogged down in profit and a vacationing civilization. Awfully ugly, looking like overgrown babies, completely bald, cowlike tits, flabby paunches, fleeing on short stumps, fleeing, pushing their broken-down cars, the children pushing their obese parents. Ambulances and firemen transporting peoples, races, and continents between vineyards and Cathar castles.

Agathe can't take everything in with a glance. This superabundant reality in motion fascinates but disturbs her. She delights in a thousand emotions, powerful perceptions, but her demand for order and classification remains unsatisfied. So many treasures are unfurling past that need to be told separately, named, labeled, so many men who need to be questioned about their country of origin, their province, their family, their profession and the legends of their land, the myths of their race. A great world craving tortures

Agathe. She experiences this divine curiosity that intermittently threatens the structures of her memory. She'd like to explode these limits, open up her barns and smash her granaries, enlarge her treasure chests in order to welcome the universe and the infinite. But then a dizzy spell seizes her. She takes measure of what she's losing, these meticulous archival perimeters, this perfect mosaic where each narrowly circumscribed fragment fits into the following with an implacable logic. She'd like to quest for the adventures of totality, of the cosmos—why not?—open up, fling wider her arms, surrender to a limitless lust. She's too old, too puny. She makes do with looking at this flood of naked, dazed tourists, gesticulating in their clownish fear while the flames dance on the hilltops. The fire greets, smokes out, plumes, multiplies, clicks its spurs, rears up, streaming with embers and bitten by desire. The police and firemen's helicopters coursed above these Luciferian spells and pirouettes. Large ruby breaches stab the earth, rippling black suint. The maniac is caught on film . . . Military strategies are drawn up. Assaults, retreats and pitched battles. Agathe likes war. Through her telescope her eyes are peeled, a small, frail Napoleon, death-cicada with feverish antennae. Her nostrils twitch in the scorching blast, the sulfur gusts, the phosphors, the russets. With the people escaping, the birds, the animals, the rodents, the rapers of shepherdesses and young she-goats, witches, water diviners, the poison mushroom gatherers, the breeders of buzzards and crows, the shepherds, goats and sheep, wolfhounds, the engineers and executives on holiday in their second homes that they must abandon: their beautiful furniture and libraries, rare cherished old-fashioned things, hoarded booty, well-polished copper, staircase of sculpted oak. The fire has a feast, gobbles up millions, dreams, lives, comic utopias. It sings in death. And the field mice, the rats, the hares, the quails, the weasels, the snakes, the crickets flee. The missionaries and colonists, the guys from Amsterdam and Hamburg in their deluxe trailer homes... shrieking, crying, shitting, distraught hordes of kids. And teenagers camping illegally, the resorts all full, battalions of little lads and lassies come from the black cities of the north, decamping with their Boy Scout leaders, their high-powered priests, their female counselors in panties and their spastic nuns. And the flies, ants, tarantulas and garden spiders, unicorns and chimeras, the angels and demons, the roving teachers and paleontologists hunting stones and gold, the evil genies, fairies, djinns, the ladybugs, the maybugs, the fireflies and glowworms, the phoenixes, the fauns and the sylphids, the naiads driven from the waters stark naked, nymphs such as are no longer, thighs taut and pink, Fragonard divinities fleeing from rural boudoirs. What an outcry! Male and female fleeing... cymbals and lightning bolts, tolling horror... Keen Agathe adjusts the eyepiece... peeping, braying, whinnying, bleating, squealing. And the babies blubbering, dehydrated, traumatized by the large eagle of fire, its bitchy claws, its nasty beak, its venom-shot eyes . . . pissing, farting. The whole while the sky is frozen in a miraculous azure as soon as you gain some distance from the arena where the tournament of flames is being fought. A perceptible paradisiacal light from which the fire was perhaps born, where it drew youth and strength, its warbling of a colossal robin redbreast. The thick clouds, the heavy, complicated wreaths were hemmed in by this circle of clear, immobile skies. A vault of eternity swelled beyond the putrid fumes, the soot, toward the abyss of other suns, a sea of invisible blue stars. And frogs, lizards, toads, weasels, grasshoppers, old ladies chased from their cottages, woodcutters from their huts, fishers and poachers, beggars, thieves, stream otters . . . There was some hope that the terrorist would pop up. He would have been immediately recognizable among the others, marked by a special seal, torso tattooed with his victims' names. A magnificent torturer running in front of the fire, displaying his golden scars, jewels of murder and cutthroat's gems. And then they were awaiting the lynx, anxious about the feline. Amid the fleeces of goats, sheep, people thought they spied its sweet, ferociously feline face. Unless the terrorist is clinging to the belly of some big ewe, concealed in the woolly tide. Agathe remembered the ruse, she'd read the major books, the essential sagas. Or disguised as a woman, a Norwegian in braids, a beautiful Gretchen out of Goethe, that's how the wily killer must have dashed past. Or endowed with sparrow hawk wings he might have flown off or . . . made iridescent by Aurèle's light . . . The panic favored substitution and metamorphoses. All it would take is killing a fireman, borrowing his helmet and uniform, tossing his corpse into the flames. Now a helmeted captain, he would have tricked his public. Sue would have lusted after this svelte savage fireman with all her concentrated fury and strident joy, she would have sucked him off to reward him for his bravery during a big thanksgiving ceremony. She would have pumped the prodigious reserves of pure blaze that he breathed in during the battle. Sue the sucker of igneous sperm. Drinking fire, war, glory, Dionysian liquor and sun-nectar. Agathe, black among the ashes, in a halo of black magic, in a gown of soot, but whose eyes blink while piercing the centuries and overloaded parchments, for the ash envelops all with a great shroud of signs as if the Word were supine upon the world, unfurling its immense black wings riddled with language.

At a crossroads the gold prospector stopped his ramshackle cart crammed with utensils out of some Western movie. Sieve, screen, rifle, ax. A recently tamed talking magpie was flitting around the vehicle. The hermit exhibited his coat of mystic grime. Attached to his side he wore the archaic statuette of the Virgin, while under his arm was the big precious book that visitors were allowed to look at but never touch. The fire was threatening the ninth-century church. The hermit fled. However, where the paths intersected he'd come upon the prospector. Sitting, they shared bread and a hunk of hard, smelly cheese . . . The prospector kept a myriad of tiny nuggets in a bag. He showed them to the hermit, reassured by his biblical paraphernalia. The hermit gazed upon the gold without batting an eyelid.

"I drew it out of the springs, filtered from stones, months on end, all alone out in the scrub."

"I'm a man who's filtered the divine, alone, in the cool darkness of the church . . ."

"We're rare solitary souls, the very last of our kind. But we're fleeing. We ought to have died in the gold of the flames."

"The divine fire!"

"I must confess, the loneliness was making me go mad. I had visions, stones turned into nuggets in the sunlight. I saw fish made out of gold swimming in the streams. The lynx sprang around my camp fire. I'm heading back toward the city, I'm going to sell the gold to bankers. Over my tiny transistor I heard that the price of gold is rising."

"You needed a transistor?"

"Oh, now and then it connected me to the world. I haven't got a Virgin or a Father . . . So I'd occasionally betray the silence in order to listen to other people, their worries. But I would go days at a time without listening."

The Virgin stood waiting in the middle of the path beside the secret book. A worn, blue-tinted statuette, an ashen black flecking its veil, with a rigid peasanty look when viewed from behind. For she had her back to the two men.

"You ought to sell them, her and the book. They'd fetch a good price and you'd be able to help out a lot of poverty-stricken people."

"You're antagonizing me!" said the surly hermit. "Such sacrilege!"

"Yes, but it'd help the poor. Where are you going to settle down with those two? Especially since they look so heavy and fragile. You'll get them stolen from you one of these days, it's inevitable. And then you carry them so egotistically, a person feels that they belong just to you, that you've taken them over. That's not very Christian."

"I defend them from impure attacks. That's all. And what do you plan on doing with the profits from your gold?"

"I'm going to buy myself a small fishing boat, maybe something bigger. I'll make a living off my catch."

"You'll always need to forage the waters for treasure. Sieve, net, it's one and the same. Then with the money you've earned, what are you going to do?"

"Pay for the boat's gasoline, its upkeep . . . I want to live in a cottage surrounded by dunes and reeds. Kept very dry by salt and wind."

"Salt! Wind! That's close to God," says the hermit in the tones of a sermonizing monk.

"Yes, and the fish?" added the prospector dubiously.

"Even closer to God, haven't you ever read the sacred texts?"

"So then we're very similar, right? Look at them all running away with their gear while others cut down trees around houses to hamper the flames. They're fighting over their plots of land, their steaks. While we clear off with no fuss and bother. Where are you headed?"

"I'm going to the heart of the city."

"For a hermit . . ."

"At present I want to be a hermit amid crowds. To show them the book and the statue."

"You mustn't tempt them too much, they'll swipe them from you, maybe that's what you're after . . . to be completely destitute."

"No, they'll kneel before them. No one will resist me, look, I'm as strong as a Turk, a Hercules of God, armored with vermin and filth. They'll fall to their knees before my boulderlike corpulence and I'll speak about Her and Him. In the heart of the cities now. The whole time I remained in solitude I stored up an incredible strength, heavy layers of wisdom. Ears will be pricked toward me . . . There's a large modern pagan district now being constructed with banks and offices. A circle of glass towers, Babels of cash and cold in the middle of the old city. It's to that place I want to carry the book and the Virgin. I'll live on alms. I'll be a beggar, a truth-shower. They'll feed me the way pilgrims and saints were fed in bygone days."

"I've been to those districts, that's where I exchange my gold. They won't listen to you, you'll be lumped in with the packs of roving acrobats, jugglers, portrait painters, flute players that put on a show in the concrete squares at the foot of the towers. Those sections of cities are for business and voyeurism. Artifices, grimaces. Everything's phony there, plated, plastered with makeup."

"Right from the start they'll spot what makes me different. The statue will frighten them and the book . . ."

"They'll take you for some old crackpot."

"First, if need be, I'll submit myself to every possible blasphemy, but I'll convince them all, simply by casting my gaze upon them. The visitors at the old church were terrorized by my authority, my gestures, my heavenly despotism."

The two men fell silent. The crackling fire grumbled in the distance, a vast volley of ashes and soot traced a confusion of sentences in the azure. At times a great intense burning sensation made itself felt. Everything dazzled. Suddenly the puffs of smoke were reabsorbed into a supernatural brightness, a mystic menace. They almost expected to see the trees spontaneously explode into flames. They had the impression that wonders of every kind would be theirs to witness. A spell of lightning and light haunted the world. The terrorist was purer than Christ.

"If you put the Virgin's statue in front of the fire, would it stop in its path, brought to a vertiginous halt by the old Christian fairy? That would be beautiful to see: the circle of fire petrified before the Madonna of Ages. Petrified! Huh . . . that's a professional tic. I'd like to turn everything into enormous nuggets. The fire mineralized before the Virgin's gaze. A mountain of fire transformed into gold before the sacred hussy. Now I'd like to see that."

"I don't thirst for such miracles. I want to miraculize the most restive crowds. Those from the towers, the bureaucracies of glass, the champions of trade and numbers. Those are the people I aim to metamorphose."

"You'll fail, they can't tell bluff apart from the real thing. At the very best you'll pass for a serious madman. You could do better, come on. For example, sticking your statue up there in the pithecanthropi's cave. Amid the ancestors' bones she'd find her place. The Ministry of Culture and Research would protect your girlfriend."

"Take it easy with your labels, take it easy . . ." said the hermit with a grumble.

"So the cave doesn't attract you! Yet it attracts those others—whole families at a time, crowds, schools, packed busloads, tourists from all over the world and elsewhere. Who don't give a damn about the Virgin and the book. Who want ancestral skeletons! And not fakes! Shock elephants, cave lions, strapping bison . . . And then (ha! ha!)," the prospector took several dry, breathless laps of laughter—"Ha, ha! They want Man, the first men, none of those Adam-and-Eve knickknacks, your worn-out nonsense, but cavemen, evolved primates, something with a sturdy build, you know, veracious, apes missing craniums, bones, hermits, relics not from saints or bishops but from beavers and Australopithici. And then, hermit, your book and strumpet can find their way into the Grévin Museum! Because what magnetizes everybody from all lands is tibias, thighbones from the very start of things. Polished bleached bone is a benefactor! It fertilizes, oh yes it does! . . . Then instead of ogling the Holy Shroud, kissing Mary's toes, dipping their peckers into holy water, they show up to get a look at the behinds of the beginnings, touch their ash, their splinters, their fragmented molars, sniff the odor of their heats, of their brawls, of their lynx hunts. That's what captivates them, primordial stuff, so old you can't even calculate because it goes all the way back to the stammerings of sunrise. Compared to this the Bible's as new as the latest detective novel. They want older than old from back before the Flood and alluvium, the dove and your twaddle, from the times people ate each other, emptied-out, brain-chocked skulls. They were a strange lot, full of darkness. Yellow-bellied and very touchy. Loudmouths. Big babies who know how to stand up, hands already playful, grasping and molding the world. Did you ever go up to the cave? It disturbs you . . . You feel brand-new beside it, with your Galilean gadget."

"Enough, prospector. Enough! You're raving!" exclaims the hermit, red with shame. "You'll be cursed!"

"Oh, I'm not afraid anymore. Maybe you'll send a shiver through the greenhorns of the new city. They're superstitious creatures in their way. My own superstition is the scrubland, the sea, gold, fish, the great everything. I remove its lice with my screen and nets. I filter it, it lets me have my way with it, even goes so far as to reveal its hiding places, its little secrets, its lodes. I pass a fine comb through the infinite. Streams, ocean abysses. I unearth the grains, collect the seeds, the sperm of the titans. No need for a book, effigy, intermediaries, anything personal, divine or whatever. I work on the whole heap, I finger the universe, probing, running my hands over it, my precision tools, my magnifying glasses, lorgnettes, scissors, fishhooks. I gaze into its bowels and brain. I gather up Leviathan's amber. I live off it, balanced on the great ship, I feed off it. I don't do any preaching. I sleep on the bridge under the stars. I don't give any sermons. I don't train any apprentice prospectors. I nibble away at my chunk of the universe without asking for leftovers. But I live close to those great intimidating things: wind, salt, rocks, lightning, sunken streams, the ocean of storms and giant fish. I'd be ashamed to spoil that with bookish bluster and pious puppets."

"Pagan! Pagan! . . ." the hermit shrieked. "You're a pagan beast, worse than a billy goat, fouler-smelling than a lizard, that's what you are . . . You'll rejoin the great everything, your carcass will rot in it like those of weasels and foxes."

The hermit disgorged his wrath. A profound, flatulent expulsion of divine fury. The pages of the book trembled, the Virgin's robe almost fluttered upward. And the gold prospector imagined the monstrous pubis of the immaculate broad, this Virgin seen from behind, rustic, stubby, a wood-carved vulva sculpted by wintry blasts, frost, racing through the forests under the robes of monks who were fleeing before the invader, the barbarian, Hun, Viking . . . What Madonna's sex, intact asshole, unbearable hymen? The Virgin's cunt—had the hermit ever seen it? Depraved and visionary in his crappy tunic, had he ever posed the big question about his protege's femininity? This ancient, age-old Virgin, worn, moth-eaten, threadbare, lashed by rains, frail frosts, torrid summers, from church to church lugging her spiritual, gangrened cunt.

"Have you ever seen the Virgin's cunt?"

The hermit brandished his fist toward the prospector, rushed upon the blasphemer in a whirlwind of strength. Catlike, his adversary bounded off, made tracks.

"Take it easy, take it easy, saint! Once you start landing punches, heaven won't be too happy and your lady'll start crying, so take it easy!"

The hermit gazed at the prospector for a long moment: "You're going to fish up the Devil in your nets!"

"He's already totally gnawed away your filthy rags. You're as proud and black as Satan. Plus being perverted with your fantabulous trollop, more jealous than a boar. You must do dirty things with her in your mystic intimacies. You're going to make those selling inflatable dolls in the city burst out laughing."

The hermit hitched the statue to his side, wedged the book under his arm and strode off. After a moment the prospector heard him break into a religious hymn. He walked along briskly, rotund but long-legged, his statue in its basket, the big book pressed against his left hip. He reeled on the slope of a hill. The fires hissed in the pines, sissed, chattered their teeth and twisted their red tails, the rocks exploded, revealing their crystal secrets, at the cores, a brilliant scarab or—who knows?—an angel's eye, a drop of hominoid sperm, a nugget, a smile, a word, a key, a spider or a living snake.

The gold prospector sat down again on the side of the path. He talked to his magpie, then stretched out in the grass, got drowsy. His thoughts turned to the fire; he flicked on the transistor to make ready his entry into the city. He wanted to reaccustom himself to the noises of his brothers. And what a racket they made, tireless, on all fronts, sea and land, at both poles . . . Eskimos, Zulus . . . and in the skies. The radio vibrated. The magpie, perched on top, beat its wings while beaking the antenna. It all had to be seen: the struggles, asthmas, hostilities, plots and free-for-all brawls, summits, treaties, carnage, hunger, thirst, hordes of unemployed, arid overpopulated cities, assassinations, athletic tournaments and cooking recipes, gregarious enthusiasms, the lyricisms and alarm bells of nations . . . the teeming catastrophe: shipwrecks, earthquakes, smashed planes with two hundred dead, volcanic eruptions, presto, twelve thousand dead, you want some you got some, ecological massacres, hygienic incinerations . . . And famines, scourges, modern plagues, one hundred thousand dead, cancer wreaking havoc, ten corpses a second, reaching into the millions, the chronometer goes haywire, a performance at every hour . . . The inexhaustible flood of horror that the gold prospector listened to without shuddering. The world must be entered, the clamor confronted, the herd of the mawkish, the weak, martyrs at the barbecue, and tyrants holding sway, hunchbacked, vociferating, outraged ogres, drunk with pride, human barrels haranguing the mob of gawking cowards from their rostrums. The news-in-brief was charming and even bloodier, ticking off the daily melodramas, full of carnage and endless pandemonium.

Shepherds were fleeing before the fire, sheep, goats and wolfhounds, three German engineers stopped their blue Mercedes, two Danish campers emerged into the crossroads, then kids, little guys from a camp with Boy Scout pennants, giddy and stamping, happy about the disaster . . . and others . . . A group winds up forming, a few people whose chance converging paths and concomitant scares had dumped in the crater of pines where the gold prospector listened to the cosmic Word. They came up to him. The radio mentioned the blaze. They were very proud to be participating in the event. They listened to the news of a fresh war, just born, broken out in all innocence between England and Argentina. How nice this face-off was between old Europe and El Dorado. A beautiful war, not too big, girlish, coquettish, progressive, patient and promising over the Falkland Islands. Replete with patriotic fanfare, verbal hysteria, young lads catapulted on sea and into diving planes. A war that could be followed with no trouble, clear, not like the conflicts in the Middle East where you get lost in the melting pot of races, warring camps, clans, like in Lebanon, the Israeli territories and all the complications of history. This was out at sea: yes, over islands, the Falklands, clots of ice fought over by English and Argentinians. A lovely tango . . . Casualties, not too many, a boat sunk here and there, reprisals, bombast. Very solemn negotiations, missions, go-betweens, appeals and trips by the pope, holy water on the cannons.

The listeners huddle together. When all is said, the blaze is everywhere, the excess, the exodus, the massive outflow. They managed for themselves a little better than all the people the radio mentioned who were killed, shattered, stricken by disaster, beheaded, the latest news bulletins. The big nuclear villains trade fulminating polluting threats.

The sheep and goats had virtually sat down themselves, horned, cute, and the blond-chested wolfhounds, the two Danish giraffes in skimpy shorts with their slalom thighs, the shepherds from a nativity scene, the chubby engineers framed in the window of the German Mercedes . . . each and every one knocked breathless by this magpie beating its wings on the platinum transistor spewing mutinies, daring holdups, robberies, rapes, lunacies, invasions, Virgins seen at Lourdes, in Warsaw, deliriums, chains of enormous incongruities, the raft of the Medusa in a deluge of hemoglobin. A little war making its way, good-natured, not too crowded, on a human scale, a kind of game for adults but with real deaths here and there, volunteer heroes on seas and in the skies, for the sake of islands with igloos and stones, but devoid of interest except for the majesty of the gesture itself . . . These small clashes have their charm, nattering out their modest machine-gun volleys and amicable corpses. Still, the seat of the island capital is a sort of stormed Alamo, feats with sabers, revolvers, axes or sticks, grenades and missiles, depending on cases, tastes and ideals. A small well-to-do seat of government, functioning with all due ceremony, the terrors of weapons, weeping mothers and trembling fathers . . . Gods and sheep bleat in this fog of information. Teats jiggling under fleece, milk, horns, the broad impression very pastoral and Vergilian, pedophilic and fresh as could be thanks to the pretty faces of the two boyish shepherds. Oh, but the cardiac claws, the train derailments, the exactions, round-cheeked multinationals sucking up everything, epileptic, the fanfare of glory, the uproars and routs. The holocausts out in the desert learned about three years after the fact upon discovering entire fields of picked-clean skeletons, spick-and-span sheaths before eternity. All well and good! The small group gesticulated, Danish and sheeplike, bleating and guttural German, amid the cooing of the Scout sparrows. Examples of alarmed humanity but at bottom cheerful, very cheerful, asking for some more terrific stuff, going farther into the fury, vibrating with delight at the idea of so many great Shakespearean events on a global scale . . . to the point that people felt so exquisitely weak, so small, so like brothers marching to the drums of a frenzied, galloping, thunderous history . . . magnificent and carnivorous . . . Oh beloved ferocity! . . . Feeling all sorts of things, shy, hunkering down before the toothed idol, its wild-eyed stampede, feeling limp all over with voluptuousness, hanging from the hot teats of death, torpid with happiness in this violent, planetary she-wolf's fur.

Alphonse shifted the radio dial, turned off the macabre spigot. Enough! A listlessness since losing Paula. Alphonse at the helm of his lifeless vessel. Yet they're all here, still some tourists in the grip of fever, vehement, recounting the muleta of flames between the rocks, that red tom-tom on the ridges. Agathe yanks details from them. Teenagers from the village, shepherdesses, Hippolyte the mailman and Lison the notary's sister, Marthe Praslin, one and all press the victims with questions, vie with each other in exclaiming, pouring on pathos . . . our vines and our valleys catapulted into the chasm, oh really how awful! Alphonse, a hollow bubble, so many echoes bursting in the shell of his brain. They speak with melodramatic gestures, a great theater of affliction, shepherds, cowherders, executives in ultramodern trailer homes, shrill females in bikinis, golden wasps . . . and the country folk sitting at tables, Aurèle's little buddies struck dumb, the priest stammers, shits the name of God in his frock, Iza, a carcass full of omens and mummy of coal, blames the cave, it's the same old madwoman's song, again and again . . . As if one night the skeletal hordes of pithecanthropi left the cavern, armed with torches to set the scrub aflame. Processions of vengeful thoraxes and malicious skulls, ancestors, ghosts, wreaking the inferno upon their descendants.

At one table, in a corner, Simon and the beautiful woman from Cameroon are involved in conversation. Calm amid the commotion. Eyes upon eyes, they see into each other, at the edge of the abyss, untempestuously, with no fancy talk. Peaceful. Mutually visible. They accept each other in their roles. They shrug their shoulders, happy with the beauty of chance, with this nascent fatality.

Alphonse's gestures are precise, never a false move. But the machine is whirring along on its own. He knows he's old now. Paula's death lays him bare to his nothingness. The void, free of tragedy or agony. He feels no pain, no torture pierces his breast, no gimlet of anguish. Absolute blankness. At his bar he governs the lapping motion of the bistro, the comings and goings of both villagers and foreigners. The fire chief suddenly pops in. He drinks a quart of pure water that Alphonse serves him in a jug. Alphonse doesn't feel like questioning him. He lets the mob do as it wishes. The noises clash around the metallic helmet. The fire chief is besieged, shouted at. He reassures, informs, pulls a long face, more allusive on certain points, he's the headman, leader, priest. He mobilizes all the region's springs against the fire, the water towers, the clear brooks, the underground streams, Melusina's wells, virgins' saliva, widows' tears and early morning dew.

Alphonse no longer has a memory. Bereft of nostalgia. No more future. No present. Alone. Yvette immediately understood when she saw him out planting endives in his garden. Gestures drained of vigor, aroma. Exact, certainly, irreproachable, but without zest, without love. Paula having passed away, they could hope to live together or at least see each other unhampered. But now Paula separates them far more than she did in the past. As if in order to see Yvette, Alphonse needed to keep Paula alive in her bedroom, Paula sick and slow, alert for sounds seeping through the blinds.

Paula was that lamp, that consciousness, that memory . . . Alphonse split in two, between Paula and Yvette, had established a balance, facing double mirrors that reflected his existence. He suffered over betraying Paula, for possibly bringing on her death. Failing Yvette disturbed and exasperated him. But it was this double flight, this back-and-forth wavering tolerated by both women that allowed him to recognize himself. He felt faithful to the person he was, his past, the secrets of his Moroccan life and farther back still, he stayed close to his childhood and first loves. Now severed from this former oscillation, he could move or love no longer. Nothing. There was this emptiness in Paula's bed, this hollow in her sheets. At night his hand instinctively groped toward her, his round, good, eternally dying spouse. It would encounter nothing but folds of cloth or smooth surfaces, the liquid expanse of the bed as far as the eye could see, a ghostly ocean. Alphonse couldn't sleep anymore. His sleep, as his waking, required an equilibrium. Without a partner to balance the pendulum of his dreams, he remained petrified in his corner. He felt himself stretched prone upon sleep. Nothing moved under him anymore, the bed had ceased breathing, drifting. Without masts or wind. Settled on the boulder. And the ditch at his side widened. At such times he had the impression that his skinny body was rising, protruding, exposed to a terrible lucidity which precisely prevented any sort of abandon, any warm slippage through the valley of the sheets. Union with the heavenly bodies was becoming impossible, and with the white spouse, the sated village, the circle of vineyards and hills, the pleasant snoring of bones and rocks in the gorges, the caverns, the moons and planets. He could no longer surrender to the shipwreck under the greatcoat of blond algae. He tried sleeping in Yvette's bed. But his mistress, though indulgent and with flesh so soft, was transformed alongside him into a glaringly new presence, full of arrogance. It was as if she had never wrapped her arms around him. The great cosmic, maternal balance was no longer in effect. Yvette's body loomed with such luminous sharpness that it dazzled Alphonse. It would have been likewise with a virgin, a vigilant maiden, quick to scream out and feel resentful. Paula's death brought Alphonse back to distant shores, to the anguish of the very beginnings that he was hard put to analyze. But he was conscious of having returned to some acute, painful origin where this very peace of mind, its felicitous refluxes were forbidden him, now lying exposed, offered for sacrifice. The night no longer danced in its wool of dreams, its white peaks of little bells and lambs. Insomniac, he had his eyes wide open upon the cavern of an empty sky.

And here, at this bar, the sounds broke upon him like waves, the voices, the worries of the groups, the frenzies, collective hopes, the distress of local families, of foreigners . . . a bedlam of angry, verbal men, or those resigned and sniveling as they blew their noses, hugged each other, spouses, mothers and children . . . the whole thing a hoax, hollow, for Alphonse. The great fire burned in the wheel of the void. He no longer saw the vines, the devoured houses, the scorched campgrounds. The life of the flesh attacked on all sides, emptied of its substance, reduced to black soot. He saw a desert whose undulations of sand turned to fire, raging, boundless dunes devoid of human beings, human suffering. Or else an infinite sea unfolded whose every wave became a flame following the same metamorphosis, the same monotony. Burning sea and desert: such was the image of the blaze in his mind. He no longer was able to imagine people, concrete existences. Of course he heard the babel and its branching networks, its knots, its outbursts so like the rings of a hydra made of words. He recognized the mailman, Dr. Chany, the notary, Marthe Praslin, Auréle's father, the fire chief, old Ludovic's granddaughter, Agathe. He knew it was them. He wasn't senile. Nobody worried about his health. He served the wine, the pastis. He lived just as they did, but separated by a cold mirror. Agathe badgered her world, collected anecdotes exaggerated by fear and the legend already spreading with the fire, its breath of some drunkard, hoodlum. Reinforcements from other cities were announced, great measures never before seen, a call to action, First Aid units . . . From the mountaintop, on the stage of the rock, the director and directress of the excavation, a lovely couple, saw the swift passage of the flames. They dreaded nothing, located far above the vegetation, sheltered by a rampart of sterile minerals. The fire ran below the bones, the heaped ancestors, the vestiges of monsters and beasts. The hurricane rolled along under Aguilar's skull. And the blaze moved in arches, half-mile long crawls, writhed, flew up, took from the rear a battalion of firemen, endlessly zigzagged and swarmed through other centers, other messages, frightening mythologies, miracles. The terrorist was under suspicion, or those bikers, for multiplying their own furor this way. The young people of the crew decorticate the skulls of Mosbach horses and bison ossicles while contemplating the herd of flames. And maybe one day, in a million years, paleontologists would arrive and dig up the substratum of the plain, rediscovering the complicated skeleton of the fire, paws clutching the hills, claws sunk in the schists, the imprint of its pikes, its horns, its fantastical scales, the supine length and suppleness of its dragon's body chiseled in the strata.

At night the village teenagers don't manage to get to bed. These are the grandsons of Polyte and Raoul, one of Aurèle's distant cousins, one of Yvette's nieces, one of Alphonse's female second cousins. All great-greats and once-removeds, scions, recent branches in blossom, twigs, birds hopped out of the nest, new fruit, a leafy race, delicate green buds, little runts and damsels. The blaze doesn't keep them from listening to their records. They're frail, even the sturdy boys who slave away on the farms, even the future matrons already potbellied dreaming of marriage. Their frailness springs from their youth, an inner haze, a flaw of matter, a scatter-brained skittering, an easefulness of gestures and forgetfulness. No end to their laughing amid sorrows. They booze it up, tell each other off, wriggle their backsides and flaunt their balls and tits. No end to veiling or unveiling themselves in shy or brazen arabesques. They gather round the fountain. Friends, enemies, rivals. They have their clans, their jealousies, their swift, scorching hatreds and their muddled tendernesses, their colossal modesty under all the masks and tawdry flash. They can hear the fire moving through the night, a high-pitched rustling at times, or heavier like a mass, a background purring that turns into fur, part dry, part creamy, between rust and soot. It can be sensed by a sort of heat more imagined than real, coiled in the atmosphere. The fountain quakes, cold, beautiful cords and ice-webbing. A girl dips her bare foot in the basin. A guy dares her to stick in her boobs and ass. She hesitates . . . then they hear a motorcycle racket. The teenagers stand up. Their feelings about the bikers are split. Hostility toward the strangers. But the fringe element of the group is more tolerant, warms up to the bikers. The cycle emerges, they recognize Paloma with Lynne behind. They're slowly cruising through the evening coolness. They love each other. The teenagers could care less, but the amazon and the maid fascinate them. The other bikers follow a little later, the guys. They look peaceable. Roving through the night. The teenagers fall silent, some stretch out along the sidewalk, others in the street. Two are standing on the basin coping. From time to time a joke breaks out, reverberates in little waves and dies in gentle laughter. The boys get hard-ons in their undershorts. The girls daydream, their breasts harden under the spindrift, minute splashing that the breeze pushes and plasters against their busts. Fingers of water, dripping cocks lash them. A snickering, two guys trade secrets about the hardness of members. The girls know full well what they're talking about. They like this atmosphere where everything grazes the surface without bursting into action. A gentle, tentacular presence. Some couples have formed, already old, viewed with indulgence and irony. They'd like to get married, flirt nonstop. Licking and groaning, a little goofy, moist from loving. Little islets of caresses and intertwined tongues. Strange how their outworn antics have stopped exciting the others. Their embracing no longer incites anybody. Part of the furniture. Eroticism is found elsewhere, in what weighs heavily or waits, in everything that has yet to occur, bodies untouched, breasts unseen. A fog of unstable, insidious desires that creates an oil stain, seeps in everywhere, mutually electrifying. The plane tree has spoken in the wind. The old men's bench stretches out, an empty plank. The teenagers looked at the small craft. The giant anchor of the trunk, the beautiful moorings of the branches and the infinite sails.

One by one they rose and went over to sit on the bench. At this time of night the old men were asleep in their houses, separated, dissociated from the royal seat. Wizened in a slumber of tightly crooked fetuses, of shriveled monsters, scattered along the streets, above shops, the glorious souls whistle and cough, ruminate their glaucous dreams. Nimbly the teenagers settled on the large bench. They feel the wood's power under their loins. Ludovic's leather, Polyte's piss, Alexandre's godawful stink, Julia's sweat impregnates this august belvedere. Knots swell under the uprights; molds dried by haunting fears and obsessions are encrusted in the pleats, small mushrooms populating the corners. The friction of asses gently indented the plank. The kids' rumps slide into the eroded cisterns. They touch lesions, scars and folds, ligaments blackened by frost and sunlight, the impact of very old clogs, scorches, knife cuts. There are marks dating from before the wars, from the time of smithies and glades. In ages past perhaps Melusina sat on this bench of the centuries. Here the first lovers exchanged a primal kiss. The teenagers fall silent, listen to this stubborn living pedestal which their fingers constantly, tirelessly brush against and explore, discovering cavities, cusps, blisters, ligneous jaws. Bumpy all over with vermin, dampness, encrusted with stains fallen from the tree: autumn leaves, the smallest stems, baby birds tumbled from the nests, droppings, buds, and all that the high branches snatch from the wind, sands, flints, thistles, twigs, dead insects, dashed objects, elytra, angels' piss, fragments from caves, caverns, mountain and sea, words fallen from the lips of the gods. The tree is a screen that catches seeds, sucks them into its riddle of leaves, makes them run along its limbs down to the base, to the bench. Each morning the old men wipe the seat, but every night the active caustic residues lay down their grime, tattoo the elderly gentlemen's nave. Initials, hieroglyphs and magic formulas can be read both on the legs and back. In hidden nooks words of love are nested, seven league-long peckers are carved as well as large solar cunts bristling with beams. Generations have peopled this bench, chains of human beings come to sit, wait and watch, but especially to listen to the wind and the world whose mirror is the tree. Gods descended from the heights or arisen from within the trunk have meted out justice and prophesized from this trivet. Horned, sylvan creatures, fauns with green-misted eyes, dryads disheveled with leaves. Errant knights, vanquished warriors, preachers and pilgrims, barbarians, invaders rigged out as aggressors or saints have rested here along their path, and with their staffs, swords, wretched bundles, with their war gear have tapped the millennial carcass of the bench adrift upon the years, veering with the stars. People say its legs sink far down into the soil like roots, thus explaining its strength, its resistance to the cycles, the seasons over which it holds sway. The living legs of a billy goat set upon two underground boulders similar to Saturn's knees.

That's what connects it, attaches it . . . the teenagers are settled into the craft. When they raise their eyes they probe the inextricable floating forest, its well-set framework, flying buttresses of a fortress or basilica, but possessing a delicate interlacing, infinitely branching network, its fragile textures, cocoons of mists, footbridges where the night dreams upon the down of leaves. The old men's past is engraved in the deep barks, their coarse integuments, their lumpy tumors . . . Tunnels can be sensed, caverns, heaped boughs of twisted guts, chasms of memory. They have deposited their wars and their loves here, their families, their homes, their tools and their deaths. The tree remembers in a black wavelike rustling. The foliage beats against a muffled drum, whispering the epics, the exoduses, the encampments, the alliances, lineages and first fires . . .

The naked teenagers tingle in their flesh. Sexes, asses thrilled with joy, fright. The moon looms large like an egg forking open the branches. White, gently rolling while the tree pitches and tosses, the stars wriggling with the leaves, tracing wakes of milk, punctuating immense pools of shadows. They can be seen disappearing and being reborn, multiplying in aigrettes, gravel and gleaming seeds. At times a plant scabbard seems to sheath an astral stone. The blackness is so dense that the well's blaze has been extinguished. Supine, garnering its flames in the shell of branches, curled like a big black hedgehog, ready to be reborn and shine when morning comes and the star of day rises. The blaze sleeps in the sheath of the tree. The teenagers and angels sway in this dream of moonlight, sunshine, these plunging reminiscences . . . they see the lynx and the pithecanthropi walking on the cables of time. Agathe and Iza have appeared, their mothers, their sisters and brothers. The bench makes them drunk, drugs them with its saps, star-liquors. A flux drips out, inebriates brains and makes muscles ache while the tree softly cracks and dances . . . in which the birds cheep, dream about their tournaments, their flaunting feathers, their combat songs . . . jays, crows, pigeons, chaffinches, starlings, blackbirds and thrushes, invisible but innumerable with their eyes, claws, beaks, stubborn instincts, queer habits, bickering and ferocious animals. Sects of ancestors.

And the future opens an avenue into this nest of memory. The teenagers slip into a channel between the somber carbons, the ancestral deposits, the palimpsests and illegible scrawls. One door opens, then another, broad corridors where the breeze comes to life and moons germinate. The tree is the terrace of the future, a telescope where loving and dying take shape . . . where frescoes are sensed, stones whispered, omens spun out . . . Agathe and Iza remain far behind this slender virgin stream, tender wave of fresh years in which girls' breasts stir, the smooth hard pricks of boys full of sperm. The bench jerks them off, the hand of an old man and eternal youth. And the blaze contorts into a dream, a silk of its fur suddenly flashes iridescently, then dies out. The fountain divulges its secrets under the leaves. It seems to be carved into the very tree trunk. Squirrels and marmots abruptly budge, stirrings of round warm things, discreet shadows shifting. Screech owls . . . winged mice . . . moles of heaven . . . The tree looks to be redistributing its limbs, its forces, rearranging its gloomy lungs. Whole cosmoses circle upon themselves and ball up like dogs dazed with dreams. Hands creep toward the naked thigh under the back and torso-stalk, the beautiful underbelly cloves, the fruits of the bust. The big billy goat, the big bench, this wild sow bristling with splinters grumbles, a dream-rush, breasts swell and pricks spew their semen. The tree disperses in anguish and happiness. It wobbles with its barge laden with the centuries, trophies, ancestors, bones, weapons of war, grain reserves, its colonies of children and animals. It changes into a chaos of roars and clashes, shaking its fantastic burden. Fear-struck, the teenagers await the verdict of branches and bench. The shades of Ludovic, Polyte, Raoul and Julia loom up above them, followed by other old people, gnarled colossi, bowed, wrinkled statues. They see the skeletons and mummies emerging from the caverns. Great-grandparents, their backs stooped with the centuries, chests crumpled with famine. They're very beautiful with their breasts of bark, their cruciform tendons, the ancient brambles of their loins, the calluses of their palms, their sallow faces and their greenish knees. In their wake, inexhaustible ranks of skulls slowly pushing the boat-bench of the children in love. A procession emerges from the cave, a whole population of branching apes and men towing the nave of the lovers toward the lustral waters, this milk of stars opening the tree and the sky beyond moons and suns.

Sue, swaddled in dust, smooth all over with ashes, has almost entirely freed the vestige . . . Slabs of earth, scabby crusts still conceal the lower left member. But the ribs are visible, the pelvis, the head . . . Gilles, Pier, Myriam, the director, his wife come each in turn to contemplate, scrutinize, take measure of the immemorial child. An architecture of bone rife with gaps like a sketch. It seems that some Tom Thumb out of Genesis put together these ghostly remains with white stones. Not much to it, a pattern of sand-encrusted shells . . . The flesh, the muscles, the furors of blood, the network of nerves, the facial expressions, the heartbeats have been absorbed. Time has attacked the crust of the bones. The chemical reactions of the soil, seepage, acids, guano have opened hollows filled in by sediments. All that survives is a frail essence, a child's reflection in a mirror of deposits. And each and every one marvels at this enchantment, kneels for a better look, admires the fragile puzzle telling of the families back then, the children clinging to their mothers' breasts, the squeals of pleasure, the greedy suckling.

It's right there, left behind, betrayed by these fingers of ossicles. I was a child five hundred thousand years ago, before Adam, before the angels, before . . . at the very base of the spiral, at the root, a first step, a shy questioning, a prelude, a cry . . . notes of bone on the stave of the ages.

And Sue, the very young, very loving mother, nibbles away at the last ergots of earth, strips off the light scales. The occiput is still sunk in matter. Bulges, bumps hamper the skeleton. The stripping process proceeds slowly, gently, tenaciously. Sue the midwife.

Myriam will need to imagine the kid based on these archives, draw the features of a face, sketch out a gesture, a posture, extract the child from the chasm. A temporal twister whirls above her, a colossal spiral she must ascend, translate. A fantastic salvaging operation; she tosses the lifesaver to those drowning in the abyss. The ones at the very bottom are lost, going under, calling out . . . Seven hundred thousand years down, eight hundred thousand years down a tooth might be discovered, a breath, a limestone knob. A million years deep, five million years, their presence can be sensed, small erect humans who hunt and think. From even farther down their cries reach us, muffled, subdued, a soft muddle of speech . . . at seventy million years the first primate and even before, at the threshold of the sea, of oxygen and the sun, a chirping. Voices interweaving in the hair of the algae, a murmur of miraculous microbes. And Sue tosses them a rope, Sue offers her breast. And Myriam paints them, fashions them, breathes in life. They're about to walk on the large leaves of drawing paper.

Simon is seated at the cave entrance, Myriam stretched out beside him on the terrace overlooking the Verdouble valley and its herds. Simon watches the black woman whose secret he had pierced. But he knows only the substance of a fact. All the rest eludes him, Myriam's motivations, feelings, the genealogy of her choice. He gives no thought to articulating his discovery to her face. She must know that he knows, but how far does her personal knowledge about him extend? No doubt there's something essential she's ignorant of, a mission he's kept hushed up since his arrival, even if his primary purpose was to carry it out surreptitiously. He watches her and now that he has evidence, Myriam's black face opens upon a frightening whiteness. What he knows resides in this whiteness, yet it's a closed circle he must in turn cut through in order to go down deeper, burrow toward other enigmas, other links, these phenomenal layers of thickness that a face hides. Myriam, beautiful and sculpted in smooth wood, her skin agleam. She conceals an infinitude of life. Simon hates her for all these mysteries, this perfect play-acting. What did she give by sleeping with him? By lending a surface, the most visible envelope of her being? He thought he had flushed her out of her fleshy depths as if being in heat might extract the treasure of a secret. He fathoms to what extent reaching orgasm distracts from the essential, like digging in the wrong spot, drilling alongside the lode . . .

The cave whispers in its shadow. How beautiful they are, the girls and boys laboring away. Insects and sages. Angelic ants. They're pure and innocent. Their hands precise. Their gestures . . . Teenagers with a sense of solidarity. And their scruples. The cave transfigures them. Pale in the night, slow. They pass by like peaceful phantoms. Simon never wearies of this circumscribed activity, compressed into the rock orbit, officiated by magicians and tightrope walkers. Above all, familiar motions. Free of tragedy. He's astonished by so much calm, precision. Gentle, peaceable . . . sheepfold of skeletons. He, the stranger, envies them.

Myriam fashioned a latex cast of the Aguilar skull. Several duplicates of the original mask exist. Myriam and Simon contemplate the effigy, this hollow dome with two holes for eyes. A remake shorn of sacredness, a soon-to-be standardized product. Skulls will be sold to tourists the way Madonnas are at Lourdes. And the visitors arrive, panting, sweating, at the summit of the sheer slope, proud of their climb, they've earned this gaze over the plain. They pass inside, displaying precaution, a respect, as into a sanctuary, ask questions in hushed voices, don't always dare to inquire. They forget the beaches, the noise, the furnace of heat, the mobs . . . their commonplace vacations. All at once they change planets. Enter time on a grand scale. They too become beautiful. Their gaudy shorts, their comical bonnets, their bouncing folds of flesh, peeling epidermises slip into the background. Their breathing quiets, their exclamations die down. They find themselves in the cave. Moved. Told about the bones, the encampments, the fratricidal struggles, the hunt. They descend deeper, confident, credulous. Avoiding abrupt gestures, laughter. Travel along the wooden footbridges above the ditches, between the strings gridding the soils. They grope along, balanced, dizzy . . . The years flash past beneath, torrents of centuries. The figures stupefy them. They wobble, undermined, far from the present. The fat ladies, the jokers, the braggarts, slenderly built men, ludicrous clowns in pathetic getups, packs of thunderstruck gawkers in all shapes and sizes, crooked, pot-bellied, youngsters or retirees, the cave swallows them up, short sleeves and bermudas. They plunge out of sight into the chamber of the dead. And the details of their attire, the summer folklore disappear. The darkness ennobles them. They sense things, graze the surface of truths. Shed their self-identities. Naked in the naked cave. And when they leave, they blink their eyes in the sunlight. Looking out upon the valley a nostalgia sweeps them. The universe has lost its obviousness, the landscape is suspended. An expectation hovers in the air, a vague anguish matched by a veiled joy. A presence settles within them, the hand of the millennium, footsteps of the ancestors, parents . . .

Simon touches a patch of wall. The Aguilar men lined the caves with stones to protect themselves from wind and ground moisture. They took shelter, sought warmth, set rocks in rows so they could stretch out on top. Then they slept, played, threw themselves into petty tasks . . . made love . . . the embrace of the first humans . . . Who had the upper hand over whom? Ritual precedents, hierarchies or anarchies of sex? The second hypothesis is very unlikely. The etiquette of coitus is punctilious and eternal. What about those beings? Did a large male, as Freud wrote, rule the clan, imposing law upon the sons, possessing the females of his choice? A large incestuous male? Did the famous taboo exist five hundred thousand years ago? Unlikely . . . He mounted his daughters, his sisters, his mother, fought over them with his sons and brothers . . . What a crazy stew! Or else did the power of this chief ensure the reign of order? Haughty, ferocious, supervising exchanges. Whom did he fuck? At what time? And the females: were they docile or nasty, tying the knot with everybody or just a special favorite? Was there a large dominant female grandmother of the clan, doddering and toothless, scolding the pack of brats, clawing the males, grunting, shitting in her corner, sucking the leftover bones?

Hardened shafts aiming for the vulvas of the clan's girls sheltered in the cave, on the bed of stones, all fucking in front of each other amid those excluded members, trembling, belligerent. Unless they went off searching for a more ephemeral companion among the members of another group? Did the children remain with their parents? Did a mother recognize her sons and daughters her whole life long, preferring them to all others, assuring them protection? And a father, was he at the head of an indistinct swarm of bastards sown in nature, depending on the passing seasons and hordes? For this was the very beginning, sexuality existed, but love? . . . Long before Cro-Magnon man, long before Neanderthal, long before . . . Orgasm was brutish, short. The female mounted without ceremony or subsequent to some nuptial fanfare, movements, rubbings, laughter, signs to draw near, invitations. They get erections while carving their stones. While fashioning their weapons they dreamed about the cunts of these human she-monkeys. Already with preferences, values . . . At what moment did little girls lose their hymens? Who took them? Did they have a prince of their dreams? A charming ape, a warrior, some strong and crafty hunger.

They all fucked in packs, whole heaps, exciting each other in the bone-crammed cave, bloody carcasses, in the aroma of sweat, grease, sperm. Sisters, brothers, fathers and mothers . . . between wars, hunts, in hot seasons when the sap is boiling. And the great herds were undulating through the plain. Or else, legislators already, instinctively ritualized . . . Orgies are not the forte of beasts.

Getting hard in the broad sunlight, jerking off in sight of everybody. The females gazing at the members with fright or malevolence. Did they desire these poignant arrows vibrating in the males' hands? Did they dare touch the living rod, suck it? No trace of eroticism back then. Did obsessed creatures, maniacs and shaggy Don Juans, already stand out from the lot? Screwing specialists, gluttons, errant destroyers. Their vices were quite minute. They climbed on top of each other with no masks or theater and surely buggered each other. But kisses didn't exist. What about caresses, gratitude? There must have been niceties, affectionate signals.

The horde, the gang, the mob . . . Who's to know? Twenty, thirty individuals? What chaos if a little authority isn't introduced. Murder, retaliation. Devouring each other after the massacre. Creatures who ate themselves. A cannibalism that was systematic or codified, pre-religious . . . Were there special cases, conditions? They didn't bury their dead, that's a fact. Burial rituals came long afterward, hundreds of millennia later, four hundred thousand years are going to pass before tears of mourning and this desire for eternity at the threshold of ourselves. These beings exist before the age of fire, incest and graves. Uncivilized, the real thing. Since so little about them is known, their existence is the stuff of dreams, their absence delineates the shadow of our presence. Their skulls are the cave of our future ideas. Eons have been folded in their neurons. A great saga of genesis is brewing in the lair of their brains.

From the cavern can be seen the dancing fire. The cave terrace resembles a bench looking out upon the world. You have the impression of being in a miniature night above the flames.

The terrorist is walking in the sunlight. He's less suspicious of each rock, of the countless crenels carved in the limestone. He knows that the police surveillance network is closing in. He discovered the pair of binoculars in his den. He circles in his flight between the hills. No escape possible, there are cops at the borders. He doesn't really feel like struggling anymore. A sense of relief overwhelms him. Liberation. Walking in daylight. He dreams about the lynx joining up with him. Man and beast leap upon the rocks. Out in front, the happy lynx gallops to the top of a hillock, inspects the horizon, returns, his fur beats against the escapee's thigh. A circaetus crosses the sky, hovers. The bird is hunting asps coiled on the stones. The terrorist contemplates this African migrant. The bird of prey is going to swoop down on the snake which darts out its head, tries to bite, an open, enraged triangle. Jewel of fury. The beak seizes the neck, pierces the skull. The long reptile writhes, a spasm of horror. The beak swallows the coppery rings very slowly. And the bird flies off with the snake in its belly. And the serpent sleeps in the sky, borne aloft by the eagle's wings.

The terrorist remembers the beach in the blazing heat, women, kids, all that sunlit din. Naked, welded bodies gleaming with lotion. That torpor of the dead offered up. Beautiful, golden. He walked amid the tomb-statues. Breasts, rumps, altar of love. The killer with his solar bomb. The motionless sea; each wave proffered its sword. Upon arriving he'd seen the ice-cream man, all the kids gathered around the refreshing scoops. Then the families in queer tepees with their arsenal of drinks, tanning creams, bath towels, curtains against the wind. And the sum total swarming, languid, and monotonous. A sense of life slowing to a stop bore down upon the beach of the dead. Except for the kids zigzagging about, licking their ice creams. He'd seen the banners at the top of a row of masts. Those triumphant colors pleased him, that sound of snapping silk. For a long while he'd looked at the wings of flags. No sea gulls, no surf. Naked flesh, skin. A silence populated with myriads of plangent insects. A hubbub of frail pebbles, the voices, cries, shouts swirled together by the distances, the sea. Echo, as if so many sounds no longer belonged to the living. A cloud of inaudible words, feelings, fears, that became detached, drifted. Ghosts . . . these were the voices of all beaches and all times. There was no present . . . A mature breast, ambered, protruding from a bra, swelled in the sunlight. He stared at it with its coarse tip, light rippling breeze. Heavy, distended with vitality. He remembers a pair of tiny panties encrusted in the furrow of an ass. Bold red material and cone-shaped buttocks, long, fragile. But the rustling voices, wind, water leveled everything. The details sank away in the eternal whorls of the sand. A gigantic torrid hourglass disgorged the seed of the centuries. The beach was now ageless. The bomb would revive time. A big bang of the beginning. The blood of the origins. The sea washing the corpses, boats towing them toward the horizon, the other shore.

The lynx runs. The snake gleams in the African eagle's belly. The terrorist rambles. He laughs. He touches his beard. With his hand he strikes his assassin's torso. He'd gladly see the woman emerge from the boulder. Long back, birdlike ankles. Strength molded in the slab of her buttocks, her upthrusting throat. The spacious stomach, curled with inky hair. And this fragrance of straw, pollen, both sacred and excremental. The lynx sat down. The female giant kneels before the idol. She strokes the quiffs decorating its ears. Bacchic brushes. She wraps her arms around its neck, the animal lets himself be tumbled in the sand and the black woman touches, breathes in the thick withers and coat . . . mass of sparks, odors. The lynx is supple, he shudders, stands back up. On all fours the woman arches her back, thrusts out her bronze loins. He sniffs her gash, her hair, her vermilion liquor. His speckled paws climbing the back of the black female sphinx. The sweating skin sticks to the wild beast. She feels the animal's balls knocking against her body. And the lynx mounts the carina who sways in all her fullness, roundness. She cries out, sings. The lynx bites her neck, draws blood from her sides. Flanking her hips she sees the shaggy red arrows of his thighs. The convulsion of nerves. The lynx grunts, shoots its sperm . . . She's supine in the dust. Her wounds of happiness, long body of brambles in the desert whiteness. He takes a few steps toward her, heavy and growling, head bowed. He licks the blood from the sand.

The circaetus landed on a ridge, puffing its breast, lifting its beak in a spiral as pure as a snake's neck.

The terrorist is going to sip some cold water from a ring of limestone. The cops' helicopter passes above the Corbières. The fire, toward the east, forms a thin wind-bristled pelisse. A border of almost motionless flames. The terrorist would like to climb to the cave and touch the bones of the first men and the great herds.

The gold prospector passed through the eastern door. An old medieval postern which defended the city during times of plague, invasions, religious wars. The hermit headed westward. On that side there stretches a rampart topped with crenels and machicolations. The metropolis immense inside, with its old districts, and toward the center its modern zone. Audacious architects created a city of glass, a cone of limpid, futuristic towers. A ring of ancestral walls encircles this Jerusalem of mirrors. The prospector and the hermit make tracks toward it.

The prospector pushes along his gold-rush junk cart. The nuggets crackle in the leather pouch. The swaying magpie keeps its balance on an eccentric perch above the old man's mess tins, ice axes and sieves. He entered fearlessly. Tourists and bureaucrats look at the tramp, his composure and serenity. The closely packed cars lengthen their lines of traffic. Chrome, windshields shoot blinding flashes. The clangor of horns. The city rumbles, protean and metallic, interlinking its outer shells, its asphalt rhizomes, shop windows, facades. The ensemble stubbornly interlocked, materials and colors weaving glassy smooth mosaics. The crowd itself belongs to the puzzle; its flux, its knots, its folds are the soft mobile pieces of a chessboard, at times rigid, at others more pliable. The city welded together in sidewalks, walls, streets, men, flesh and concrete. In the breaches, little squares, people coming out of bistros, an effusive outburst takes place, turbulence, a mutation of molecules into living atoms, human scraps. Bunches of gesticulating passersby. Walking along, jostling each other, laughing, getting riled up, shouting. It's been a while since the prospector has seen so many people. They move about, swift, active, full of desires, ogling and despising each other. Some wear narrow suits, ties and smooth-shaven, calculating faces. Squeaky clean they are, odorless, no shit or lice. The white-collars with eyeglasses, briefcases. Bodiless, no assholes or nostril hairs. Took their one last shit quite a long while ago. Presently strict and scoured. More android than human. The prospector pushes his cart, the magpie squawks, his ice ax falls on the flagstones with a chinking tinkle. The cars envelop him, a trellis grating of shock absorbers, hard, brilliant, hoods. Heads turn toward the wanderer, his grime, the feathered babbler with the long keeling tail. The frying pan, two pots, the bundled tent, two pitchers. The prospector isn't afraid. He's going to sell the gold, he'll buy his fishing boat. He'll sell his catch. He doesn't feel all that old. The city hurts his ears and knees but it's bearable. Let them look at him—kids, teenagers, adults! He is confident of his intimate superiority. A spirituality radiating within him, his wrinkles act as nests of benevolence. His torso full of sunlight and pure water. His forehead has the rigor of rock. His magpie is his capacity for taking flight, for infinite sagacity.

The hermit is going up a broad avenue; an expanse of automobiles stops at the traffic lights of one block, then is off again. An entire perimeter of car bodies darting forward, halting. A large slice of chrome-studded pie that cops' arms cut, the gash of a pedestrian crossing. He steps onto the sidewalk. Tall, heavy, in his filthy robe. The Book under his arm, the Virgin hooked to his side. Rows of customers at outdoor cafés, seated, legless, nothing but busts and heads eyeing the face of the Madonna in her rotted blue veil. The old puerile expression bounces to the rhythm of his strides. The giant unfurls a halo of stench. A blend of piss, sweat, mane. And the Madonna jiggles about, gentle and rudimentary, with her peasant's back. Her Oriental profile . . . The shop windows display bikinis, light silken tissues, skimpy bras for dragonflies, and swimming trunks with holes, ants' asses, laces upon bald, svelte mannequins. The hermit contemplates this cluster of dolls, garbed in finery. They rather seem like martyrs in their beauty. And paradoxically, before these denuded Venuses, he muses upon those who were once tortured, Christian saints. And the Virgin also, sisters of the queen statue. Because they are all stiff, humiliated, flashily decked out, offered to the torture of stares, commerce. He walks on, people look at the book clenched against his side, a worn leather volume in an old-fashioned gold binding. He's a monk, they whisper. A real one? asks a child. And the man advances in his big black sandaled feet. The robe beats against his scrawny calves, tendons covered with a tangle of grey hairs. He gives off a fragrance of soot, billy goat musk. The saint's balls swing under the mystic robe. He smells of God's pubis, dry dung. Proudly striding, sparing of his treasures, fanatical and cantankerous. He spotted two women sitting at a table of an outdoor bar. One, a redhead, arrogant, with a fleshy mouth, the other blonde, with periwinkle eyes. And all at once their lips melted in slow, avid union. With a sidelong glance he saw their shorts, their naked thighs cuddling against each other. The hermit is not stricken by any stupor. Any furor. The scene has a miraculous quality. This gluttony of women arouses him in his course, opens up a beach of love in this urban chaos of automatisms and deafening dins. The hermit stumbles against the big black bike that his robe envelops.

The city as yet knows nothing. Caught in its frenetic gears. Spewing and swallowing its people, chewing them up in its circuits, spouting them all, spreading them along every floor. It slogs away as usual, an anaconda of reflexes and signals. Only the windows of bars, of stores, the eyes of stray passersby reflect the image of the two old men. The city welcomes them without scandal, without altering its rhythm. The sticky frock, the verbose magpie and the bag of gold. They entered the city, heading for the modern center.

An enormous square opens out in the heart of the old city. And in that spot, equally distant from the crenels and posterns of the east and west, looms the new zone, the glass fortresses. A stack of offices, gangways and subways. Fantastical spiral of walkways and terraces. Babel of the year 2000. It's the seat both of business and of culture. A large theater has been ensconced, a mausoleum of pipes, organs made of plexiglass and metal. An exhibition hall displays abstract paintings and sculpture. A flood of various kinds of music streams from the honeycomb cells inhabited by computers, dials, video screens.

The hermit and the prospector contemplate the vessels' glass. Icebergs and prows carved in the rarest materials. Boulders of limpidness. Transparent, colossal skulls. And virtually silent overall compared to the shop-lined streets. Heavenly . . . It's the new city, the lofty district of dreams, trade and exchanges. Speculation bustles in this rectangle of frost. The sun illuminates the mirrors, the aerial interchanges, the pilasters, the cornices, the synthetic gardens, habitats in glass bubbles, shells, all sorts of gadgets, artificial fountains with a view, concrete oubliettes. Here the new world shoots skyward, the world of space shuttles, satellites, telematics, ultrasophisticated missiles. The sons of the hermit and the prospector are the magi of future ages. Their efficiency is stunning. Their science of figures. Yet they are very simple children, they like tennis, swimming, such terrifically healthy kids, not a depraved creature among them, founders of families . . . with bright eyes, lively ways, childish laughter. But top-notch calculators, real virtuosos. Strong in algebra, resourceful, revolutionary inventions all day long, and most of all rapid. The hermit and the prospector understand that by coming into the city they haven't come to take on the money-changers in the temple, the miasmas of Sodom, the Babel of vices. These sites are pure. The spirit in an archangel's garments holds dominion. Acrobatic displays with no falls or foul-ups performed by a human race of telamones aiming for the power of the stars. It'd be easier for the hermit to convert decadent and lecherous mobs. The Madonna would put them in their place, any such salacious descendants wallowing in their disgust. But these people here are so clear, so positive, spotless, free of nostalgia, what will they say upon seeing the Mater from the East, enveloped in a veil of blue molds? They betray that sort of purely material curiosity before the object, the incongruity of the remnant, the worn quality of the wood. They'll estimate the age. Judiciously and sympathetically they'll scrutinize the interesting statue, the amusing ruin, the thingamajig from back when. The Virgin, truly long forgotten, going back to their grandparents' days, to childhood and Christmas. In the large exhibition hall where the bronze, the metal fittings form harsh angles or tough tumors, who would see the small Madonna in beggar's rags? She would be crushed by the scale of the stelae, the space, the awesome purity of the materials, curves and geometry of smooth surfaces. While she simply stands there, so tiny, mire and stains, robe splotched by the saint's embrace, body rubbed by his beard and sweat, the old man's ruminations. The hermit advances... So much light purifying the glass, so much sky reflected by the high spheres give him hope. He'll open the large book and the mirrors will endlessly ricochet the text, the sacred calligraphy of letters, rare and precious illuminations. The Word in its original Hebrew. And she'll extend her worm-eaten stumps and her desert mother's face. The futuristic fortresses will be the tabernacle of icons. The holy devotion will be transported into the cities of the sons. Their supersonic spaces, their computers, their rockets will transmit the message of Galilee.

Thus the hermit will wander, hugging the Virgin in a shaggy, sweat-blackened arm. And the prospector with his magpie, his gold, looked fondly upon the mute, hyaline citadel. At a bank window he'll cash in his nuggets. He breathed deeply. The wind from Africa had crossed the sea and deposited its sands on the snows of the Pyrenees. It was soon going to take back the migratory circaetus and their reptile feast. It hovered around the fortresses, announcing miraculous catches, tracing the oval of fish bellies...

The next day, early in the morning, stationed in front of her window to breathe in the odor of embers and resin, Agathe saw police vans passing by. The escapee must be feeling the heat between the cops and the conflagration. Fresh information reached the inspectors' ears. Spies are lying in ambush everywhere. The tourists are phonies. Watch out for the hilarious Germans, the phlegmatic Scandinavians... Agathe gathered a whole bunch of newspaper articles on him, the daylight assassin . . . Clippings, tidbits. Accounts of the trial preceding his imprisonment are mutually contradictory. The testimonies cancel each other out. The terrorist confesses, retracts, multiplies his antithetical, fragmentary statements . . . Spanish Basque, perhaps, born in Morocco, fine... a bastard born of an impoverished mother. Another version lends credence to a Middle Eastern birth. The man precociously leaves his native land to lead a vagabond existence about which nothing is known. In this blank space, hypotheses and wild speculations proliferate. He turns up in Mexico, trafficking in Aztec artifacts. A long stay in Paris, late in life majoring in literature and archaeology. Same name, similar photographs. But without the beard. A woman marks this period, a student from the suburbs in love with theater, studying math and economics. Tall, beautiful, a very pure face. Fifteen years younger than he, a long affair. But is it really him? He was said to be a teacher for a while. Instructing nice little girls and boys in our classics. A weakness for little girls. A killer with a thing for Alice and Ophelia. Then, as a journalist, working for different magazines, he drops out of sight, reports become muddled, his face grows murky, multiplies. The photos are no longer convincing. The very beautiful math major always showed herself to be discreet and modest. How old is she at present? Living with a new guy, holding down a regular job. She camouflages her original passion, her beautiful love for him. The only admission that could be pulled out of this upright young woman was that he was prone to violent outbursts, fits of rage. A mixture of frenzied idealism and cynicism. Capable of everything, lying, traps. But an irrepressible frankness from another viewpoint, a frightening ingenuousness which at times made her smile. But is it really him? Is it her? Did they value and love each other despite the lapse of time? Their ardent, unfortunate adventure during one brief period, a fragment of sad suburbs and delights.

Another love, always love, thinks Agathe, it fascinated her, these pieces of flames, these magical islands. Never been in love personally. No regrets. But magnetized by their ecstasies, their horrors, their deliriums. This garble of confessions, hysterical jealousies, impulses, letters . . . He embraces the Basque cause. Exactly when is unknown. Throws himself headlong into the movement. Bold, suicidal. The worst missions, in places where death shimmers. But is it him in Barcelona, in Marseilles, Toulouse, Madrid? Plundered banks, gunned down policemen, bomb in a trashcan that decapitates a child. Explosives going off in bistros, making mincemeat of people sitting outside.

On the wood table Agathe lines up her sundry pack of small rectangles, lobes, biographical fragments, rachitic amendations and droplets, or a profuse apocryphal chronology. She clipped articles whose layout forms zigzags, extending into appendices and further notations, "continued page 7," "continued page 22," Tom Thumbs between the magazine ads, the thread must be kept track of, the link flushed out, the final reappearance. Some leaves are completely yellow as if a flame had grazed them, others cooked and recooked, blackened to the color of tobacco butts. But also pieces of brand-new, brilliant paper, precious, top-quality publications. Murder presented in a jewel box. In Mexico, he pillaged Aztec tombs, resold statuettes to rich collectors. Middle East, agricultural ancestors, oranges, citrus fruits. Herds of goats, a pastoral scene with little bells. Other fables . . . Lebanon. The terrorist woven out of lacerations, a lace of countries, an archipelago shredded across several seas and continents. A beautiful myth. One source suggests a far more wretched destiny, bounced around, running aground, precarious moorings. Taste for violence, craving for blood. Spanish Basque, since when? for what purpose? His brothers have repudiated the monstrous attack. Not a one laid claim to the horror that summer, the light blue sky, the very gentle sea, all the desires, beautiful bodies, the somewhat idiotic innocence of beaches at such moments.

Agathe patches this stuff together, tatters, rags, a mosaic of quilted newspapers. It looks pretty in its faded hues, sepia tints, grey and off-white monochromes. Flakes, shavings, word-blackened bone splinters. Scraps of hypothetical, questionable messages. Everywhere these densely packed flies telling the epic of the Orient in Mexico. Agathe revels, arranges her puzzle, recites the terrorist's life out loud, certain Aztec or Lebanese passages. The very beautiful, young mathematician whom he loved and was to hurt and shed tears over. What ever became of her? A distinguished economist, actress, mother . . . How old is she now? Agathe gathers lots of articles about her, some newspapers are so taken up by extravagant exploits that her only problem was which to choose concerning the noble, pure Dulcinea, the so-very-lovely teenage lover. A core of Tristanian legend. But do the photos really show her in her younger years and her lofty vigilant silhouette? Her desire to be and her doubt, her tears of joy in her pleasure, her fear of him and his silence and flight?

The Spanish prison escape took place without spectacular tunnels, uprising, or full-scale assault. He was slipped a revolver with which he threatened two guards. He dumped his hostages later; the police lost his trail. Nothing is known about the person who passed him the revolver. He received no visitors. People shunned him. So many dead, maimed for life, martyrs in broad sunlight, the listless dance of the waves . . . all that seed of the ages, sand of erosions, ancient shores, the drifters of the deep, reddened by this blood. Time suddenly congealed in an immense stone. The summer blocked. The affront of sunlight. The macabre blue sky. How was he able to go through with it? Gunning down cops, strictly speaking, is all part of the game, but those cretins, absolutely naked and on exhibit in their swaddling of sand, all silky with oil and happiness? . . . Was he struck by such a terrible loneliness after losing the beautiful suburban Aude who must have fled before the furious lover, fornicator, seized by an all-consuming madness, surrendered to the unbounded agony of love?

Then Agathe looks out the window and forms an impression of the world he's hiding in. Hills and rocks, gorges, craters, caverns obstructed by thorns and nests of birds of prey. And Agathe loves this loner, she'd offer him her gnarled hands so he might drink. She'd pat his sweaty nape and ask him . . . now . . . tell me the truth, look at what state my files are in, nothing but clippings and scraps, a bunch of mismatched fragments . . . help me, delete, clean up, expand where need be, light my way. You tell me . . . blasphemer and destroyer . . . were you ever pure enough to proffer a beautiful love to that young girl who's supposed to be a geometer, fascinated by its art and nuances, so white with black hair, so divided and so true in her quest? For her locks of rain the tears of a king. So afraid of losing herself in you, in your fanatical glamour, this fire of images that slayed her. I, Agathe, want to find out, to see you, to know you from head to toe, your killer's soul handed over, oh miracles, virgin under my gaze . . . your soul and memory for Agathe's archives. I won't repeat a thing, I swear, I'm only a poor old woman whose life is drawing to a close. I'll keep the big secret. About your love and death. A perfectly sensible woman, soon to be paralyzed, blind, but I'll know the essence of your life, the truth of these deserts, the key of your madness. Come and drink from my cupped knuckles. You'll have bread. Tell everything, you'll feel better. Tomorrow I'll be all shriveled up, black with the years, hiding inside this awesome youth of knowledge. Tell me, artist, wanderer, splendid murderer and beggar, plague carrier, traitor, oh Judas, oh Jesus, you are Osiris in pieces, tell me all about the white lover, show your beating heart to my eagle eyes. I'm keeping watch from my threshold, tiny greedy scarab. I won't even look at you. I won't move, I'll play dead, lying on the stone doorstep in the broad sunshine . . . you'll talk in my ear. Nobody will see from the outside this freshness of origins being born within me. I'll remain stone-dumb under my elytra, my insect armor. Enshelled in shadows. But nearing birth! Birth! Primal, howling . . . I'll be your infinite survival, your immortality, killer. I, the grey lady, sterile, rotted virgin, dry vine tendril bearing no grapes, I'll be the womb of an eternal mother. Come and drink in my mirror. I'm all ears.

When a police van stops, Agathe has the time to stuff her papers in a drawer. A knock at the door. She comes out with her bundle of laundry. They question her, she who knows everything, a net of multiple curiosities, information garnered from all homes. Plus, her house is the last of the village, at the edge of the highway. She acts the weary old lady, bowed under her burden, touches her painful knees. She laughs, she quavers. Come on now! You're not claiming that an old granny like me, at the end of her road, might have seen things, understood God only knows what? . . .

They are three young proper policemen. They don't look like they're interested in their investigation. She holds it against them inwardly. These generations have no souls, devoid of burning curiosity. The sense of the sublime totally escapes them. A soccer game and a glass of beer puts them in paradise. They're absentminded. The old woman amuses the smallest rosy-skinned fellow. You think I'm funny, you squirt, keep laughing . . . She doesn't know these officers, from Perpignan probably, noses in the air, made tipsy by the smell of burning, the hem of smoke. All they got on their minds at that age is screwing. Telling each other about it in their wagons, bragging and dreaming about movie stars, orgies with harebrained whores. They don't believe in the terrorist anymore, it's routine. They don't imagine he's out there, in this circle of blazing stones. Don't give a damn, any pretext is good for stopping cars, preferably with young women inside. Checking IDs while ogling the low-cut necklines. Cerebellums in uniform caps, belts wrapping emptiness. They hope they'll stumble upon nudists.

Agathe begins to hang out her wash. Nightgowns dating back to her youth. Unexplored shirts, threadbare lingerie. Washed and rewashed, tirelessly stitched up. Fabrics constellated with big segments of string, pieces endlessly resewn . . . Camisoles, narrow dresses, husbandless bride's bodices, a hope chest of an eternal fiancé who withstood the wars, decolonization, space satellites. She hangs the adorable remnants from a rope between two posts. They'll dry in five minutes. The clothespins beak the rinsed, overripe thrift store tatters, the beggarwoman's austere, swishy things, her prophetess's rags . . . this never replenished wardrobe has dwindled, a misshapen farrago, colorless volutes of an aged Colette, of some proletarian woman out of Brecht. It looks like modern art, you can easily visualize graffiti scrawled upon these eaten fabrics, Rimbaud's poems, calls to arms, uprisings, the new *Illuminations,* the ukases of the year 2000 . . . tattooed on these fossil clothes dangling in the wind, the flight of sparrow hawks, flames, voices emerging from caverns. All these rags whiten in the sunlight, stiffen in islets . . . discreetly triumphant, an old woman's pennants, wriggling indefatigably, whispering like tongues in fits of immortal gossip.

They unearthed it completely with the utmost precaution and placed it in a special trunk, an ambulance of skeletons. It was raining that day, a warm, gentle stream. The countryside was fragrant. The rock sang like a skin swaddled in drops. Beforehand, they'd taken measurements and photographs, opened cross sections, produced sketches, drawings, molds. The trace of the child was repeated in a throng of mirrors. It would escape memory no longer. There he was, recorded in notebooks, seized by latex, numbered, dated, situated between monstrous jaws, mastodons' maws, murderous choppers, feline molars . . . in its cradle. In laboratories it would be subjected to rays, experiments, ultra-accurate tests. Driving behind so many others alongside the sea, it entered the city, penetrated into the great centers of power and glass . . . It had left this cave of love, the happy layers of the ages, Sue's long hands. Cold, lucid, clinical experts awaited the ghost. Through the city, amid thundering mosaics of chrome and glass, hard, brilliant auto bodies, it journeyed. Into the violent splendor of the future it rolled along, the doubtful, immemorial object, paler, more nebulous than a watercolor of ossicles, with its total burden of millennia and gloom. The passersby and drivers, the shop windows, the cog wheels of the modern anthill know nothing of this atavistic intruder crossing through. Memory as frail as an index finger of night, a dew of chaos. Launched amid limpid buildings, new motors, banks, contracts, exchanges and circuits. The giant Plexiglas walls reflect the truck where, invisible to the crowds, the fabulous child was being born, the ape-kid, the link of the world. It was a step away from dissolving, ghostly in its swaddling, enormous and wretched, between the origins and the end, between flight and eternity. Nobody knew that in this rapacious metallic avenue five hundred thousand years were opening their white wake of centuries, of dust, their swarm of seeds and ashes. He was walking.

A great silence gaped in Sue's heart. She no longer felt like tackling a new task. To her eyes the cavern grid held nothing more than squares of banality. The dig site pursued its insectlike weaving, but its soil was missing the kid's magic. Of course she knew that only twenty or thirty yards below there were virgin deposits waiting, down toward the cave bottom, strata, regions . . . more eyes, skulls . . . They enveloped her in a large circle of promises. Their message was both humble and ferocious. Remains, sorry-looking fragments, skulls crammed with nothingness but also rare relics, awesome presences lodged in the remote zones.They will have to be desired during the course of time. The future will come forward to meet them. The dead will see daylight in twenty or thirty years. The phantasmagoria of unforeseeable vestiges. We're far from done with these ancestors, these chattering sands, this eloquence encased under tons of lithic debris. They will speak, the precise moment is unknown. They'll emerge from the hands of other girls when Sue is a woman on in years, elderly or dead herself, a child in a tomb. They'll be born under other caresses, thanks to other techniques, other curiosities. The cave will endlessly offer its modest, colossal treasures. The entire world will have changed in appearance, covered with edifices and materials as yet unsuspected, with utterly different sorts of roadways and vehicles. A new mumbo jumbo of signs and exchanges that a person of today would be unable to decipher. Machines, metals, speeds, channels and networks of things. But the cave would still ruminate its confessions. Slow and stubborn, emptying its bag of secrets. Muttering its refrain of gossip from the centuries. Indifferent to the flight of space shuttles, the epic of new men, their meetings with other planets, their wild third-millennium imaginings. Bustling about always and everywhere, races of people neither more nor less wise, crisscrossing scaffoldings and cupolas above the planet, wakes and braids of languages.

She really earned her virgin lad. She'd spotted him two weeks ago in a remote forest farm. Quite high up, above the multiple stenches and stains, far from tourists, miasmas. A Pyrenean shepherd cradled by the peaks, with a torso of snow, blue wind in his eyes, and knees round as tide-smoothed stones. Sue has a thing for knees, their coarse, ingenuous surfaces. Especially side by side with their traces of black-and-blue marks, old blows, their purple scars. It's knees that catch it during falls and kids' soaring flights. Each to her own obsession. She petted, patted them, listened to the bone-hump echo, genuine little gongs. The boys held them squeezed together like virgin girls. Big janissary knees of a sacred pilaster. With their look of bonzes' shaven skulls.

He was a shepherd . . . When the virgin boy turns out to be a shepherd he's as soft as milk, and if he plays a reed pipe, ecstasy is guaranteed. She'd seen him on a boulder in the middle of a meadow. He was blowing into his flute. Around him a swell of sheep ebbed and flowed. The bleatings, fleeces, tinkling of bells, a black dog racing about, harassing strays, the whole scene swept her with a surge of tender feeling. She would have liked to weave him a crown of stream irises and stick a daisy in his ass. Let no one cast stones at Sue, such a nasty biblical habit. She toiled as the priestess, delivered the engulfed child from the cave. She is fully entitled to voluptuous delight. Cocks are her hobby; each to her own. Better than stamps, butterflies, and postcards are these rural members drawn from fresh pastures, amid clouds, in places where snow-struck summits thrust their rock needles into the azure. Cocks from slopes pattering with springs. A she-wolf's craving lashes Sue in the odor of grasses and sheep. She crouches at the edge of a wood. The gentle shepherd is playing his flute. The white animals graze in an idyllic light. She dreams of a beautiful glans, corpulent, mauve, square-headed, a massive, ultraviolent glans . . . that she'll undo for the first time. A strawberry popsicle popped out of its wrapper. She smiles. Eyes peeled, lying in the ferns. The pasture rustles in the wind of the peaks. The beautiful black dog, seated on its haunches, looks like Anubis. She's going to suck you, her rustic archangel, and stick her fingers up his ass, this simpleton, and shove his pipe between his buttocks. Play on, my shepherd! Play us some flute, get your ass all puffy-cheeked by your blowing on the tip. She laughs. She loses a little bit of saliva. The boy's macabre fairy, a divine milkmaiden and sucker. The tender Herculean mountain lads will be swallowed raw, their shafts gulped down, balls and all. She's got Saturn's throat. A very greedy English ogress. She likes her shepherd boy, toes in the water of a brook pinking against his calves. A shepherd in sauce. She senses a delicate girlish duvet upon his alabaster loins. His sleeping shaft, beautiful maggot which Sue will deftly unknot, gradually transforming it into a passable python. She garners pricks of the highest order. She would have made countless, precious bouquets, swollen stems of diverse calibers and colorings ranging from dark to bright. She'd have put living specimens in crystal vases and sucked them every day so that they wouldn't die. Each to her own roses, cats, games of tennis, jogging. For Sue it was cocks, just cocks, she'd have made them into garlands, members woven into bowers for wiling away hot summer days. There are worse fantasies than Sue's. I know some that are virulent, unwholesome, rotting the soul in the end . . . cramped, poisonous fantasies, vinegars that make you rancid. Oh, Sue was pure in the kingdom of mountain pricks! An innate sense for scepters, heavenly aspergillum. She savored the aroma of semen. More or less dense, with their odors of ivy, of budding Amazon lilies, their swampy blandness from the origins. This taster highly prized and gargled with the elixir . . . She eyes the teenager whose pipe has fallen in the grass. His head tilts forward. He dozes in the gusts amid mauve digitalis. Tall flowers whose corolla in strings of bells dot the meadow. Lyricism. The bacchante draws near. The cur spots her. She possesses a power over beasts. For two weeks she's been cajoling this dog from a distance, insinuating her voice, her scent in stages. He doesn't bark. He wags his tail furiously, plumes of dusky hair. It's a fine shepherd dog, a beater who does a flawless job keeping his sheep together. Each to his role, with mutual respect. She pets him under his belly . . .

She goes up alongside the shepherd. The tip of the pipe lying in the grass is still moist from his lips. He has a broad face, part lamb, part calf, but crystal-sharp. He looks like he doesn't think much. A forehead free of ideas. He sleeps to his heart's content, united with the slumber of plants, with the very slow swaying of the flock's udders. Stupid, oh delights . . . a mountain mossy stupidity like a big meander dozing under a willow's shade. He's sleeping like a salmon. A little spittle glimmers at the corner of his fleshy lips. She keeps watch, doesn't quite know how to attack the idol and his ribbed shorts, studded with stamens. The fabric shows a hole above the knee, gentle scratches have torn his thigh. Nails of eager dryads, Melusina's claws. He knows nothing. Motionless, dreamless, heavy with aimless seed. He reeks of sheepfold sweat. At his feet the stream, a viper of raw water. Sue cut a blade of grass, a horsetail with which she tickles the shepherd's mouth. Very lightly at first, as if a dragonfly's wings were grazing the boy. He quivered in his sleep, his forked snores shift register, nuanced with a cute sniffling. His nose moves, his eyelashes thick. He has dull blond hair, a very pale Lorelei shade, a night-light blond, soft lantern over a dark sea. He sleeps in his skiff. Moss or shepherd, it comes to the same thing. Part sea gull, part sheep. Sue finds that he has a fish's round mouth. And it is as if the ocean were beating in a dream against the mountains, enveloping them in a rosette of waves. She drifts upon these images of an ark and youthfulness. Freshness of the Flood.

Now she lashes his cheek with the horsetail. He jumps awake, eyes wide open, divinely blue and empty. No musing clouds his gaze, not the least stain of thought. It's all brand new inside his skull, a virgin hive of neurons rinsed in the great rush of wind and streams. He looks at her like an enchanted fairy. He's a touch scared. Throws his dog a glance. The very calm animal reassures him. The sheep bleat, a close-packed cluster of curls . . . The dog's coat shines, hemmed with black tufts. She looks at him. Her blouse is open upon her pointy breasts. She's wearing a skimpy skirt. And then the wind, the wing of gulls, schools of fish amid the clouds, the spindrift bathing the pines, the smell of salt, semen. Divine lamb . . . a small knife and I'll cut your throat, Isaac. My god wants it. See the immense ark aground on a mountain slope. The wood smells good, the algae and ferns. With her finger she touches his chest, part marble, part silk to the touch. He trembles, a little nervous all the same. She kisses his mouth. Instinctively he wipes it off with his hand. A brusque gesture, as if swatting an insect. He's got to learn to tolerate the sting, let the bee land and linger on the inside of his lips. He could be off in one bound. She senses this and is afraid. He must be able to run fast, the bugger, in a jumble of sheep and dog barking. And she, an abandoned shepherdess, weeping in the stream . . . brooks' tears, the ark rising amid the pines, with gulls perched on the masts, everywhere upon the mooring, white birds, transparent Aurèles. The ark shaped like a sperm whale harpooned by trunks . . . She thinks of yellow trout floating at lake bottoms, of eagles' eggs in the mountains. Bears are said to live in reserves nearby and slow terrorists climb the rock and breathe in the air, very pure, wind-cleansed killers who swim washed of their blood by spring water.

Much later, when Venus rises, when owls' hooting haunts the ark and large fish emerge from the forest to circle around the mountains, he'll have removed his velvet shorts. He's got a tiny penis and moonlike buttocks. An androgyne whom in other times Sue would have disdained with a bitter pout. She likes thick, heavy saplings, virginal milk abruptly gushing from trunks. He's tiny but his buttocks are taut and circular . . . She slipped her tongue toward the sphere. He groans at the touch of her stinger. There are big fish swaying just above the slumbering sheep. The swelling streams overspill their beds into the grass, as wild and curious as otters. The digitalis exhale whiffs of witches and poison. Now Sue approaches the pipe. Christmas night in midsummer. Magi can be sensed journeying between the stars, a gathering watchfulness, glimmers traveling, crisscrossing, whisperings upon moon-tracks and circles of darkness. The pine tops speak . . . The fish lay eggs in the trees. The stream is a silver branch. The pipe sinks into the shepherd's ass. A lyre of stars sings in the circle of moonlight.

Aurèle's sister is playing in her brother's bedroom with the window open. She tickles awhirl dust balls in patches of sunlight. The flurries settle. With a drumstick she stirs them up, sends them flying in all directions. She's bored. She yawns. She's got two bedrooms now. Her brother's death makes her very important, an owner of grandiose spaces. The house is all hers. Her friends are jealous of this promotion. The adults vie in kindness toward her. She's the little sister of a dead boy . . . a sort of queen, poor dear. Mimicking their parents' compassion, her little girlfriends gaze upon her. They've found the right expression of delicate pity. They like putting on this air: holding title to a secret knowledge makes them feel more grown up. They play with the sister of a dead boy. His name was Aurèle. Alive, he was a lot less interesting. They barely remember him. Shy, a bit babyish. Aurèle's sister doesn't really think about her brother. When her parents abruptly burst into silent tears, sometimes the weeping infects her. She tells herself: "Dad, Mom are crying because of Aurèle, who's dead. He's in the cemetery but at the same time he lives up with the angels." The sister told her best girlfriend one day: "My brother became an angel." "Did not!" answered the other girl instinctively, forgetting the consideration she owed to the sister of a dead boy. "Did too! Dad and Mom are the ones who told me and Father said the same thing at confession." "What did they say?" asked the girlfriend, half suspicious, half envious. "They told me Aurèle was an angel."

What both girls know about angels is limited to church statuettes and the holy cards given out to kids making their first communion. Angels got wings —that's the most important thing—and gold circles around their heads. They got curly hair, sometimes as long as girls', plus a white robe. They're darling. They fly through the air. But they don't make honey. They aren't birds. They're angels. They like landing around the Blessed Virgin or on plump white clouds. And when it rains, then who knows where they are because people always see them in sunbeams and ribbons of light. The girls repeated at home that Aurèle's sister was saying how he'd become an angel. The parents gave each other the sort of look they do when about to lie for their children's own good, and with hypocritical gentleness, they said that yes . . . Aurèle lived up above with the angels. The dads cutting their rare steaks, the moms bringing the cheese . . . The girls then wondered what had really become of Aurèle. He's in the cemetery and that's the end of that. He's asleep in the hole . . . However, even if they knew it was untrue, they like to make angel Aurèle a part of their games. It's a good idea, an angel with wings mixed up with dolls. It's practical like an intelligent bird; you make him do things a normal doll couldn't.

At times Aurèle's sister starts awake during the night. She cries out. She's afraid. The parents rush to her side, console her, wipe away her tears. They gently question her. "Were you dreaming, honey? Were you having a nightmare?" But Aurèle's sister never remembers her dream. She can't say whether something specific frightened her. She doesn't know why she's crying. The next day she completely forgets her screams, her tears. She becomes the queen again, the girl who earns glances, combining respectful pity and admiration. She's the sister of a dead boy. When she crosses the street, runs an errand for her mother, other people's faces always remind her of this. Sometimes she's ashamed. She'd like to be a little girl like any other. Sometimes she thinks it's fun and nice having two bedrooms and parents all to herself. She feels very rich and very lovely despite everything. When Aurèle was there, at dessert, he was entitled to a serving of custard or rice pudding that she craved because she always found it to be bigger and more beautiful than her own. Since he became an angel, the servings are all the same size and she can eat everything. But it's not like it used to be. It's not as good, and she doesn't understand why. She feels that she's in a world where something very important is missing . . . Her parents aren't the same anymore, their smiles are less profound, incomplete. The sister feels like a princess, yet guilty. Since he became an angel, there are only surfaces. The world is like a picture. How annoying! She's the queen of a kingdom that doesn't exist anymore.

Simon and Myriam now felt that the terrorist was a goner. Simon wasn't in any position to understand just what had turned Myriam into the killer's accomplice. And as for the reason he himself was the man's voyeur—this also escaped him. Ten thousand, one hundred thousand footpaths, a million possibilities crisscrossed in those black, torrid places. He and the African woman, settled under the boulder's white dome and the night of the ancestors.

Come sunset, their desire to scale the heights awakened. After nightfall the cave was unguarded. There was nothing to steal except the shadows. The air smelled good . . . the wind-licked grass. Yet the cicadas, as soon as you became aware of their song, testified to a tension, a keen relentlessness. Pools of moonlight bleached the limestone, huge stars quivered. Their footsteps stumbled over roots and bumps. They supported each other in the warmth of this night climb. They felt their way along a kind of continuous hollow, a furrow that seemed constantly to disappear only to spring up between the pitfalls. All the footsteps of the men who had trod this path guided them. The mountains appeared to be slowly circling in the emptiness like pyramids. Simon experienced a sensation of immersion, of colossal gravitation. The mountains might well have opened like portals and the stars loomed larger to become a tangible crystal. And the insects, transformed into dragons, gilded by the suns. In the neighboring gorges could be made out the sound of flowing water. Then it all became simple and familiar. The metamorphoses ceased. The large astral ship glided along in its hull riddled with cicadas. The cave opening was blacker than the night. Myriam and Simon hesitated at the edge of this mouth. They discovered to what point the shadows are an attribute not so much of heavenly darkness as of the earth's innards. They were as afraid of entering the mountain as of the world's womb, of passing through this crevice, this grimace, this gargoyle's hole. Their flesh remembered the ancient terrors. Beautiful stars slept on the backs of the hills. The man and woman dreaded leaving them behind. Even the chirring cicadas took on an intimate, reassuring meaning. The great vessel had much to recommend it with these sounds of wave and wind. Where were they going to enter? Through what porthole? Simon squeezed Myriam's hand. The cavern no longer betrayed the toiling teenagers' traces. The gridded space of the excavations reverted to a savagery that preceded any gazes. A bottleneck of uncalculating gloom. The naive and monstrous mountain snatched them up. Inside it was cold. There was a sense of something alive and listening. After they advanced a few steps, the outdoor darkness loomed against the cavern porchway in a bluer oval. And they missed this great glimmer covering the earth. Now it was pitch black. A pall fell upon them, orphans cast into the abyss. They had a nostalgia for cosmic lightness. The deep shadows weighed heavily. They dreamed of this vast shell of air fractured with light called "sky," constituting the universe itself. They burrowed to the bottom of a heavy core. Kept sliding forward to the base of the deposits, into the ditches. Under their fingers they felt the bones breaking the surface. They told each other these were ordinary animals from Genesis. They repeated the names: lynx, Etruscan wolf, bear, cave lion, ancient elephants, beaver, Mosbach horse, reindeer, bison, musk ox. They recalled the teenager's decorticating labor. But all these signs disappeared, engulfed by the subterranean night. They were no longer remnants, familiar forms. However, in one final vision, they glimpsed the herds moving through the blue night of the plain. Large phantom creatures in the dark grass under the diadem of stars. And then it died out. The bones now referred only to themselves and became horrible like the vestiges of a fantastical pulverization.

They stretched out upon a smoother layer and embraced. The black woman smelled good, of honey and mane. He breathed in the perfume of her armpits, skin, bowels. What solace did she find in this pale man's arms? And the cavern watched them. An extraordinary presence encircled them. Neither herds nor primitive hunters, but rows of vigilant bones. Skeletal voyeurs. They pondered those who lie sleeping there, five hundred thousand years earlier, in a living heap, this primal heat. They failed to rediscover the protective virtues of the cave. What had once been a refuge had become a sly trap, a cowl of death. They embraced in death. All this coldness wrapping the hot core of this black woman. Good heavy buttocks, vulva swollen with curls, dug out in the dampness. Her chest filling his palms. And Simon understood the overwhelming power of the life that mingled with his terror. The black woman drew on his member with a violent gesture, she squeezed it in her hand. Fitfully she kissed Simon's mouth, overcome by thirst, and hardened him between her fingers. She plunged him within her, speeding the living bone of the penis by a thrust of her loins. And gradually the dead grew mellow. And the animals returned and circled around the lovers in a lunar dance of bison. At times Simon's and Myriam's arms reached out to touch the relics. This contact didn't frighten them anymore. On the contrary, it rekindled their desire. The cavern was no longer death, its bony envelope became the thin limestone membrane around an egg of happiness.

When they awoke, the dawn sunlight was coming in the porchway, coating with blood the remains from the beginnings. No fright seized them at the sight of this placental compost and these red skeletons. Elsewhere the cave was brighter. Its calm dusts, its sand deposits took on grainy hues in some spots. Myriam made out the latex mask hanging in a corner, the double of the Aguilar skull that she had reproduced. She went over to place it on her face. Simon gazed at this skull-born woman. Her body seemed to gush alive from this punctured stone. Simon wasn't afraid of the mask. He contemplated the effigy of this twenty-year-old man who had once lived here. He no longer knew whether he saw the black woman, the young hunter or himself. He stroked the mask with his finger, recognized the occipital ridge, the recessive chin, imagined the strong jaws and retreating forehead. Myriam moved the skull away from her face and set it upon Simon's. She broke free and lay upon her lover. The mask's sockets weren't synchronized with Simon's eyes. He didn't see Myriam. He didn't know what she thought, what she desired. She also touched the mask. He heard her fingers rustling. In the night of the skull, Simon waited. He had the impression that Myriam was showing her truth, was speaking to the Aguilar hunter. Jealous, he kneaded the black woman's buttocks and grabbed hold of her breasts while she cheated on him with the young man from five hundred thousand years ago. But later on these differences became blurred in the warmth of sunlight streaming into the cave. The three partners merged beyond embraces in a daydream telling of the young sun, the pines on the slopes, the birds, the springs, the sky and the large quartzes under the cold water. Another love united them, painlessly. They all three could have come down from the mountain hand in hand.

And the bikers leapt amid the flames. They did stunts between the boulders. They adored the fire, its coppers, its torso, its cymbals. Paloma and Lynne lead the gang, then a tall naked guy twirling his rifle, followed by others: squat, tattooed hoodlums, or eellike with an aquatic dexterity. They howled in the clangor of accelerators, the growling of gases. They hunted the herd of flames. The villagers were afraid. People went up the old watchtowers, the medieval ruins and the Cathar spurs to see the invaders, the javelins, the pouncing shields, the Barbary Coast raids. At times they halted, formed a circle, a camp amid the smoke upon strips of land cleared to isolate the fire. They ruminated their wrath. But a great gust swept away a firebrand which relit some tufts of arbutus. The bikers worked at the fire as if with lassos. Periodically enshrouded, they managed nick-of-time escapes by plunging into the flaming row, reappearing on the other side, bitten on the necks. They jumped in the red fur, leaping, wriggling. They seemed besieged by giant foxes and laughing hyenas. When the fire galloped into a valley, they liked riding out in front. Boastful warriors leading the disaster. They surged into the dry streambeds, bikes jabbering over the backs of stones. The flames halted, for want of food. Running back and forth along the rut. Down the very center, water still flowed. And the bikers bathed while thumbing their noses at the blaze and its Sioux headdresses. Paloma smelled of ash and sweat. Lynne squeezed against her in the zigzags, the racket, the almost horizontal skids. The big guy shot his rifle into the fiery furnace. He aimed at the flames like lionesses' throats. Paloma, bursting with revenge, spurred her cylindered mount. She raised her loins, calves arched, hips tacking, spine dancing, spotting in the distance brand-new red fire zones. The police helicopter witnessed the game, crisscrossing the sky, impotent and voyeuristic. The firemen fought on toward other hills. They could have seen the metal of the roaring machines through the flames. The terrorist was fleeing somewhere, or perhaps took shelter out toward the beaches and the sea. In the city, on maps, the policemen imagined the trail he had followed. Accounts by peasants and wanderers furnished contradictory information on his passage. More reliable data corrected these rumors. The fire flushed him out but erased his tracks. They were waiting for him at the mouths of ravines. Police vans in ever greater numbers were stationed in the scrub, at the foot of mountains, in rarely used paths and out-of-the-way hamlets. They were lying in wait at springs, beside sheepfolds. Kids and cowherders were questioned. Precise orders poured in from Madrid and Paris. He was a common-law murderer. No mercy for the foul leper. His cause was considered a mere pretext. His ancestors could not have been the original seafaring Basques. A people of telamones and kings of the oceans. He was a traitor, a coward, an insane egoist. He was identified with evil itself, with the fire. In his person he concentrated the craving for expiation. They wanted his hide, that trophy of muscles. Under the sunshade of the boulders, the pithecanthropi watched . . .

Simon came to fetch Agathe before the heat overwhelmed everything. It was an awfully cheerful morning, one a trifle disturbing nevertheless for the old woman. She'd slept little. However she was in no way averse to hearing that long thumping of night between the shutters left ajar. She kept watch and felt beautiful in her bed beside which glowed a wisp of moon. He drove her to the foot of the mountain. The teenagers in the camp looked confident at the sight of her. Simon simply blurted out: "We're going!" The die was cast. She'd climb or croak. In the village all the inhabitants were far from approving. Some nodded their noggins while muttering that it was madness. Simon gave incontrovertible proof of the harm it would do. The elderly ladies were especially jealous. The young ones laughed, finding Agathe barmy.

They started out onto the first loop which tackled the steep slope. The sun was already beating down. But the fragrance of night and dew still lurked under the pines. Agathe watched where she set her feet, aiming for the track running between stones, ducking thorn branches. The little hike up proved harsh right from the start. Although the zigzags vainly attempted to outmaneuver the slope, often the terrain loomed sheerly, uncourteously. A chamois trail. Slowly she ascended, saving her breath, arranging for breaks. Simon calmly accompanied her. "I'm slowing you down! Oh, I'm slowing you down!" she apologized. "Not in the least!" the traveler replied. "I'm taking in the countryside at an easy pace and enjoying it." For Simon liked the cave path. This scatter of vines on the neighboring bumps. Agathe's black dress kept scraping against the rock edges. She used her hands for help, clinging to the bushes. They spotted berries, thistles, yellow flowers, copses chubby with leaves as round and shiny as boxwood, followed by arid stretches, seeds of stone where the first rays ricocheted. She set off small landslides that made her laugh. At times Simon supported her, discreetly backing her up. She squeezed his hand like a fiancée who knows her lover is leading her to some hiding place where he'll take her virginity. She stopped to contemplate the village huddled below, beyond the vines and fruit trees. A meander of the stream flowing out of the gorges was visible, its course gradually drying up. A rail of immaculate vertebrae. They decided to sit a moment. Agathe's heart beat louder. But it was bearable. They had to go at it slowly as if it were nothing. A tenth of the path had been covered, the first link, at least that much is done, thought Agathe. Instead of envisaging the global distance, the idea was to fragment it into modest segments. From time to time all the same, she stole a glance toward the summit. She measured the ramparts where the skinny furrow of the footpath slipped through. All that remained afterward was a chaos of boulders that seemed impassable. She chased away these unreal visions that belonged to the future. Simon posed questions about her youth. Ordinarily she was the one who did the asking. She was surprised.

"I don't have anything to tell," she said. "Nothing remarkable happened in my life, no really noteworthy events, no catastrophe . . . time passing, little by little, and then that's all, but I was happy."

"You're lying to me, Agathe, you're hiding things from me, you're hiding love affairs!"

"Don't act like such a ninny! You know full well there's nothing of the kind, love's never been my affair. Oh, I have no regrets! But you see, you won't find it the least bit surprising if I confess to you that the great love of my life was curiosity."

"But lovers," Simon repeated in a teasing wheedling tone, "when you were a girl . . ."

"Stop singing the same song, I tell you! A young girl, a grandmother, it's all the same. I was always too interested in everybody to settle on one person. My father was a customs agent at the border, my mother kept a vegetable garden, I helped her out, we sold what we grew at market, I harvested grapes and even did housework at the druggist's. Maybe that's where I really learned curiosity, by listening to people's sicknesses. I'd have liked to be a druggist, prepare potions, listen to patients recount the long list of their woes. Little troubles are very interesting, they paint a person's character better than outward acts. But how I'm going on!" she exclaimed. "Look at me losing my saliva when I need it most of all."

"And don't you have any more questions for me?"

"I know quite a lot already!" said Agathe with a short snigger. "And anyway up there I'll see everything, right?"

She gazed at the cavern mouth, that stone-lipped shadow staining the whiteness. The hole couldn't be seen, the passage, but only a gap in the wall, a touching weakness. That's where the others were . . . in the place where the stone became almost curtainlike. Behind, they were waiting. Like antique actors, in buskins and masks.

They continued on their way. She snuck a glance at Simon, his skinny face. To bring her along this way—she whom nobody wanted—showed he must need affection. He was at the end of his tether in his own way. She almost knew why. He had a too-personal memory, full of painful individual recollections . . . That's where he went wrong. Never had Agathe been interested in herself. Mirror, joy of seeing. But she liked the tragic dimension of certain men. As if they had chosen remorse for the rest of their lives. She wasn't going to explain it to him. She was there to see, and he to live, supposedly . . . clearly he liked the sunshine, she surmised that he'd left at dawn only to suit her. She saw his face lift skyward. Instinctively he solicited the star. A tunic of sweat, a killing ardor.

Things were going well, a rhythm of sorts, a somewhat imbecilic taste for obstacles, heaving upward, getting hooked on nettles. And then breath, this piston running wild, controlled by inhaling, slowing down, an acquired discipline. At such times their objective was not present to their minds. They became one with each difficulty, with each instant in their obsession with self-mastery and pacing. Their temples pounded against the hot stone. Layers of odors had settled in the blue-tinted greyness of thyme. There were no animals, birds. The silence could be heard echoing in the nearby gorges. A vast silence uncoiled like a boa's belly. Agathe's right knee suddenly hurt. He surmised that from now on he had to help her continuously. She leaned on him. He was almost carrying her when they had to cross a slab. They neither talked nor laughed. Agathe was solemn . . . every yard was a point scored, a stage, a pain-inducing victory. And then a new terrace, and this narrow footpath, ill-defined and enveloped by a lattice of other trails even vaguer and more winding that the youngsters must follow in order to move faster, fly through the loose stones . . . Alert with their notebooks crammed with figures, complicated codes, carrying cave fragments described down to a fraction of an inch. To clear the way and hoist her from above, Simon often jumped into this network of childish, fugitive tracks.

She was in pain. He saw this. Her breath was halting in her thorax. She was old. She was not going to make it to the peak and take her vast, decisive sounding. They stopped. "You've really got to help me, Simon." Simon made her understand that they'd reach the end even if it took them several days. They'd take shelter under the pines. The young people would bring them something to drink. She was touched to see him so resolute, determined. She surmised he was all too happy to succeed in at least this, to be loyal on this particular occasion. He was as pure as a thief toward his lifelong accomplice. He climbed up above with the old woman, like a mother being led to a sanctuary. Even if he himself no longer believed. In advance he redeemed himself for what in truth he had come to see in the region. With his car, at nightfall . . . Soon it was her other knee and then her back, a cramp like a saber. Agathe no longer made out anything except for the details of the ground vibrating in a mist, countless, minute mirrors reflecting her pain. She was sorry about nothing, had no aspirations anymore. Stubborn, tortured. And Simon so easy, so light. He was young—it was as simple as that. Sturdy muscles and organs springing forward. She, an aged combatant. She missed a step, he held her, but her thigh had grazed the sharp tapering point of a rock sculpted by storms and lightning. She felt the blood flowing under her skirt. She pressed her hand against the fabric. Simon sensed her injury. They sat at the edge of the guilty boulder. He forced her to raise her skirt. Her thigh appeared extraordinarily fresh and white above her gnarled knee.

"You've got beautiful thighs!" he said to her with a pat.

"Don't get carried away," she gently gasped.

And he looked on, surprised, her skin under her mourning dress had preserved its youth while her narrow face was caught in a densely wrinkled reticulum. He dabbed the blood with an end of his shirt. She protested, forbidding him to soil himself. He kept at it. They pulled down the cloth over the cleansed wound. And then they very slowly resumed the last segment of the slope. Tortuous loops twined around large mineral protuberances. Neither cave nor footpath was in sight. They were confronted with immediate reliefs that hid the future, hemming the traveler and the old woman in a colossal, opaque ring. But, on the other side, the cave reappeared close enough to touch. The last slope was extremely easy, free of stones, gentle and sandy, marked out by very green bushes. But Agathe could no longer enjoy this happiness. Exhausted, she almost came to a standstill. And this miraculous path running toward the porchway of all secrets struck her as forever inaccessible. Simon made her stretch out along the border of the footpath. He whispered tender words and deceptive promises. She thought she ought to have stayed back in her house with the road passing in front, the neighboring village, the town population. A perfectly circumscribed, snag-free fiefdom. She'd wanted to take wing, hover above the world, cast a glance over the other side of the mountains, to do what, to see what? In her overwhelming state of fatigue, no matter what world wonder might have been mentioned she would have dismissed it with indifference. She'd lost her curiosity. She looked at the few yards separating her from the cave. A few steps, trifles that in normal times she would have strode without a thought. But doing so now seemed vain and interminable. And Simon waited. A group of ten or so teenagers brought water and cookies. Simon told her that they were both fine right where they were, at the threshold of things, that they mustn't hurry, that they had all the time in the world and that indeed they could go back down without seeing the porchway. Gradually he soothed her. Reclining in the dust, aching. A branch protected her from the sun. The teenagers were pleasant. Their faces attentive but devoid of pity. They didn't get overwrought, they understood. The water was good, the sugar from the cookies. A great emptiness opened up around her where her breath rose, fell. Unreal mountains, weightless scenery. Her tiredness still left an aftertaste of bowels in her mouth. And that alone existed. This savor between birth and death in which her whole being wavered. He also had stretched out and was gazing at the sky where a circaetus circled.

Small signs of returning life, swaying lamp halos that steadied, weaving a fragile yet continuous web. Myriam had come down. Agathe saw the fearsome black woman whose strength seemed awesome. Breasts, buttocks, an athlete of the caves of heaven . . . But so calm. This serenity awakened Agathe. A questioning was born, but at a distance from the old lady. As if this query was not quite coming from her. It was within her reach, a temptation, possible reunions with her being. All she needed to do was stretch out her arms. Agathe didn't make any such motion. But she sensed that she was going to, either now or later. The seductive interrogation loomed larger.

And the skein of thoughts and desires was reconstituted . . . interlacing designs that branched out from the cave to the village, with Agathe at their center. She hadn't yet confessed her best to Simon. But Simon must have known. He hadn't moved, the bird circled, saw the precipices, torrents, wadis, the coarse crust of the scrubland, the holes, valleys pointed seaward. A mosaic of images for Simon. Indistinct, blue-tinted by the distance, a mist of inappetence. Agathe was the one who found her hunger again . . . For Myriam was leaning over her. The old woman scrutinized the Cameroon lady's eyes. Behind their circles of innocence dwelled anguish. All was in play, but not yet accepted in the depth of her being. And Agathe perceived that here, supine, in this posture of abandon, the truth came toward her, was easily tamed. The old lady became porous. She who had tackled beings and things, scrutinized them, wrung them out atom by atom, now only needed to allow this flux to stream toward her. The obvious facts fell into place by themselves. She could have fallen asleep bearing the world in her womb.

When she got up she walked effortlessly toward the porchway. Her black grandmotherly footsteps were a slap of terror for Simon's soul.

All was ready inside Agathe's brain, an entire lifetime's data, patiently reconstructed deductions, tied threads. She circled in the cave, driven to hallucination by the ancestors. She sated herself on archives, bones, recognized everything she had imagined, concocted in her calculations of a planetary gossipmonger. The enormous deposits trembled under the heel of this old visionary. It was as if the battalions from Genesis were watching her. She welded the first links to the rest of the chain. The shadow enveloping her was a great cradle of centuries. A nest of millennia. She knew herself to be the mother of this abyss of men.

It was upon coming out abruptly onto the sun-drenched porchway that she let out a cry. Villagers below saw her through their binoculars. Black Agathe in the broad sunshine. An almost animal shout of joy resounded, far-reaching, as strident as a spasm. In the heart of her thought, Simon, Myriam, the terrorist, the lynx, the pithecanthropi and the world were clear filings of intuitions, facts, memories abruptly crystallized. In the sunlight Agathe beamed. Myriam and Simon heard her cry of victory echoing. Free of pity, it was the elation of total power. Agathe understood the universe. The village at her feet revealed its structures, joined houses, gardens, gaps, troops of shacks, lines of streets, enclosures, the church and town hall, a chain of tiny dwellings she could have held in her palm. The town in its least details, interconnections, the tree of its families, the saga of its races. All this matter arranged in the circle of her hand, brilliant in her gaze. The terrorist, Simon and Myriam formed a surrounding triangle of gold. And the mountains hiding other valleys, other villages, the gullies leading to the sea, the borders, Spain, all those peoples along rivers whose route and source she still knew nothing of, the backbone of the state highways, those out-of-the-way estuaries, immense cities frightening her. They no longer challenged the central truth. This hamlet of truth that was hers alone. Transparent rock. Agathe was the queen of things. Her joy rose like a flood splattering her bones, soaking her breast. She exulted, stamped on the stone, in the face of the star of daylight. She possessed the key . . . one she herself had chiseled, whose contours she had tirelessly purified. She was opening the universe. This cosmic village in her triangle of gold. The herds could run past in the primal plains, the pithecanthropi disappear far back in Genesis with their ever-more receding heads, their torsos of puny apes, pitched in the savanna for around three million years and more . . . fear-stricken ghosts in the vessel of the ages . . . and the constellations amassing their unimaginable ciphers, at great distances, quasars, millions of other suns, other dusts and hamlets encircled by animals, satellites and gazes. She sensed the presence of oceans, trails, immense rifts in the nights, the gigantic ditches, the twinkling skeletons of Milky Ways on the sand of orbits. But what mattered was this node of light, this village truth, armoire of the infinite which her joy opened wide. Distinct houses, contiguous or detached, at times agglomerated like atoms, with the bench and the tree, the museum, the fountain, the lattice of small streets and the highway. The whole, limpid and minute. But possessing an absolute certitude. And the terrorist, Simon, Myriam, even they, the confused buggers of the beginnings, must have been happy knowing themselves to be understood this way, allied to geometry and light, docked ships, asleep on the calm waters of language, for their fate was already determined, their destiny sealed. All that remained was to utter the words. It came all by itself, was born from the mouth of happiness.

Simon brought Myriam to the seaside, toward nightfall. After a long hesitation she followed him. At any rate, events had gathered a momentum in which they had no part. The man and woman were relegated to the background. Myriam looked at Simon, Simon at Myriam, while the police vans passed by. They had never directly spoken about the escapee. Simon didn't know why she abandoned the terrorist. But couldn't she still help him? The least attempt to communicate with him ran the risk of being spotted and bringing harm his way. Other reasons may have explained Myriam's behavior. A mutual agreement between her and the runaway. What pact had bound them, how deeply had it involved them?

They avoided overcrowded beaches. Simon left the roads, took a pebbly path between two hills. The sea appeared below. After parking they walked along a steep incline. A slender fringe of sand joined the purple rock to the water. Waning light, violet sea. Unblocking space, the water made matter undulate and gave breath to long braids of atoms. After the dense tangle of the mountains sliced by gorges and gridded by vines, it felt good looking at this skin where nothing was written. Tested with a bare foot as if it could bite or sting. In terror, like an unknown body. Shreds of surf, a light lapping fritters away the outermost edge of this uniform mass. Timid net. The sea brought to birth these fragments of spindrift, white mice skittering along the sand, describing a semicircle, flowing back, vanishing, as another small wave spills out. Myriam and Simon meditated upon this infinite discretion of the sea. It scribbled such light alphabets on the beach, composed such frail messages alongside the enormous mystery of waters. And they were struck by the recognition that their own words were just as small compared to everything their silence concealed, everything they didn't know about the other and themselves.

They stretched out along the sand, ears attuned to the waters' beating, the docile dinosaur breath coming and going, purifying thought. The Milky Way extended such huge trails above their heads, with larger pools here and there, clouds of suns, surf of stars. They were caught between the hand of sea and of heaven. They didn't speak, feeling the weight of their bodies resting on the pivot of worlds. Anecdotes faded, the panting of history, all those police vans in every corner of the mountains. Myriam got undressed and went into the sea. Simon followed. She swam slowly, creased the brilliant surface. Her body curved like a core of darker sea. Island, flotsam, a fish's side. Black jewel in the ring of white waters. Swollen algae. Black jellyfish. Simon grazed Myriam's hip with his mouth. The African woman's fragrance had disappeared, swallowed up by the deep salty odor of the ocean. Wrack, stirred sands, a hint of silt, insipid taste of grounded vessels, slaughtered gulls. Water and night intercoiled, stars hatched in the womb of the swells. Myriam's breasts glimmered and Simon thought of the Cameroon woman's first name which evoked myriads, pleiades . . . violent or diamond constellations encrusted in bronze, brilliances sprinkling this oiled flux like a seal's throat. Where water and air meet, Myriam became a world, magnetizing denser molecules, binding them into a spindle, an umbilicus. Flesh was born of this fusion of stars and sea, like a bodily rim indefinitely modulated by the same caress.

When they returned to the sand and made love, Simon sank into a living piece of the cosmos, a sticky concretion of stars and shadows.

After embracing, their thoughts turned to the terrorist. Their consummated lovemaking ushered back noise, ephemeral perceptions. The escapee was huddled out in the rocks and shrubs, with the vans and their glinting metal bodies and those helicopters on their landing fields. The whole pack waiting. He, not far from them, or perhaps nearer than they think, in his zigzagging wiles, the arabesques of his fears and his desire. A mile or so away, the blaze had galloped to the sea, arriving in a cirque. The flame in the mirror of the waters. A wave driven by a current thrust its torso against a boulder and sprayed up, a cold flare. The sparks and spindrift caught fire, died out. A virgin hell of contrary elements . . .

The couple in the oneness of night lacerated at present by a humming motor. The boat emerged from limbo. They saw the fisherman's shadow loom up. They rose and the man came toward them. They weren't suspicious. He was tall, skinny. Simon thought he recognized this silhouette. He rejected the idea: through what magic had the gold prospector become a sea hunter? The fisherman merely paused a moment. He announced he would soon be off again. Simon offered him money so that they could go along. Tractor-drawn by the motor, the boat swiftly crumpled the waves. The coast disappeared. Slowing down, the fisherman emptied his trawl net hooked to the poop. The skiff continued on its way, the mechanical growl didn't thwart the vast circular sound, orb of the sea, silence populated with depths. They slipped across the roofing of an immense edifice whose moving layers were superimposed, with varying volumes and temperatures, floors of currents. An architecture of transparencies and eddies, of columns whose energy ceaselessly wavered and reformed, distended with swells at the shores. The fisherman didn't break his silence. Myriam shivered in the coolness emanating from the water. Her flesh hardened and united against the sea. The young woman's scent returned. Large planes of water and moonlight spread across them. The fisherman brought in the trawls with a winch. A shower of fish tumbled into the bottom of the boat. Silver-sheened bellies, supple writhing, thick lines, hopping with life. A mound of creatures expelled from undersea caverns, spawned there, suddenly, a magnificent reeking harvest. Old seadogs and gilt-heads in a sinuous heap. Myriam's and Simon's eyes widened. The fisherman grabbed hold of the biggest catch. Its mouth opening and closing, body swelling, muscled under its scaly sheath, shaken by brutal spasms. The fisherman admired his prey. Myriam and Simon thought of all the others below them, multitudes of animals, colonies, schools, playing their part in the invisible regions, armadas of devouring fury, great and small creatures as in the jungles. The vegetation of waves camouflaging the carnage, the bluff of gorgon masks, the war tunics, Scaramouche noses, swordfish and garfish, their flourishes of death and grandiloquence under the ocean. The silence and serenity masked an abyss of terror. And perhaps the stars themselves, calmly beaming, watch themselves closely in the firmament, clashing their helium blazes, exploding, digesting planets, galleons of voracious suns and celestial pillages. But the overall impression was one of remote gentleness, diluted in its milk, like the back of the sea, the dome of a summer night.

Their romp echoed on the pebbles, they threaded their way through, slender Sioux between the pines, along arbutus, on rock ledges. Faces scrunched. Eyes scrutinizing every least recess. Defying their parents' orders. "Absolutely not!" they had declared in threatening tones. "You're not going to go traipsing around the scrub with the police closing in and the terrorist in a panic and getting even more dangerous." But the kids are tempted by Hippolyte the mailman's story, who got it from the prospector living in the area. They say that the lynx himself contains in his bowels a jumble of jewels called ligures or lynx stones. He shits his fabulous treasure in the mountains, stashes it in his lair, in the hollow of a tree stump, a hole in the limestone. The kids launched an expedition without further delay. The lord of the bench Ludovic's granddaughter, Polyte's, plus Yvette's grandniece, the mailman's youngest boy, a second cousin of Julia, finally Aurèle's sister because they thought she'd bring good luck with the marvel of her dead brother. She was a sort of miraculously cursed creature, endowed with special antennae. They needed nothing less than the angels to conquer the lynx's diamonds. In his belly they took shape, it was written in very old books, the prospector had said, Latin volumes from antiquity, from the time of Rome and Caesar. It goes without saying that there couldn't be any mistakes. For it was far back when, therefore true. Like the ancestors' cavern . . . A pile of brilliant pebbles that he forges in his belly. From the blood of hares and old eagles he's devoured, wild trout in the torrents, he produces these gems. With his claws, rage, fangs sunk into the heart of goats' stray kids, he can engender rare and violent minerals . . . At times in the streams you can see round stones speckled with sparkling crystals. Nothing to do with the lynx. Indeed, very little is known about these famous ligures except that the lynx lays them at dawn. Out there, beyond the vines, out toward the gorges, beyond pathways, toward the Cathar ruins perhaps, Galamus and the frontiers. The kids were in despair over not being able to travel that far. But the blaze ravaging the whole border region must have driven the lynx into the circle of Aguilar. Some have spotted it, that's a fact. Agathe in Hippolyte's car. Simon the traveler admitted so to Paula before her death. She evidently told Alphonse who repeated it to Lynne and so on. The student burst out laughing and fiercely denied the stones' existence. "These vulgar superstitions must be dispelled!" he said. But he's a cuckold, wasn't able to hold on to Lynne, sorry-looking, he can't be believed. He's too weak, his hairs are withering in his beard. The bikers are also probably out searching for the treasure, that's why you can hear them racing deep into the mountains and the scrub. They're hunting with the lust of pirates, they want to unearth the lynx's precious pile. Thieves know where real things are stashed, the stuff that counts. At every moment the kids think they've discovered the hideaway, what all the talk's about. There, under this suspicious slab, that crust you only have to listen to, in that fault . . . First they ram in a stick to see if a snake might have stuffed itself inside, then thrust in their hands. Nothing, the casket is empty. In this immense setting, how can the spot be guessed? Could be that the lynx has lodged his treasure in an invulnerable kingdom, in the heart of the blaze, in a chest of flames. The precious stones are proof against the fiercest furnaces. They don't melt like metal. In a thick mantle of ashes the children scatter, rummage, gambol, climb through the complexes of loose rock. Light-footed fauns leaping above crevasses, javelins of kids with archangel ankles. The predators of the air see their rock-minuet. Tom Thumbs hopping along crenels, in fissures with freshwater springs, imponderable and high-spirited, flailing about, catching themselves in time. They bend over watery surfaces to glimpse a ruby's sparkle. In the rubble of an old sheepfold they move the beams. They come out of the lair in single file, impish, giddy, like the letters of a bewitched alphabet reduced to purely musical signs. Does the mountain hear the minute cascade of these single notes falling one after the other?

While dashing down the slope, they made a mistake. Behind the ridge blocking the view, a road passes with two police vans stationed alongside. The cops caught the kids and hauled them off. They came back to the village. The old men of the bench recognized the faces of their great-grandchildren through the windows. It causes a scandal in the hamlet, a rain of slaps and shoes flying into rear ends. "Ain't it just too sad when so many misfortunes come tumbling down, the blaze and the mad terrorist. And these here, skedaddling off, defying the police . . . throwing themselves into the wolf's jaws. The slightest shift in the wind could have blown the inferno back toward them. And if they'd stumbled upon him, that ogre of sunlight . . . On the beach he didn't even spare the children. Nobody escaped. The democratic bomb catapulted people of all ages." And the children are shaken, insulted, cuffed. And they cry like sows whose necks are being cut. The big ones squeal more discreetly. Others, restive, clam up, take the beating, their gazes glinting with malevolence. Chins hard-set. Mulish. Future bandits. And her mother gave it to Aurèle's sister: "Oh my God, now isn't this a disgrace . . . you, with all our woes, our great misfortunes . . . you, the sister of a dead boy, you didn't even give one thought to us, your little brother . . . Don't we have enough with your father out there fighting the fire!"

"Ain't it just too sad! Ain't it just too sad!" the villagers repeated in chorus.

The small bunch of kids trembles in the middle of the square, not far from the bench that the old men have left to surround their fragile issue: these tender shoots, elder stalks, willow torsos, innocent branches, branchlets and elbow-shaped stems of green holly. The veterans scold, a row of tree barks and wattles. But Julia remains silent, it looks as though she's smiling. The lords of the bench recall old times, their fathers, the wars, the scourges from the origins to our days, the clash of clans, plagues, violated treaties, families taken refuge in the church during invasions, the ever-dependable absence of happiness. "And her, her . . . even her too, his sister . . . when you think about Aurèle under the wheel of the colossal . . . she, the sister of a dead boy . . ."

"Ain't it too sad! Ain't it too sad!"

But Aurèle . . . How to express Aurèle . . . Sketch, bird . . . fragile angel, golden bough. How express his essence, spirit, fire, transparency, and the phoenix, the living soul. Aurèle who is all that is lightest in the world . . . What can't even be touched, what brushes past in a burst of sunshine, pollen, the down of a cloud, wing of snow, Aurèle, when he appears on the church roof in these blazing plumes, this armor of air and sunlight . . . dove-woven mail. And when the bird settles on the ship of the dead . . .

Everywhere in the village the sounds of making ready for the hunt. Hurled orders. Cars crammed with journalists. A thirst for death quivers at the windows of homes. What importance does a more or less imminent denouement have for Agathe now? Aguilar in an uproar is unable to nonplus her. She recapitulates things such as they'll be tomorrow. The storm will pass without changing anything. The terrorist, Myriam, Simon are presently cards already played, out of the game. All she need do is recount the world yet one more time. Without haste . . . to repeat the chain of things . . .

There's the goldsmith, the carpenter, the mason and the butcher. Their shopfronts and rooms behind the scenes, their kitchen-dining rooms and their pantries with peppered pickles. The raspberry or peach bathrooms. Agathe sniffs their gardens from the other side of the street, in the back where they plant their cabbages, carrots nibbled by Bugs Bunnies. The lust of foxes come down from the forests into the turkey pen. There's the building painter, the shrewd locksmith and the skinflint clockmaker, the spendthrift stamp-collecting pork butcher, the cuckolded, waxy-faced electrician. Their supersecret closets, the orifices where they stash the tribe's gold, ancestral jewels, magic books, talismans, shell shards from 1914–1918, antique manuscripts, dildos with cranks or motors, miscarried fetuses in jars, a two-headed lizard in formaldehyde . . . There's the well-read, temperamental druggist, the crossword puzzle fan and assistant manager of the supermarket in Perpignan, the widower Alphonse, his concubine Yvette, immortal Ludovic . . . There's the spider under the main beam of the dining room in the sixth house from the northern entrance to the town, where the sleepwalking gamekeeper lives. The chicken feathers from Léonie's pillow, the truck farmer's mistress who confided to Agathe that she's suffering from an allergy caused by the plumes of red chickens . . . that and nothing else was the root of her sinus trouble, exclusively red, exclusively chicken . . . With the johns over the streams, ivy-topped wooden blockhouses on piles above trout and eels. You shit in open sea. Turds drift on, sharks, the drunken boat will have to await another day. There's the engineer for the Forestry Commission, who sodomized shepherdesses. The notary's walking stick, the stuttering chessplayer, the one-eyed man, the immigrant and the albino spy, the fire chief's helmet. And the Henri II sideboard, the barrels of wine in the cellars, color TVs, attics full of garlic and mice, gutter cats death-rattling in love, rats always underrated by the carpetbeaters, moles under lawns and slugs in heads of lettuce. There's a new caterpillar in the folded leaf of a water lily.

Agathe weds the world. Their beautiful family linens in century-old armoires exuding a scent of violets and starch. Granny nightgowns, chaste and Carmelitic knickers. There's an aviator, a daredevil who just bought the mill in the so-called coachman's street. The priest's threadbare cassock, one long love letter from Iza dating back fifty years. Three cancers, four cirrhoses, a sclerosis in meticulous patches eating away Lison's brother-in-law, nicknamed Tonkin because he fought in Indochina. Segments of sagas, boughs of wars, bits of massacre. Thermopylaes in cosmic battles, you'll surely love it, yes, tomahawks, proton revolvers! Agathe visits, spells out, turns the pages, there's the suppository going into Raoul's horribly constipated ass. There's his grandson's pecker coming out of the buttocks of Eugénie, the mailman's girl. There are the blackbirds in the lilies, sputtering candles of mauve flowers, fragrance of wisteria and black currant, well copings, the goldfinches chirping, the hedges abuzz with bees. The grease-blackened gas station owner who crams multicolored cars full of fuel, the family of a surgeon from Brest full of themselves in a diesel Mercedes expelling fumes, polluting the blue wind inhabited by insects, grasshoppers, nighthawks and swallows . . . A scarab and a lizard nap in the bowels of a dead dog.

There would also be a snake charmer, an obese fakir, a matador and a muezzin, a star dancer in country clogs, a Hindu dancing girl and a hetaera in asbestos panties, a part-time maharaja, interim executioner, a memoir-writing galley slave, a gladiator with large kohl-rimmed eyes, a paludal janissary, an overshaggy ephebe, an odalisque with penis and an American gun-chomping slave trader, the balls of an embalmer, a flutist, a water diviner, a mule driver who is into screwing young ballerinas from the Opéra, Tuareg and Zulu in their birthday suits, big shots in the triangular trade, spices and silk, leatherworkers and glassblowers from Venice, righters of wrongs, dyers who tattoo hips and breasts, potters, madams with beribboned bottoms and indiscreet scribes, bird catchers.

There are invisible beings, ghosts, doubles, vampires, phantoms, zombies. Creatures from the fourth dimension, from the fifth and so many other universes parallel to the village that Agathe prefers to place between parentheses. Legions of Aurèles. Without mentioning the future where there'll be unimaginable houses, habitats up in the air and underground, impalpable lairs of electrons and cities of frequencies, livelihoods that are not very commendable or else mind-boggling and redemptive, professions of ultracunning robots, magnificent mathematicians, acrobats of ciphers, trapeze artists of pure abstraction. Swarms of astronauts, disintegrators, galactic telepaths, skirtchasers of the infinite, stagecoach drivers moving at hypercosmic speeds . . . Priests still proud, shamans as always, prophets for the taking. They'll come to rest a while in the grass, tickle the snakes, worship the pithecanthropus who'll be a stale, insipid idea, or some god, an idol of a fifth-millennium religion. Maybe a cathedral of rare atoms, unknown until now, imported from some quasar or black hole will hover above the cave with its promising apes.

Once there were plow horses, blacksmiths and drum majors, eel fishers, cowherd wizards, nesters, otter trappers, child snatchers, geese-keeping girls, prince charmings, the wasteland witch who concocted remedies for backside tumors, hunters of stinking beasts, mole catchers, exorcists, tinkers . . .

Agathe, Agathe when you hold us . . . Agathe, oh I love you, darling, my twin with black piplike eyes. There will still be bombs, missiles, occupying armies, endless peoples deboned, butchered into tiny pieces, ultrashrieking sophisticated tortures, poor souls bumped off by tidy neutrons, war veterans from the twelfth millennium, knights who fought for just causes with laser beams. Agathe will not be forgotten, nor her homemade computer brain. She was the last woman. They say there once lived a woman on this site occupied by a village called Aguilar, back in the days when a writing system existed. She was ugly, small, skinny and dark. But possessed the vivaciousness of a visionary weasel. A fox, she stole every cheese. An old lady from the times when death set a limit to life, investing it with that stunning tragicomic brevity. From the age of the human condition, permanent melodrama, and art, that mania of an ailing species. Agathe was her name. She lived to be quite old. In the end she no longer remembered anything. She remained silent to conceal her colossal loss. Supposedly she died at the age of ninety-two, totally idiotic, incontinent and amnesiac. Or else, or else, differing legends clash. Another version has it that she abruptly stopped on the day when she turned one hundred, at noon sharp, having retained a caustic lucidity. She's said to have called the whole village together and recited its story without a single mistake, from the origins to her birthday before all the assembled inhabitants, astir with emotion, choirs from the equator to the North Pole, televisions from all over the world and elsewhere, a camera from Cameroon come for the express purpose, plus beings from friendly constellations. At last, after having narrated the story in every last detail, in all its volume, every least facet, its multiple spaces, subterranean and celestial, she stopped, a fantastic clock . . . oh those funeral orations, the procession of pithecanthropi garbed in gold surplices, grand style togas and banderoles, royal androids, penitent robots, cavalries of angels and mutants come to pay homage to the Homeric corpse. It's said that the hoary-headed lady maintained a murky relationship with Iza, another old woman, not a memorialist but a prophet, insane, a convulsive contrary sister, a subtle bond linked them which might explain a good many phenomena from the savage times when men died like flies for love . . . It's said, it's said . . . Agathe witnessed a pharaonic world. Black Eve, Lilith of the dark locks, Isis of soot, logical lynx, holy gossipmonger.

For excitement, manhunts beat by far the pursuit of lynx or elephants: tracking the beast who experiences remorse, that thinking biped alarmed by his conscience! In Perpignan, along beaches, in offices of the prefecture or police stations, all departments are on red alert. Drastic measures have been taken, those reserved for truly destructive criminals of the first order. The final assault has been sounded. Shilly-shallying, coordination foul-ups come to an end, every category of petty conflict—diplomatic, technical, or personal—that slowed the ultimate outcome are all at once smoothed out. The league is vast and flawless. The net stretches over the mountains, along seas and borders. Now five helicopters are hedgehopping. The cops went out early in the morning from every corner in the country. They can be seen emerging from trucks, in single file, swift and concentrated, fresh from the Academy, fledglings for justice. Booted, with dogs on leashes, hand radios that receive and emit, establish communication along the whole front. All that're missing are fanfares, battle fifes. The terrorist is done for, except for some miracle, some demoniacal act of audacity that only children imagine, and poets, those criminals who sing when great civilizations die, the pride of morbid dreamers who always take the side of the savage and of the weak, transformed into wolves. Orders have come down from on high. Let this rebel business be wrapped up once and for all! The abominable beach butcher. The sunlight martyrs called out for vengeance, the widows, mothers and fathers, the whole damn pack of pain and moaners. They banded together into an association of tears and rancor. After all, motives existed for their hatred: in cemeteries the corpses from the terror. They demanded immediate reparations. The wild beast must be quickly handed over to these sheep baring their fangs. A just quarry. Every resource thrown into action. Peace would reign at the hearthside, vacationers would experience trouble-free snoring. The summer would be beautiful after his death. The fragrance and sweetness of the world would be reestablished after the stain is washed clean and the scorpion of the sands has exited the world of the living. A squadron of sharpshooters specially dispatched from Paris arrived in Aguilar. They'd participated in daring and victorious operations in different hostage-holding situations or embassy attacks. Their precise bullets nail in their tracks anarchists, executioners, sadists, escapees, madmen, the just. With fraction-of-an-inch accuracy, struck right in the skull. Their brains explode and there's an end to the escapade, the bid for power, the racket of rebellion. They came out of the van two by two as in wartime, real bruisers, highly trained, with micron-honed eyes. No one made merry in the village. A great silence spread over the old people, the punished children, the foreign tourists, the mothers lining up at the bakers' casting sidelong glances upon these state assassins. They were metropolitan murderers in a way, since France itself was only one big mayoralty. Trashmen armed with submachine guns to empty society's garbage bins. The din of boots, the perfect rows, the orders, the weapons brought back to mind episodes from the last war such as still could be seen at the movies. People admired the unsurpassable beauty of force when it deploys its ranks of automatons likewise, a mass of rumbling muscles sculpted by intensive world champion training. These Olympic heroes hung their gold medals on legal corpses. Sharpshooters, but now cowboys. Not muddleheads, prone to whimsy, not a hitch in the way they drew their guns. But cold, professional, obedient, death was their job. For example, they were never drunk like those fellows out in the Wild West. They had no attenuating circumstances. Free of folklore and legends, they massacred cleanly. Between the barracks and the canteen these housekeepers of death were as submissively devoted to the State, their master, as Merovingian spouses. The truly mean creatures were perhaps the husbands in government minister costumes, Dior perfumes, brilliant conversationalists at cocktail parties. The servants were after all nothing more than pawns set into action by delicate palates. The spectators lining the sidewalk glimpsed fascinating mysteries and scandals. They were split into two camps, in appearance diametrically opposed. On one side, the fervent partisans of order, those keen on cop clubs; on the other, the romantic individualists, fanciful young people, impenitent Bovarys and violent dreamers. Those who supported the lawmen's cause and those who more or less consciously identified with the terrorist. In the middle there existed a more hesitant, more depraved fringe wavering between these two extremes, thus managing to double their delight by adopting each role in turn. There's something for just about everybody in this large-scale tournament. It was a lot better than the horse races, erotic vaudevilles, or Sunday jogging. The terrorist and the sharpshooters, who might also be killed, were performing a great service. They'd pay for all private and collective repressions. They'd compensate for countless bitternesses, humiliations, stinging failures, ranging from love affair fiascoes to blocked careers. They were going to restore triumph and fertility to a population of abortions. A person simply needed to become one spontaneously with the game's players . . . Once unity was created, the nervous stamping and feverish mastications could be observed. A gluttony of belligerence, blows, murders. A bestial unventing too long contained. Some faces betray almost sexual flashes of lust when gazing upon the patrol of justice-meting rifles. A splurge of targets, bullets crackling and human dolls riddled like sieves. This muffled desire overcame the simplest hearts. They virtually exhorted the new gladiators into battle. This truthful detail must be confessed: some members of the audience applauded the cops coming out of the trucks! In short, die-hard fans. Human faith is cause for admiration. The only thing missing was the priest blessing the apostolic brigade of murderous musketeers. But that dotard's dribble would have upset the show. At any rate, one and all loved the ever-growing promise of blood on the verge of blossoming like happiness.

In this gamut of sweet pleasures it would be wrong to forget the dogs, which added a more primitive touch. Of course, the animals were trained, docile as the sharpshooters, but their chops, their fur, their tongues, the glimpse of their gullets when they yawned, the quiverings of their long muscles encircled the scene with blatantly savage connotations. The huge archaic curs compelled visions of slaughter and quarry. The splendors were set to the rhythmic din of the helicopters. Orgiastic blasts of motors. The TV reporters, the amateur or professional photographers, the print media gesticulating in swarming crushes. Messages were sent out for news flashes. There was a secret hope that Aguilar would be the top story on the eight o'clock news . . .

But what couldn't be seen was the ferment at command headquarters where computers processed the slightest information. Thousands of cards arrived, issuing from the most varied sources: shepherds, tourists, strollers, anonymous tips, bikers, campers, pranksters, hunters of carved stones, women out gathering thyme and lavender. A trail was traced in the region of Queyribus, in the outskirts of the ruins of the last Cathar stronghold. An officer had delivered some final info which matched up with a body of testimonies. The police army moved into action. State security patrols and local cops, dogs and sharpshooters. It was ten in the morning. The heat was firmly ensconced, solid, shimmering.

And Simon imagined the man . . . all alone out among the rocks. He's hungry, it's quite simple. Armed with a rifle and a knife. An explosion now runs the risk of signaling his location to the pack. He can't even shoot at birds and hares anymore. He uses a bit of horsehair and a hook to attack trout in the streams. He even avoids making fires whose smoke might be visible. He eats raw fish. But he had to remove himself from areas surrounding water which would be especially patrolled. He vanished into limestone scrub. In places where the chaotic rocks keep visibility down to ten yards. The fortress of Queyribus intently stares from the top of its belemnite guard. Here the Pure Ones withstood the last siege. No more than a spur of ruins inhabited by clicking crows. He lay under a squat, round hillock in the low shadow. He slunk like a fox between the branches and roots. He hears the helicopters. He knows they're heading in from everywhere with the dogs, the crack hit men. He is well acquainted with state practices. He'd assumed the risk for a long while. They lost no time in launching the assault for political reasons, mutual plots hatched between Spain, France and the parties. The field is open now. The terrorist had been somewhat forgotten. They rediscover and greet him. Never has he been newer, more handsome . . . The trouble is that he no longer correctly defines the why of his death. The glamour of the cause has tarnished during the course of those lonely nights. It occurred gradually, a doubt seeping in, then an abrupt fracture completely shattered the tree of his motives. To die for the freedom of the people has just lost its meaning. He no longer believes in history, in its logic, its finality. His death doesn't enter into any programs; reality has no architecture. His imminent death is due to happenstance, a network of psychological and social circumstances, a horde of petty facts that pitch and toss. However he feels no remorse about what he perpetrated on the beach. He can hardly imagine the convictions of the wild-eyed killer he once was. He is here now, devoid of memory, innocent in the center of a web that he no longer understands. He doesn't feel much like living anymore, but he's repelled by the thought of handing himself over, enduring the consequences, the interrogations, their asinine deductions always lagging behind the deeper reasons and the only mysteries that matter. He'd really like to kill himself. But an instinct still checks him. He'd like to be left wandering, fleeing only to die no doubt a little later after he's caught his breath, better fathomed his life's insignificance. He doesn't know who he is anymore nor does he have a clue as to whom he'll kill. Every time he wants to think about those people on the beach, a sort of fog descends. His mind stumbles and drowns in a murky mass, a sound of sun and sea, the slipping of a billion grains of sand. He's nostalgic for remorse. A little while ago the intermittent presence of the woman attached him to the world. Planted in her body, he felt as if he were drinking. He told her not to come back anymore. He'd become perfectly impotent. A sort of hunger lurked inside, purely biological, a hunger he had to nourish while awaiting the real choice. He was no longer ripe for suicide. He wanted to give a meaning to his death. He wanted to have time left for reflection. To flee not in order to kill or betray, but to gather the minimum of being before dying. He knows full well such things can't be explained to the police. You can't peep a word during wartime. He'd loved war too much and his own relentless, farcical rebellion against others. So he was hungry, suffering from a terrible stomach cramp that had to be soothed. He couldn't remain indefinitely in this gully of thorns. He pulled himself free, stood, listened. His hearing had sharpened since going on the run. He recognized the noises of the scrub. He walked along clinging to rock surfaces, bowed, furtive. He knew about a half-mile on there was a "mas"-style house set on a hillside. He'd observed it during his previous roamings. The police couldn't keep watch over every farm. He hopes this one still escaped their control. He advanced. He was hungry, it was a goal of sorts seeping into the center of his belly. A circle of pain. He crawled inside as into a garret. The farm seemed peaceful on the hill slope with its sheepfold on the right. He spotted the dog by the pen. The animal would bark as soon as the man approached. He had to act swiftly, run, dash, so as to keep the barking to a minimum. He kept moving forward downwind as he'd learned to do for game. The dog heard nothing for the moment. The farm appeared deserted. The masters were working no doubt in the vines or the fruit gardens that could be made out on the other side. With a little luck . . . Unless they've barricaded themselves in upon hearing what the radio was surely blaring out. The dog was fifty yards off. It was a black German shepherd, somewhat mongrely. Untethered. The terrorist sprang suddenly with his rifle butt and his knife. The animal shot forward at the same instant, barking. They met after a few seconds. A terrifying fear and rage bristled the dog. The butt struck it on the skull and the dagger sank into its throat. The barking ceased. The terrorist ran toward the sheep pen. He shattered the door. There was a press of ewes and kids squeezing in a panic, bleating hysterically. With his rifle butt he stunned the smallest among them and, grabbing its legs, made his escape. Upon reaching shelter he disemboweled it with his knife and ate the liver, sucked up the blood, bit into the raw meat. Then he walked very quickly, almost without hiding. He lengthened his strides, he fled far from the animal murders. He didn't regret leaving obvious traces of his passage. He knew they were circling in on the territory with every means at their disposal, men, machines. The crucial point was not being hungry anymore, not remaining paralyzed under a bush until sinking into delirium. The blaze whipped a broad swath of mountains toward the east. An outlaw also, but phenomenally better armed than the runaway. He had to get closer to the fire. Run the risk of those flames, find refuge at the side of this ferocious extra playing its part. And he didn't take his eyes off the fire, this unforeseen savior . . . He heard them in the distance . . . a tapping upon stones. He flattened himself against the ground, slid toward a knoll. There were five of them, with two dogs . . . behind, eight hundred yards away, a van could be seen on a pathway and other men advanced, more numerous. They were following a curve that led them away from the fire. The terrorist pressed himself against the ground, keeping track of them at eyelash level. It was imperative not to move, to let them pass while hoping that the dogs would discover nothing. He waited. Some stopped to inspect the vicinity with their binoculars. He felt the lenses sweeping the rare clumps of grass, the slightest movement along the backbone of rocks. They progressed steadily without hurrying, self-confident, supported by the others. Such cohorts must be multiplying throughout the region. They wove cordons, roadblocks, formed stoppers, executed the plans of their chiefs back in headquarters. Their mistake was in not hugging the fire tightly enough. At the edge of the flames, menaced by their stingers, there zigzagged a furrow of freedom. When the head patrol passed him by, before the bulk of the troops arrived, he dashed forward, raced straight to the other side, heading for the inferno. He ran for five hundred yards, in a complete crouch, obstinate, head bowed. The others followed their curve toward the ruins of Queyribus. Did they think he was romantic enough to go perch himself up there, trapped like the prophets of yesteryear? It was the fire he had chosen, the luxuriance of its gold. A helicopter arrived. No cover offered itself. He stretched out among the pebbles. His thorax became one with the vertebrae of the ground. The machine passed without spotting him. The echo reverberated, propagating a clangor of grapeshot. A nausea seized him, he vomited the kid's blood. He drew nearer. The blaze swayed in the wind. A cavalry of torches and plumes of smoke. A vast odor of resin and ashes swirled outward. The fire appeared stable. No perceptible progress. Stationed within its perimeter. Composing a landscape wholly unto itself, a place, a climate. It didn't frighten the terrorist. However, the animal multiplied itself with pauses, stagnations. It digested on the spot before shooting out other banderillas of flying sparks. Cracklings, snappings, breaths enveloped the terrorist. An immense body distended with air and embers, impalpable and fleeting, with its accelerations, its hollow organs throbbing, an intermeshing mechanism of lungs that writhe, swell, spew a searing wind.

Nightfall. The terrorist lay in a field of ashes. In the orange glow he no longer saw the stars. He stripped stark naked and sweat covered him. He remembers nothing. In his bowels the taste of the kid. He'd like to recall a few points of his past. Moments of life. Tatters of dream. His mind drifts . . . He sees a stream of black goats. Never-ending discussion under a fig tree. And Fifth Avenue in New York that he walks down with an aging, vanquished woman. On the avenue street sign there's the black crepe of mourning. Then he walks on the sea over a glass surface that separates him from the waters. Gently rolling fertile hills loom clearly beyond Manhattan.

The terrorist confuses dream and memory. He runs, crawls, brandishes a rifle, rolls in the dust, crosses through barbed wire, a crackling of weapons . . . Cries, bogeymen, slogans, encampments . . . blows, blood, the lamp and the question . . . The fig tree, the old men's bench, the jackass, the shameful mother. Why New York and its draped avenue and this worn-out woman? Her thick curly fleece. Moaning of loins. And the Aztec statuettes gaze at him from the bottom of a vine-crammed ditch. They eye him scornfully, motionless and vain, stocky, pug-nosed, indecipherable faces in the cavity of flowers and stems. Lined up, lucid, secretly humiliated deep down in their hole. Then later, arranged under glass in the apartment of a crooked collector, rich and obsessed, in Mexico. They are still looking at him from their transparent prison. Delivered from the vines, molds and humus and fragrant corollas. In a halo of stable light where hovers an odor of wax, of memory. Images slip past. Cameroon, New York, glass museum, prison, the bomb, the beautiful summer explodes, foot resting on the sea. The jackass, the pleas, litanies of the mother, the Yucatán, the hard prick wedged in the tufted African woman's sheath. Dark swell and black heat . . . The rocks in all countries, those limestone expanses that recur and the raw sunlight. And those gorges and caves and billy goats and those green leaves of the big fig tree. And the red poppies of the Atlas valley. Four or five to a room, bunk beds, a smoky stove and a pungent reek of sperm, socks and balls. Wooden walls, wind, sand. The laughter, the toothless mouths . . . the overripe canvas, the rancid, heady urine. Then a dank suburb, the sky low and never any sunshine. Greyish, cold. Weaponless. The books, the knowledge. The well-dressed comrades . . . The embassy that protects him in Paris, with its grand salons, its Arabian Nights carpets, the fanatical security check at the entrance, armed soldiers, target apertures, hidden cameras scrutinizing you. But the beauty of the immense rooms and of the tapestries and the soft rich nuances . . . delicate monochromes and velvet rosettes. Then the image of that vigilant girl springs up, the one he met in a northern French suburb where he was a teacher . . . so white, slowly looking around with those eyes that devoured his face. Her fervor and her doubt. Her desire for being . . . Now an obsession with this young Madonna. She detested companions, hated the purity to which the beauty of her features condemned her. She wanted so badly to be guilty for at last loving. She chose him and his vices in order to be born in the slime, shame acting like a fresh spring. In the ashes he saw her face, almost cast in white wax. But all the rest, the other women passed into oblivion, engulfed nights, raging possessive passions, every sort of tyranny. His childhood and his wanderings. He didn't manage to firmly fix any scene. And the pictures receded, riddled with stones and almond trees and seas bleeding under glass. There was nothing but this vigilant image . . . for your locks of rain the tears of a king. This epitaph of water in the grave of ashes.

The fire swept along like a thousand torches of the dead. A mausoleum of flames. In the shroud of ashes his heart thumped harder. And he found her again, along with his thirst for happiness. He wasn't able to give her everything. Then the bird had landed in their room. A gold lapwing that he'd offered her, but that he must have destroyed in his delirium. She'd forgiven him. All violence brought her to birth. She thirsted for joyful impurity. So lofty in her whiteness.

He'd forgotten about his mission and history, his tenacious war against the law . . . this chirping of all the world's voices in the pools of blood. All that survived was this image of a woman to be born in the shadow of the flames and the bird.

The killer elite set up camp, seven guys at a slight remove from the sizable police encampment. They played cards while waiting for dawn. They checked their weapons, turned the parts around again and again, adjusted, oiled. Scrupulous craftsmen. They spoke a little about him, of his fragile survival. They found the dog's corpse, a bit disappointed over such paltry carnage. Even though for these men, superstitious in a way all their own, the remains of a dog are more unusual than a human being's. Disappointed in appearance, a little anxious underneath. This dog-corpse is a bad omen. This fleeting, obsessive fear makes them snigger. They shine their swords. They are masters of the game. The most wily wolves always wind up surrendering to them. They are the fatal brigade of positive killers.

When all is said, a skull is something abstract in a rifle's sights. There is hardly any thought given to all it contains by way of memories, images, loves and tears, comic and tragic clichés, all those networks, neurons harnessing wild fancies. The exploding bullets blow up an unreal puppet. The sharpshooters are not thinkers, but exceptionally gifted athletes. They take aim, they're accurate. They excel at their job. They get straight A's in their macabre discipline. The skull bursts the way it ought to. A stranger's brains. Everything evaporates: agonies, militancies, the emancipation of peoples gurgle away, a heap on the ground. A blanket is thrown on top and it comes to a chaste end. One less delirium in the world, therefore a bit of air, a chance for those left behind in their deferred survival.

People feel like total morons upon hearing of Homeric gangsters' deaths. They've gotten accustomed to their continuing saga of nose-thumbing at the cops. They've prized the latest developments and the clever ruses of the villain who always finds a way to dodge around and slip through the trap in a hair's-breadth escape. They've wondered how long it'd go on, hopes pinned on never-ending sensationalism. But comes the time when the head office tolls the bell. Then the rebel's days are numbered. And the party suddenly ends. Disappointed, they return to their humdrum routine. A little older from all the excitement. Going into cold turkey as they withdraw from the epic. When the haze of victory dissipates, the most revenge-minded sulk bitterly as after a significant coitus. They also miss the hunt, the episodes, the suspense, the stairway leading to the ass of the beloved woman . . . the small hope that it'll come to a different end, with some tiny novel twist.

But it always ends up by ending. And if it doesn't end, people weary of it in the long run and that's the worst of all possible endings.

Now the terrorist—oh this giddy rush!—is still going strong. His fairy-tale magic lasts on, holds out. Families at eight P.M. in front of their TV sets are not cheated. Forks miss mouths and noodles dribble down. The kids, wide-eyed with murderous naïveté. More hypocritically, the parents rein in their pleasure a little, but their brilliant eyes betray them. The special chief superintendent of the sharpshooters' brigade is laconic but firm during his interview. A crack at mopping up, the champion of national dry-pressing. The most beautiful creases in the land. He was already seen in action on similar occasions. Dead or alive is not his specialty. He erases the second useless adjective. On high he's advised to respect both terms of the expression, form in short, the rights of man. But the statement is accompanied by a most peculiar blank expression, a gone-flaccid look which leaders alone know how to adopt whenever intimating that their subordinates must do whatever needs be done regardless . . . even if it's painful. Of course.

Agathe rests in her bed. She's lost nothing of the happiness of knowledge. She delights in this small eternity. An egotistical old lady, an ant of memory. So scrawny in her white bed. She hears the night of their vigilance. They haven't yet laid their hands on the lynx of the limestone. The villagers are afraid despite the awesome police defenses. The terrorist incarnates everything within themselves that terrifies them. Agathe virtually left her door open for the vampire. She knows he's coming to an end and that therefore it's already over. She's filed away this adventure. "During the time of the terrorist." But he's alive and the mystery of this still intact life, violent and full, fascinates her. He's alive and tomorrow he'll be dead. But his life remains whole. Her head is crammed with archives, details, places, men. These flourishes form a consciousness. Agathe rose. She contemplates the horizon through her window. She makes out the border of flames fissuring the gloom. She likes this sign. This wound in the world's side—the fire: this insomnia of matter. She ponders the pithecanthropi who watched the blazes after storms. They hadn't yet tamed this violence. For it was before Prometheus. Neither man nor gods were born. It was before the time they dare draw near the blazing ardor to touch it, take it, keep it. Before the lovely tale of the home hearth. For they had no hearth, being really no more than barely evolved apes, yet far more gifted . . . Their house was a black cavern without fire. A house of the origins, long before light. And a person dropped out of sight in this darkness. Drowned in this mystery.

Myriam and Simon are stretched out on the bed. They don't take each other's hand. Soon they are going to separate. They have nothing more to say to each other. They'd like to utter magnificent words. They've lost the childhood that would enable such words to be said. They know forgetfulness will overcome them. Already it consumes them. It's as if they were going to die to each other. Unsentimentally they'll judge this episode in which they silently lied to each other. The truth of their bodies is short-lived compared to that old dream of transparence and soul mates. Greedy for carnal pleasure, they failed to speak each other . . . But the other man was superfluous, the one out in the scrub, an errant creature laden with horrors. How dare to speak each other and find true union alongside this cursed soul who ruins language and leaves you agape before an abyss of blood? Soon he will be dead. It's good for the executioner to rejoin his victims. Forgetfulness can occur only when this final balance is struck.

They took advantage of the night. Paloma and Lynne crossed the border. They'll travel through Spain along the highway. One night will do. Lynne carries Arthur strapped to her belly. The bike races along. The child, stirred by the motor's sound, stays quiet, listens. Soon he'll sleep in the rolling motion, securely sheltered between Lynne's side and Paloma's back. The fragrance of orange trees, lemon trees in the nocturnal valleys. The median strip of the highway quivers, vibrates. And time is abolished. The star of the dykes whirls vertiginously. They've decided to realize this dream: to go to Gibraltar, see the coast of Africa being born upon the sea at sunrise. They fled. The highway hugs the coast and gravitates, a great galactic groove. They rock to a cosmic cadence. The water shines, the immense black ocean aglimmer. A large egg rolling in the orbit of noise that the motor circumscribes. A nice big racket, stable and strong. A node of sea between the lovers' thighs. The wheel, the immensity. Great pupils dilated with energy, water, flesh. Mute, enormous bliss. Lynne and Paloma feel it beaming all around. A firmament of black stars of happiness.

And Gibraltar in flower, at dawn . . . Africa, odalisque supine on the violet stone of the sea.

He doesn't know if he's slept. For one moment reality became dream. He's not able to gauge how long this moment lasted. But he got scared at the transition point between these two universes. He found the fire, which had moved slightly away from him and fallen off during the night. The field of ashes is broad now. A dew makes the soot ooze over his torso and thighs. The odor is good. He gets up. At the horizon's edge he sees, way out, the mouth of the cave. And the sight mysteriously reassures him, the image of the first men. On the stage of the rock, the horde watches him . . . He walks toward the flames. He hears the boots on the stones. The helicopters spot him. He runs. A long line of cops emerges in the whiteness of the desert, which sharply contrasts with the outlined expanse of ashes. He has time to catch the blaze. Soon they'll be near, within firing range. Sharpshooters adjusting their sights. But he's already galloping in the wind before the flames. The cops won't venture out there, for the least gust could engulf the men. He escapes them. The helicopters alone make him out intermittently beneath the fresco of smoke. He runs before the fire. He knows nothing but this flight. He's stopped fleeing. Upon awaking this very morning he made his choice. If he's running now, it's because he's already the fire, in terror and in happiness. Eyes wide open. He weeps. He'd almost burst into song. He yells. And nobody hears him. He runs in rhythm with the inferno. He doesn't know when he's going to stop. But his flight is already a pause. An immobile lightning of life. He thought he saw the lynx nearby. Flame or animal mane? The man and the feline run before the fire. He shouts again, a howling song. Armor of sweat, helmet of ashes. He bleeds. The lynx sings . . . He comes to an abrupt halt. The place is in the open, an altar of rocks. And they hem him in and devour him.

The cops and firemen searched for the tracks of the solar killer. They would never have found him if he hadn't chosen to die on a bed of stones. When the blue sky returned, the man's remains were discovered, black bones, stumps of soot. Not far from him a matching twin vestige was recognized, later identified by the police lab as belonging to the lynx. Lots of cop cars, journalists and voyeurs had parked on the sacrificial site. A large moving ring of men had formed, a host of puppets, coming, going, circling. The silhouettes became confused, their noise and gesticulations interknotted in macabre, sorry-looking swarms. They hopped, leaped, doubled in number, dwindled . . . like shadows, like large puddles of ashes, with their gossiping mouths, their covetous gazes. And the clicking of the snapshots, the sputtering of the movie cameras, the crackling of the microphones drilled the silence with a thousand murders, deft, startling stabs . . . like birds of prey, vultures . . . Not the large circaetus of the azure, the pure, haughty sparrow hawks. But a race of ignoble, croaking birds, rending to pieces this holy circle of death. And Agathe had come, armed with a camera that she was using for the first time. She took pictures of the reporters, photographed the voyeurs. She grew giddy with an incredible voluptuousness while snapping photos of these professional gawkers. She liked the hubbub and this mess, this swirling in place. Men squatting, standing, bent over, gathered together, fluttering around the sacred enclosure like macaques, pithecanthropi or unruly, thieving chimps. For when the hordes descended from the cave, they were imagined to be nervous, feverish perhaps, hesitating along their trot out toward the great herds of the plain. Those very first men, the young simians, the leading ingenues, the superstars, the magical bumpkins, when their gang armed with stakes and carved stones came tumbling down . . . And they would perhaps be the ones who, by some marvel and devil's trick, would appear on the negatives developed back in the laboratory night. Emerging from a blur of nebulas and genesis. Gradually, one after the other, future supermen, masks of ourselves, living founders and prophetic doubles. Up there the cave stirred, was seized by a deep trembling. And they were going to appear, the leading lights and the Quasimodos, the genius dwarves, the knock-kneed tightrope walkers, the Gargantuas from the very beginning . . . Obtuse, and how! Stupid, of course, but with a luminous stupidity, camouflaging those surly angels, the pearl of lucidity under tufts of hair and the hump of eye sockets. They were going to pay homage to the slain terrorist. The photographers will take a step backward, terrified before this herd of Abels and Cains . . . The only one left would be Agathe, fearlessly photographing until the last moment, even up under their open jaws while the corpse of the prince lies garbed in soot like black flies . . . abuzz with words.

The lenses, machines, somber and brilliant instruments, metallic protuberances like beaks, big spurs, horns rigging out the press officials, along with the ground-level cameras scouring, violating the mysteries, screwing death—all brought to mind the burning eyes, the claws, teeth and hunting spears and sharpened stones which at one time fiercely set upon the remains of hunted animals, beautiful prey of the origins reclining in their wool and blood. And they circled around, jiggled, jabbered, grumbled, gluttonous, showered with sticky clots. God photographed them, the azure in its infinite transparency capturing the image of the men, of those who would be us, who quaked at the thrill of being us . . . Five hundred thousand years away from us, who existed in their every nerve, in an upheaval of ravenous bowels before the tracked beast, pierced with blows, and who drank its blood and swelled with youth under the grey maternal eye of the caves. Such was the spring preceding our seasons, our tales, long before legends, in a genuinely intact meadow. Pure loophole of daylight. No thought conceived this beginning. The world was virginal, untouched by musings and sentiments. It was being born. It was one, dense, brand new . . . a mirror of itself.

Beautiful electronic tools, silver-plated pieces . . . calibrated to the fraction of an inch, sliding. Agathe had the impression of a vast swallowing action, a numberless ingestion. Recording countless details, looks of places, things. Each crumb of ash was inscribed on the ribbons of film, the velocity of reloading, flash-bursts gashing like fangs, the gluttony of grapeshot devouring this corner of the world, immortalizing it. The ghastly banquet was engendering eternity, memory frozen, images, tomb of a flawless present.

Agathe, who knew everything now, took full scope of the sadness of knowledge. The masks had fallen and she was deprived of the greatest secret. The only thing left her was this struggle against the holes of memory; this light everywhere frightened her, so pure, hemming in the mountain and black caves.

Myriam showed up on the scene. She'd been required to identify certain details. They made her examine the mutilated skull, shorn of its chin, forehead scraped down, a thick ridge of bone and soot agglomerated above the sockets. A few negatives in the police files and photographs (the publication of any close-ups barred) preserved this image of the skull of Aguilar man.

Myriam stole some ashes from the skeleton. She borrowed a car and headed seaward. She wanted to spread the terrorist's remains out there. But perhaps they'd precede her, a procession, a caterpillar of stubby men, jabbering their chaos of words, with loony gestures, tripped up by rocks, heading toward the fish at the bottom of the rumbling waters. Before the oceanic immensity, the fistful of dust struck Myriam as forlorn. It was impossible to reconcile the sea and the man's memory. She walked along the shore and spotted it, moored to the rocks. At sunset the black woman poured the loner's ashes into the fisherman's boat. But maybe they'd already piled into the skiff's hollow, nestled in the wave-encircled shell. Credulous and shivering suddenly, surprised by this enormous presence of shadows and waters. Huddled together, shaggy and trembling. Setting sail in the floating cave. A gust of wind drives them toward the shores of Man.